D1335186

THE CUSTOM
HOUSE MURDER

By Mike Hollow

THE BLITZ DETECTIVE SERIES

The Blitz Detective
The Canning Town Murder
The Custom House Murder
The Stratford Murder
The Dockland Murder

a&b

THE CUSTOM
HOUSE MURDER

Mike Hollow

Allison & Busby Limited
11 Wardour Mews
London W1F 8AN
allisonandbusby.com

First published by Lion Hudson as *Enemy Action* in 2017.
This edition published by Allison & Busby in 2020.

Copyright © 2017 by MIKE HOLLOW

The moral right of the author is hereby asserted in accordance with
the Copyright, Designs and Patents Act 1988.

All characters and events in this publication,
other than those clearly in the public domain,
are fictitious and any resemblance to actual persons,
living or dead, is purely coincidental.

All rights reserved. No part of this publication may be reproduced,
stored in a retrieval system, or transmitted, in any form or by
any means without the prior written permission of the publisher,
nor be otherwise circulated in any form of binding or cover
other than that in which it is published and without a similar
condition being imposed on the subsequent buyer.

A CIP catalogue record for this book is available from
the British Library.

10 9 8 7 6 5 4 3 2

ISBN 978-0-7490-2692-9

Typeset in 11/16 pt Sabon LT Pro by
Allison & Busby Ltd.

The paper used for this Allison & Busby publication
has been produced from trees that have been legally sourced
from well-managed and credibly certified forests.

Printed and bound by
CPI Group (UK) Ltd, Croydon, CR0 4YY

For my parents, who are not here to see this book but whose world and war this was

CHAPTER ONE

Broken glass slipped and crunched beneath his boots. It made him feel queasy – like when the rain brought the snails out onto the pavement and you trod on one in the dark. Only this was like stepping on a thousand snails, all the way down the street, and it felt peculiar because it wasn't how things were supposed to be. This glass he was walking on was people's front windows, smashed all over the road.

And yet he couldn't help but find it exciting too – exciting in a bad way. Breaking windows was something you got told off for – as he'd discovered playing back-yard cricket the summer before last – but now windows were being shattered everywhere, every day, and people took it as normal. Everything was changing; rules didn't seem to be rules any more. He kicked some of the glass to one side, just because he could. All in all, war seemed to be quite a lark. So far.

Not for his mum, though. She was poorly, and he

began to worry he might have left her on her own for too long. It wasn't the same as when he'd been little – if he woke up with nightmares then, she'd be there in the dark by his bedside, like a fairy, singing him gently back into peace, her voice fading into a whisper as he drifted away to sleep.

Now he was big enough to be out on his own, and she was the one who didn't like the dark.

She said she was glad he hadn't been born a girl, because men did bad things to girls in the dark, but she never said what. At night, when the warning sirens went and they were alone in the flat, her eyes would twitch round the room, looking for somewhere to hide, and she'd cling to him – not like she used to, holding him tight to comfort him, but more like the way you'd cling to someone if you'd fallen in the river and couldn't swim.

He came to a corner. This would be how all that glass got smashed – as far as he could make out, the street he'd just come down was one house shorter than it used to be, possibly two. Some of his friends reckoned they could tell from the damage what size bomb it had been, a fifty-pounder, a five-hundred-pounder or whatever, but he wasn't sure whether they were making that up. All he could tell was whether it was an incendiary or an HE – if an incendiary landed on the roof and wasn't seen to it could burn the place out, but high explosives would blow it to bits. This one looked like an HE, because all that was left was a mountain of rubble and splintered timbers, littered with the smashed-up remains of what had been someone's home – a kitchen sink, a toilet seat, a twisted iron bedstead. He hoped no one had been in the house when it was hit.

Mum had been asleep in the street shelter when he slipped out this morning, dozing at last after probably being kept awake half the night by the noise, but he'd been longer than he should have. It would be light soon. He didn't have a watch, but it felt like he'd been out for a good half-hour. Quite a profitable half-hour, though.

It was a boy he knew from school who'd given him the tip. The best time for nicking things was to nip out of the shelter just before dawn, he'd said, and he was right. There was no school any more, of course – the council had closed it down when war broke out so it could be used by the Air Raid Precautions people for the wardens' post and what-have-you. But that advice had been a good bit of education.

Not that he'd popped out for nicking. Definitely not. He could've done – there was plenty of stuff on offer in that last hour or so of darkness, when the bombs had done their worst and the sites hadn't been cleared up, but he knew what it would do to his mum if he got caught.

He'd come out to get shrapnel. You could find it all over the streets if you were out early enough, and you could swap it with the younger kids. They thought it was bits of German bombs or aeroplanes, but it wasn't – Dad said most of it was just what fell to the ground when our own anti-aircraft shells exploded, and Dad knew, because he'd been a soldier in the Great War.

Shrapnel was good for swapping – he used it mainly to get cigarette cards. The best were from just before the war – famous cricketers, cars, warships – and they were worth more now, because the paper shortage meant the cigarette companies weren't giving them away any more. Sometimes if you swapped a set that lots of kids wanted – speedway riders or RAF aircraft – you could even get something like a Dinky Toys car.

He had a grimy hessian sack stuffed inside his jacket. Mum was going to use it to make a rag rug for the hallway as soon as she had enough bits of old cloth, but she wouldn't be needing it yet. Besides, she used to tell him off for ripping his trouser pockets by putting shrapnel in them, so he reckoned it was fine to borrow it for carrying today's haul. You had to be careful, though – if a copper saw you prowling round in the blackout with a sack over your shoulder he might jump to the wrong conclusions. So he kept an eye out, and if anyone in authority came close – which these days basically meant his dad and anyone else wearing a tin helmet – he'd drop it smartish and run like the clappers. There wasn't much chance of anyone old catching him.

The sudden interruption of the all-clear siren made him jump, as it always did. Not quite as creepy as the warning signal, but even so, such a dismal sound. You'd think they could've come up with something a bit more jolly to let people know the bombers had gone. A week or so ago they'd had the sense to cut it down from two minutes to one, but it was still a dreary moan. He dropped a last couple of decent bits of shrapnel into his sack. Now his mum would definitely be awake – he'd have to get a move on.

He started to head back home. On both sides of the street the rows of gloomy old houses looked spooky in the morning twilight. They reminded him of the one the family used to live in – dark, poky little places that always smelt of boiled cabbage and rising damp. Where they lived now was much nicer. The council had put them into one of the new flats off Prince Regent Lane when he was little, when their old house in Canning Town had to be demolished to make way for the new Silvertown Way. A road to the empire, that's what they called it, because now it was easier for lorries to get in and out of the docks and factories. Before, everything had to go across the old swing bridge over the entrance to the Royal Victoria Dock from the Thames, but now the Silvertown Way flew straight over it, on concrete legs. It was the only road he'd ever seen that went up in the air. His dad said it was the first one like that in the country and it would be great for the borough, even though it meant thousands of people had to have their houses knocked down.

The flat was all clean and modern, with plenty of light. The only problem was that you didn't have your own back yard, which meant there was nowhere to put an Anderson shelter. True, they weren't much use from what he'd heard – just little tin boxes, really, half buried in the ground, and in Custom House they always got water in them, because it was marshland, lots of it below high-tide level on the Thames. But at least an Anderson was your own, and you could make it a bit homely, with beds and blankets and an oil lamp. If there was an air raid and you lived in the flats you had to run to the nearest public shelter, the brick-and-concrete ones built on the street, and squash in there with fifty other people all night. There'd be babies screaming, old ladies crying, and people with smelly feet and clothes all in together, and no beds or lights either.

Where he lived, the nearest ones were in Nottingham Avenue. There were three of them in a row, and he'd left Mum in the one at the far end from where he was approaching. She usually went straight home when the all-clear sounded, to see if the flats were still there, but sometimes she might stay for a chat with a neighbour. He put a couple of pieces of shrapnel in his pocket ready to show her, just in case she asked what he'd been up to, but then he stowed the rest under a bush in front of an empty-looking bomb-damaged house. He could pick it up later – he didn't want her seeing how much he'd got and telling him to put it in the salvage collection.

He reached the last shelter and looked inside. It was darker in there than outside on the street, and his eyes took a moment to adjust. It was empty. She must've gone home, he thought. He'd go too, but first he'd have a look round in here and the other two shelters. Most people rushed away as soon as the all-clear had gone, especially if they had jobs to go to, and if there were no ARP wardens around you could sometimes find some good pickings on the floor. He'd once found a cigarette case that must have been dropped and then kicked under a bench.

No such luck today, it seemed. There was nothing in this shelter, nor the next. He came to the third and went in, again waiting for a moment so his eyes could adjust to the gloom. It was the same as the others – nothing but the bare brick of the walls, and wooden benches along them where people had spent the night trying to pray the bombs away.

But this time there was something else. He peered into the far corner. It was a sack or something, right at the end of the bench. He switched on his flashlight and went closer, then stopped. It wasn't a sack – it was a man, sitting, leaning with one shoulder against the wall, looking like he was asleep. Or maybe he was drunk. You didn't go flashing a torch in the face of drunks in a place like this – like as not they'd give you a clip round the ear as soon as look at you.

The boy slid his thumb onto the button to switch the torch off, but stopped. There was something else. The man's coat was open, and there was a dark patch on the front of his white shirt that glistened as the beam of light passed across it. Slowly, cautiously, he moved the light upwards, and then froze. He could see the man's face right in front of him – it was set in a contorted grimace, and the eyes were staring straight at him.

He felt his own eyes blink several times before he realised the man's had not moved at all. They were wide open, but he wasn't looking at anything.

CHAPTER TWO

Detective Inspector John Jago pushed open the door to his bathroom. It was small, but a luxury to be thankful for when he thought of the old zinc bath that had hung on the back of the kitchen door in his childhood. That was what many people in West Ham still had to make do with, taking it down on bath night every Friday and laboriously fetching hot water from the copper to fill it – unless the fire had gone out, in which case there was none to fetch. He was lucky, with hot water from the tap whenever he wanted it.

His back was stiff from another night in the Anderson shelter, and a soak would do it good. All he had to do was get the geyser going. He struck a match and tried to light the gas, but nothing happened. One of the night's bombs had probably broken the gas main somewhere, and when the Gas Light & Coke Company's men might be able to mend it was anyone's guess. He'd just have to wash in cold water, but he'd done plenty of that in his time. Should've had that back boiler put in, he thought. If he'd done that a couple of years ago, as he'd planned, he'd be heating his water with coal now, not relying on the gas supply. One way or another, though, he hadn't got round to it. There was no chance of getting anything like that done now the war was on, and what was the point if you might be bombed the next day? Anyway, the country had already had a taste this year of what the government liked to call 'short-term rationing' of coal, so there was no knowing how long that would stay available.

It was Sunday morning, and he'd woken at precisely six-fifteen. Before last September, in what increasingly seemed to have been the good old days, he used to wind up his bedside clock on a Saturday night but switch the alarm off, in reasonable hope of getting a lie-in the following morning. Sunday was still his day off, as far as it could be for any police officer, even in peacetime, but there was precious little hope of sleeping in nowadays, even when he'd remembered to push the alarm button firmly down. Who needed an alarm clock when you had the sirens? The all-clear had woken him today, just when he'd dozed off after lying awake for what felt like hours.

He decided to go for a walk to loosen his joints. The park wasn't far away, so he headed there – it ought to be quiet at this time of day, especially on a Sunday. It was the twenty-ninth of September 1940. Soon they'd be into the second winter of the war, he thought, and if the air raids went on things would be a lot grimmer this year than last.

He'd put his overcoat on as he left the house and was glad he had – there was a definite chill in the air. It looked as though the Indian summer that had warmed the weeks since the Blitz began was over. All around, the leaves were starting to fall, except where bombs had already blasted all the foliage and half the branches from trees in what had once been quiet residential avenues. Now there was only the usual damp autumn to look forward to, and after that the fog and frosts of winter.

The park was a tonic. The sun, still quite low in the sky, was gleaming through the trees, and the grass smelt sweet with early morning dew. He enjoyed the space, the openness of it, and the fresh air began to lift his spirits. It could still be a good day.

He walked once round the park, thinking back over the weeks since the Germans had launched their first big raid on the seventh of September. West Ham had suffered grievously, with the docks in the south of the borough seemingly the main target, and the whole world had been in turmoil. There was nothing much to celebrate. But then his thoughts turned to Dorothy – meeting her had brought a bright light into the darkness that seemed to swirl around him, and getting to know her had begun to change him.

He'd realised how much he liked being with her, and in that realisation he'd had to admit to himself that he found her very attractive. There was a strength about her that seemed to spill over into those around her, and he felt as though she'd brought him back to life after twenty years in an emotional limbo.

He wondered what she'd be doing today. At this time of the morning he hoped she'd still be sleeping peacefully in the safety and comfort of the Savoy Hotel, unless the Luftwaffe had chosen to roam over that way in the night. And later on? He pictured her in her grey woollen suit, sitting at her typewriter, pounding out a story for some hungry editor on her newspaper across the sea in Boston, or scribbling notes with the telephone receiver wedged under her chin. The one thing he couldn't imagine was her lounging about doing nothing – she had such energy that she would surely be working.

It wasn't just this morning in the tranquillity of the park that his mind was on Dorothy – she was increasingly filling his thoughts. And yet there was also the constant presence of someone else in the picture, or perhaps more precisely just out of it. It was as if Eleanor were there too, looking over his shoulder and seeing what he saw. The woman who'd been physically absent from his life since 1918 inhabited his memory still as the nineteen-year-old nurse who'd cared for him in a hospital in France, a bittersweet distraction now elevated beyond human frailty and shorn of imperfection by the passing of time.

His circuit of the park brought him back to the gate where he'd started, and he wondered whether his thoughts had done nothing more than meander round in a big circle too. He decided to head for home and breakfast, trying to make plans for the rest of his Sunday on the way – plans that if he had his way would not include the investigation of crime on K Division of London's Metropolitan Police. He wasn't accustomed to having a whole day to use as he pleased. Ever since he'd been a detective his working day had started at nine in the morning – earlier when required – and regularly gone on till ten at night. Perhaps he would just go home and sleep.

He reached the main road and waited for a red double-decker bus to grind its way past before he crossed. It reminded him of the tram ride he'd taken along the Embankment with Dorothy, and the pledge he'd made to himself to break free from the restrictive tramlines on which he'd been content to let his life run. He began to wonder whether the unseen presence of Eleanor might itself have been one of those tramlines, steering his life over the past two decades. If that was a fact, it was a hard one to face.

He tried to push the spectre of Eleanor out of his mind and refocus his thoughts on Dorothy, but thinking of her was troubling too. It was madness. He was surely too old to fall for her, in fact too old to fall for anyone. And yet it wouldn't go away. Would he have to tell Dorothy what he felt about her? He paled at the thought – some things were just too difficult to contemplate. It was all so complicated – and yet there remained the simple, undeniable facts, like the strangely warm feeling he got when he thought of her gentle laugh and her smile.

He was still lost in these thoughts as he approached his house, head down, eyes on the pavement at his feet. He got to his front gate, lifted the latch and looked up to find a uniformed police constable waiting on his doorstep.

'Sorry, sir, but you're wanted. Suspicious death in an air-raid shelter down in Nottingham Avenue. Shall I tell the station you're on the way?'

Jago sighed, nodded, and went into the house to find his car keys.

CHAPTER THREE

The night's damage to buildings and roads alike was substantial, and it was five to eight by Jago's watch when he arrived in Nottingham Avenue. The road ran along one side of the West Ham Greyhound Stadium in Custom House, down in the south-east corner of the borough, close by the docks. He peered at the shelter through the windscreen of his Riley Lynx. Like the other two identical structures farther down the street, it was about twenty feet long, nine feet wide and eight feet high, and had been built in the road, leaving just enough room for vehicles to pass on one side. It looked strangely out of place, as if a householder had decided to flout all rules and regulations and erect a large shed in the roadway to save taking up space in his garden. Jago's mouth felt dry as he cast an eye over the squat building. There was something brutal and ominous about its windowless walls – more like a tomb than a refuge.

It was one of the public shelters that he tried to avoid – built on the surface and exposed to blast, with a flat concrete roof in danger of collapsing if the walls gave way. Death traps, he called them.

He parked the car a little farther down the road, where it wouldn't obstruct the traffic, and walked over to where he could see Detective Constable Cradock standing by the shelter doorway, waiting for him.

'Morning, guv'nor,' said Cradock. 'Didn't expect to see you today.'

'Nor I you, Peter. So much for our day off. How long have you been here?'

'About twenty minutes, sir. They tried phoning you at home from the station, but apparently there was no answer – so they ran me to ground in the section house. I wasn't long out of bed and I'd just made myself a bit of breakfast in the mess room but I had to leave it and come straight down here, so I expect one of my dear colleagues will have scoffed the lot for me before I get back.'

'So you've had about as much breakfast as I have. The station must've been phoning when I was out for a walk.'

'Yes. I told them to send the local PC to wait at your house until you came back, and to get the police surgeon down here – oh, and I told them to contact the pathologist. He should be here soon.'

'Good. And where is the police surgeon?'

'Been and gone, sir. You just missed him. Wasn't too

pleased to be called out so early on a Sunday morning as far as I could tell, and I don't think that was because it'd make him late for church.'

'So he's tucked up in bed again at home by now, is he?'

'Couldn't say, sir.'

'All right for some. I've never met a poor doctor, but some of them do seem to work harder for their money than that man. He did manage to certify death before he went, I suppose?'

'Yes, sir, that's right. He says he reckons it's death from a stab wound to the chest.'

'That sounds fairly straightforward. Let's have a look, then.'

Cradock led the way into the gloomy interior. Once they were inside he sniffed the air and greeted it with a loud expression of disgust.

'Hope it won't take long, sir – it stinks in here.'

'Not a patch on my local park, that's for sure,' said Jago. 'And these places might be a bit more tolerable if the council had put some electric lighting in them. Give me that flashlight of yours.'

He took the flashlight and swept it round the inside of the shelter.

'The body's over there, sir, on the bench,' said Cradock.

They walked to the far corner of the shelter and stood over the corpse. Jago shone the light onto the dead man's face. He appeared to be in his twenties and was clean-shaven, with dark hair, shiny with cream. His hair was ruffled and at one side it hung down over his forehead, but not far enough to cover what looked like an old scar above his left eye. His black overcoat was unbuttoned, revealing a grey jacket, a white shirt, and navy blue flannels. As the beam passed across his chest, a large patch on his shirt glistened. Immediately above this a gash about an inch long was visible in the fabric.

'I haven't touched anything,' said Cradock, 'since the pathologist hasn't had a look yet, and as far as I could see the police surgeon didn't disturb the body – he just had a quick look at the wound. You can see the blood on the shirt there.'

'Yes, and plenty of it,' said Jago, taking in the scene.

'There's a bit more on the floor, too.'

Jago pointed the flashlight to the area at the dead man's feet and saw the blood, splashed over an area about two feet across. At the edge of the pool of light he noticed something else. It was a man's hat – a black fedora. He stooped to pick it up and turned it over in his hand.

'Hmm,' he said, examining it with the torch. He judged the hat to be a medium-priced example, the kind a professional man on a tight budget might buy. It wasn't new, but apart from the dust and dirt it had picked up from the floor it was in decidedly better condition than his own battered fedora – possibly an indication that this man had spent less time out in the recent bombing raids than Jago had. He ran his finger round the sweatband. It felt greasy, and one sniff confirmed the oily smell of Brylcreem. He couldn't see the point of slapping on hair cream every day himself, but half the male population did.

'I reckon this was his,' he said, placing it on the man's head. 'Knocked off in some kind of struggle, do you think?'

'That would make sense if someone attacked him. And there's no weapon to be seen in here, so it looks like he didn't kill himself.'

'We might assume murder, then. Who found him?'

'A boy, sir. Local lad. We've got him waiting outside.'

'Let's go and see him.'

Jago left the shelter, followed by Cradock, and took a deep breath of fresh air.

'There he is, sir,' said Cradock, pointing across the road.

Jago followed Cradock's finger and saw a boy sitting on the pavement, his feet in the gutter. He looked about twelve or thirteen and was wearing a shabby dark jacket, threadbare trousers, and scuffed boots. He jumped to his feet as the two men approached, his face apprehensive.

'Hello, sonny,' said Jago. 'I gather you found the body in there.'

'Yes, sir.'

'What's your name?'

'Jimmy, sir – Jimmy Draper.'

'Address?'

'7 Barrington Road – a turning up the road there.'

'Telephone number?'

Jimmy laughed.

'Not likely – we use the box round the corner if we have to make a call, and that's not often.'

'So tell me what happened.'

'Well, I went in there and saw that man sitting all on his own. At first I thought he was asleep, but then I realised he must be dead. I ran out and found a flattie – a constable, I mean – and told him, and he said wait here, so I did.'

'And how old are you, Jimmy?'

'Thirteen.'

'What school do you go to?'

'Don't go to any. I used to go to Custom House School in Russell Road, but then the war started and the council closed it down – made it into an ARP post. I got evacuated out to some place in the country.'

'But you didn't stay evacuated?'

'Not for long, no. My mum needed me back here, so I came home.'

'And you haven't found another school you can go to?'

'No. When I came back there weren't any proper ones open. Some of the teachers that hadn't been evacuated said I could come to these classes they'd set up, but it wasn't with my mates – it was down some draughty old mission hall and only half a dozen kids in the class, so that didn't seem like much fun to me. Besides, it was only about an hour and a half a day, so I wasn't going to learn much, was I? In any case, I'll be fourteen soon and I've got a job lined up – my uncle's got a stall up Rathbone Market, and I'm going to work for him. Fruit and veg, you know.'

'Tell me more about what happened. Were you in this shelter overnight?'

'No, I was in the one up the end there with my mum, all night.'

'Until the all-clear sounded?'

'Not quite. I nipped out a bit before that when it was getting quieter outside – for a bit of fresh air, like. It was smelly in there.'

'What time was that?'

'That would've been about half past five, I suppose, but I haven't got a watch, so I can't say exactly.'

'And how long were you out for?'

'I don't know – an hour or so, maybe. I know I was still out when the all-clear went, because I heard it.'

'That's a long time for a bit of fresh air.'

'Yes, well, I collect shrapnel, see. Lots of my mates do, and we swap it sometimes – we have a little competition to see who can find the best bits.'

'And what happened when you came back?'

'I popped in to see if my mum was still in the shelter. She wasn't, so I had a quick look at the others. When I went in that one over there I saw a bloke curled up in the corner, and it looked like he was dead.'

'So how long after the all-clear siren was that, do you think?'

'I reckon it was half an hour, not more.'

'Did you recognise the man?'

'No, never seen him before.'

Jago heard footsteps coming from behind and saw the boy glance past him. He turned round to see a woman approaching. She looked perhaps forty and walked with a kind of poise that struck Jago as perhaps not elegant but certainly self-possessed. She wore a tailored overcoat with an ARP armlet on one sleeve, and a white steel helmet with a black letter W painted on the front. A duty respirator was slung over her shoulder.

It seemed to Jago that for a moment she glared at them, her lips pursed and her brow knitted in an expression of hostility. The boy looked nervous and keen to be gone.

'All right, my lad,' he said, 'you can be off now.'

Jimmy turned and hurried away down the street. The woman watched him go, then strode over to Jago and looked him in the eye.

'Good morning,' she said. 'Are you the police?'

'Yes,' said Jago. 'And you are?'

'I'm the post warden. They told me you were here and that someone had found a body, so I thought I'd better look in. My name's Hampson, Mrs Maud Hampson.'

She removed one glove and held out her hand to shake his. Her gloves, close-fitting and made from brown kid leather, looked as though they might have been expensive, but now they were scuffed and white with plaster dust.

'Good morning, Mrs Hampson. I'm Detective Inspector Jago of West Ham CID, and this is Detective Constable Cradock. Which post are you in charge of?'

'Post 1Q, at Custom House School. We cover the area from here down towards the docks.'

'Thank you for stopping by. Tell me, that boy who's just gone – do you know him?'

She looked again in the direction by which he had gone.

'No, but I know his sort.'

Jago waited for her to elaborate, but instead she sighed, moving her hand across her brow to tuck a lock of hair back under her helmet. He noticed that this movement left a faint streak of grime across her forehead.

'Look, Inspector,' she said, 'it's been a busy night, and I still have a lot to do – I've got nine of these shelters in my area and I've got to finish doing the rounds for my damage report before I can go off duty. I just wanted to check whether you need any assistance.'

'Thank you, but I think we have everything in hand.'

She stepped past him and peered in at the entrance to the shelter.

'Don't go in there, please,' said Jago. 'I don't want the scene disturbed.'

She stopped and turned back to face him.

'Very sorry. Just instinct, I suppose – one gets to feel very responsible for these places. Mind you, if you've stuck your nose in there you'll probably have realised it's pretty disgusting.'

'Yes, it was a little unsavoury.'

'That's a nice way to put it. To be honest, it's a disgrace, and it makes me very cross.'

'What's the problem?'

'Bad planning before the war started, that's the problem. I blame the government – they decided in their wisdom that if we ever had air raids they'd only last an hour at the most, so these public shelters were just for people caught out on the streets who couldn't get home. It seems no one imagined hundreds of local residents would end up spending all night in them, every night, so as a result there's no lighting, no heating, no lavatory, and most people have to sit on newspapers on the floor. There'll be trouble if something's not done about it soon, you mark my words.'

She paused, as if sensing she might have said too much.

'Forgive me, Inspector, I'm sure you haven't come down here to listen to my gripes. Is there anything you actually do want to know before I go?'

'There is one thing, yes – were you by any chance in this shelter during the air raid?'

'No. We have an unwritten rule in the ARP service, you see – a warden doesn't take shelter during an air raid. I was at the post quite a lot of the time, because there always has to be someone there to answer the phone, and apart from that I was roaming around here and there wherever I was needed.'

'Well, if anyone reports seeing anything suspicious here in the early hours of this morning, please get in touch with me at West Ham police station, if you'd be so kind.'

'Certainly, I shall. But now if that's all I can do for you I'd be glad to get back to the post.'

'Of course. May I just take a note of your address, and your telephone number if you have one?'

'Yes, I have a flat at the top end of Freemasons Road – number 213. No phone there, I'm afraid, but you can generally find me at the post – I'm on duty six nights a week and on call for sirens all day too.'

Jago closed his notebook and slipped it into his pocket.

'Thank you, Mrs Hampson. You've been most helpful.'

'Well,' she said with another sigh, 'that seems to be my job – being helpful to everyone. Nine months ago people were calling us the Darts Brigade, a bunch of army-dodgers and busybodies getting paid for doing nothing. Now they expect us to save them from the bombs, hold their hands, clean the filthy shelters for them, and be at their beck and call day and night. I'm tired – all I want to do now is help myself to a bit of sleep.'

She turned and walked away. As she did, Jago

wondered briefly about the faint smell of whisky he'd caught on her breath when she sighed. Still, he thought, she can't be the only one who needs a bit of Dutch courage to deal with a night's bombing.

CHAPTER FOUR

'Right, let's get back in there and have another look round – if your nose can bear it,' said Jago as Mrs Hampson disappeared round the corner. He and Cradock entered the shelter again.

'One more check of the floor,' he continued, 'just to make sure you're right and there isn't a weapon lurking somewhere.'

The concrete at their feet was littered with cigarette ends, crumbs of food and dog-eared sheets of newspaper.

'That post warden was right,' said Cradock. 'They'll have rats in here soon if they don't keep it a bit tidier than this.'

'Nothing of interest for our purposes, though, I think,' said Jago. 'Let's take a look in his pockets – see if we can find out who he is.'

They returned to the corner where the corpse was still seated on the bench. Cradock carefully reached into the dead man's coat pockets and pulled out the contents.

'Not much here, sir,' he said. 'A wallet, a diary and two keys on a ring. No sign of a national identity card, though – that's a bit unusual.'

'Yes, but there must be lots of people who forget to take it out with them sometimes, especially in an air raid – and they get two days to produce it at the station before it's an offence.'

'He's not going to be doing that now, is he?'

'No, and we shan't be sending him to the magistrates' court either. Now, pass me that little diary and check the wallet. And let's go outside – we can see better there, not to mention breathe.'

They stepped outside into the early morning light. Nottingham Avenue itself seemed to have escaped the bombs, but the noise coming from a nearby street suggested not everywhere had. They could hear sounds that a year ago would have been out of keeping on a Sunday but had now become commonplace: baskets of rubble being dumped into the back of a truck, and shouts from rescue workers coordinating their efforts. Then, abruptly, the shouting ceased, everything fell quiet. Listening for someone trapped in the wreckage, Jago thought. He'd seen it several times – the men digging would call for a brief silence in case anyone buried was making their presence known. He found himself instinctively listening too, even though he was far from the scene. As he listened, he became aware of birds calling and responding from tree to tree, and for that moment only it could have been a normal Sunday morning after all. Then the noise started again.

He opened the leather-bound pocket diary and found a name written inside the front cover.

'Right,' he announced to Cradock, who had crouched down beside the shelter's wall and was examining the contents of the wallet. 'His name seems to be Paul Ramsey, assuming this is his diary. No address here, though. I wonder what he did for a living. Any clues in that wallet?'

'No, sir,' said Cradock. 'There's not much in here at all. Just some cash. Two pound notes and a few bob in coins. But if his money's still here, I suppose we can rule out robbery, can't we?'

'On the face of it, yes,' said Jago, 'unless perhaps it was an attempted robbery that went wrong. But not many people would kill for a couple of pounds in cash, would they? And the keys?'

'They look like Yale door keys to me. Probably the keys to his house, I shouldn't wonder.'

'Good. If we can find out where he lived and it turns out he was local, we should be able to take a look this afternoon.'

Cradock took that to mean that the rest of his day off had just disappeared in a puff of smoke.

'Yes, sir,' he replied, trying hard to disguise the weariness in his voice.

Jago opened the diary at the ribbon page marker.

'Here we are,' he said. 'This looks like the most recent entry – two days ago.'

He passed it to Cradock, tapping the right-hand page with his index finger. 'What do you make of that?'

'Friday, eleven o'clock in the morning, "T. H. Hampson",' said Cradock. 'A meeting of some kind, I suppose. With someone called Hampson – that's the same name as that ARP woman's, isn't it?'

'Well done, Peter.'

Cradock thought he noticed a touch of sarcasm in Jago's voice, but wasn't entirely sure.

'Not her, though,' he said. 'Her name starts with an M. Could T. H. Hampson be a relative?'

'It's possible. Something else for us to find out. The only T. Hampson I know of is Tommy Hampson.'

'Local villain, sir?'

'No – he played in goal for West Ham back in the early twenties.'

'Oh,' said Cradock, nodding as if grateful for the enlightenment. 'I was just a kid then.' He hoped this might be a good enough excuse for the fact that he'd never heard of the man. Since working for Jago he'd formed the impression that the DI found his lack of interest in football strange. 'Good, was he?' he added, to show willing.

'Yes, but not as good as Ted Hufton, so he didn't get to play in the 1923 Cup Final, which must have been a disappointment for him.'

'Oh,' said Cradock again. 'Yes, of course.'

He leafed back a few pages from where Jago had opened the diary.

'There's some more things written in here for

September, sir,' he said, his voice brightening. 'Ah, yes – I think I may have found out what he did for a living. Look, there's an entry here that says "staff meeting", and another one a bit further back that says "start of term". He must have been a teacher, don't you think?'

'Quite possibly – or perhaps a headmaster, but he looks a bit young for that.'

'There's something else here too, sir, for last week. It says "Drink with Shaw, POW".' Cradock's voice reflected his puzzlement. 'He went for a drink with a prisoner of war?'

'Unlikely, I would say. I believe the government's quite strict about prisoners of war, and in any case, the way things have been going I don't imagine we've got many yet.'

Jago thought for a moment.

'No, I know what that is – POW, the Prince of Wales. And before you ask, I don't mean he went for a drink with the Prince of Wales, because we haven't got one now – I mean the pub. It's not far from here – down the other end of Prince Regent Lane, by Cundy Road.'

He glanced at his watch. It was nearly half past eight. He looked down towards the far end of the street.

'Where's that pathologist got to?'

'He should be here soon, sir.'

As if on cue, a black Austin saloon turned the corner and stopped. A young man got out, clutching a leather bag, and strode briskly towards the two detectives.

'Good morning, Dr Anderson,' said Jago as he joined

37

them. 'I'm sorry we've had to drag you out so early on a Sunday morning.'

'Think nothing of it,' said Anderson. 'I was up already, and it's a fine morning, isn't it?'

Jago envied the man's energy, and could only assume the doctor had somehow managed to get a more peaceful night than he had.

'Where's the body, then?' said Anderson, looking round the street.

'In here,' said Jago, gesturing towards the shelter entrance. 'Young man, looks in his twenties, may have been a schoolmaster. The police surgeon says he died of a stab wound to the chest. There's what look like traces of blood on the floor, by his feet, and we found a hat that fits him on the floor, so there may have been a struggle. No weapon to be seen, so we assume someone killed him. I'll obviously be interested to know your view on what kind of weapon may have been used.'

Anderson followed him into the shelter and began to examine the body by the light of Cradock's torch.

'Yes,' he said, pulling open the dead man's shirt, 'definitely a wound to the chest, as the police surgeon said, and that seems to be the source of the blood.'

'And would you say he was stabbed with a knife?'

'Rather than something like a chisel, you mean? It looks very likely, but I'll be more certain when I've taken a closer look at him and his insides at the hospital.'

'And he was murdered?' said Cradock.

'That's for you to say, I think – I assume you

wouldn't rule out manslaughter at this stage, for example. But as the police surgeon said, it certainly looks as though this was the wound that killed him. I suppose you'll be wanting to know if I can say how long he's been dead?'

'Anything you can tell us will be helpful,' said Jago.

'The short answer is not yet. If he's died of a stab wound, it's notoriously difficult to say. I'll take his temperature in a moment, which may help me to estimate, and I might also have a better idea when I've done a post-mortem examination.'

'This shelter would've been crammed full of people all night, so it's unlikely he'd have been stabbed then, isn't it?'

'I suppose that's a reasonable assumption. The assailant would have had to use some force, and if you're right and there'd been some kind of struggle too one would imagine it wouldn't have gone unnoticed, but obviously that's not something I can establish. When was the body found?'

'About a quarter to seven.'

'And what time was the all-clear? I didn't note the time myself.'

'Quarter past six.'

'So there was about half an hour between the all-clear and the moment the body was found. Was the shelter empty by then?'

'Yes.'

'So subject to what I find in the post-mortem, we might surmise that he was killed sometime during that period, between six-fifteen and six-forty-five, on the grounds that it would have been easier for someone to kill him when the shelter was empty rather than full.'

'Could he have been stabbed outside and staggered in here looking for help, or been dragged in here if the killer wanted to hide him?' said Cradock.

Anderson took the flashlight from the detective constable and directed its beam downwards, first at the floor by the body and then at the surrounding area.

'As Mr Jago said, there's blood on the floor beneath the body,' he said, 'but nowhere else. That would be consistent with the victim having been killed right there, where he's sitting. If he'd been dragged in while he was bleeding we might expect to find some trace of blood elsewhere on the floor, but it doesn't look as though there is any. As for staggering in here by himself, that would depend on how quickly he died. But in any case, I imagine you might ask yourselves why, if he was desperate for help, he would seek it in a shelter that was likely to be empty. Wouldn't he have more chance of finding help outside? And which is the more likely place for the killer to attack him – out in the open on the street or in a shelter that was empty because the all-clear had sounded half an hour ago? Those are questions for you rather than me, but on the basis of what I can see I'd say he was killed right here.'

'Is it all right for us to move him now?' said Jago.

'Yes, I've almost finished. I just need to take his temperature, then I'll get the mortuary van to take him up to the hospital. I'll have a more detailed look at him there and see what I can come up with. You can join me for the examination if you like.'

There were few things Jago enjoyed less than watching a pathologist cut into a cold corpse in an even colder mortuary, so he shook his head.

'If you don't mind, I think I'd rather join you when you've finished. I need to find out whether he has any family so I can get someone to identify him. OK if I join you in a couple of hours?'

'That should be fine. Now, where's my thermometer?' said Anderson, rummaging in his bag.

'I think I'll leave you to it,' said Jago. 'Come along, Peter.'

He led Cradock out of the shelter as Anderson bade them a cheery farewell. Watching a pathologist taking a dead man's temperature was another scene he had witnessed enough times already in his career.

'Shall I get some men to search the area, sir?' said Cradock once they were outside. 'See if we can find the weapon? Dr Anderson seemed to think it was probably a knife.'

'I'm not very hopeful,' said Jago. 'If the weapon's not here the killer must have taken it away and could've tossed it anywhere.'

'Chucked it on a bomb site, for example?'

'Exactly, and then how do we spot it? There are knives lying around all over the place – how do we know what's a murder weapon and what's just the contents of some poor soul's kitchen drawers scattered in all directions by a bomb? And blood too – in the old days we might've found a bit of bloodstained cloth, and that would've been suspicious, but now you can walk round the corner and find curtains, sheets, clothes and Lord knows what else all over the place, and blood on half of it. Besides, right now I should think every man we've got is likely to be looking after the living who've been bombed out of their homes last night or helping to dig out the dead.'

'Still got to try, I suppose?'

'Yes, you're right. Just do what you can with whoever can be spared. And there's something else you can do. I want to know if this Ramsey fellow really was a teacher, and if so what school he taught at, so find someone who knows, and get me the home address of the headmaster or headmistress or whoever's in charge. You'll have to speak to the council, but the only people they've got working today will probably be doing a duty shift at the ARP headquarters in Stratford High Street, so start with them. If you have to get someone out of bed at the council do so, and tell them we need to know now, not next Tuesday.'

'Yes, sir,' said Cradock, mentally adding an interview with a school head to the list of the day's forthcoming pleasures.

'And before we go, let's pop back in and check his other pockets. Dr Anderson should've finished that temperature business by now,' said Jago.

They went back into the shelter and found the

pathologist wiping his thermometer with a cloth and replacing it in his bag.

'All done, Doctor?' said Jago.

'Yes,' said Anderson. 'There's just one thing I think might be of interest to you.'

'Oh, yes – what's that?'

'I had to move him a little to take his temperature, and adjust his clothing, of course, and that's when I saw his right-hand trouser pocket for the first time. It looked as though there was something quite bulky in it, so I had a careful look. But I didn't touch anything – I thought I'd better leave that to you.'

Jago nodded to Cradock, who put his notebook down and stuck his pencil behind his ear, then eased open the pocket. He gave a low whistle. Using his pencil, he carefully removed a dull black object and held it up for the other two men to see.

'It's a gun,' he said.

Given that they could now all see it, Jago found the comment superfluous. But to be fair to Cradock it was unusual to find firearms in air-raid shelters, or indeed anywhere on the streets of West Ham, so he let it pass.

'Yes,' he said. 'A revolver.'

He took a step forward and examined it more closely.

'A Webley Mark VI, by the look of it.'

'You know your guns, then,' said Anderson.

'I wouldn't say that. I'm no expert, but this one's easy to identify – it was standard issue to British Army officers from 1915.'

He took the pencil from Cradock and scrutinised the weapon.

'If you look down there below the cylinder, just above the trigger, it's stamped on the side – "Webley Mark VI". See? And those little arrowheads mean it was for military use. I had one myself when I was commissioned – it saved my bacon more than once.'

Jago pulled a clean handkerchief from his pocket and covered his hands with it as he lifted the weapon off Cradock's pencil. With one hand holding the grip and the other round the barrel, he pulled the hammer down and broke the gun open with as light a movement as he could. He showed it to Cradock: all six chambers were loaded.

'Right,' he continued, tipping the rounds out of the cylinder and handing the gun back to Cradock, 'keep this wrapped up so no one touches it. When we get back to the station, make a note of the serial number, then pack it up properly with the cartridges and send it off to the fingerprint boys at Scotland Yard. And take this dead man's prints and send them too – I want to know if anyone else has handled this gun apart from him.'

'Will do, sir. I wonder how he got his hands on this – not exactly a toy, is it?'

'No – it's a deadly weapon in anyone's hands. But there must be hundreds of them around, if not thousands – so many men brought them home when the war ended.'

'Even so, sir, it's not what you expect to find in a place like this.'

'On the face of it, no, it's not.'

'Especially loaded. Do you think that means he was planning to use it?'

'We don't even know if it was his – someone could've put it in his pocket after he died. And if it was his, it doesn't necessarily mean he intended to fire it – he might've just wanted to frighten somebody.'

'Or maybe he was frightened of someone who might want to harm him?'

'Yes, or perhaps he just found it in the street and was going to hand it in to us – who knows? Whatever the reason, it didn't help him much today.'

CHAPTER FIVE

By mid-morning Cradock had the information Jago wanted. One of the council staff on weekend duty at the ARP headquarters worked in the education department and confirmed that Paul Ramsey was a teacher at the secondary school in Prince Regent Lane. The headmaster was a Mr Jeremy Gilroy, who lived in Garvary Road, in Custom House. By eleven o'clock Jago and Cradock were sitting with him in the front parlour of his modest terraced house.

The room was neat and tidy, and Gilroy struck Jago as being the same. They had called on him at short notice on a Sunday morning, but he was dressed in a smart grey suit with spotlessly polished black shoes. His dark hair, parted in the centre, looked recently cut and had a speckling of grey at the temples. His face was lean, well proportioned, and intelligent, and he wore a pair of round tortoiseshell glasses. He seemed poised and self-controlled, but Jago noticed that every few seconds he fiddled with his shirt cuff, apparently trying to ensure the correct amount showed beyond the sleeve of his jacket.

'I understand you're the headmaster of the local secondary school,' said Jago. 'Is that correct?'

'Yes, although only since the beginning of this term, so I'm what you might call a new boy. The school was shut down when the war started, like so many others, but then the council decided to reopen it as an emergency school.'

'What's that?'

'A temporary solution to what we hope will be a temporary problem – I don't think it was an easy decision for them to take. The thing is, as you know, all the children were evacuated to safer parts of the country when the war started, but then when the mass air attacks that we'd been expecting didn't happen and people started talking about it being a "phoney war", a great number of children began drifting back to the borough. But with no schools for them to return to, their education effectively came to a halt.'

'I don't know much about children, but I imagine they weren't too concerned about that.'

'No doubt, but in my profession we can see that it's a disaster. We risk having a whole generation of children growing up unable to read or write. There was a national survey at the beginning of the year, and it found that only half of elementary-age children were getting regular schooling. That's shocking. What's the future of this country going to be like if our children are denied education?'

'So the council are reopening the schools? I haven't seen much sign of that, but then I don't have any children.'

'Well, that was the problem, you see. For one thing, they couldn't reopen all the schools, because so many are being used for things like Air Raid Precautions and the Auxiliary Fire Service, and several have been damaged in the bombing. And even if they could have, they didn't want to, because it might tempt still more parents to bring their children back from the evacuation, and that would be dangerous for them while these air raids are going on. On the other hand, the council couldn't just have hundreds of children in the borough with no school to go to, so they're opening a small number of emergency schools – it means there'll be children of all ages lumped in together, but at least they'll be taught.'

'I see – so that's what your school's doing.'

'Yes, and they brought me in to be the head teacher. It's a big challenge, but to be honest with you, I felt honoured to be appointed – there are so many children who've had their education disrupted, and these emergency schools are vital for getting them back into learning.'

'I can understand that, Mr Gilroy. Now, I believe that your staff at this new school includes Mr Paul Ramsey. Is that correct?'

'Yes, indeed. Is there some problem?'

Jago gave no reply as he pulled the diary from his pocket and opened it at the first page.

'Take a look at this, please, Mr Gilroy. It has Paul Ramsey's name written inside the front cover. Do you recognise the handwriting?'

'Yes, it's his,' said Gilroy.

'And these entries here,' Jago continued, turning to the September section. 'Where it says "start of term" and "staff meeting" – are those the correct dates for your school?'

'Yes, they are. That must be Ramsey's diary. But why have you got it?'

Jago slipped the diary back into his pocket.

'It's come into our possession because a man was found dead this morning. There was no national identity card on him – just the diary. I'm sorry to say this, but we need to establish whether the man in question was Mr Ramsey.'

'What did he look like?'

'In his twenties, I'd say. Dark hair, clean-shaven.'

Gilroy looked apprehensive. 'Did he have a scar – here?' he asked, tracing an index finger across his forehead above his left eye. 'At a kind of forty-five-degree angle?'

'Yes.'

'It must be him, then. But dead, you say? That's just awful – the poor man. How – what happened?'

'We suspect foul play. We're treating it as a case of suspected murder.'

'Oh my goodness. That's terrible news.'

Jago waited for Gilroy to calm himself, then continued.

'We need to trace his next of kin for the formal identification, so I'm hoping you'll be able to help us. Can you tell me anything about Mr Ramsey's family? Was he married?'

'Married? No, he was a bachelor, and I don't recall him mentioning any woman in his life, but then again that's not the kind of thing he'd need to tell his head teacher. As for other family, I don't think his parents are still alive, but I do know he has a brother, Joe Ramsey. He's a local businessman, and I believe he's the only close living relative. I imagine he's the man you'll need to speak to.'

'Thank you. Do you have an address for him?'

'As it happens, I do,' said Gilroy, his voice subdued as he took a notebook from the inside pocket of his jacket. 'A sign of the times, I suppose. We've already lost one colleague to the air raids, so I've taken to keeping a note of all my staff's next of kin on me in case of emergency. It's just a sad necessity in today's world, but still a rather morbid thought, I feel.'

He opened the book and turned over a few pages.

'Yes, here it is.'

He tore a blank page from the back of the book and wrote on it, then handed it to Jago.

'There you are – his home address and a telephone number.'

'Thank you, Mr Gilroy. That's most helpful.'

'Is there anything else I can do?'

'Yes, there is, actually. I'd like you to tell me a little

about Mr Ramsey, if you don't mind. Did you know him before you moved to this school?'

'No, I didn't – I've only worked with him since the beginning of September, when I started this job.'

'Your impressions will be valuable, even so. What kind of man was he, in your view?'

'I can't say I was closely acquainted with him – I only knew him as a member of the staff – but he was a capable teacher. Overall I'd say he was a confident man, with ambitions for the future, for his career. It's so, er, so difficult to believe he's not . . . well, that he's not here any more. Forgive me, Inspector, but it's all rather a shock.'

'How old was he?'

'Twenty-six, I think. He'd been teaching for a couple of years, and before that I believe he worked in a commercial business of some kind.'

'What did he teach?'

'English – he was recently promoted to head of the English department.'

'After two years? That's rather soon for promotion, isn't it?'

'In normal times I'd agree with you, Inspector, but needs must, as they say. It's difficult to insist on years of experience these days – especially when we can look up at the sky every day and see that the only thing standing between us and defeat is nineteen-year-old boys. We needed a replacement suddenly because the previous head of department was killed in the first big air raid in September, and I had to make a decision. I think one thing this war's taught us is that whatever our responsibility, we all have to be bold and decisive, and when I've made a decision I stick to it. Mr Ramsey got the job – he was the best person available.'

'And now you have to start again.'

'Yes, it seems we have a double tragedy on our hands – two heads of department lost within a month. It was only last Thursday that I told Mr Ramsey he'd got the job, and now I have to find a replacement for him too. It's not going to be easy, but we'll find someone. To be frank, no one is irreplaceable.'

'But I assume he was good at his job?'

'Oh, yes, he fulfilled all the duties of his post satisfactorily. I wouldn't say he was outstanding, but then to be quite honest the teaching profession in general is not what it was, Inspector. I find the current generation of schoolmasters leaves rather a lot to be desired. Far too easy in their manner, most of them. When I started teaching, the world was very different. Then we still believed we were raising children to serve a great empire, to be a credit to their king and country. Nowadays, though, I don't know. A lot of teachers have some funny ideas.'

'Did Paul Ramsey have funny ideas?'

'Not about teaching, no. He knew how to teach, and when all's said and done that's what he was paid to do. But there were just one or two times when I had occasion to talk to him about anything other than the day-to-day work of the school, and then I found a certain contrariness about him.'

'For example?'

'About the war, for example. I was talking to him after that terrible air raid, the one that started all this trouble we're having now. I knew he had certain principles that he thought a lot of, particularly concerning the war, but I was quite surprised by what he came out with. Remember, his own head of department had just been killed, and I remarked that the only way to deal with these Nazis is to give them a taste of their own medicine. I mean, it's perfectly simple – they're bombing us, so we should bomb them even harder. It's the only language they understand. Ramsey got very upset when I said that – he was a regular peacemonger. He said, "All they that take the sword shall perish by the sword," which I must say sounded a tad pompous to me. I said I was more inclined to agree with Theodore Roosevelt – you know, "Speak softly and carry a big stick." If your country's strong, others won't trouble you.'

'What did he say to that?'

'He said if we bombed them back we'd be stooping to their level and would lose the moral high ground. Forget the moral high ground, I said – at a time like this when our very existence depends on it, we need to fight fire with fire. He didn't like that at all, got quite animated about it. So you see, he could be a little prickly at times. But forgive me, Inspector, I shouldn't speak ill of the dead. Is there anything else you'd like to know?'

'I'd be grateful to know his address, if you have it.'

'Yes, I have it here.'

He looked through his address book again.

'Here it is – 47 Tree Road.'

'Tree Road?' Cradock interjected. 'We passed that on the way to the shelter, didn't we, sir?'

'Yes, it's quite close,' said Jago. 'And only a couple of hundred yards or so from the Prince of Wales, so maybe that was his local.'

He turned back to the headmaster.

'Was Paul Ramsey a drinking man, Mr Gilroy?'

'I believe he enjoyed the occasional glass, but as far as I know he wasn't a heavy drinker, if that's what you mean.'

'Thank you. Did he have any colleagues at school that he mixed with socially or was particularly close to?'

'I'm not sure – I don't know much about my staff's life outside school. I imagine his closest colleague would have been Mr Shaw – Harold Shaw. He's another English teacher.'

Jago assumed this would be the Shaw whose name they had found in Ramsey's diary, but kept the thought to himself.

'Very good. I'd like to talk to Mr Shaw, but there are some more pressing things to do today. What would be the best time to catch him at school tomorrow?'

'He should be free at lunchtime, and if not then, at half past three. That's when the schools shut now, and they don't open till half past nine in the morning – it's been like that since the air raids started.'

'Thank you. Do you know of any other friends Mr Ramsey had?'

'Apart from school colleagues, you mean? No, I don't think I do.'

'Could he have had any enemies?'

'Enemies? Not that I know of. I suppose there might be people who took a strong dislike to his views on the war, but I'm not aware of any particular individual who wished him harm.'

'Do you know if he had a gun?'

Gilroy's eyes widened in alarm.

'What? A gun? Why no, that would be completely out of character. My goodness, what a thought.'

He sat in silence, staring straight ahead as if having difficulty taking it in. His right hand strayed to his left shirt cuff and made a minuscule adjustment.

'Just another couple of questions, Mr Gilroy,' Jago continued. 'Did you notice anything unusual in his behaviour recently?'

Gilroy thought for a moment and shook his head slowly.

'No, not particularly – but then he was a teacher, and teachers have to act a sober and serious part for most of the day anyway. Although there was one thing I noticed. You know what it's like when a man has something on his mind but doesn't want to talk about it? It was like that. It reminded me of a colleague I had years ago who was running up gambling debts and didn't know what to do about it.'

'You're not saying Mr Ramsey was in that position?'

'No, no, not at all – or at least not to my knowledge.

I only mentioned it as an example of the kind of impression I got. I couldn't put my finger on it, but it was as though he were haunted by something – or perhaps hunted would be a better word for it. I'm sorry, Inspector, that must sound terribly muddled. It was only an impression, you see. I've no evidence to back it up.'

'There was something weighing on his mind?'

'Yes, he seemed preoccupied, worried about something. It was almost imperceptible – perhaps he was good at hiding it – but in the last couple of weeks I had the sense that in some way he was looking over his shoulder. Not literally, of course, but he seemed different. It was as though he felt someone was after him.'

CHAPTER SIX

What can this one tell us? Jago wondered, gazing at the lifeless face lying before him on the white porcelain mortuary table. Its eyes were closed and would never open again, its expression frozen. If only the dead could tell their story, he thought, how easy this job would be. If only those confident enthusiasts back in the last century who thought the face of a murderer was imprinted on the retina of his victim had been right – he'd now be waiting only for Dr Anderson to perform the necessary procedure on these hidden eyes and present him with a photograph of the killer. But no matter how great the pathologist's skill with his scalpel, how extensive his medical and scientific knowledge, Jago knew that today's post-mortem examination would not result in a conveniently detailed description of the man or woman he was looking for.

A quiet sigh beside him snapped him out of these thoughts.

'Yes, that's him,' said Joe Ramsey. 'That's my brother.'

Ramsey was a tall, wiry man with unruly dark hair. His face and what could be seen of his arms were tanned, and his mouth seemed permanently turned downwards in a way that made him look sullen. Jago quickly scanned his face for any sign of emotion, but he found little.

'Thank you, Mr Ramsey,' he said.

'Would he have suffered?'

'No. It would all have been over very quickly.'

Jago didn't know this for a fact, not having heard Dr Anderson's findings yet, but he felt it a reasonable thing to say about a man who'd been stabbed in the chest, and more importantly these were words that might be of some small comfort to the bereaved. It was like the letters he'd had to write from the front to the widows or parents of men who'd been killed in action – letters that said what they would want to hear about their lost husband or son. He gave Paul Ramsey's brother a few more moments to linger by the side of the body, then took him with Cradock into an empty office adjoining the mortuary.

'Mr Ramsey, would you mind if I ask you a few questions about your brother, until the pathologist comes back? It's just to help us build up a picture of him.'

'No, that's all right. What do you want to know?'

'Was Paul your only brother?'

'Yes, there were just the two of us.'

'And I believe he was twenty-six?'

'That's right – two years older than me. He'd have been twenty-seven in November.'

'Is there any other family?'

'No. Our dad died three years ago, and our mum before that. Dad worked himself to death, literally – he was gassed in the Great War and was never a well man, but he was a fighter. He built a business up from nothing, because he wanted to have something to pass on to his sons.'

'What kind of business was that?'

'Building.'

'But your brother didn't work for the company?'

Ramsey's laugh seemed to be laced with an edge of bitterness.

'No,' he said. 'Not him. Paul always had different ideas. He fancied he was cleverer than that – too good to get his hands dirty, you might say – so it was up to me to carry the business on when Dad died.'

'Is that something you would've preferred not to have to do?'

'No, I didn't mind at all. I like building, and I'm good at it. Paul always did better than me at school, but he ended up full of fancy ideas, and I've got no time for that. Roll your sleeves up and do an honest day's work, that's what I say. Building – that's man's work, not sitting round all day talking about poetry, or whatever he did. He might've passed more exams than me, but I reckon I've made more money than he ever did as a schoolmaster.'

'So you feel you've proved you're his equal?'

'No doubt about it. I used to envy my brother, used

to think I could never have what he had – but now I know there's nothing Paul had that I can't have too, and more so. In fact if he'd lived a little longer, he'd have had reason to be jealous of me. He might've been good at reading books, but that doesn't put food on the table. When all's said and done, I reckon my life started when I left school.'

'It wasn't your favourite place, then?'

'The masters were bullies, a bunch of thugs – and so were some of the older boys.'

'So it was useful to have a big brother in the school to protect you?'

'I thought it would be when I first went there, but it soon turned out I was wrong. He was just the same as the rest – a bully. He had a real vicious streak in him – you know what I mean? Made my life a misery, he did.'

'But I've been told he had strong moral views – on the war, for example.'

'That's one way of looking at it, I suppose, but I'm talking about when we were kids, not now. When we grew up he decided he was going to be a pacifist, but I don't know where he got that from – he was never afraid to swing a fist when he was young.'

'He was a pacifist?'

'Yes, I believe he was involved in that Peace Pledge Union thing – I expect you've heard of it. Just another of those fancy ideas I was talking about, I reckon, like books and poems and plays. He was probably just in it to get the girls – he always had an eye for the women. Too much spare time on his hands, I reckon – not like me.'

'He must have been of an age to register for military service, mustn't he? The government's been calling up the different age groups all this year, and I'm pretty sure they've already told the twenty-six-year-olds to register.'

'Yes, that's right, but his job was schoolmastering, and that's a reserved occupation. So's mine, for that matter.'

'So he reckoned he was safe from being called up?'

'Yes. When the government published that list of reserved occupations last year he was very pleased with himself for not being born a year later. He'd already turned twenty-five, so he was just old enough to be in the reserved-occupation category. I remember him saying he'd do anything to avoid going to war. I think he was planning to register as a conscientious objector too – he said it was all about his principles as a pacifist, but I'm not so sure he'd have got away with it. The tribunals are a bit fussy about how many conchies they'll allow, aren't they? They don't want us all trying it on. I wouldn't be surprised if he'd seen it coming years ago and decided to be a teacher just so he'd be safe if all the rumours about a war came true.'

'Did you have any sense that your brother was preoccupied or worried about anything?'

'No. We didn't see each other very often. But look, Inspector, I think I'd like to get out of this place, if it's all the same to you. Is there anything else?'

Jago could see over Ramsey's shoulder that Dr Anderson was standing in the mortuary and looking in his direction, apparently waiting for him to finish talking.

'Not just now, Mr Ramsey,' he said. 'I can see the pathologist waiting out there and I expect he'll be wanting to speak to me. But there are one or two other things I'd like to ask you about, so could I call on you at home later today?'

'Yes, be my guest,' said Ramsey. 'But if that's all, I'll go now – I'll see myself out.'

'Of course. Just before you go, though, could you tell me where you were overnight?'

'Yes – in my Anderson shelter, like everyone else. Same as I am every night, lying there trying to get to sleep while some bloke up in the sky's doing his best to kill me. And now if you don't mind—'

He muttered a curt farewell to Jago and Cradock, gathered up his coat and hat, and with a nod to Anderson waiting outside he left, closing the door behind him.

'Not exactly distraught, was he?' said Cradock as the pathologist joined them in the office.

'No,' said Jago, 'but he made no pretence of being close to his brother, so maybe what we got was just his honest reaction. There's no law that says brothers have to like each other.'

'I hope I'm not interrupting,' said Anderson, 'but I thought you'd want to know the results of my examination before I dash off.'

'Yes, of course – what did you find?' said Jago.

'Well, first of all I can confirm that he was stabbed once, in the left side of his chest – his left, that is – in the fourth intercostal space. That's the bit between the fourth and fifth ribs to you. And the weapon went straight into his heart – the left ventricle. It's likely that death would have occurred within a few seconds.'

'That's good.'

'Good?'

'Sorry – I've just assured his brother that it would all have been over very quickly, so I'm glad to hear your findings bear me out. Do continue, please. What was the weapon?'

'The shape of the wound suggests it was indeed a knife, as we suspected, and a sharp one at that. It looks to me as though it probably had a sharp point and a single cutting edge, so my guess would be something like a kitchen knife – and the blade would need to be five or six inches long to do that kind of damage.'

'So the murderer hit just the right spot first time. Does that mean it was an expert job? The killer was someone who'd done it before?'

'The position and angle of the wound are not inconsistent with that supposition, but equally it could have been a lucky stab by an amateur, or what you might call a first-timer. I can't say on the basis of the evidence here. I did find some fresh scratches on the man's hand and neck, though – that could indicate a struggle between the victim and his assailant.'

'And what about the time of death?'

'I can't be sure, but from what I've seen I'd stand by what I said earlier, that he was killed where he was found, and that it was likely to have been after the shelter had emptied. His body temperature would suggest he hadn't been dead long by the time I first saw him.'

'What does "not dead long" mean?'

'I wouldn't be able to say with any precision, but my observations would indicate he'd only been dead for a couple of hours or so by the time I took his temperature. That doesn't prove he was killed in the half-hour after the all-clear sounded, but I can say my findings are consistent with our assumption that that's what happened.'

'Any idea whether it was done by a man or a woman?'

'No, it could have been either.'

'So all we know is we're looking at a case of murder by stabbing.'

'Yes.'

'Not suicide?'

'I don't think so. People attempting suicide usually aim lower down, where they think the heart is, and they also tend to lift their clothing before inflicting the wound. Neither of these conditions applies in this case, so I think it's unlikely to be suicide. Besides, I couldn't see a weapon in the shelter. Did you find one?'

'No, no sign of one.'

'Then if I were in your position I'd assume I was looking for a killer unless I found evidence to the contrary.'

'Indeed.'

'I hope that gives you enough to get your teeth into.' Anderson glanced at his watch. 'Talking of which, it's a quarter to one already. If that's all you need to know, I'm off to get a quick bite to eat – would you chaps like to join me?'

Jago saw out of the corner of his eye an eager smile breaking on Cradock's face. He stepped forward to shake the pathologist's hand.

'No thank you, Doctor – we need to take a look at the dead man's home. Come along, Peter – no lunch for the wicked.'

CHAPTER SEVEN

Jago started the Riley, with Cradock in the front passenger seat, and pulled away. The drive from the mortuary at Queen Mary's Hospital in Stratford to Paul Ramsey's address in Custom House would mean crossing almost the whole length of the borough, and these days there was no knowing how long that would take – it all depended on how many streets were closed because of air-raid damage, unexploded bombs or any number of other hazards the overnight attacks might have caused.

Cradock was staring out of the side window and had his arms wrapped tightly across his stomach, which suggested to Jago that the boy was hungry. A few hundred yards down the road they passed a mobile canteen parked at the roadside, and Jago pulled over. He climbed out of the car, strode quickly to the counter and bought a threepenny round of cheese sandwiches and a Mars bar, then returned to the car and handed them to Cradock.

'Here you are,' he said. 'I hate to see a young man starving.'

'Thanks, guv'nor,' said Cradock, biting into the first sandwich as soon as they got underway again. 'Not having anything yourself?'

Jago shook his head.

'Hanging around in a mortuary full of dead bodies with a man who spends his time cutting them up to examine their innards does nothing for my appetite,' he replied. 'I'll get something later.'

Cradock paused before taking another bite and gazed at his sandwich for a moment, but then just as quickly seemed to recover and took another bite.

'Boiled baby,' he said brightly when he'd finished chewing.

'What?'

'What you just said about those dead bodies – it reminded me of the stuff we used to have for school dinners. Disgusting, it was – always seemed to be liver, full of veins, and then suet pudding for afters. We used to call it "boiled baby" – I suppose that's what we thought it looked like. Still, an army fights on its stomach, eh, sir?'

'So they say,' said Jago. 'But all the same, I think I'll eat later. And it's not "fights", it's "marches".'

'Whatever you say, sir.'

Jago drove south through Plaistow, and after only two substantial detours they arrived at Tree Road. He parked the car outside number 47, where it became clear that the terraced house was actually two flats.

One of Ramsey's keys opened the front door, and the other the internal door at the foot of the narrow staircase. They climbed this to the upper flat and went first into the living room, at the front of the house. Jago scanned the contents. It measured about fifteen feet by twelve and was sparsely but neatly furnished: a red-and-cream carpet, a square wooden dining table with two chairs, and a three-piece suite upholstered in a grey fabric. He walked over to a small bookcase and ran his eye along the book spines. Shakespeare, Dickens, Chaucer, Milton, a selection of Romantic poets and a few lengthy novels from the previous century – exactly what he supposed an English master would be likely to have on his shelves. He moved to the dining table, where an empty glass and a plate dusted with what appeared to be toast crumbs indicated that someone, presumably Paul Ramsey, had eaten there before leaving. Jago wondered whether Ramsey had been a tidy man in a hurry who'd had to depart without clearing them away, or an untidy man who'd thought he'd do that later, not knowing that there would be no later.

He picked up a thin yellow booklet that was lying, closed, beside the plate. 'What are you going to do about it?' asked the title. The front cover added that its subject was 'The case for constructive peace', its author was Aldous Huxley and its price was threepence – the price of a cheese sandwich, thought

Jago. He wondered what Huxley made of the value the world put on his writing, and leafed through the first few pages. The argument was familiar: war is not inevitable, pacifism makes the outbreak of war impossible, a world conference to settle the justifiable claims of the dissatisfied nations will avert war. The sort of thing that might well have provided fodder for Paul Ramsey's views on war, if his brother was to be believed.

Jago moved into the bedroom, followed by Cradock. It was as spartan as the living room: a single iron bedstead, a cane chair, an old figured-walnut wardrobe and a matching chest of drawers, with a marble-topped, tile-backed washstand in the corner, on which stood a wash bowl and jug for the dead man's ablutions. The only striking feature in the room was a group of three small framed photographs on the chest of drawers. Jago examined them while Cradock investigated the contents of the wardrobe. The pictures all appeared to be of the same young woman, fair-haired, with an open, attractive face, and one of them showed her standing next to a man. As far as Jago could tell, this was Paul Ramsey: he stood about a foot taller than her, and his face seemed locked in a much more serious expression, almost a scowl.

'Here, look after this,' he said, passing the photograph to Cradock. 'Anything of interest in that wardrobe?'

'Nothing much, guv'nor,' said Cradock. 'There's three

packs of playing cards in here, still sealed. Maybe he played for money – to top up his teacher's salary, perhaps? Apart from that there's just the usual kind of clobber you'd expect a schoolmaster to wear. I found this in one of his jackets, though – looks like a letter.'

He handed an envelope to Jago. It was addressed to Ramsey and stamped with a local postmark dated the previous week, and was open. Jago took out the sheet of paper inside it and unfolded it.

'It's from someone called Wilfred Morton,' he said, 'group leader for the Peace Pledge Union, inviting him to their next meeting – and it's next week, so he won't be making that. It starts "Dear Paul", so he must already know him, and the address at the top's in Barking Road. That's on our way back to the station, so we could drop in on him – he might be able to shed some light on Ramsey's life outside school, and if he knew him well there's a chance he'll be able to tell us who the young lady in these photos is too. Anything else in that wardrobe?'

'Just this,' said Cradock, hauling out a small suitcase. 'Feels like there's something in it.'

He swung it onto the counterpane that covered the narrow bed on the far side of the room. From where Jago was standing the suitcase appeared to be a cheap cardboard affair, somewhat battered at the corners.

'Have a look, then,' said Jago, 'while I just check what's in this chest of drawers.'

He opened the first drawer and began rummaging, but there was little in it: just a small collection of handkerchiefs, socks and underclothes. The second drawer too was half-empty. He was beginning to doubt whether this search would yield anything of interest when Cradock spoke from the other side of the room.

'That's interesting.'

Jago closed the drawer and turned to face him.

'Yes?'

'It's half packed. Looks as if maybe he was planning to go away somewhere – he's even put his shaving kit in here.'

The open lid of the suitcase was facing Jago, so he couldn't see into it, but Cradock held up a safety razor and a badger-hair shaving brush, like trophies.

'Interesting indeed,' said Jago. 'I wonder if he—'

'Hang on,' Cradock interrupted. 'There's something else in here.'

He moved some clothes aside and produced a pair of small cardboard boxes.

'Well, well,' he said, reading the words printed on the front of the boxes. '"Twelve cartridges, revolver, .455 inch". I'd say that suggests he didn't just find that gun on the street. Wouldn't you, sir? I mean, having a revolver in your pocket's one thing, but keeping a store of ammunition in your bedroom is another. His boss said he was a man with no enemies, didn't he? That doesn't sound like the kind of bloke who'd feel the need to take a gun and a pile of cartridges for a weekend away, does it?'

'Hmm,' said Jago. 'Curiouser and curiouser. I wonder where he was going – and what he was planning to do when he got there.'

CHAPTER EIGHT

Beckton Road was the main thoroughfare running across the southern part of the borough and on into neighbouring East Ham. Jago guessed that its extra width offered their best chance of getting to Wilfred Morton's home without delay, and he was right: they only ran into one blockage. A sizeable bomb must have landed in the roadway during the night, leaving a large crater, demolishing the two closest houses, and rendering those nearby uninhabitable. Now workmen were busy with shovels, wheelbarrows and handcarts. He had to wait until he could ease the Riley through the remaining gap, avoiding the debris and rubble, but after that they made good time. Within minutes they were at the junction with Barking Road and could see on the opposite corner the distinctive Gothic spire of Trinity Church, which had so far escaped the bombing.

They turned right and parked just past the church, then crossed to the other side of Barking Road and found number 174, Morton's address. It was a bookshop – closed, of course, as it was Sunday, and the only person in sight was a woman sweeping the pavement in front of it. She was dressed in a long, black-and-white floral-patterned dress that looked more like the kind of thing Jago imagined women wore to cocktail parties. This was combined with red high-heeled shoes and a vivid red turban incongruously adorned with what he took to be a peacock feather tucked into the knot at the front. They passed her and headed for a black door to the side of the shopfront and rang the bell. The woman stopped sweeping and approached them.

'Can I help you?'

'Yes, we're police officers – we're looking for Mr Wilfred Morton. Am I right in believing this is where he lives?'

They held up their identity cards for her scrutiny. The woman's eyes twitched from one card to the other, then back to Jago's face.

'Police? There must be some mistake, surely. Mr Morton is a very law-abiding man and wouldn't harm a fly – he can't have done anything wrong.'

'I haven't said he has, madam. We just need to speak to him.'

'I see. Well, he's just popped out to catch the post. He's very dedicated to his work, you know, with a lot of correspondence, and I expect he's been using his Sunday to catch up.'

'And you are?'

'I'm Mrs Garside – Olivia Garside. This is my shop – I sell books, as you can see. I live upstairs, on the first floor, and Mr Morton rents the top-floor flat from me. Would you like to come inside and wait for him? I don't expect he'll be long.'

'Thank you,' said Jago, and removed his hat as she led them into the shop. It was small inside, and packed from floor to ceiling with bookshelves, which in turn were crammed with books, apparently a mixture of new and second-hand.

Mrs Garside positioned herself in front of the two men, with one hand resting on a shelf at head height and the other on her hip, as if she were modelling women's fashions in a mannequin parade. Indeed, thought Jago, while she looked a few years older than himself and perhaps twice the age of Cradock, she cut a very smart figure, and her choice of clothes suggested sophisticated if perhaps eccentric tastes. She seemed markedly less tense now that she'd been reassured that they hadn't come to arrest her lodger.

'Let me get you something to drink while you wait, gentlemen. What would you like?'

'A glass of water would be fine,' said Jago. 'We don't want to put you to any trouble.'

'A glass of water it is, then.'

She wove her way between the bookshelves and disappeared to the back of the shop, returning shortly with two glasses of water.

'Thank you,' said Jago, taking one and sipping it. 'Now, Mrs Garside, we're here merely to ask Mr Morton for his help in connection with our enquiries. We think he may know someone we're trying to find out about. Has he lived here for long?'

'A year or more – yes, it was the spring of last year that he moved in, so about a year and a half.'

'Do you know him well?'

'Well enough to know that he's a good tenant and a man of sensitivity and taste – the kind of man who understands the importance of books. I believe that a man who has no books has no civilisation – don't you agree?'

'I'm fond of reading, Mrs Garside,' said Jago, casting his eyes over the shelves that surrounded him.

'Do please call me Olivia,' she said.

She perched on the edge of a table, trailing one foot on the floor, and crossed the other leg elegantly over it. She looked at him carefully, as if perhaps wondering what kind of literature he read.

'I couldn't live without books,' she continued. She picked up a leather-bound volume from the table and caressed its cover absent-mindedly, then abruptly put it down again. 'Unfortunately, however, not everyone in this part of the world agrees with me. Before the war, some of my friends were quite fond of Mr Hitler and couldn't understand why I detested him so vehemently. I told them why – it was because he and his Nazi thugs burnt books. Anything they deemed "un-German" was fit only for the flames – even books by some of their finest writers if there was the slightest whiff of the synagogue about them. They behaved like animals. I prefer more cultured souls, like Mr Morton. He's a poet, you know.'

'Really?'

'Yes, and I believe we need men like him now as much as we need miners and soldiers. I mean, where are they? In the last war our poets were giants of men. I once met Wilfred Owen, you know. It's a coincidence, isn't it? Wilfred Owen, now Wilfred Morton – it's as if they were kindred spirits. He was serving in the Artists' Rifles when I met him – Owen, that is. A whole regiment of artists, poets, musicians and the like – such a noble idea, and yet so sad. Do you know of them?'

Jago nodded thoughtfully.

'I do, actually – our paths crossed once, although I didn't meet Wilfred Owen, of course. I was at the front near Cambrai in November 1917, until a shrapnel wound put me out of action for a while, and there was a battalion of the Artists' Rifles in the line not far from us. They had a hard time of it – mud like glue, and shell craters so deep the tallest men could drown in them. They took very heavy casualties, I believe.'

He fell silent, lost in reflection, then noticed a look of distress on her face.

'I'm sorry,' he said, snapping himself back to their conversation. 'I shouldn't talk about such things.'

'On the contrary – men of your generation don't talk about them enough. If we'd heard more of the awful reality we might have been more determined to prevent it happening again. How many great men were lost in that war? How many future Mozarts, Miltons, Rembrandts, all cut down in their prime because our politicians and generals made them walk into machine-gun fire and shelling? And now here we are all over again – the government takes our art treasures away from danger and puts them in places of safety, yet the men who are destined to create the great art treasures of the future are sent by that same government to be slaughtered like cattle. How many of them are lying dead in France already? It grieves me to think of what Wilfred Owen might have achieved if he'd lived, and how many men of talent in this generation have already been lost.'

Jago saw in his mind some of the men he'd known who were neither great nor famous who'd been cut down too, but said nothing.

'I shall never forget that day, you know,' she went on. 'It was in 1916, and my husband was away at sea – he was a sub-lieutenant in the Royal Navy. I was staying with an aunt who lived in Romford, and she invited some officers from the Artists' Rifles to tea – they had their training camp at a mansion nearby called Hare Hall, you see. I believe it's a school now. One of the young officers was Wilfred Owen. All I noticed then was what a charming man he was, and terribly handsome too. It was only later I read his poetry and realised how magnificent it was. Have you read his work?'

'Just a little.'

'What did you think of it?'

'I liked it – the way he wrote about the war was how most of us at the front had experienced it. Not like some others who dressed it up romantically for the people back home. It's sad that he didn't live to see the war's end.'

'Oh, yes, so sad. A tragedy – killed just one week before it ended. His poor mother received the telegram telling her on Armistice Day. What could be more awful than that?'

'And your husband?' said Jago. 'Did he come through the war?'

Mrs Garside looked down at the floor and sighed, then shook her head.

'No,' she said, glancing up again, her face now sombre. 'His ship was HMS *Hampshire*. Less than a month after I had tea with my aunt that day, the *Hampshire* was sailing for Russia with Lord Kitchener on board. I'm sure you'll remember. She was hit by a mine off Orkney and sank in heavy seas. There were six hundred and fifty men on that ship, and only twelve survived. In fact, the newspaper reports at the time said there was even a detective sergeant from Scotland Yard on board.'

'Yes, I heard about him later, when I became a detective. He was in the Special Branch, so would've been there to protect the field marshal during his visit, I imagine.'

'Not much protection against a German mine, though, was it? Your detective was lost, Kitchener was lost, and my husband was lost. I was just twenty-five years old, Inspector. I got a war widow's pension of two pounds a week and was thankful for that small mercy. Now all I have is these books. I feel an affinity with them. Each has a story, but they're all completed, finished, some of them many years ago. I feel I'm like them. My story was completed in 1916, when my husband died. He was a wonderful man, all I'd dreamt of, but my story stopped then. I've spent the last twenty-four years envying young women, because they had a future and I didn't – I stopped having a future at the age of twenty-five.'

'I'm very sorry, Mrs Garside.'

'Thank you. It was all a long time ago – or so it seemed until this war started, and now it's as though it all happened only moments ago. That's why I find myself asking where the poets of this new war are. We need them, to remind us what war is really like. Why do you think we don't seem to have them, Inspector?'

'I don't think I could say,' said Jago. 'In the last war men like Owen wrote because the people at home had no idea. Perhaps this time it's different. The civilians in places like this probably know more about seeing people around them maimed or blown to pieces by bombs than most men in uniform do.'

'You may have a point, Inspector. But I still want us to hear the voice of the poets, and I think young Wilfred Morton could be one of them. So go easy on him, please.'

She gazed out of the shop's front window, then hopped off the table.

'I think I can see him coming now. Slip outside, gentlemen, and you'll catch him.'

Jago picked up his hat and moved to open the door. She took a step towards him and placed her hand on his wrist.

'Just one other thing, Inspector.'

'Yes?'

'Wilfred is a good man, and I don't want to see him getting into any trouble. I was – well, I was never blessed with a son, but if I had been, I just want you to know he's everything I would have wanted a son of mine to be, and I don't want anything unpleasant to happen to him.'

'Thank you, Mrs Garside. Goodbye.'

He turned the handle of the shop's front door and walked out into the afternoon sunshine, followed by Cradock. He didn't turn round, but he heard no movement behind him and had the sense that she was standing still, with her eyes fixed on his back as he left.

CHAPTER NINE

'Mr Morton,' Jago called as he strode across the paving stones in front of the shop.

The man was putting his key into the lock of the black door they had observed on arriving, but turned round when he heard Jago's voice. He was young and hatless, wearing a wide-lapelled blue overcoat and a colourful scarf in a large check pattern. It was a warm day to have something like that round your neck, thought Jago, and he wondered whether it was worn more for effect than for comfort. The man looked puzzled, as though struggling to recognise the stranger who had just called him by name.

'Yes?' he said.

'I'm sorry to disturb you on a Sunday, Mr Morton, but I need to speak to you. I'm Detective Inspector Jago of West Ham CID, and this is Detective Constable Cradock.'

'Sounds urgent. What's it about?'

'Could we come in first?'

Morton pushed open the door with a somewhat theatrical gesture and directed Jago and Cradock up a narrow staircase to a cramped landing, then up a second staircase to the top floor. Here he opened another door and showed them into a living room that ran the width of the flat and looked onto the street. Jago ran his eye over the room. The wallpaper was grubby and faded, as was the carpet, which was nailed to the floorboards here and there at the edges to stop it curling. The furniture was a hotchpotch of pieces that looked as though they had seen many homes and were now in the final stages of useful life. Most striking of all was the fact that every flat surface seemed to be covered with books, upright and in rows on the shelves, but for the most part stacked or scattered in heaps. The room looked like a set for a play about Bohemian literary life, but it reminded Jago more of what his mother would have called an unholy mess.

There was something about Morton's face that made Jago feel he'd seen him before, but when he began to trawl through his mind for a connection he realised that wasn't the case. The sense of familiarity was because Morton looked like someone Jago had seen in photographs and newsreels. Yes, that was it, he thought – the face of a far more distinguished poet. He smiled to himself. How appropriate – the man shared a name with Wilfred Owen and a face with W. H. Auden.

Morton's appearance suggested he was in his twenties, perhaps nudging thirty. He was slim, of no more than average height, and his face was angular and pale. His hair was a little longer than most men wore it and was combed to one side, appearing to be in danger of falling over his left eye. His nose was slender and patrician, but there was a hint of weakness around his mouth that added an element of indecision to his expression. He took his overcoat off and threw it on a chair, to reveal a shapeless sports coat and flannels that looked probably of an age with his battered brown brogues. The pipe he picked up from the sideboard completed the look of a poet or some other form of intellectual, but Jago wondered whether this last detail was a sign of the man working just a little too hard to create that impression.

Morton moved some books from a couple of armchairs and invited his visitors to sit, then began gathering up a sheaf of paper from the top of a wooden stool, his back towards them as he spoke.

'I'm sorry I wasn't in when you arrived, Inspector,' he said. 'I hope you didn't have to wait too long.'

'No need to apologise, Mr Morton – you didn't know we were coming. Besides, Mrs Garside entertained us in your absence.'

Morton twitched a glance back over his shoulder at the mention of her name.

'Really? Of course. A most hospitable lady.'

He sat down on the stool, facing them.

'Please excuse the flat, Inspector,' he said, looking round it with a forlorn expression. 'What with my work and the difficulties of life these days I don't seem to have much time left for keeping things tidy.'

'That's quite all right, Mr Morton. What is your work?'

'I'm a librarian – I work down the road at Canning Town public library. It's very convenient, only a couple of minutes' walk. And before you ask, these books are not purloined from the library – they're all honestly acquired, and mostly not new. The inevitable consequence of a man of letters living over a second-hand bookshop, I suppose.'

'Don't worry, Mr Morton, I haven't come to question you on your book collection, although I must say it looks impressive, even if in quantity alone. Now, I understand you've been living here for about eighteen months – is that correct?'

'Yes, I suppose it must be. Mrs Garside's been very kind to me. Not the most astute businesswoman in the world, I think – not that I'm competent to judge – but a terribly creative person, and in a small way a patron of the arts. I believe she keeps the bookshop going as a kind of haven for those with literary aspirations in West Ham, and she lets me have this flat at a reduced rent. You can imagine how a woman who loves books and owns a shop full of them must feel at the thought of incendiary bombs raining down every night. I think she finds it reassuring to know I'm on the premises, although to be honest, when the sirens go my first thought is to take shelter – and to make sure I have my own writing with me.'

Jago's eye roamed across the low table in front of his

chair and noticed a poetry magazine with the names of its contributors on the front cover. Towards the bottom of the list was the name Wilfred Morton.

'May I?' he said, leaning forward to pick it up.

'Please do,' said Morton.

'So you're a published poet.'

Morton gave a self-effacing smile.

'Only just – I haven't had a book published, but even to have one poem in a magazine like this is tremendously exciting. It's a serious poetry magazine, you see, not just something for housewives.'

Jago turned the pages until he found Morton's name again, and read.

War Sonnet No. 1: Air Power
Bright dawn, when first we slipped our mortal ties,
Hope's dream to gird the earth about began:
Cleave nation unto nation through their skies
And vault each bounding wall conceived by man.
Yet swift, with swords uplifted now they fall,
To loose the shaft of hatred from their bow,
To take their certain aim upon us all
And pierce a hundred thousand hearts below.
And who shall judge the measure of our spite,
When vengeance is our one intention left?
And shall we visit death to death requite,
Their mothers of their sons by ours bereft?
For we are lost in nature's darkest night,
And evil's wrong can scarce make virtue's right.

'What do you think?' said Morton.

'Well,' said Jago, 'I can see it's a sonnet, although the title rather gives that away.'

'Yes, I intend to write a series as the war goes on.'

'Apart from that, I hesitate to say. If you think you're not competent to judge Mrs Garside's business skills, I certainly feel the same way about a poet's work. My knowledge of sonnets doesn't go much further than "Shall I compare thee to a summer's day". The bit about "to gird the earth about" reminds me of *A Midsummer Night's Dream*, when someone says he'll put a girdle round the earth in forty minutes. But I probably only remember that because when my father took me to see the play I was too young to understand and thought it was something to do with ladies' undergarments.'

Morton laughed. 'Anything that gets a little Shakespeare into your soul is good for you, Inspector. There are lots of other references to his works in my poem, but you might not spot them.'

'Probably not. My father loved Shakespeare and took me to see one or two of his plays when I was a boy. I don't know them well enough to quote them, except the odd line he used to come out with all the time – but then he was an actor *manqué*.'

'French too? One doesn't expect to find policemen using French in West Ham.'

'It's my mother's fault – she was French. It's not exactly every day you come across a poet in the Barking Road either.'

'Sadly true, I agree. However, Gerard Manley Hopkins was born in Stratford – our Stratford, I mean, not Shakespeare's one – so there's some hope. He must be one of our greatest poets of more recent times, don't you think?'

'I bow to your judgement on that, Mr Morton. I wouldn't know. But look, I don't want to take up too much of your day off. Fascinating though this talk of poetry is, I've come to ask you about some rather more mundane matters.'

'Of course, Inspector, and forgive me – I haven't offered you a drink. Would you like something? I have coffee, but I don't drink tea. Mrs Garside drinks a gallon a day, so I buy my ration and give it to her. Can I get you a coffee?'

'No, thank you,' said Jago. 'We've already been watered by Mrs Garside.'

'Ah, yes. Most hospitable, as I said. I'm surprised she didn't offer you something stronger.'

'Water was fine. Now, Mr Morton, I understand you're involved in the Peace Pledge Union.'

Morton's open and friendly expression changed in an instant. He narrowed his eyes and studied Jago's face carefully.

'What if I am?'

'I'd like to ask you a few questions about that.'

'Why? It's not illegal – not yet, at least, although your people seem intent on making it so.'

'My people?'

'The powers that be, the authorities. The people who think they run this sceptred isle. Let me assure you, Inspector, I haven't broken any laws and I'm not a traitor to my country. But you've probably got a file on me anyway, and you'll know that.'

'I assure you I don't have a file on you, Mr Morton, and I haven't come to take you to task for your convictions.'

'Well, what is it then?'

'I want to ask you about one of your colleagues in the PPU.'

'If this is some kind of police snooping operation I'll tell you now you'll get nothing out of me. While this country still calls itself free I'll defend my right to privacy and that of any of my fellow members.'

'It's nothing like that, Mr Morton. Am I correct in thinking you're an acquaintance of Mr Paul Ramsey?'

'Yes, that's correct,' Morton replied cautiously.

'Then I'm afraid I have some sad news to report. Mr Ramsey was found dead this morning, and we believe he was murdered.'

Morton looked shocked. He got down from the stool and moved hesitantly towards the window.

'Murdered?' he said. 'But that's dreadful. Who would do such a terrible thing?'

'That's what I'm trying to establish, and I'm hoping you might be able to help me.'

'How did you know we were acquainted?'

'We found a letter from you in his flat, after he died.'

Jago took the letter from his pocket and passed it to him. Morton read it and handed it back.

'Yes, of course. He was a member of the PPU, and I'm the local group leader, so that's how I came to know him.'

'Both pacifists, then.'

'Yes. I've been involved in the PPU since 1934, and I'm not ashamed to say so. Ever since Dick Sheppard wrote that letter.'

'What letter?'

'His letter to the press. He said war was a crime against humanity and he asked everyone who agreed with him to send him a postcard. I knew he was a good man – he was the vicar of St Martin-in-the-Fields and he'd opened up his crypt to the poor and hungry years ago – and it was a simple thing to do, so I did. Thousands of other people did too, and we all wrote the same – "I renounce war and never again, directly or indirectly, will I support or sanction another." You can see how deeply I felt it – I can still remember the words.'

'So is it a religious conviction?'

'For him it was, but not for me. I don't believe in God, but I do believe in human beings' potential for good. That probably sounds a bit airy-fairy to someone like you, but to me it's as plain as a pikestaff that the whole world's in a mess, but we could make it such a different and better place if only we'd change the way we think. There are too many old men running the world – men who believe in empires, armies, fleets of warships, planting their flag on other people's land. People like Churchill. They belong to the past and we should leave them there. Ordinary people want peace, not war – if we have real freedom and socialism we can all get together and solve our problems peacefully without recourse to violence.'

Morton came to a halt and took a deep breath.

'There, Inspector – that's what I think. You may laugh at me if you wish, but I'm not alone in my convictions, and I'm not about to change my mind.'

'I assume you've applied to be registered as a conscientious objector, then.'

Morton nodded. He seemed to have calmed down, Jago thought – perhaps he was used to having to justify his position and was relieved now he'd got it off his chest.

'Yes,' he said. 'I didn't have to when the war started, because I was born in 1909 and too old to be included in the first round of registration for military service. But then in May the government said men aged up to thirty-six had to register in July, so I went down to the labour exchange – but I registered as a conscientious objector. I'm expecting my tribunal any day.'

'And hoping for full exemption?'

'Hoping, but I don't know whether I'll get it. I've heard that for every man who gets unconditional exemption there are twenty or more who don't.'

'Did Paul Ramsey have the same convictions?'

'He was against war, just like me, and that's why he was a member of the PPU too.'

'We're trying to get a picture of the kind of man he was. How would you describe him?'

'If I had to sum him up in one word, I think I'd say passionate. Things were black and white with him – he knew what he wanted out of life and he was determined to get it.'

'Ambitious, then?'

'Definitely.'

'Did you like him?'

'We're all different, Inspector. I try to get on with everyone.'

'But some people are more difficult to get on with than others. Was he difficult?'

'He was a strong-minded man. That can be a good thing and a bad thing. I think perhaps he was the kind of man you wouldn't want to cross – he could be your best friend or your worst enemy.'

'So what was it that he wanted out of life?'

'Quite simply, I think he wanted to be successful.'

'You mean he wanted to make money? Teaching doesn't seem the obvious route to riches.'

'I think that was perhaps part of what he wanted – he certainly seemed to want more money than he had. But I think it was broader than that. I think he wanted to be successful in his work, successful with women, just generally successful in whatever he turned his hand to. He had a lot of energy – a man of action, I'd say.'

'And a man of duty? His headmaster seemed to think so.'

'I can't comment on his professional life – I only knew him socially through the PPU. I'd say he saw his highest duty was to himself – I got the impression he'd do anything to get what he wanted.'

'That doesn't sound very much like a pacifist, if you'll forgive my saying so.'

'He could sound like the perfect pacifist when he wanted, but I'm not sure his convictions went beyond his own purposes. Look, Inspector, to be perfectly honest with you, I didn't trust him.'

'That's a harsh judgement on the dead.'

'Harsh perhaps, but I have good reason to believe it.'

'What would that be?'

Morton paced the length of the room, saying nothing and staring at the floor. He stopped and banged his fist against a bookcase, then turned to face Jago, his eyes filled with anguish.

'If you must know, he – he stole my girl. I'd been seeing a young teacher. I really liked her, and I thought she liked me. Then all of a sudden she seemed reluctant to see me – I'd ask her for a date, and she'd always be unavailable for some reason. In the end I challenged her. All she'd say was she'd found someone else and we'd have to end it. Then I found out the someone else was Ramsey.'

'How did you feel about that?'

'How would you feel? I felt betrayed, of course. It's not the kind of thing a friend should do – not a gentleman, anyway.'

'Did you feel angry? You're looking angry just talking about it.'

For a second time Morton took a deep breath and calmed himself. He looked at Jago suspiciously.

'You're not suggesting I . . . really, Inspector, if you imagine I would want to harm him, you're very much mistaken. I'm a pacifist. I couldn't do such a thing.'

'I see. So what did you do?'

'I got over it, of course. I realised Gloria – that's her name – didn't mean that much to me, and if she could drop me just like that for another man, maybe she was too fickle to be worth pursuing. In any case, I meet plenty of very nice girls through the PPU. I just turned the page, if you know what I mean, and got on with life. I've rather avoided Paul Ramsey since then, so I don't know whether they stayed together, and I haven't seen her either.'

'Do you know whether Mr Ramsey had any plans to go away?'

'No.'

'We've got a photograph we'd like to show you.'

Jago motioned to Cradock, who pulled the photograph from his pocket and handed it to him.

'We found this in Mr Ramsey's flat, and I assume it's him in the picture. Is that young lady with him the one you're talking about?' said Jago.

He offered the photo to Morton, who took it and stared at it, then looked up.

'Yes,' said Morton. 'That's Gloria. I told you he'd taken her from me – well, there's the evidence.'

Jago took the photograph back.

'Thank you. Can you tell me her full name and where she lives?'

'She's Gloria Harris. As for where she lives, she used to lodge with a lady called Mrs Grove in Kildare Road – number 112. But she's not there now – she was evacuated. She's a teacher, and she was working at a junior school not far from here, but most of the kids were evacuated to Buckinghamshire, I believe, so she's up there with them.'

'When did you last see her?'

'I can't remember – it was some time ago.'

'Thank you for your help, Mr Morton. That will do for now.'

Morton moved towards the door and grasped the handle.

'You're welcome,' he said. 'If there's anything else I can do to be of assistance, just let me know.'

He opened the door to let Jago and Cradock out, and looked a little startled to see Olivia Garside standing on the landing. She was holding her broom, and pushed it lightly across the floorboards as they emerged.

'Just doing a little tidying, gentlemen,' she said.

Jago and Cradock eased past her, then Jago stopped and turned back to Morton.

'Just one other thing, Mr Morton. Where were you last night?'

'I was in, all evening.'

'And overnight, until seven this morning?'

'I was down in the Anderson shelter, all night, until

the all-clear went.' He turned to his landlady. 'We were there together, weren't we? All night.'

Olivia stopped brushing and looked up.

'Er, yes, yes, that's right. All night. Wilfred knows that I sometimes get a little anxious in the air raids and he stays with me when he can.'

She stared at Morton, as if waiting for him to dismiss her.

'Will that be all, Inspector?' said Morton.

'Yes, thank you,' said Jago. 'We can find our own way out from here.'

He and Cradock continued down the stairs to the street door. At the bottom of the staircase, Jago turned back to see Morton and Olivia standing motionless, side by side on the landing. He raised his hat in a parting gesture to Olivia, and she lifted one hand a few inches in what he took as a hesitant acknowledgement before he stepped out onto the street and closed the door behind him.

CHAPTER TEN

Cradock sat hunched in the front of the Riley. He was hungry, and it felt as though he'd spent the whole day either bumping round the streets of West Ham in Jago's car or talking to people about a dead man they didn't know very well, his ability to concentrate fading as the hours marched by. He tried to glance at his watch without Jago noticing: it was already past four o'clock. His day off had been gobbled up by this perishing teacher, and it seemed Jago still wanted to pay one more call on their way back to the station. The thought of gobbling made his stomach rumble, and if it hadn't been for the roar of the Riley's engine Jago would surely have heard it. Where his boss got his energy from was a mystery, especially as he hadn't eaten at all, but he was always like this when he got the bit between his teeth – a new case seemed to bring him alive. Whatever energy Cradock's body might have derived from a couple of cheese sandwiches and a Mars bar, however, seemed long spent.

'Sir,' he said. 'Any chance of grabbing another bite to eat?'

'Patience, Peter,' said Jago. 'I'm not expecting this to take long – just a quick word with our builder friend Mr Joe Ramsey on the way, then I'll treat you to a slap-up meal, the finest fare the station canteen can offer.'

A picture of a slap-up meal drifted briefly through Cradock's hungry imagination – a creamy mushroom soup, then perhaps a fish course, say salmon, followed by a main course of roast beef with all the trimmings and finishing with a sizeable helping of apple pie and custard. His fleeting enjoyment of this image came to an abrupt halt when he pictured instead what the reality would probably be in the West Ham police station canteen on a Sunday evening – sausage and mash. Still, he thought, a plateful of that with a nice drop of gravy would certainly keep the wolf from the door.

'Very kind of you, guv'nor,' he said, and hoped Joe Ramsey would be brief and to the point. Even better, he thought, Ramsey might be out when they got to his house – but then again, if he was, Jago might decide to chase all round the borough again trying to find him.

Jago glanced at his young colleague and could see he was suffering. The boy's mind was clearly too focused on his stomach.

'What did you make of Mr Morton, then?' he said.

'Interesting bloke, but a bit odd with it,' Cradock replied. 'Everything you'd expect a pacifist to be, I suppose – apart from that moment when he got a bit cross, he looked like he wouldn't say boo to a goose. And a poet too – I can just see him sitting up all night writing poetry. I've never met a real poet before. A timid bunch, if he's anything to go by.'

'Yes, and Crippen was a mild-mannered doctor, wasn't he? Still waters, Peter.'

Joe Ramsey's address was in a turning off Manor Road, which ran beside the railway line along the western edge of Plaistow. It wasn't far from Olivia's bookshop, and Cradock was comforted by the fact that at least they were heading in the right direction for the station. He studied the shops and houses on the way to take his mind off his appetite. Jago turned left from Hermit Road into Star Lane, where they passed the barn-like Victorian structure of Star Lane School, and as they came to Manor Road a long brick building with a mansard roof, followed by another identical structure, caught his eye.

'They look smart,' he said. 'Very modern. I wouldn't mind living there.'

'Council flats,' said Jago. 'Been there ten or twelve years, I think.'

'Don't see many that high round here, do you?'

'Four storeys, you mean? Highest in the borough, I believe.'

'You'd probably get a nice view from the top floor.'

'Of the gas works, yes. I wouldn't fancy being up there myself, though, especially these days – I think we were intended to live on the ground. I just hope they don't get hit – imagine living on the top floor of a pile like that and having it collapse. They must be at risk, right next to the railway line like that.'

'But some people say blocks of flats are safer than houses in air raids, don't they? It's because they're made from steel and concrete.'

'Yes, well, I didn't see these flats being built, so I wouldn't make any assumptions about what they're made of. All I can see is brick, and that doesn't seem to stand up too well to the bombing, from what I've seen lately.'

'Joe Ramsey lives just up the road here, doesn't he? I wonder if he built them.'

'If he's anything like some of the builders I've known, he'll have made sure he never builds anything too close to home – won't want people to know where he lives when the roof starts leaking. Anyway, here we are.'

He turned into Godbold Road, pulled up outside the house where Joe Ramsey lived, and switched off the engine. Ramsey was at home and welcomed them both in.

'I'm sorry to disturb you, Mr Ramsey,' said Jago, 'but as I said, there was something else I wanted to ask you – and I'm afraid you may find it a rather surprising question.'

'Try me.'

'Well, it's this – did your brother own a gun?'

'Paul, with a gun? Blow me down. I wouldn't have thought so – in fact I'd be very surprised if he did. You know what his views were, I imagine. I mean, the man was a pacifist.'

'I'm aware of his views, but whatever they might have been and however deeply he might have held them, the fact remains that we believe he had a gun.'

'What kind of gun?'

'A Webley revolver.'

'Webley . . . Is that a type that soldiers use?'

'Yes – it used to be British Army standard issue.'

'Ah,' said Ramsey, and gave a knowing nod.

'You don't look so surprised after all,' said Jago.

'No,' Ramsey replied. 'I think I know what it might be. Our father was a lieutenant in the army during the Great War and he brought a revolver home at the end of it. He was very strict with us – used to drill us like conscripts – but when we got a bit older he'd let us play with it. We didn't have any bullets, of course, so it was safe for games of soldiers, or cowboys and Indians. Later on we grew out of that sort of thing, as boys do, and I didn't see it again – I assumed our dad must've put it away somewhere. Maybe he passed it on to Paul, though, before he died – Paul was the elder son, so I suppose Dad might've felt that was the thing to do. Whatever happened, I haven't seen it for years, but that's the only way I could imagine Paul having an army-issue revolver. He'd probably just put it in the cupboard and forgotten about it.'

'But it wasn't in a cupboard – it was in his pocket when we found him.'

'No,' Ramsey gasped, 'surely not. If what I've said is right it could explain Paul having a gun at home somewhere, but I can't imagine him carrying one about with him. It's just not possible.'

He looked shaken. He sat down on a chair and stared at the floor, twisting the end of his tie with his fingers as if his mind were elsewhere.

'Is that all you wanted to ask, Inspector?' he said at last, looking up. 'I'm sorry, but it's all been a bit of a shock.'

'Yes, that will be all for now, Mr Ramsey,' said Jago. 'We'll be on our way.'

Jago and Cradock moved towards the door. Ramsey took a handkerchief from his pocket and wiped his palms, seemingly no longer aware of their presence.

CHAPTER ELEVEN

Betty Draper sat in her favourite chair by the fireplace, unpicking an old jumper. She pulled at the wool, unravelling it row by row and winding it into a ball. Her husband George was sitting a few feet away across the room. He had the shaft of a cobbler's last gripped between his knees, and on the last itself was an upturned army surplus boot, one of the pair he wore to work every day. The metal heel plate had worn down on one side, and he was nailing a new one on so he wouldn't have to replace the heel itself.

'So who's that for?' he said, putting his hammer down on the table and watching Betty.

'It's for Jimmy, love,' she replied. 'I'm going to knit him a new pullover – he's growing so fast I can't keep up with him, and the one he's wearing now stops three inches short of his wrists.'

She thought of her only son, now up to her shoulder but still a child.

'I'm worried about him, George – finding that dead body this morning. A kid shouldn't have to see things like that.'

'He'll have to get used to it. You can't keep him wrapped up in cotton wool all his life. I don't like it any more than you do, but it's the way the world is.'

'I just don't like to see him frightened. He won't let on, but I could see he was really shocked. It must've been awful for him.'

Betty knew that if she said any more she'd get upset, and she didn't want Jimmy to come in and see her crying. She wound the ball of wool silently, and George continued his hammering. It looked as though he'd said all he wanted to say.

She felt her chest tightening – it was that blasted cough again. She didn't seem able to shake it off. She tried to smother it but failed, and looked apprehensively at George.

'You all right, love?' he said, half rising from his chair.

'Yes, I'm fine, dear. You sit down.'

'You should see the doctor about that – it doesn't sound right to me.'

'No, it's all right. I'll get some linctus from the chemist – we haven't got money to throw around on doctors.'

'We'll find the money. It's not right – if I can go, they ought to let you go too. We should've put something to one side.'

'Don't be silly, George. When have we ever had money

to put aside for anything? I've been thankful we've been able to pay the rent and keep ourselves fed.'

'But what's the point of that national health insurance if someone like you still has to pay, even just to see the panel doctor?'

'I don't know, love, but I can't see the government changing everything just for my benefit – can you? Especially now there's a war on. That's the way it is, and we have to like it or lump it. I mean, it must cost a fortune just to cover working men like you, so how are they ever going to let wives and kids see the doctor for nothing too? And even if they did, what would the doctor say? Go and get some medicine that you can't afford either, and probably wouldn't do you any good anyway. We shouldn't complain – it's the same for everyone.'

'Yes, but even so. You having to put up with all this – it's not what I wanted for you. You deserve something better. I'm sorry, Betty.'

'Don't say that, George – I've got no complaints. You're a good man, a loyal man. You've always been faithful to me, and that means more to me than a nice house or fancy clothes. And this is only a bit of a chest cough – it won't last long.'

'I'm still worried, love. Gasping like that – it's not good. That's what my mum was like.'

'I haven't got that, George, and I don't want some doctor telling me I have. They'd pack me off to that sanatorium in Dagenham, and – and I'd probably never come back. I'll be all right, dear, you'll see – it'll clear up soon. Now, has that tea brewed yet?'

Betty got up from her chair and inspected the contents of the teapot, which was sitting on the table, keeping warm in a tea cosy she'd made when they were first married, twenty-two years ago. She heard a creak from the hallway as the front door opened.

'That'll be Jimmy,' she said. 'Don't say anything about my cough in front of him.'

The sound of boots approached, and Jimmy appeared in the doorway, a bulging old sack over his shoulder.

'Hello, Mum,' he said, putting the sack down on the floor. 'What's for tea?'

'You and your food – that's all you think about,' she replied. 'I don't know where you put it. If you must know, we're having tripe. At least they're not rationing that yet.'

'Lovely – tripe and onions.'

'No, my love, just tripe. You try going into a greengrocer's these days and asking for onions – they'll just laugh at you. And if they do get some in, d'you know what they want for them? Tenpence a pound – I ask you. This time last year it was a penny-ha'penny. I wouldn't pay tenpence even if we had it, which we don't.'

'But why can't they get them? We grow onions, don't we?'

'Don't ask me, dear. All I know is they're very short, which means they cost a packet. And you don't see those onion sellers going round with their bikes any more, do you? They were always coming over here from France and Belgium or wherever it was, but the war's put a stop to that – I expect the Germans'll be eating all their onions now.'

'Yes, well, never mind, Mum – I'm sure you'll make it nice. And look, I've got you a present.'

He opened the top of the sack and pulled out a blackened wooden block the size of a house brick.

'There you are,' he said. 'Some tarry blocks I found – that should keep you going for a day or two.'

'Oh, thanks, love,' said his mother. 'That's very thoughtful of you. They'll do nicely on the fire, what with coal being short too – just put them over there in the corner, out of the way.'

'Watch you don't put too many on, love,' said George. 'All that tar and creosote'll start a chimney fire if you're not careful.'

Jimmy picked up the sack to move it, but noticed his father was giving him a look he knew well, over the top of his wire-framed glasses.

'And what exactly do you mean by "found"?' said George. 'Where did they come from?'

Jimmy put the sack down again.

'Salvage,' he said.

'What do you mean, "salvage"? Are you telling me you've been out collecting saucepans for Lord Beaverbrook so he can make them into Spitfires, and someone gave you these for the propeller?'

Before Jimmy could reply, Betty handed George a cup of

tea and then returned to the table to pour one for herself.

'They're not having mine,' she said.

'Your what?' said George.

'Saucepans, love. Someone told me they'd been down the WVS and seen a great big pile of aluminium pots and pans there. That means loads of women must've donated them, but the shops are still full of them. Where's the sense in that? Why's the government asking us to give up our own when they could just take all the new ones? It took me a year to save up for my aluminium saucepans – I'm not going to put them on a pile of old scrap just because Beaverbrook says so. I'd have to buy some enamel ones to replace them, and where will I get the money to do that? Someone needs to have a word with him, I reckon.'

'Answer my question, Jimmy,' said his father.

'Like I said, it's salvage. I was passing this place where a bomb had landed in the road, and the wooden blocks had been blown all over the place. With all that tar on them they should burn up a treat. The council would only take them away to the dump, so I've saved them a job by bringing a few home.'

'You shouldn't do that, Jimmy,' said Betty. 'You know I worry about you. I don't want you to get in trouble.'

'And I don't want to find myself down the police station watching you get a birching,' said George, 'which is what you'll get if they catch you. Listen to what your mother's saying – she's having a bad enough time with all this bombing as it is, without you getting in trouble with the law.'

'I'll be all right, Dad. I can run faster than those old coppers.'

George Draper looked at his son and saw himself at the same age. In those days he'd reckoned his legs could get him out of trouble too – and they did, until a German machine-gun bullet smashed up his thigh in 1917 and put paid to his running days. He'd had the same cockiness as Jimmy too, at that age. But then he'd learnt a painful lesson – life laughs at that kind of confidence and finds its way of dragging you down. He didn't want that for Jimmy.

'Look, son, I know it's a lark for you, but I don't want you to end up like me. People like us, we're always at the bottom of the pile. It's all right when you're young and strong – you can get any old job labouring or something, and think you'll be earning money for ever. But it doesn't always work out like that. My old dad – your grandad – thought he had a job for life stoking furnaces in the foundry at Thames Ironworks. They were building ships in Bow Creek for the navy and everything before the last war, but then it all came down like a house of cards – in February they were full of themselves, launching a Dreadnought, but come Christmas the firm had gone bust. Thousands of men suddenly unemployed in Canning Town, and he was one of them. Do you think I want that kind of life for you?'

'But you've never been out of work, have you, Dad?'

'Not since you've been born, no, but that's only because one man gave me work when no one else would. If I lose my job, we'll be out on the street – that's what real life's like, and you need to get it into that head of yours, my boy. I want you to have a proper job and a house of your own, earn a decent living so your wife doesn't have to worry every week about where the rent's coming from.'

'Don't worry, Dad – Uncle Ted's said I can help him on his stall in the market when I'm fourteen, and he does all right for himself, doesn't he?'

'That's not a proper job, Jimmy,' said his mother. 'Not the kind of job your dad's talking about. You need education to get a proper job. I do wish you'd go back to school. Won't you do it – just to please me?'

'But I haven't got a school to go to, Mum, not since the war started. It's not my fault.'

'I don't like to see you running wild on the streets, that's all.'

'I'm not running wild. I'm just doing a bit of this and that, to help out. Besides, soon I'll be a soldier, if it carries on like this.'

'You're not old enough to be a soldier for another five years. You can't really mean you want another five years of war.'

'I don't mind. It's quite fun. Besides, we'll be winning by then, and I'll be able to go and kill a few Nazis before it's all over. I don't want to miss out.'

'Believe me, son, you don't want to do that,' said George.

'Why shouldn't I? You did, didn't you?'

George couldn't look at his son. He closed his eyes, but sprang them open again because of what he saw – the pictures that still violated his sleep. That was why he'd volunteered to be a part-time air-raid warden – so he'd have an excuse to be up and about in the night. Even on his off-duty nights he was often thankful to be woken from his sleep by the bombs or the ack-ack guns on Beckton marshes, if only to be free of the dream. He'd be drowning in the mud, or buried with his trench collapsing under shellfire, and then he'd see the eyes of Germans he'd killed, staring into his own with the surprise of death. Even Betty didn't know what he saw in these nightmares that had stalked his sleeping hours for over twenty years.

He wanted to tell Jimmy the truth. Yes, he'd killed some Germans, but that was only because the army had turned him from an honest labourer into a foot-slogging soldier who knew better than to disobey orders. He wanted to tell him that the war had destroyed his life, used him up and spat him out, left a generation of men either dead or maimed for life, but he didn't have the words. And besides, how could anyone ever talk about things like that to a child, even one who was almost grown up now? He felt his stomach churning and set his face so as not to betray what he was thinking. He had to be strong, for Betty.

'Yes, I did,' he said quietly. 'But it was no picnic, and I lost a lot of good pals. I don't want you to have to go to war – you might think nothing can hurt you, but that's not the way it is. And I don't want you to have to struggle like I did, in and out of work, living in the gutter. You're right – it's not your fault they closed all the schools down. Perhaps we should've made you stay out in the country with all those other kids, but I know you wanted to look after your mum. You're a good lad, Jimmy. I just want you to have a better chance than I did. There's no free rides in this life – you've got to work for everything you want. The people who run things have no time to give people like us a leg up – they're all too busy looking after number one.'

'Not everyone's like that, George,' said Betty.

'There's enough that are,' said George. 'It was the people with all the money that sent us off to war, and plenty of them managed to find safe billets for themselves until it was all over. And it's not so different now.'

'What do you mean? The King and Queen have been bombed, haven't they? And the Duke of Kent's in the air force.'

'That's as may be, but what about all those people who live up West? Gone off to their country estates, haven't they? Or fancy hotels as far away from the bombs as they can get. And from what I've heard, half the councillors in West Ham have packed themselves off to the country out of harm's way too. Like I said, looking after number one.'

'All right if I go now, till tea's ready?' said Jimmy.

'Yes, you cut along – but mind what I said.'

'Yes, Jimmy,' said Betty. 'Your dad's right, you know.'

'Don't worry, Mum, I'll be all right – never you mind.'

Betty watched her only son as he moved the sack of wooden blocks into the corner, then headed back towards the door. She picked up her ball of wool and resumed winding it, then felt her chest tightening again.

CHAPTER TWELVE

Jago thought he must be weakening – he'd found himself feeling sorry for poor Cradock. The boy must have known the hours that detectives worked before he applied to join the CID, but on reflection, perhaps keeping him on duty all day Sunday was a little harsh. In a moment of what he could now regard only as weakness he'd not only bought Cradock supper at the station the previous evening but also told him he could have a lie-in on Monday morning and meet him for breakfast at Rita's at nine o'clock. He hoped word didn't get round the station.

While Cradock was catching up on his sleep, Jago was on his way to Maud Hampson's ARP post at Custom House School, hoping to catch her at the end of her shift. On arriving, he was directed to a squat brick building with a flat concrete roof occupying a corner of what just a year or so ago would have been the playground. Here he found Maud sitting at a wooden desk. She rose to greet him with a handshake, and he noticed the redness in her eyes. He wondered what had caused this – tiredness, smoke from the night's blazes, or something else altogether? Whatever it was, she'd clearly had a demanding night. He also noticed that this time there was no discernible trace of alcohol on her breath.

'Inspector Jago, how nice to see you again,' she said, as if she were welcoming him to a tea party. 'Welcome to our post. It's not exactly the Ideal Home Exhibition, but it's a bit more suitable for air raids than what we had before – when the war started we were in the school secretary's office. As you can see, we have everything we need – a desk, a telephone, and three old chairs that nobody else wanted. Won't you sit down?'

Jago sat on a cane chair in one corner of the small room while she took her seat at the desk.

'Can I get you a cup of tea?' she said.

'No, thank you – I'm on my way to work and I'll be having a spot of breakfast as soon as I leave here. I don't want to take your time – I can see you're tired. Has it been a bad night?'

'A bad night? Yes, I suppose so. Every night's bad these days, though. It's because we're so near to the docks – people round here have taken a real pasting, and there's no sign of it letting up. The Luftwaffe seems to be trying to destroy everything.'

'It must be very difficult work for you – I mean, I don't imagine it's what you're used to.'

'You mean seeing people killed every night? No, I'm not used to it – but then none of us is used to death and

115

destruction on this scale, are we? Not even the police.'

'No, but police officers have chosen to do the work they do. People like yourself have had this forced on them by the war.'

'You could say that, I suppose, but ARP workers are all volunteers, so we've chosen it too, at least until the war's over. I certainly didn't feel forced into this by anyone – it was quite clear to me what I had to do. I remember listening to the nine o'clock news on the BBC after the Germans had marched into Austria in 1938 – I felt so angry and so helpless. But then straight after the news the Home Secretary came on the wireless appealing for a million men and women to be ARP volunteers, and I knew I had to be one of them. I agreed with him – if there was going to be a war I couldn't stand by and do nothing. Obviously I couldn't go and fight, and I wasn't anything really useful like a nurse, but at least I could do something to help us all get through it.'

'I expect it's probably turned out to be more demanding than you expected.'

'It certainly has – but to tell you the truth, even though it's exhausting and distressing, I'm really glad I'm doing it. It's as though for the first time in my life I've come alive, I'm confident and bold. My husband's not very happy with that, but then all he ever thinks about is work and money. He's fifteen years older than me and quite old-fashioned too. He believes a woman's place is in the home – you know the kind of thing. It might sound an awful thing to say, but this war's been a godsend to me – for the first time I've been able to get out of the confounded home and do something worthwhile with my life. It was like escaping from a cage and spreading one's wings after years of being locked up. When I put this helmet on, I feel I'm doing something good, I'm a person in my own right, people need me and depend on me – I'm leaving a mark on this earth instead of just passing through unnoticed.'

She slumped back in her chair and let out a sigh.

'But you didn't come here to listen to my half-asleep musings. What can I do for you?'

'It's just a small matter,' said Jago. 'A couple of quick questions, and then I'll leave you in peace. First of all, that boy at the shelter, the one who found the body. You said you didn't know him.'

'That's correct – I've never seen him before.'

'But he lives in Barrington Road – isn't that part of your post area?'

'Yes, but there's something like two thousand people living in my post area, and I probably only know a handful of them.'

'You said you know his sort. What did you mean?'

'I meant he seemed to me like so many boys today – a typical street urchin. They stay out of school and roam the streets causing trouble and thieving. This war seems to be breeding a generation of lawless youngsters – we'll pay for it one day, you know. I blame the parents – working-class people today seem to have lost their sense of decency. They let their children run

117

wild and expect someone else to be responsible for their upbringing. It's a scandal. We're all supposed to be pulling together at a time like this, and a boy like that is probably round the corner looting a bombed property as we speak. Why you police aren't stamping down on it I don't know.'

'We are, Mrs Hampson, I can assure you of that. If you have any evidence against that boy or any other, report it to the police station and it will be investigated.'

'I haven't got time to do your job for you, Inspector – I've got more than enough on my plate as it is.'

'Of course.'

She paused and calmed herself.

'I'm sorry. I shouldn't speak to you like that. I haven't had much sleep recently, and I think it's taken its toll on my patience. I just don't like to see what's happening to boys like him – these air raids are putting temptation in their way, and far too many of them lack the moral fibre to resist it.'

Jago wondered how this woman would adjust if and when the war was over and she had to go back to the sedate and private life of a housewife. She seemed to have risen enthusiastically to the challenge of war, but how would she cope with peace? However, this was not a question he intended to put to her.

'What else did you want to know?' she continued.

'I just wanted to check whether the name T. H. Hampson means anything to you.'

'No. Should it?'

'Not necessarily. We've come across it in the course of our investigation and thought it might be someone you knew.'

'Because it's the same surname, you mean?'

'Exactly.'

'Is it a man?'

'We don't know.'

'Well, it's a common enough name, but I don't know anyone who's a T. H. Hampson. My husband's initials are R. G. – that's Robert George – and we have no children, and I'm not aware of any relatives with those initials in my husband's family.'

'Thank you – it was just in case you happened to know. Now I must be on my way and let you rest. Goodbye, Mrs Hampson.'

'Goodbye, Mr Jago – and thank you for listening.'

CHAPTER THIRTEEN

Rita's cafe was warm and cosy. For Jago it was a kind of haven, a place where he could be away from duty, reports, and the whims of his boss, Divisional Detective Inspector Eric Soper. Here he could settle down in peace with a cup of tea and some of Rita's fine cooking, slow down a little, and think about things other than police work.

Cradock had not arrived yet, and as Jago took a seat at an empty table he found his thoughts filling again with Dorothy, and especially their last conversation. There was a clear picture in his mind of the two of them standing alone that night just a stone's throw from the Thames in Savoy Place, the street bathed in moonlight. He'd admitted to her that ever since his affection for Eleanor came to nothing he'd avoided getting involved with women. He'd never told anyone that, yet there he was, disclosing his most private secrets to her. There'd been a strange intensity in the moment, but now, in the early light of a West Ham morning, sitting in Rita's cafe, it seemed unreal.

This image was promptly dispelled by the very real presence of Rita, who appeared beside the table and greeted him with a warm smile.

'Morning, Mr Jago. Lovely to see you. How about some nice eggs and bacon to start the day, just the way you like them?'

Her familiar voice brought him down to earth. She was homely and comforting, and seemed to have an unconscious knack of making him feel relaxed.

'That would be perfect, Rita,' he said. 'And do some for DC Cradock too – he'll be here in a minute.'

'Two lots of eggs and bacon it is.'

'And tell me, do you ever think about life?'

Rita raised her eyebrows in mock horror and gave a hearty laugh.

'That's a big question for this time on a Monday morning,' she said. 'Can't say I do, to be honest – not much, anyway. Life's what you make it – that's what they say, isn't it?'

'That's right, I suppose. But do you think we're ever really free? Can we choose our future?'

'Search me. If we could, though, I know who I'd be – Vivien Leigh. Have you seen *Gone with the Wind*?'

'No. Too long for me.'

'It was wonderful. She got an Oscar, you know.'

'So I heard, but some people said Greer Garson should've got it, didn't they? Wouldn't you rather be her? I mean, she's a local girl – born in Manor Park, went to school in East Ham. She's one of us who just happens to live in Hollywood now.'

'Yes, but she died in her film – I don't fancy that. And she's a redhead, isn't she? I couldn't be a redhead – wouldn't suit my complexion. No, I'm sorry, local girl or not, it's Vivien Leigh for me every time. If you can wave a magic wand, that's who I'll be for my future.'

Rita began to weave her way through the tables back to the kitchen, leaving Jago to his thoughts. Abandoning those restrictive tramlines in his life, whatever they might be, seemed alarmingly like living as a free spirit, something he'd never done. When he was a soldier he'd been subject to King's Regulations, and as a policeman he was bound by the law and by Judges' Rules. He couldn't imagine a life where he just did what he liked. But Dorothy? She seemed a lot closer to that than he was – a talented woman with a professional career who'd done exciting and dangerous jobs as a journalist in Spain, Czechoslovakia, Poland, France. Apart from one small and deadly corner of the latter, these were places that he'd never even seen, let alone worked in. She'd faced peril and even death, yet clearly didn't seem to feel the need of a man to protect her.

In truth, if there was anyone who could teach him how to break free of his past it was probably this educated Boston girl turned war correspondent, but he wasn't sure he could ask her. If those tramlines were everything that was familiar in his life – the things he did, the places he went, the role he played – they were also the things that determined who he was. Without them, would he even recognise himself? His life might not be ideal, but it was the life he knew how to live. He was a police detective. Rita might fancy swapping her kitchen for the life of a film star, but he wanted to be a detective tomorrow, the same as today – interviewing witnesses, piecing together information, tracking down the person or persons unknown who had temporarily upset the proper order of things. If he did his best and had a bit of luck, he'd be able to restore that order, at least in this little patch of south-west Essex. But was that all he wanted in life? He wasn't sure.

Rita appeared at his side with a tray from which she deposited a plate of eggs and bacon on the table, followed by a mug of tea.

'I've done you a bit of fried bread too,' she said. 'That should get you off to a good start. You'll have noticed I didn't turn into Vivien Leigh in the kitchen, so it looks like you're stuck with me.'

She took a step back from the table and studied his face.

'You don't look your usual self. A bit down in the dumps, I'd say. Is something troubling you?'

'Just thinking.'

'About what?'

'Oh, I don't know. About life, I suppose – about what makes it all worthwhile.'

'Love makes the world go round, you know.'

'Yes, I know that's what they say. But sometimes love lets you down, doesn't it? You think perhaps you love someone, but life gets in the way and somehow you never manage to tell them, and then suddenly the chance is gone and it was all wasted.'

He looked up and caught a glimpse of something in her eyes. He wasn't sure whether it was sadness or disappointment, or both.

'Don't worry about me, Rita,' he said. 'It was all a long time ago.'

Rita nodded silently, gave a fleeting smile that seemed half reassurance, half pain, and walked away.

Jago sat alone at the table and began to eat his breakfast. Shortly afterwards, Cradock appeared.

'Still all right if I join you, sir?'

'Pull up a chair,' said Jago.

Cradock had barely sat down before Rita returned, her tray replenished.

'Good morning, Constable,' she said with a smile. 'Here's some eggs and bacon, and a nice mug of tea for you.'

'That was quick,' said Cradock.

'Mr Jago had already ordered for you. We don't want you going hungry, do we?'

She placed Cradock's breakfast before him, arranged a knife and fork neatly either side of his plate, and moved the salt so it was within easy reach. She looked down at him in a caring, maternal manner as he began to eat.

'We were just talking about the films, Mr Cradock,' she said. 'Do you go to the cinema much?'

Cradock glanced at Jago, worried lest he get into a

conversation that might make them late for work, but Jago's face was blank. He turned back to Rita.

'When I can, yes.'

'On your own?'

'Er, yes, usually.'

'Not like it used to be, though, is it? Not with these air raids. Quite dangerous, really. Even going to the pictures means you have to be quite brave these days, doesn't it?'

'Well, I suppose so.'

'I bet you're not the sort of man to let Hitler and his air force stop you having a good time, are you?'

'Certainly not, no.'

'That's the spirit. I like to see that in a man. My Walter was like that – nothing frightened him. My Emily loves films too, you know.'

'Emily?'

'My daughter, dear, she's a lovely girl – but then I would say that, wouldn't I? About your age, she is. She's always had this thing about going to the pictures. Best way to spend an evening, she says – but these days she gets a bit worried about going on her own. A girl's got to be careful in the blackout, hasn't she? Breaks my heart to see her having to sit at home every evening. What she needs is a nice young man to go with her, just so she'll know she's safe. A nice brave young man who isn't afraid of those silly old sirens. You're not, are you?'

Cradock looked anxiously at Jago again, but still his boss's face was expressionless. No help was coming from that quarter. Cradock felt cornered, and an unexpected sense of panic began to grip his stomach. He looked back at Rita, whose face in contrast was creased by an affectionate smile.

'Well, no, I mean—'

'I knew I could rely on you, Mr Cradock.'

She turned to Jago.

'He's a good, reliable young man, isn't he, Mr Jago?'

Jago said nothing, but gave her a slow and considered nod. It seemed to Cradock that he might just as well have given her a thumbs down, like Charles Laughton did to the gladiators' cries for mercy in *The Sign of the Cross*.

'That settles it, then,' said Rita. 'In that case you may, Mr Cradock.'

'May what?' said Cradock.

'Take Emily to the pictures, of course. I think she's free tomorrow evening – is that all right for you?'

It seemed to Jago that Cradock was having difficulty knowing how to reply, so he stepped in and spoke for him.

'Yes, Rita, I'm sure I can spare Detective Constable Cradock tomorrow evening. That will be fine.'

He rapped his knuckles gently on the table and pointed to Cradock's breakfast.

'Come along, Peter, eat up. We've got work to do.'

CHAPTER FOURTEEN

Alex Hedges sometimes wondered whether it was right to have ambition. He'd been brought up to be modest, quiet, reserved – what his mother used to call 'respectable'. Now a married man and twenty-seven years old, if he felt he'd done something good at work and wanted to let Sally know, he'd still hear his mother's voice in his head saying, 'Don't you go blowing your own trumpet,' and as often as not he'd keep the news to himself. His father's advice about work had been similar: 'If you want to succeed at work, keep your head down and don't speak out of turn – then you'll get on.' But now that he was a working man himself, it seemed clear to Alex that if you wanted to 'get on' you did need some ambition, otherwise you'd take no steps to improve your own prospects. Surely it was no sin to want some of the good things in life, especially for your wife, and your children if you had any? As long as you didn't do anything dishonest to get there, of course –

he'd been brought up not to break the rules, and that was a principle he'd never abandon.

He fastened a fresh starched collar to his shirt: he felt at his smartest at the start of the week, as Monday morning meant a clean collar. But it could be difficult making it last for three days, especially in the warmer weather, and even more so if he had to run for the train. Ever since he'd got the job at Stratford town hall two years ago he'd had to walk to Connaught Road station and get the train to Stratford Market, then walk at the other end, and the trains didn't wait for you if you were late getting out of bed. The new job paid better than his previous one, but the fares took quite a slice out of a clerk's wages.

Last week he hadn't even been able to complete the journey. The trains had only run as far as West Ham station, because of bomb damage to the line, and from there he'd had to take a bus. He hoped he'd find it repaired this morning.

When the last collar stud was in place he stood in front of the mirror and knotted his tie. He used the straightforward four-in-hand knot, as he had done every day of his working life – the Duke of Windsor might go in for a more extravagant style, but he was sure this would not be looked upon favourably in the office. As a senior colleague had pointed out to him when he started his job, the majority of councillors who made up West Ham Borough Council might be Labour, but the dress for men employed in the council's various departments tended to be conservative.

He pulled the knot tight and checked it in the mirror to make sure it was straight, then picked up a pair of hairbrushes and smoothed his hair flat.

'It's ten to eight, dear,' his wife called from downstairs. 'Nearly time to go.'

No one had ever looked after him like Sally did, he thought. She was one in a million – and it wasn't just her looks. She was smart, probably smarter than he was. He went downstairs and gave her a kiss on the cheek.

'No hurry, my love, I've got five minutes yet.'

Sally studied his face.

'You've got bags under your eyes again,' she said. 'Are you sure you ought to be doing that fire-watching duty? You were out all night on Saturday, and I don't suppose you slept a wink, did you?'

'I managed to get one little nap. But we don't want the library to burn down, do we? I'd like to think that if an incendiary bomb lands on it I'll be there to save it.'

'But you can't work without sleep – you'll wear yourself out.'

'Well, just make sure you don't wear yourself out too – I need you to keep me going. Mind you, it's washing today, I suppose.'

'Yes, I've just been out in the scullery, getting the hot water going. I don't know how I get through so much of it on washing day, but I seem to be constantly shovelling bits of wood and coal under that old copper. And the steam – this place is damp enough already, without me making it worse. We definitely need to do something about that.'

'Move, you mean? I can't see us getting anything better than this – what can you rent on two pounds sixteen a week? We'll have to wait till I get promoted.'

'Yes, but that might not be for ages. Supposing we started a family, what would we do then? We couldn't bring up a baby in a place like this – it's not healthy. Can't you talk to the landlord?'

'I did, love. He just says there's a war on, there's no one to fix it, and we'll have to be patient. He said if we don't like it there's plenty more who've been bombed out and would move in at the drop of a hat.'

'Well, what kind of attitude is that? I think we need a plan. I was talking to that nice Mrs Draper last week. Do you know her? She lives in one of the council flats over the road. They're very cosy, and no damp at all. Couldn't you get one of those for us? You work for the council – can't you pull some strings?'

'Sally, how could you say such a thing? I can't do that. There's people more deserving than us who need those places.'

'Why doesn't the council build more, then, so people like us who aren't deserving enough but still have to live in a house with water running down the wall can get somewhere decent?'

'I know you think I'm too loyal, but I reckon the council's done everything they can to get rid of the slums – they've built more houses than just about any other council around London since the Great War. There's just too many of us needing help. If it hadn't been for this new war they'd probably be building more right now.'

'No, Alex, I don't think you're too loyal. I think you're an honest and decent man, and I'm glad I married you. I just think we need to take this into our own hands and do something about it. But not now – you need to get off to work.'

She put her hands on his shoulders and turned him round to face the door.

'Be off with you, Mr Hedges,' she said. 'I'll see you later.'

He left the house and with one last wave he headed briskly down the road towards the station. He arrived in time to catch his usual train, but at West Ham it stopped again and he had to take a bus. Standing room only, but at least they were moving.

He was still a mile from work when the bus conductor turned all the passengers off. The road was blocked by the remains of what had until sometime during the night been the Duke of Gloucester pub, and for the time being there was no way round it. Some passengers complained loudly to the conductor, as if he could do something about it, but Alex decided to be pragmatic – the walk would be good for him.

He set off, thankful that at least it wasn't raining, and thankful also that even if he lived in a slum he had a roof over his head. He thought about the day's work ahead of him, about what a fortune this war must be costing the country as a whole and West Ham Borough Council in particular. He wondered whether there'd been any damage to the town hall over the weekend –

these days you couldn't take anything for granted.

The street he was walking down seemed to have survived the night unscathed, and one woman was even out whitening her front doorstep. Like most of their neighbours, Sally had stopped doing this, because she said the amount of dust and smuts in the air from the fires meant it just got filthy again, but for some older women, he supposed, it was still like a kind of religious practice.

The scene in the street was beginning to feel almost normal, like peacetime. But then he turned the corner and stopped in his tracks. Down the road he could see police, rescue workers and passers-by at work on an unidentifiable mass of wreckage. He hurried forward to see if he could help. When he got close he saw what it was. A huge slab of concrete about nine inches thick was resting at a drunken angle on heaps of rubble. One glance at the concrete was enough to tell him it was the roof of a public air-raid shelter, and the rubble would be the shattered remains of its brick walls, now holding the roof only two or three feet above the ground.

The rescuers had managed to prop the heavy concrete roof with timber on one side and clear part of the rubble, and they must have removed some of the people from the wreckage, because he could see on the pavement beyond the shelter a row of blankets covering what could only be corpses. He couldn't imagine anyone escaping the sudden collapse of this building that was supposed to protect them. He wondered how many bodies would be found.

He felt suddenly guilty that he'd been hurrying to work, concerned about getting somewhere better for him and Sally to live at probably the very moment some of these dead bodies were being dragged from the ruin of their shelter. He felt helpless, too, because he knew there was nothing he could do for them.

He walked slowly round to the other side of the lurching slab and looked down at the ground. There was something sticking out between the broken bricks, something unrecognisable, covered in grey dust. He stopped and looked again. It was a leg, with a sock still on the foot. He couldn't tell whether it was a girl or a boy – all he knew was that it was dead.

He felt a retching in his throat and had to turn away.

CHAPTER FIFTEEN

It was half past nine when Jago and Cradock arrived at West Ham police station. As they were about to go in Jago saw the familiar and substantial figure of Divisional Detective Inspector Soper approaching from the opposite direction – probably on his way back from breakfast with some local dignitary at the town hall, he thought.

'You go on, Peter,' he said to Cradock. 'I'll join you when I've spoken to the DDI.'

Cradock hurried into the building, leaving Jago to wait for Soper.

'Good morning, sir,' said Jago as his boss arrived.

Soper stopped in the middle of the pavement and stood facing Jago with his hands clasped behind his back, looking him up and down as though inspecting a constable on parade.

'Morning, John,' said Soper. 'I hear you were called out yesterday morning.'

'Yes, sir. Suspected murder.'

'Who was the victim?'

'A schoolteacher, sir, by the name of Paul Ramsey, aged twenty-six. He was found stabbed to death in an air-raid shelter down in Custom House.'

'Any leads?'

'Not yet, sir. That's pretty much all we know about him. The only other thing of potential significance is that he was a pacifist – a member of the Peace Pledge Union.'

'A conchie, eh?' Soper sniffed, with a look of distaste. 'Don't hold with it myself, you know.'

'Really, sir?'

'No. You may not agree with me, but in my humble opinion when we're fighting with our backs to the wall as we are now, a pacifist's about as much use as a chocolate fireguard. If you ask me, we've gone too soft on these conscientious objectors. They want to live in a free country but they won't fight to keep it free. Meanwhile, Hitler's doing his very best to bomb the living daylights out of us, and I don't think it's the conchies that are going to stop him. The only thing that'll do that is when he works out that every time he drops a bomb on us we'll drop five back on him. Then he might start conscientious objecting himself and we can all get a good night's sleep again. There's a war on, dammit, and we all have to do our bit. But I don't have to tell you that – you were in France. Two years, wasn't it?'

'Yes, sir.'

'Jolly good – well done. I was only sorry I couldn't go myself.'

'Of course, sir. You were already serving in the police, weren't you?'

'That's right – all the way through. We had some tricky moments here too, what with the suffragettes and everything, not to mention the Zeppelins, but I envied you chaps who could go to the front and give the Boche a taste of their own medicine.'

'Indeed, sir. Of course, whatever we may think about conscientious objectors, some say if we're fighting for freedom, we must be fighting for people to be free to live according to their convictions, even if we don't agree with them.'

'That's as may be, John, but I think half these people adopt their convictions the way a normal man puts on a winter coat – they just want to save their own skins when the going gets tough. Anyway, this fellow of yours seems to be one conchie who didn't manage to save his own skin. Unlucky for him, but I can't say I have much sympathy when there's men out there on the front line dying so that he can exercise his precious convictions. Don't spend too much time on it, John – he probably just got into a fight with someone who didn't like conchies. And anyway, if he was stabbed in an empty shelter in the middle of an air raid, with all that chaos going on we're unlikely to find out who did it.'

'Not in the middle, sir – it was after the all-clear had sounded, as far as we can establish.'

'Well, whatever it was, just get it wrapped up somehow and don't get bogged down in it – we've got plenty more to do without fretting unduly over a dead conchie.'

'Yes, sir.'

'Which reminds me, there's something I want you to look into.'

Jago felt a sudden wariness based on past experience, but was careful not to let his face betray it.

'Yes, sir?'

'It's a case of fraud, and it involves a builder. Something to do with putting up an air-raid shelter. I don't know yet whether it's an unscrupulous builder or a bogus one, but I'm sure you'll be able to find out. The point is, a local resident has been fleeced of five pounds by some confidence-trickster, and I want you to get his money back – and make sure the scoundrel who did it is taken off the street.'

'Do we know who the culprit is?'

'Irish, I believe – you know the sort. Don't have a name, though.'

'Didn't the customer ask for identification?'

'I believe not.'

'So this man could be in Dublin by now. With respect, sir, there are bigger fish to fry – for example, I have a murder to investigate.'

'Well, put that boy Crampton onto it.'

'Cradock, sir.'

'Yes, yes, I know. Surely you can spare him.'

'I'm not so sure, sir. This local resident – who is he?'

'His name is Mr Guy Hunter, of The Firs, Romford Road.'

'And would he be an acquaintance of yours?'

'Well, yes, actually he is. As it happens, we play golf together, or at least we did until the council dug the links up and stuck poles all over it to stop the Germans landing stormtroopers on it. Anyway, he told me what had happened, and I've assured him I'll put my best man on to it. There's far too much profiteering and fraud going on these days – we need to drive these crooks out of business.'

'Your best man, sir? Cradock?'

'It was a figure of speech. I don't expect you to do all the leg work yourself, but you're responsible for the investigation.'

'Very well, sir. I'll do what I can, subject to operational requirements.'

'What's that supposed to mean?'

'I mean I'll make every effort to make enquiries, as circumstances permit – as with all such matters, sir.'

Soper stared at him uncertainly, as if trying to read the meaning behind the words, but Jago's face was inscrutable.

'Very well, then. Right, good day to you, John. I must be on my way now – time, tide and in-trays wait for no man.'

'Yes, sir. Thank you, sir,' said Jago, and waited until the DDI had bustled through the front door into the station before making his own way in.

By the time he stepped into the front office, the DDI had disappeared. Station Sergeant Frank Tompkins was at his habitual post behind the counter and gave Jago a broad welcoming smile.

'Ah, good morning, Mr Jago,' he said with a slight bow of his head. He glanced round at the corridor to make sure Soper had not returned. 'How nice to see you.'

Jago noticed Tompkins' almost imperceptible emphasis on the final word of his greeting, but thought it prudent not to rise to the bait.

'Morning,' he replied.

'Nice day off yesterday, sir? Pottering about in the garden like me, were you?'

'Very funny, Frank. Pottering about in the mortuary, more like.'

'Just my little joke, sir. I know how much you enjoy that place. A suspected murder, I gather. A young man, wasn't it?'

'Yes, only twenty-six.'

Tompkins looked thoughtful and nodded his head slowly up and down, as if weighing the value of twenty-six years in the balance of life.

'Well,' he said, 'always sad when they're young – in their prime, as you might say. But at least he had more of his threescore years and ten than a lot of our mates did when you and I were both in khaki. Mind you, I've always thought being killed in a war's different, isn't it? At least you're dying for something, for a cause, not just done away with because someone takes a dislike to you.'

'I don't think this one would've agreed with you, Frank. I imagine he'd have seen all war as murder.'

'Oh, I see – one of them pacifists?'

'That's right. He'd probably have said he was fighting for peace.'

'Well, that's as may be. I don't know what to make of people like that – but what I do know is that some of them conscientious objectors who ended up as stretcher bearers at the front was as brave as any soldier, and that's a fact. So no one can tell me they're cowards – just a bit more complicated than the rest of us, I suppose.'

'I certainly find it complicated, Frank – I can understand why they want peace, but how can you stand by and let evil men do whatever they like?'

'Exactly, sir. But that's you speaking as a copper, isn't it? Same as me. We both took the same oath, didn't we, when we got sworn in as constables? To preserve the peace and prevent all offences against the persons and properties of His Majesty's subjects – and that meant giving cocky young upstarts a clip round the ear and putting the bad 'uns inside. Our job is to nick the villains so the rest can live in peace. Keep it simple, that's what I say. Maybe if someone had done that with Hitler years ago we wouldn't be in this mess we're in now.'

'You may be right, Frank. Still, if I've found it a complicated question for the last twenty years I'm unlikely to get it sorted out this morning. I must get to my desk.'

'Very good, sir. But before you go, I've got someone waiting to see you. I've put him in an interview room and told young Cradock.'

'Are you going to tell me who it is?'

'Yes – it's a vicar. You been putting buttons in the collection again, sir?'

'Not guilty, Frank. And I've got an alibi too – when the vicar was taking his collection yesterday I'd have been out preserving the King's Peace, and there's an upstanding local headmaster who can vouch for that.'

'I'll let you off, then, sir. Actually this vicar said he wants to speak to you about something to do with a school.'

'What's his name?'

'He's a Mr Cardew, and he's the vicar of a church down in Custom House.'

'Right, I'll go and see what he wants. See you later, Frank.'

Jago collected Cradock from the CID office, and they made their way to the interview room. Jago entered first and found a tall, ginger-haired man of lean build, a little older than himself. Their visitor wasn't dressed in a conspicuously religious way – just a dark two-piece suit and a dog collar. The suit struck Jago as rather shapeless, and he noticed that the turn-ups on the trousers were frayed.

'Good morning, Vicar. Detective Inspector Jago,' he said. 'And this is Detective Constable Cradock. Sorry to keep you waiting, sir.'

'Not at all,' said the vicar. 'I've only been here a few minutes. My name's Cardew – Henry Cardew. I'm the vicar of St Thomas's Church in Custom House, near the greyhound stadium.'

'Right, Mr Cardew, how can we help you?'

'Well, it may be of no significance, but there's something I'd like to show you. I should explain that I'm also a member of the board of managers for a secondary school. The head teacher, Mr Gilroy, told me yesterday that one of the staff, Mr Paul Ramsey, had been killed, and that you were treating it as a case of suspected murder.'

'That's correct.'

'A terrible waste, especially in times like these. I felt I should come to see you, because something happened last Friday which seemed nothing out of the ordinary at the time, but which now might possibly be of significance.'

'I see. And what might that be?'

'The thing is, I received a letter from Mr Ramsey.'

'You knew him, then?'

'Yes, but only slightly. He'd been to my church occasionally – he wasn't a regular communicant, but he lived in the parish and would attend on a Sunday morning from time to time. We had a few chats after he'd told me he was a teacher at the school. And then I received this.'

He pulled a crumpled envelope from his pocket and passed it to Jago, who noted that it was stamped with a local postmark dated the previous Thursday and had the vicar's name and address handwritten on the front. He opened it, then removed a single sheet of notepaper and unfolded it.

'He said he was writing to me in my capacity as a member of the board of managers, not as the vicar,' Cardew added.

'Yes, so I can see,' said Jago, beginning to read the letter. 'And then he says, "There is a matter that is concerning me and that I would like to bring to your attention at your earliest convenience." So did you meet him?'

'Well, that's just it, you see – I didn't. I received the letter on Friday and was intending to write back to him on Monday – today, that is – suggesting when we might meet, but of course in the meantime the poor man's been killed.'

'So you don't know what it was that was concerning him?'

'No, I'm afraid I don't.'

'What can you tell me about Mr Ramsey?'

'Not a lot, really. He was a teacher, of course, and he'd been promoted recently, and I understand he was a bachelor. I also gathered that he was a member of the Peace Pledge Union.'

'You're familiar with the organisation?'

'Yes, I am. I know the local group leader.'

'Mr Morton?'

'That's the chap.'

'What's your assessment of him?'

'Of Morton? Well, I'd say he's a man who means to do good. Rather a sensitive fellow, though.'

'What do you mean?'

'Nothing really – I just have the sense that one has to be careful what one says, that's all. But I think we need a few people with strong principles in today's world.'

'I'd like to keep this letter if I may, Mr Cardew.'

'By all means, Inspector. It's of no use to me now.'

Jago folded the notepaper back into the envelope and put it in his pocket.

'You say you had a few conversations with Paul Ramsey. What sort of impression did you get of him?'

The vicar paused in thought for a moment before replying.

'If I had to describe him in one sentence, I'd say he was quite a talented young man, good at his job no doubt, with a promising future ahead of him. But on the other hand I couldn't help feeling he was also somewhat troubled – or perhaps I should say in conflict with himself.'

'What do you mean?'

'He seemed to be struggling with what he was, in himself. Why do you ask?'

'It's been suggested to us that his commitment to non-violence may not have been quite what he said it was, and I wonder whether you'd seen any evidence of that.'

'Do I think his pacifism was a pretence, you mean? No, I wouldn't say that. I think he wanted to be a man of peace and he wanted peace in the world – but he wasn't at peace with himself. I think when he joined the PPU he was making some sort of personal pledge to become a better man, because he knew himself too well. It was as if he'd seen something in himself that frightened him. I think perhaps he had looked into his own heart and been shocked by what he saw there.'

'What do you think he saw?'

'Who knows? Pride, greed, jealousy, hatred? Only he could have answered that question, and now he can't. But I can be fairly sure he saw some kind of darkness, because that's what I think we all see, if we're honest.'

'Are you suggesting something criminal?'

'Not necessarily, Inspector. The law of England is one thing, the holiness of God is another – and I suspect you're more concerned with the former. But if you want me to speculate on why Paul Ramsey seemed in conflict with himself, in my experience a man who looks into his own heart may find things for which he cannot forgive himself, and which he thinks even God cannot forgive. That's why when I preach on Sundays I talk about the grace of God, his ability to forgive the unforgiveable – if a man discovers that, he can perhaps make peace with himself, but if he doesn't, he's lost.'

'Did you know Paul Ramsey had a gun?'

'No, I certainly did not.'

'Do you think he might have seen a firearm as a way of securing peace?'

'I don't know, but then people are always doing things I don't expect – good things as well as bad. It depends what you mean. Are you suggesting he might have used it against someone who was threatening him, or threatening someone else?'

'You tell me, Mr Cardew.'

'I find that question very difficult to answer. I must emphasise again that I didn't know him well – in fact, the more you talk about him, the more it makes me think I didn't know him at all.'

CHAPTER SIXTEEN

Jago watched from the police station entrance as Cardew walked briskly away up West Ham Lane. The vicar looked like a man on a mission, as he supposed a vicar should. Meeting the pastoral needs of the people in his parish, and possibly beyond, must be ten times the work it had been in peacetime, he guessed. Comforting the bereaved, helping the survivors who'd lost everything but the clothes they stood up in, having to find time and compassion for everyone – not a job Jago would like, but now he had his own small excursion to make into such territory.

'Come along, Peter,' he said with a sigh. 'We need to track down a young woman and break some bad news to her.'

They drove to Canning Town and stopped outside Mrs Grove's house in Kildare Road. A plain-looking woman in her fifties opened the door in response to their knock, drying her hands on a floral-print apron. Her sleeves were pushed up above her elbows and her face was flushed. Washing day, thought Jago.

'Yes?' she said.

'Mrs Grove?' said Jago.

'Yes. Who are you?'

Jago raised his hat.

'I'm Detective Inspector Jago, from West Ham police station. I need to speak to Miss Gloria Harris, who I understand was your lodger before she moved to Buckinghamshire with the evacuated children. I wondered if you might be able to give me her address.'

'Certainly I can. But she's not there.'

'I'm sorry – I was told she was.'

'Well, she's not. Leastways, she is usually, but right now she's not. She's upstairs. Shall I fetch her?'

'Yes, please.'

Mrs Grove stumped up the stairs and shortly returned, followed by a slim and poised woman who looked in her twenties.

'Here she is,' she said. 'If you want to have a talk with Miss Harris you'd best use the front parlour. In there,' she added, gesturing to the door beside Cradock. 'And mind you wipe your boots before you go in – I only beat the rugs two days ago and I don't want the place messed up.'

She looked at her lodger, gave a peculiar sniff, then walked back down the hallway towards the scullery.

Cradock opened the door to the parlour, and the young woman walked in, followed by the two men.

'Gloria Harris – Miss,' she said, shaking Jago's hand. 'Mrs Grove tells me you're from the police.'

'That's correct.'

'Don't mind her, by the way,' she added with a smile. 'Mrs Grove's quite sweet, really. And she must think you're all right, otherwise she wouldn't let you use her parlour. I rent a room from her, but I'm rarely allowed in here.'

Jago was surprised – Gloria Harris was nothing like the person he'd expected to find. On the way there in the car he'd been recalling some of the female teachers of his own early youth, and their strait-laced and forbidding image was still in his mind when she appeared. The woman before him was dressed in a neatly tailored light grey suit, sheer stockings which to his untutored eye were either silk or rayon, and a pair of unblemished black court shoes. Instead of the tightly pinned bun of his childhood teachers, she wore her fair hair in loose curls to her shoulders, Hedy Lamarr-style. What struck him most, though, was her face. There was something of the famous American actress about that too – something he couldn't quite put his finger on. It was delicate and composed, yet in the eyes there was a hint of distance, detachment. She looked him up and down and waited in silence, her head tilted slightly to one side and eyebrows raised.

'Do take a seat,' she said.

The only things to sit on in the room were four upright chairs positioned round a square wooden dining table. The table was bare except for a dark brown vase standing on a small cloth in the middle and holding a clump of dried honesty seed pods. Their frail silvery-white discs reminded Jago of maiden aunts, spinsters and widows, and seemed strikingly incongruous in the presence of this vital young woman. She sat down on one side of the table, then Jago took the chair opposite her, and Cradock another to her side. Gloria smiled again.

'How can I help you?'

'We're here in connection with an incident we're investigating—'

'An incident? Does that mean a bomb? It's what the ARP people always say when they're talking about bombs.'

'No, it's not a bomb in this case. I understand you're a teacher, Miss Harris, and your school has been evacuated to Buckinghamshire, so you're living there. Is that correct?'

'Yes. We're in a place called Bradwell – it's a little village in the middle of nowhere.'

'May I ask why you came back to West Ham this weekend?'

'It was to see Paul – my fiancé. He's a teacher too, and he'd just been promoted.'

'Would that be Mr Paul Ramsey?'

'Yes, that's right. Why?'

'I'm sorry, Miss Harris, I didn't know you and Mr Ramsey were engaged. His headmaster seemed to think he was unattached, and we were only told that you'd been seeing each other.'

'That's all right – nobody knew. We got engaged three weeks ago, but we haven't told anyone yet. But look, why are you here? What interest can the police have in why I came here for the weekend?'

She stopped speaking, and her eyes widened.

'It's not . . . this isn't something to do with Paul, is it?'

'Yes, Miss Harris, I'm afraid it is.'

'What . . . what's happened?'

'There's no easy way to say this,' said Jago gently, 'but the fact is, Mr Ramsey's body was found in a public air-raid shelter yesterday morning.'

Gloria's composure evaporated. An expression of shock and disbelief crossed her face, and she stared at him as if struck dumb. Then slowly it seemed as though the meaning of his words sank in, and she buried her face in her hands, sobbing. Jago wished he could have brought a woman police constable with him to comfort her, but with only five of them on the whole division there was little chance of that. He could only wait until Gloria felt able to speak. When she did, her voice was a whisper.

'I'm sorry, Inspector, but it's such a shock. You always think it'll be someone else who . . . someone else who's taken. I can't believe it. Was it an air raid?'

'No, I'm afraid he was murdered.'

'Murdered? Surely there must be some mistake.'

'No mistake, Miss Harris. I'm very sorry, but we're in no doubt that he was killed unlawfully.'

'But why? Who would want to do that?'

151

'I'm afraid we don't have any answers at the moment. But look, this is obviously very distressing news for you. Would you like us to come back later?'

Gloria took a lace handkerchief from her pocket and dabbed at her eyes and cheeks.

'No, Inspector,' she said, 'I want you to find whoever did this. You say you have no idea who it was?'

'No, but I was hoping that with you being close to him you might be able to help us.'

'How did you know we were seeing each other?'

'His friend Mr Wilfred Morton told us. I believe you know him.'

'I used to, yes.'

She fell silent again, seemingly lost in thought.

'You said you came back to see Mr Ramsey,' said Jago. 'When did you see him?'

A few seconds passed before she stirred herself out of her thoughts and spoke.

'Well, that's just the thing – I didn't. I decided more or less on a whim to come down here for the weekend and surprise him, to celebrate his getting the new job, but unfortunately it didn't work out quite as I'd planned.'

Jago waited for her to continue.

'In what way?' he prompted.

'Oh, I, er, started feeling ill on the train, and by the time I got to London I felt dreadful. I just about managed to get here – I kept the room on when I was evacuated, because there's no way of knowing how long it'll be before we can come back. I let myself in

– Mrs Grove wasn't about, but I still have the keys – and put myself straight to bed. I couldn't contact Paul because there's no phone here and I was too ill to get out to a phone box, and to be honest, most of the time I was just sleeping and going to the, er, well, you know how it is. I was in bed all day yesterday and only started feeling better today. I was planning to get the train back to Buckinghamshire from Euston this morning, and I was going to try to phone the school to say I'd be late back, if I could find a phone that was working and where I could make a trunk call.'

'I'm afraid I'll have to ask you not to leave the area – we may need to talk to you again. We'll contact the school and tell them, if you give us the details.'

'Yes, yes, of course,' she murmured, her voice fading.

'I'm sorry to have to ask you this, Miss Harris, but can you think of anyone who might have had reason to kill your fiancé?'

She dabbed at her eyes again and then twisted the handkerchief in her hands, as if unaware of what she was doing.

'No, no . . . No one would want to do that. He wasn't a perfect man, but he was a pacifist – he had strong views about people living together in peace. I can't imagine him having enemies.'

'Even pacifists can have enemies, Miss Harris.'

'All right, perhaps they can, but I've no knowledge of anyone who'd wish evil against Paul.'

'Did you know he had a gun?'

'A gun? But that's ridiculous – I've just told you, he was a pacifist. What would he want with a gun?'

'I don't know. To protect himself?'

'No, that's absurd. He wasn't that kind of person.'

'What kind of person was he?'

'He was no saint, Inspector, but he was a man of principle. It's not easy to stand up and be counted as a pacifist these days. It's like they say it was in the Great War – if you opposed the war on grounds of moral principle people said you were a coward or a traitor. But he was neither of those things – he was just a man who refused to bend with the wind. The mob might go off to war, but he wouldn't act against his convictions. He would never betray his country, but neither would he betray his principles.'

'So would you describe him as trustworthy?'

'Of course. Why ever not? Why do you ask such a thing?'

'Mr Morton doesn't seem to think so. I believe he knew Mr Ramsey quite well, and he took rather a different view.'

'What has he said?'

'He says he didn't trust him.'

'So? I don't know what he thinks.'

'He says he didn't trust Mr Ramsey because Ramsey stole his girlfriend, and that was you.'

Gloria laughed, but it sounded forced.

'What nonsense. We went out together a few times, but I was never his girl. If he says that, it's just his fantasy talking.'

She turned her head, and as the light from the window fell on it Jago noticed a discolouration on her right cheekbone.

'You seem to have bruised your face,' he said.

'What, this?' she replied, touching it with her forefinger. 'Yes, we were playing rounders with the children and one of them hit the ball straight into my face. It's nothing, really – I expect it'll be gone in a day or two. Now, will that be all?'

'Yes, thank you,' said Jago, rising from his chair. 'For the time being.'

CHAPTER SEVENTEEN

It was a short drive from Gloria's lodgings to the school where Paul Ramsey had taught, and they arrived just before lunchtime. After reporting to the head teacher, Mr Gilroy, they had to wait only ten minutes or so before the bell rang and they were able to speak to Harold Shaw.

He had come straight from his class and had an exasperated look on his face. He was a tall, heavily built, muscular-looking man with fair hair, wearing a shapeless sports jacket and flannels. Jago's first impression was that he looked more like a boxer than a schoolmaster, but when he instinctively ran his eyes over Shaw's clothes he spotted the tell-tale traces of chalk dust which he associated with everyone who spent their days writing on a blackboard in a classroom.

Gilroy invited them to use his study for their conversation and left them to it.

'What a shower these kids are,' said Shaw, slumping into the sole comfortable armchair in the room and letting out a noisy sigh. 'I reckon I've got enough experience of crowd control to teach your boys how to police football matches. You should send them to work here for a week in one of our classrooms – it'd be the perfect training. But anyway, time's short – how can I help you? The head told me you wanted to talk about Ramsey – my late colleague, I suppose I should say now. The man's been murdered, or so I've been told.'

'That's correct.'

'Well, well, there's an irony if ever there was one.'

'Irony?'

'Yes. I mean, a man who forswears violence yet perishes by the sword.'

'Perishes by the sword?'

'I don't mean literally – I don't know anything about how he was killed, of course. Just a figure of speech, but it's ironic all the same – not that Ramsey had a penchant for irony. Such subtleties escaped him, I'm afraid.'

'What do you mean by that?'

'Well, I won't beat about the bush, Inspector. It pains me to say this, but the impression I formed from working with him was that beneath the veneer of sophistication the man was a dullard. No depth. Do you know what I mean?'

'Harsh words to speak of a colleague who's just died?'

'Forgive me, Inspector. Perhaps I've been a teacher for too long and it's blunted my sensibilities. Ten years spent trying to drum the barest minimum of knowledge into the heads of these children takes its toll, you know. Ten years of casting pearls before swine, if you want the honest truth. If you don't believe me, how about this? One of my colleagues said the other day she'd told her class to write out their name and address, and one boy said, "Please, miss, how do you spell mouse?" She said, "Why on earth do you want to know that? You don't need that to write your name and address." The boy said, "Yes I do, miss. I live in Custer Mouse." If it weren't so pitiful it would be funny.'

He paused to pull a packet of cigarettes from his pocket and put one in his mouth. He waved the pack at Jago and Cradock by way of offering them one.

'No, thank you,' said Jago.

Shaw lit his cigarette and blew smoke towards the headmaster's ceiling.

'I mean, these kids,' he continued, 'they're the heirs to a mighty empire that spans the globe, yet they can't even spell their own address properly. And the way they speak, you wonder why we ever bothered to invent the letter H. They all live in "West Am", and the particular bit of it they happen to inhabit isn't Custom House, it's "Custer Mouse", because that's all they've ever heard at home. They probably think it's named after an American general and a rodent – except they wouldn't, of course, because they don't know anything about America and they don't know what the word "rodent" means, even though their homes are probably full of them. I tell you, Inspector, sometimes I despair.'

'But surely that's precisely why we need schools. Isn't that what inspires people to become teachers?'

'It is, Inspector – more fools we. I started out like that, full of bright hope and vision. I grew up in this benighted borough myself, but I suppose I was one of those rare birds – a boy that wants to learn. It's difficult to believe now, but even as a child I had my heart set on being a teacher. Sweet thought, isn't it? As soon as I was fourteen I was going to get one of those intending-teacher scholarships we used to have, but of course then they changed the system, so I had to stay on at school another two years. But I wasn't going to give up. At least I was learning a valuable lesson myself – if you want something, you have to work for it. Unlike a lot of the kids here. So then I got one of the new scholarships – four days a week on a teaching placement in an elementary school and the other day at school myself. After that it was two years at teacher training college. So you see, I spent years learning everything there was to know about teaching – everything except how to get the slightest bit of knowledge into row upon row of numbskulls with no interest in bettering themselves.'

'Some people say it's the parents' fault. I went to school in this borough, but I had parents who wanted me to learn.'

'Most of these kids' parents just want them to leave school the moment they turn fourteen so they can get jobs and start bringing some money into the house. Especially the girls – the parents see no point wasting time and money on education for their daughters when all they're going to do is get married and have babies. You can't blame them, I suppose – it's what they had to do when they were kids. People round here live from hand to mouth, and their biggest ambition is to have enough cash to pay the rent and some sheets to pawn so they can feed the kids. What they don't seem to realise is that if they let them stay at school for another couple of years they'd stand a chance of getting a better job and earning more. I don't know how many times I've tried to persuade them, but with some parents there's just no telling them. So I have to go back to cramming whatever I can into the kids' heads in the time available – and even that's got harder now the school day's shorter. What can you do?'

'And you've been teaching for ten years, you say?'

'That's right. I suppose I chose the worst possible decade to do it in, too – it started with a global economic collapse and ended with a war.'

'And working in this school all that time?'

'Yes – I suppose I'm what you call the faithful sort.'

'Meaning?'

'The sort that keeps on in the same job, same place, year in, year out. "Not seeking for any reward, save that of knowing that we do thy will, O Lord." That sort of thing.'

'Are you a churchman?'

'Certainly not. I just like the words of that prayer, that's all – we learnt them when I was at school. Mind you, for "doing thy will, O Lord" you could read "doing thy will, O Headmaster" – that might be closer to the mark.'

'And how long have you worked with Mr Ramsey?'

'All the time he's been here – his entire illustrious career. That would be two years.'

'In the same department?'

'Yes, both teaching English.'

'Had he taught elsewhere before coming here?'

'No – believe it or not, this was his first teaching job.'

'And I understand he was recently appointed head of the English department.'

'Yes.'

'So he was promoted over your head?'

'You could put it like that.'

'Did you mind?'

Shaw gave a bitter laugh.

'What's the point of minding? It's not my decision, and I have no influence over the head.'

'Did you feel his appointment of Mr Ramsey was unjust?'

'What if I did? What am I supposed to do? Complain about Gilroy to the chairman of the board of managers? They're thick as thieves, those two. I wouldn't be surprised if they'd cooked the whole thing up together for some reason. Gaining influence over my superiors is an area of my career that I failed to develop, so perhaps I've only myself to blame.'

'Meaning others have succeeded?'

'I wouldn't know, Inspector – you'll have to ask them.'

'But you didn't believe Mr Ramsey deserved to be the head of department?'

'I've already told you, I found him a shallow man. He lacked the breadth and depth of education that it takes to be a real teacher. I think he only went as far as he had to – just enough to pass the exams and get a half-decent job. Beyond that he had no real interest.'

'But he was nevertheless a qualified teacher, like yourself, I assume?'

'Yes, he was, but I don't think Ramsey and I entered this profession for the same reason. I chose it because I wanted to give these kids a chance to better themselves. That's why I came to a place like this.'

'And what do you think was Mr Ramsey's motivation?'

'I can't be sure. I think perhaps it was to prove something. Maybe he saw teaching as a path to social advancement. He certainly can't have been doing it for the money. Schoolmastering isn't the road to riches, you know. But whatever his aims were, I'd question how deep his commitment was.'

'What can you tell me about his private life? Did you spend time together outside school? Mr Gilroy said you were his closest colleague.'

'It depends what you mean by close. We both taught the same subject, yes, but close friends? I wouldn't say so.'

'Did you argue?'

'No. Whatever my private views about him, I know better than to air them at work and I maintained a civil relationship with him at all times. I just mean we didn't live in each other's pockets. Once in a while we'd meet over a drink to discuss some professional issues, but that's about all our contact amounted to.'

'Did you have a drink with him at the Prince of Wales last Friday?'

Shaw looked surprised.

'How did you know that? Have you been snooping around behind my back?'

'No, Mr Shaw, we just noticed the engagement in Mr Ramsey's diary. So, did you?'

'Well, yes, I did. But there was nothing out of the ordinary about it – just a drink.'

'Was it for professional reasons?'

'Yes, it was, actually. I wanted to show him there were no hard feelings about him getting the promotion. I knew there was nothing I could do about it and I didn't want it to spoil our working relationship, so I invited him out for a drink to congratulate him. The Prince of Wales is just down the road from where he lived, so I suggested we go there. It was as simple as that.'

'Right. Is there anything you can tell me about how he spent his spare time, other than going to his local?'

'He was a teacher, Inspector. He probably spent it marking exercise books.'

'I understand he was a member of the Peace Pledge Union. Were you aware of that?'

'Oh, yes, I knew he was a pacifist – he made no secret of that. He had quite strong views. I remember when we declared war he said, "They'll never get me in uniform – I won't be part of a killing machine for anyone." And another time he said, "If they come looking for me I'll make damn sure they don't find me."'

'What do you think he meant by that?'

'I don't know. At the time I thought it was just talk – he was quite het up about it, but that was a year ago. The war had only just started, so I thought it was all a bit theoretical. He clearly didn't want to do any form of military service, but there wasn't much chance of him being conscripted – none at all, really.'

'Because he was working in a reserved occupation?'

'Yes. At that time no teacher over the age of twenty-five was going to be called up for military service, whatever their views.'

'I was told something about him possibly planning to register as a conscientious objector. Is that right?'

'Yes. I think he saw it as a belt-and-braces job – get yourself registered as a conchie, then even if they change the rules about reserved occupations and make you liable for service you still won't get called up. The trouble is, from what I heard, the tribunal didn't buy it – he was hoping to get exemption from military service, but they turned him down and sent him packing.'

'How did he react when his application was rejected?'

'I asked him – I don't approve of conchies, you see. He was obviously disappointed, but he was still in the clear because of the reserved occupation business. It was only later I imagine things came a bit unstuck for him.'

'In what way?'

'The government raised the reserved-occupation age limit for teachers from twenty-five to thirty, with effect from the first of August, so now he was in the net along with all the other teachers who were under thirty – he knew he'd be called up.'

'So his plans had come to nothing.'

'Yes. With his application for exemption rejected, once he fell within the age group liable for call-up there was no way out, was there? The age limit for military service keeps going up and up – I suppose the forces have an insatiable demand for manpower.'

'And you?'

'I'm thirty-one, so they're not coming for me yet. Unlike Ramsey, though, I'm quite happy with the idea of having a crack at the enemy. After all this bombing we've had, nothing would give me greater pleasure than to bag a few Germans and even things up a bit.'

'So what was Mr Ramsey thinking once the age limit was changed and he was liable to be called up?'

'I couldn't tell you. He didn't confide in me about his feelings – although I got the sense that there was something on his mind, certainly in the last couple of weeks or so.'

'Do you think he was still determined to avoid military service?'

'He didn't say anything that would make me think he'd changed his mind about that.'

'Had he made any specific plans to that end?'

'I don't know, and again, if he had I don't think he'd

necessarily have told me. Still waters ran deep with him. He struck me as a man with one or two secrets.'

'Could he have been planning to go away?'

'It's possible, I suppose. Men desert from the forces, so I imagine there must be some who decide to disappear before they even get into uniform. Military service wasn't part of the future he saw for himself, I'm sure of that – and whether that was for purely ethical reasons or just to save his own skin I couldn't say. I suppose we'll never know now, will we?'

'Did he have a girlfriend?'

Shaw looked surprised. 'That's rather an abrupt change of tack. Why do you ask?'

'Just answer the question, please. We do appreciate your assistance.'

'The answer's no, not as far as I was aware. He certainly never mentioned it to me.'

'I see. Is there anything else you can tell us about Mr Ramsey that might help us in our investigation?'

'No, I think I've probably told you as much as I can.'

'Very well. We may need to speak to you again, so may I have your address, please?'

'Yes, it's 174 Barking Road.'

'That's interesting. I've visited that address only recently.'

'Really?'

'Yes, it's where Mr Wilfred Morton lives, isn't it?'

'Indeed it is, Inspector. I'm his lodger. I share a flat with him – or to be more precise, I sub-let a room from him.'

'You're friends?'

'No, I just needed somewhere to live.'

'Pardon me for saying so, but I'm surprised you're sub-letting a room in a flat over a shop when you've been working as a teacher for ten years.'

Shaw flashed him a knowing smile.

'Let's just put it down to unsuccessful investments, Inspector. And now, if you don't mind, I'll get back to my own little front line in the battle for education.'

'Thank you, Mr Shaw. I'll know where to find you.'

CHAPTER EIGHTEEN

Jago and Cradock sat outside the school in the car. The noise of children in the playground had faded as they finished their games and lined up in silence before returning into the building for their afternoon lessons.

'Takes you back, doesn't it?' said Jago. 'All those years ago, when we were kids – life was so much simpler then. Not so long ago for you, of course.'

'Yes, sir. Life does seem to get more complicated when you're grown up.'

'Especially when you get tangled up with women, eh, Lothario?'

'Who, sir?'

'Nobody we know. So what do you make of those two?'

'Which two?'

'Gloria Harris and Harold Shaw.'

'Well, Gloria seems a very confident young lady. It's difficult to imagine anyone pulling the wool over her eyes, but on the other hand her description of Paul

Ramsey didn't seem to tally with Shaw's, did it? I mean, she's an intelligent woman and she thought enough of Ramsey to be engaged to marry him, but from the way Shaw talked about him you'd think he was some kind of scoundrel.'

'Morton said he didn't trust Ramsey either, didn't he?'

'Yes, sir, but that was because he said Ramsey had stolen her from him. If people's emotions get involved they don't always see things clearly, do they?'

'I'm sure you're right, Peter. So do you think Morton might've been less dispassionate than he made out about losing her to a rival? Jealousy is a powerful emotion, after all – a passionate heart can send the best of principles flying out of the window.'

'Yes, sir.'

'On the other hand, Gloria's account of her relationship with Morton didn't seem to reflect quite as much passion as his, did it? I think I'd like another word with Mr Morton.'

Canning Town Library had been built on Barking Road by the Corporation of the Borough of West Ham as the nineteenth century was drawing to a close. It was one of Jago's favourite local buildings, and as they approached he was relieved to see it had escaped air-raid damage for another night. Lower – just two storeys – and somewhat less ornate than the imposing public hall next door, it had the look of a junior partner, but to him it possessed a confidence in itself which must have reflected the mood of the time when it was built. Back then the borough had seen a rapid growth in population, and he imagined the worthy councillors who governed it looking forward to further unprecedented progress in the approaching twentieth century. What they would think of that progress if any of them were still alive now in 1940 was debatable, but the building remained as a lasting memorial to their vision.

Jago parked the Riley, and he and Cradock walked the length of the library towards the entrance. He knew nothing of the architect's intentions, but he liked the way the functional red brick of the library's walls combined with the refined decoration of its white carved stonework – it seemed to say that the poor working people of this newly industrialised area were entitled to have access to culture and learning, and that the success of the future depended on providing it. As a man who put most of his education down to reading newspapers and books from the public library, he felt a personal debt to the far-sightedness and hope of that generation. Seeing this place again felt like an antidote to some of the views Harold Shaw had expressed.

He opened the front door and they went in. Jago was assuming that at this time on a Monday afternoon Morton would still be at work, and his guess was correct. Cradock found him replacing books on the shelves and beckoned Jago over. Jago crept across the silent room and whispered to Morton.

'We'd like a quick word with you, Mr Morton. Is there somewhere we can talk in private?'

Morton nodded and took them through a door at the back of the library and down a dingy corridor to a small office that was empty.

'How can I help you?' he said, speaking at a normal level once the door was closed behind them.

'I'm sorry to interrupt you at work, as I'm sure you're busy, but I'd like to ask you a little more about your relationship with Gloria Harris. The thing is, we've now spoken to her, and her description of it is rather different to yours. She says she was never your girl, and that if you believe that, it's just a fantasy on your part. Can you explain that, please?'

Morton pulled a face which Jago could only have described as a pout and sat down.

'All right. I suppose she's right. We went out for a drink a few times and I took her to the pictures once, but that's as far as it went. I wanted to see her again, but she said she wasn't interested. Is that better?'

'I see. And how did that leave you feeling?'

'How do you think?'

'Rejected?'

'Yes. I loved her, and I was angry when I heard she was seeing Paul. I wished I'd never met her.'

'You say you loved her, but the way Gloria describes it, it was more like a one-sided infatuation.'

'She may have seen it that way, but for me it was love. It still is. Have you ever experienced unrequited love, Inspector?'

Jago left the question unanswered and waited for him to continue.

'Well,' said Morton, 'I can tell you I'm not the first person ever to feel it, and I won't be the last. It's just tough luck on me.'

'Especially tough, I would imagine, given that your friend Paul Ramsey was now the love of her life. How did that fit with your pacifist convictions? You wouldn't be the first person in history to have his lofty principles challenged by sordid reality.'

'Sordid reality? Do you think I don't know about that? What's this war if not sordid reality? When I joined the PPU, Mr Jago, we weren't at war, but we all knew that's what we were heading for. I believed in peace. I didn't want to be the enemy of any man, and I didn't want to give any man cause to become my enemy. But now we've taken a decision to go to war, and through no desire of my own, whether I like it or not, a whole nation is my enemy and I'm expected to fight them. I call that sordid reality, but I don't see why it should alter my convictions one jot.'

'Perhaps not. But what Paul Ramsey did wasn't like that. It wasn't about you finding yourself at odds with a nation or a government. It was personal – it was just you and him. Perhaps it turned out that pacifism's all right in theory, when it's all about you not wanting to go to war, but not when you think someone's stolen your girl. You said you were angry – was that angry with Gloria?'

'Yes, of course I was angry,' he shouted, but then

immediately made his voice quieter. 'Look, Inspector, I'll be honest with you. Yes, I was angry with Gloria because I had a deep affection for her and I felt she knew that, and yet she'd let herself be lured away from me by Paul Ramsey. And yes, perhaps he was more charming than me, more confident – perhaps he was simply more manly or better looking than me. Who knows how a woman's mind works? Perhaps they'd all fall for someone like him rather than me. I don't know. All I know is that I'd have given her faithful love, cherished her, respected her – which is more than I think she would've got from Paul Ramsey.'

'And how did you express this anger to Gloria?'

'I didn't. I mean, getting angry and shouting and screaming doesn't solve anything.'

'You just kept it all inside?'

'Yes, of course I did. Anger and violence only beget more of the same. If we're civilised human beings we need to talk to each other and resolve these things peacefully, whether it's two people or two nations.'

'You mean if we sit down and discuss our differences nice and calmly we can fix any problem in the world?'

'What I'm saying is, even if I did feel angry, I've learnt to control my feelings.'

'And did she talk? Did the two of you sit down at the negotiating table and sort it all out?'

'No! She said there was nothing to talk about and I was just a silly boy to get such ideas in my head.'

'And did you agree?'

'Look, now you're laughing at me, just like she did.'

'So she laughed at you, did she? And how did you respond? Did you decide the time for talking had come to an end? Time for a show of force, to show her she couldn't kick you around?'

'Are you suggesting I was violent to her? The very idea is utterly abhorrent to me.'

'She had a nasty bruise on her face when we saw her.'

'What? That swine—'

'Who are you referring to?'

'If you're looking for someone who'd do a thing like that to Gloria, it's not me, Inspector.'

'Who should I be looking for, then?'

'Her cousin.'

'Her cousin? Who's that?'

'Harold Shaw, of course – didn't you know?'

'No, I didn't. That's interesting – am I right in understanding that he's your lodger?'

'Yes, that's correct.'

'And you think he was responsible for that bruise of hers?'

'I don't know. All I know is when he found out I was seeing her, he – he hit me. He said I wasn't good enough for Gloria and he wasn't going to let me ruin her life. He said he'd told her to stay away from me and he threatened to kill me if I so much as looked at her again.'

'But you didn't throw him out?'

'No.'

'Forgive me, Mr Morton, but this is becoming more and more contradictory. He hits you and threatens to kill you, but he's still your lodger? Isn't that a bit odd?'

'No, I just . . . I told him to go but he said he wouldn't. He said if I wanted him out I could try throwing him out, but he didn't think much of my chances.'

'So you decided not to try?'

'Surely I've made it clear to you, Inspector, that I don't believe in using violence. Look at Gandhi in India – he wants us out of his country but he's determined to do it by non-violence. He's a man I admire, and I hope he succeeds. Even if he's killed I believe others will be inspired and will take his place. No matter how disagreeable I find Shaw, I'd rather have the man remain in my home than strike him – that may seem strange to you, but it's my choice. And now, if you don't mind, I must get back to my work.'

He walked out of the office and let the door slam shut behind him.

CHAPTER NINETEEN

Alex let himself in through the front door. Sally came down the passage to meet him, and as usual the first thing he did on getting home from work was give her a kiss. She hugged him, took his coat, and hung it up on the old mahogany coat stand that took up half the wall space in the hallway.

'How was it today?' she asked, as she did every day.

'So-so,' he replied.

'That means not very good, doesn't it? You're not looking yourself – did something bad happen?'

'Yes. It wasn't the work – that was OK – but I was just thinking about things.'

'Well, come and sit down, and I'll get you a nice cup of tea. Then you can tell me all about it.'

She installed him in his favourite chair and busied herself with the kettle and teapot, then came and sat beside him with two cups of tea.

'There you are, my love,' she said, handing one to Alex. 'So what was it?'

'It was something I saw this morning. I had to get off the bus and walk the last bit – the road was blocked – and I came to this place where a bomb must have landed. There were rescue people everywhere, and it looked as though an air-raid shelter had come down – one of those public ones the council built on the street. There might've been fifty people in it, and the roof had just come straight down on them.'

'How awful,' Sally whispered.

'And the worst thing was I could see a leg sticking out – I don't know whether it was a girl or a boy, but it was a dead child. I was thinking what if we have a child some day and something like that happens? How would I cope? I wish we could get away from here, Sally – we're right by the docks, and they're like a magnet for those bombers. We're sitting ducks.'

'We'll get away some day, love – we'll have a nice little house, and a family, and a bit of garden for them to play in. We just have to be patient.'

'I know, that's what I want too – but the thing is, when I saw that kid lying there dead, I felt responsible. I felt guilty.'

'You mustn't feel like that, Alex. It's not our fault they're bombing us – you and I haven't done anything wrong. It's all politics, isn't it? We just have to try not to think about it all too much. One day all this'll be over and everything will change, you'll see.'

'It's more complicated than that. I think the reason why I feel guilty is because I work for the council, because I've stood by and said nothing.'

'What do you mean? Said nothing about what?'

'I'm not sure, but I think there's something going on. It's been bothering me for a while, and it's something I can't blame on the Germans. It's something at work – I think there's been some kind of fiddle going on, and I don't know what to do about it.'

'You mean something illegal? Surely not.'

'Why not? We're all weak, aren't we? Who's to say what I'd do if temptation came my way?'

She eyed him warily.

'What kind of temptation?'

'Not that kind, my love – I'd never be tempted away from you. I'm talking about money – the chance to make a bit more money on the side. Look at us, for instance, struggling to get by on my wage. I could get more as an air-raid warden.'

'But that's not a career, is it? I mean, they'll all be out of work when the war ends. At least working for the council you'll never get the sack.'

'I certainly hope not, but it's not much for us both to live on, is it? And what will it be like if we have kids?'

'Well, I won't deny it – I wouldn't complain if we had a bit more money.'

'But only honestly earned, surely?'

'Of course, yes – so you're saying you think someone's stealing money at the council?'

'Possibly – something like that. I don't know for sure, but it's happened before. Not in my time, of course, but I've heard about cases back in the old days – the head of the education department, for example. When he died they discovered he'd been embezzling council funds. There's been others too. They weren't very strict about the accounting in those days, it seems, so it was easier – but even now I dare say there are ways round it if you want to find them.'

'So what do you think's happening?'

'I'm not sure, but I think it's something to do with contracts.'

'What are you going to do about it?'

'That's the problem – I don't know. I mean, if it's to do with council money it's likely to involve my department, and if someone there's mixed up in it, it'll probably be someone higher up. So how do I report it?'

'Don't you just tell your boss?'

'But supposing it's my boss who's doing it? How long do you think I'll stay in the job if it is? He'll get rid of me as soon as look at me. And then what would become of us? I can't afford to take the risk.'

'But you can't just turn a blind eye if someone's stealing public money – people pay their rates so the council can provide the services we need, not to line some bigwig's pockets.'

'I know, but I don't know who to talk to about it.'

'Maybe you can't talk to anyone at work, but why not someone outside work?'

'Are you thinking of someone in particular, or just the next bus conductor I buy a ticket from?'

'Course not, silly. I'm thinking of the vicar. He knows

how things like the council work, and apart from you, I think he's the only man I can put my hand on my heart and say I think he's honest. He'll be able to give you some advice. He knows how to keep a secret – he's a priest, isn't he? And people say he's a good listener.'

Alex looked dubious, but eventually nodded his head. 'All right, then. Perhaps I'll go and see him.'

CHAPTER TWENTY

When Jago woke on Tuesday morning he found himself reflecting on what Harold Shaw had said about Paul Ramsey's promotion. It was of course entirely possible for a man to be promoted after only two years' service, and perfectly natural for a longer-serving colleague to suffer a bad case of sour grapes as a result. But Harold Shaw had insinuated that there was something improper about the appointment. If that was true it might cast a different light on the investigation. He drove to the station and found Cradock in the CID office.

'We need to see Mr Cardew again, Peter,' he said.

'The vicar, guv'nor? Why's that?' said Cradock.

'Because of what Harold Shaw said about Paul Ramsey's promotion yesterday. The vicar's a member of the board of managers for the school, so if there was any fishy business going on between the chairman and Gilroy, he might be able to shed some light on it. Get your coat, and let's go.'

Cradock struggled into his overcoat and began chuckling to himself.

'What's so funny, Peter?' said Jago.

'I was just thinking of that other fishy business in Custom House last year,' Cradock replied. 'Do you remember, sir?'

'No. Enlighten me.'

'There was a cat stuck on a roof down in Clever Road, and a fishmonger threw a fish up for it. The cat ate the fish but left the skin, and they said when the skin dried out in the sun it glowed in the dark. The ARP people had to be called in in case an enemy plane saw it in the blackout.'

'That sounds too fishy to be true, Peter, and it has precious little to do with our investigation.'

'It was in the paper, sir.'

'Then don't believe everything you read in the papers. I'm beginning to suspect they put stories like that in just to keep our minds off the war. In the case of our fishy business, the more light the vicar can shed on it the better.'

The Reverend Henry Cardew lived in a modest house in Leyes Road, in the south-east corner of the borough, where the relentless sprawl of West Ham housing at last expired and gave way to the Plaistow marshes. Jago expected the door to be opened by a housekeeper or a general maid of sorts, but it was the vicar himself who answered their knock and welcomed them in.

'Good morning, gentlemen,' he said, offering them chairs. 'You've caught me at a good time – if you'd arrived half an hour later I'd have been out doing some pastoral visits. Let me get you a cup of tea.'

'That would be very nice, sir,' said Jago, 'but only if you can spare one. It's not so easy to offer tea to all and sundry now that it's rationed, is it?'

'One of life's smaller challenges, that's all. Mind you, if it's true that two ounces a week is enough to make twenty-five cups, I think they ought to give vicars a special extra allowance.'

'Perhaps you should write to your MP. I'm sure you'd have a good case.'

'Yes, well, I'm afraid I already write to my MP about weightier issues probably more frequently than he'd like me to. The poor man barely had his feet under the table after the by-election before the bombing started, and of course Silvertown has had it worse than anywhere else.'

'That's Mr Hollins, isn't it?'

'Yes. Silvertown is his constituency, but it includes us here in Custom House too.'

'He must have a lot on his plate. Is he any good?'

'Oh, yes. He was a borough councillor here for donkey's years, so he's well known in the area – and he got ninety-three per cent of the vote. And here's something you probably don't know – when we had that terrible explosion at the Brunner Mond TNT factory in 1917 and all those people were killed in Silvertown, his house was destroyed and he was buried under the debris, so he's something of a pioneer when it comes to being made homeless by blast damage.'

'Very interesting. Actually I'm hoping your local knowledge will be able to help me with another matter.'

'Really? In what way?'

'After you came to see me yesterday to talk about Paul Ramsey I had a conversation with a Mr Harold Shaw, who's another master at the same school. As you're on the school's board of managers I thought you might know him. Do you?'

'I've met him, but I can't say I really know him.'

'He was passed over for promotion to head of his department – the job went to Ramsey, didn't it?'

'Yes, that's correct.'

'Mr Shaw seems to think it may have been a put-up job.'

'How extraordinary. Does he have any evidence for that?'

'None that he's offered me.'

'What do you think he means?'

'Well, for one thing, Shaw had longer service, so he thinks he had more of a claim on the job.'

'So whoever's longest in the tooth should get the job? I've had longer service in this parish than some rural deans, but that doesn't necessarily mean I'd make a good one. Are you an old soldier?'

'Yes, I am, as it happens.'

'The same as me – I haven't always been a vicar, you know. Something I learnt in France was that while the men with the greater experience were worth their weight in gold, promotion wasn't always the best course for them. I'm sure you've seen evidence of that. Perhaps that was the case with Shaw.'

'That's not for me to say, Mr Cardew. All I can say is that Shaw seems none too pleased with the way Ramsey's appointment was handled. Were you involved in it?'

'Hardly at all. I'm a member of the board of managers, but to be honest these days there's barely time to have the meetings – I find it very difficult myself, what with everything that's happening around here. In this case it was really an emergency appointment – the previous head of department was killed in an air raid at the beginning of September, and the headmaster nominated Ramsey for promotion to take his place. The chairman approved it, and that was that.'

'The board just rubber-stamped the decision, then?'

'I don't like the idea, but I'm afraid that's possibly a fair description. Any of us could have raised an objection, but I had no grounds to, and I don't suppose anyone else did. I can't say I'm a great admirer of our chairman, but I think it would be fair to say Councillor Hampson is not a man who likes to go into too much detail.'

'Excuse me, but you said Councillor Hampson. Is that the chairman?'

'Yes, that's right.'

'And what's his Christian name?'

'Robert. Why?'

'It's nothing. I just didn't realise that's who he was. Do continue, please.'

'Well, I was about to say he's also not the kind of man

you argue with unless you have very strong grounds. The headmaster knew Ramsey far better than any of us, so if he deemed him the most suitable candidate for the post, none of us was going to object. But if Mr Shaw has a grievance, he should submit it to the chairman, giving detail of his case.'

'I'm not sure there is any specific detail. He just seems to think it wasn't fair.'

'Well, none of us likes to be passed over, but it happens to all of us. I've certainly heard nothing myself to suggest Mr Ramsey was unsuitable for promotion. It may have been simply a question of professional envy – that's not the worst sin a man can commit.'

'When it comes to sin I bow to your superior knowledge, Vicar.'

'Knowledge, or experience?' the vicar laughed. 'I'm not sure I want to be known as an expert on sin. I prefer to dwell on virtue – even in the midst of brutal warfare I came across some remarkable feats of virtue and self-sacrifice, men laying down their lives for their friends.'

'Yes, but it wasn't all noble self-sacrifice. I saw plenty of cases where war seemed to bring out the worst in a man.'

'Of course – I'm not denying that at all. I'm a vicar, and for me original sin isn't just a doctrine of the church – every day I see the selfishness and cruelty of sin in every aspect of life around me. Only this morning a young man came here and told me something quite shocking. In fact I'd like to take your advice on the matter if I may.'

'Please do.'

'He spoke to me in confidence, so I can't go into detail. All I can say is he was concerned there might be some kind of financial impropriety going on in the local council.'

'You mean a fiddle?'

'Actually that's the very word he used. It was something about people making more money than they ought to out of contracts. I'm just wondering what I should do about it. I mean, how could anyone do that kind of thing at a time like this, when people's lives are at stake?'

'It was to do with contracts, you say?'

'Yes.'

'What kind of contracts?'

'I don't know, but he suspected a local builder was involved.'

CHAPTER TWENTY-ONE

Jago put his cup and saucer down and looked the vicar in the eye. Cardew held his gaze, his expression imperturbable.

'Vicar,' said Jago, 'if there's some kind of embezzlement or fraud going on at the town hall we'll have to look into it. Who was the young man you mentioned, the one who called on you this morning?'

'He was one of my parishioners, but he came to see me in confidence, as I said, and at considerable risk to his own job. I don't think I can reveal his name without his permission, but I'll ask. In fact I'll ask him to contact you, if he's willing – that would be better.'

'And the builder he suspected – who was that?'

'The young man didn't give me the builder's name, and I didn't ask him. But he did refer to the kind of contract it was, so when he'd gone I phoned a man I know in the building trade and asked one or two careful questions, and I think I know who it might be.'

'And are you willing to tell me?'

'Yes – this is a different matter. I've made no pledge of confidentiality to him, and if he's been involved in anything suspect, it's my public duty to report it. From what I've been able to establish, it seems very likely that the builder was a gentleman called Joe Ramsey.'

'That's very interesting. Would that be Paul Ramsey's brother?'

'I didn't know Paul Ramsey well enough to know his relations, and I'd never heard of Joe Ramsey until this morning. So they're brothers?'

'Yes, they are – or were.'

'In that case I must ask you – you recall my mentioning that Paul Ramsey said there was something he wanted to discuss with me?'

'I do.'

'Well, he said he was writing to me in my capacity as a member of the school's board of managers, so I naturally assumed he was concerned about something to do with the school. But now you've told me he was Joe Ramsey's brother, I wonder whether he could have been intending to raise this council contract matter with me. But that's nothing to do with me, is it? It's puzzling. What do you think, Inspector?'

'I don't know, Mr Cardew. I really don't know.'

There was nothing else the vicar could tell them, so they left the tranquillity of Leyes Road and set off in the car back to the station.

'That was interesting,' said Cradock as they turned into Prince Regent Lane. 'About Councillor Hampson, I mean. Mrs Hampson said her husband was called Robert, didn't she? So unless there are two Robert Hampsons in West Ham, she must be married to him.'

'Sherlock Holmes would be proud of you, Peter,' Jago replied, not taking his eyes off the road. 'Of course, there could be two of them. If we see her again we can ask her. But there's something else a bit more pressing that I want to check – it's about that bruise of Gloria's. She said she got it playing rounders with the children at school, but when we talked to Wilfred Morton he clearly reckoned it was Shaw's work. I want to know which is true, so I'd like to see whether she might've changed her recollection. We'll just pop back to her digs and have a quick word with her. And by the way, Peter, all this talk of shelters and builders reminds me – I want you to do something for me today.'

'Yes, sir. What's that?'

'Visit a man called Mr Guy Hunter, of The Firs, Romford Road, and find out what happened when he had some dealings with a builder about an air-raid shelter.'

'Sir?'

'The DDI's asked us to look into it – seems this Mr Hunter is a pal of his, and some rogue's relieved him of five pounds on false pretences. Just drop in on him this afternoon, there's a good chap.'

'What, on my own, sir?'

'Yes, I'm sure you don't want to be tagging along with

me all the time. It's time you handled an investigation by yourself, and I've every confidence in you.'

'Really, sir? Thank you!'

They drove on in silence. Jago knew it was risky to let Cradock loose on his own, but he was pleased that the boy seemed keen to rise to the challenge. He smiled to himself, but with the most inconspicuous of grins: he didn't want Cradock to know.

Jago turned into Kildare Road and stopped outside the house where Gloria Harris had her lodgings. He knocked on the door, and Mrs Grove opened it.

'Is Miss Harris in?' he said. 'I'd like to have a word with her.'

'In?' said her landlady. 'Of course she isn't – she's gone off back to that place where she's teaching, Bradwell. Said she's catching the eleven fifty-five train from Euston.'

'What time did she leave?'

'Not long ago. About a quarter of an hour or so. If you drive fast in that car of yours you might catch her before it goes.'

'Thank you, Mrs Grove – goodbye,' said Jago hurriedly. 'Come on, Peter, back to the car – we need to step on it.'

Cradock was barely in his seat before Jago pulled the Riley away from the kerb and set off down the street as fast as he could.

'There's not much point in trying to intercept her at a station on the way,' he shouted to Cradock over the engine noise. 'Our best hope is to try to get to Euston before she leaves.'

'But the roads in London will be terrible, sir, after last night's bombs.'

'I know, but we'll have to do our best. If we don't catch her at Euston we may have to drive all the way to Bradwell and question her there.'

Jago maintained as high a speed as he could and used every shortcut he knew as they headed for West London. When they finally arrived at the main entrance to Euston station and parked the car it was just after half past eleven. They dashed through the bronze gates of the great Euston Arch and into the station building. The train hadn't come in yet, and there was no sign of Gloria on the platform.

'Try the cafe,' shouted Jago.

Cradock's younger legs got him there first, and as he burst in through the door of the station cafe he saw Gloria sitting alone at a small table, reading a book and sipping from a cup.

'Here she is, sir,' he said as Jago caught up with him.

Fighting to get his breath back, Jago crossed the room to where she was seated.

'Miss Harris,' he said, 'when I spoke to you yesterday I asked you not to leave the area for the time being, and yet here we find you running back to Bradwell the next morning. What's the meaning of that?'

Gloria must have caught the urgency in his voice, because she looked chastened.

'I'm sorry, Mr Jago,' she said, putting her book down on the table, 'I don't think I took in everything you were saying yesterday. It was the shock of what you told me about Paul being . . . about Paul being murdered. After you'd gone I couldn't stop thinking about it, and I couldn't bear the thought of staying in West Ham. Besides, I'd told you everything I know, so there seemed no point in hanging around. I suppose I just wasn't thinking straight. You must understand it was terrible news.'

She lowered her eyes and smiled meekly at him in a way that suggested penitence, but he was unmoved.

'Told me everything you know, you say?' he said. 'But that's exactly why I want to talk to you – I don't think that's true. I want to ask you one or two more questions.'

'Very well, Inspector,' she replied calmly. 'What is it you want to know?'

Jago sat down at the table with her and motioned Cradock to join him. Cradock got out his pocketbook and pencil.

'Well, to start with, I'd like to ask you about one of Paul Ramsey's colleagues at the school.'

'Oh, really? Is it someone I know?'

'I rather think it is. It's Harold Shaw.'

She seemed to flinch at the mention of his name, but immediately resumed control of her expression.

'Am I right in believing he is in fact not only a colleague of Mr Ramsey but also your cousin?' Jago continued.

'Yes, he is. I lost both my parents, you see – my mother

died bringing me into the world, and I was told later that my father never really recovered from his grief. He took his own life when I was six years old, and to be honest I don't have many memories of him. My uncle and his wife took me in and brought me up.'

'I see. And Harold Shaw was their son?'

'That's right. He was twelve when I became part of their family, and we spent a lot of time together from then until he left home to train as a teacher.'

'How would you describe his temperament?'

'I'm not sure I know how to answer that question. I certainly wouldn't call him a placid man, for example. I'd say he was impetuous. He gambles, you know – horses and cards mainly, as far as I know – and I think he's lost a lot of money over the years. I've sometimes wondered whether that's some kind of reaction against his job – having to be responsible and serious all day, I mean. Perhaps he's wanted another life outside the classroom that's risky, even dangerous.'

'It's been suggested to me that he has a violent side. Is that true?'

'If you asked people who don't know him well they'd probably say he was a calm person, because that's the impression he likes to give. That might be a professional thing – if your job is to control children you have to keep yourself under control too. But underneath there's an intensity, a sort of passion, and that can sometimes mean he loses his temper. I have to say the change can be quite shocking.'

'How did that affect your relationship?'

She thought for a moment.

'How can I put this? Our relationship has never been entirely straightforward. When I moved into the family I think he saw himself more like a brother. Looking back now, I can see that he's been insanely protective of me ever since we were children. I think he saw me as his toy. As I got older I tried to avoid him, but he was always "looking after" me, as he put it. Then when I grew up it got worse – he wanted to marry me. I only became a teacher so I could get away from him and earn my own living, but as it turned out, I found I loved teaching, and I still do. Jobs were scarce, though, and the only one I could get was here, in the same borough as him – but at least we were in different schools, so I could avoid him.'

'So the move to Bradwell suited you?'

'Yes, when the children were evacuated and I had to go with them, it was like a heaven-sent opportunity to get away.'

'Was it your cousin who gave you that bruise?'

'No.'

'Then who did?'

'I told you, it was an accident at school. My cousin has never been to Bradwell.'

'Tell me something else, Miss Harris. Did your cousin find out about your involvement with Paul Ramsey?'

'Yes, I'm afraid he did. I think he must have found out from Wilfred Morton – Harold lodges with him. I never told him myself – that would have been asking for trouble. I was scared what he might do.'

'But how could you hope to keep it a secret if your cousin worked in the same school as Paul?'

'I see now that I couldn't, but at the time I thought if we were discreet we could. I told Paul he was my cousin and explained how volatile he could be – I was worried about what might happen.'

'Have you seen Mr Shaw since you got back to West Ham?'

'No – I daren't.'

'Do you think he might have wanted to harm Mr Ramsey?'

'I don't know. I just didn't want to run the risk of something awful happening – that's why I begged Paul to make sure Harold never found out about us.'

'It's been suggested to me that your cousin assaulted Mr Morton, because he believed you and Wilfred were seeing each other. Were you aware of that?'

'No, I wasn't. How awful. But is it true?'

'It's been alleged, Miss Harris.'

Gloria looked up at the clock on the cafe wall.

'It's nearly time for my train, Inspector. May I go now?'

'I shall have to ask you not to, Miss Harris. I need you to be available for any further questions that may arise in connection with this investigation, so I'd like you to return to West Ham and stay there for at least the next few days. If you need me to explain the situation to your school in Bradwell I'll contact them.'

'No, no, Inspector, that won't be necessary. I'll tell them myself.'

'Would you like a lift back?'

'No, thank you. There are one or two things I can attend to in London. I think I'd rather make my own way back.'

CHAPTER TWENTY-TWO

Their business at Euston completed, Jago treated Cradock to a sandwich for lunch at the station cafe before they set off. The journey back to West Ham took them through the middle of London to Whitechapel, then out to the east through Mile End and Bow. There was noticeable bomb damage in the centre of the city, but once they got beyond Whitechapel it was far worse – this was clearly where the heaviest blows had fallen.

When they got to Romford Road in Stratford Jago stopped the car.

'All right, Peter,' he said, 'here you are. Run along and see Mr Hunter. I'll go back to the station – I'd like to have a chat with this Councillor Hampson and find out whether Paul Ramsey actually went to see him. So off you go, and if you're not back before I go home I'll see you in the morning – I'm out this evening.'

He watched as Cradock set off down the road, and

allowed himself a brief smile before he pulled on the wheel and turned back towards West Ham police station.

Cradock drew his shoulders back as he approached Mr Hunter's house. He felt emboldened by the flush of pride that had come over him when DI Jago said he had confidence in him – words he'd rarely heard since he left the uniformed branch to become an 'aid to CID' and then eventually a detective constable. He would make sure he didn't put a foot wrong.

The house before him was imposing: old and double-fronted, with steps up to the front door. The door was spotless and the letterbox gleaming brass. He raised the heavy door knocker and rapped twice in what he hoped would sound like an authoritative manner. A few moments later it swung open to reveal a housemaid with a black dress, a white cap and apron, and a lined face. She looked him up and down with an expression of mild disdain.

'Yes?' she said.

'Detective Constable Cradock, miss,' he said, 'West Ham CID. Is Mr Hunter at home?'

She gave him another appraising look, and he found himself wondering whether there was an age at which the term 'miss' was no longer appropriate, even though a glance at her ringless third finger suggested that it was technically correct.

'I'd like to speak to him,' he continued. 'Police business.'

He showed her his warrant card and National Registration identity card, and after examining them she took a step back and held the door open.

'Very well,' she said. 'Please come in and wait in the drawing room.'

The maid showed him into a spacious room and departed. There were comfortable chairs, but Cradock decided it would be better if he were standing when Mr Hunter arrived. He stood in the middle of the room, rocking on his heels. A dark-toned oil painting hanging in an alcove caught his eye. It depicted an imposing-looking Victorian gentleman with a walrus moustache, who might have been glaring into the room from this vantage point for the last seventy or eighty years. Cradock peered closer, but jumped back as the door behind him creaked. He whirled round to see a tall man with a less copious but equally imposing moustache the same shade of tired grey as his oiled hair. The man examined him rather as the maid had, but with slightly more pronounced disdain.

'Hunter,' he said. 'I gather you're the police. I've been expecting you. Sit down.'

Cradock sat immediately, and only then realised he had obeyed the order unthinkingly. He took out his pocketbook.

'Thank you, sir. I understand you want to report an incident.'

'Why aren't you in uniform?'

'Uniform, sir?'

'Yes – why aren't you in uniform?'

'Because I'm a detective, sir – plain clothes.'

'I don't mean that. I mean why is a young man like you not in the uniform of His Majesty's armed forces?'

'Because I'm a policeman, sir. I'm not allowed to join up, not since June – the government said we couldn't.'

Hunter looked down his nose at him, as if not sure whether to believe him.

'Anyway, sir,' said Cradock. 'About this incident.'

'Incident, eh?' said Hunter. 'So that's what you call it. It's an outrage, that's what it is.'

'Tell me what happened, please.'

Hunter took a seat opposite Cradock and leant forward to face him. Cradock now found his immediate field of vision filled by Hunter and the portrait on the wall behind him, and both seemed to be glaring at him in the same way.

'It's quite simple. As I said to my friend Mr Soper,' said Hunter, pausing to check that Cradock had registered the significance of the name, 'a chap knocked on my door the other day.'

'What day was that, sir?' Cradock interrupted.

'Two weeks ago last Friday.'

Cradock wrote down the date.

'Thank you, sir. Please continue.'

'Right. So as I was saying, a chap knocked on the door – a tradesman, judging by his clothes, and an Irishman by the sound of him. Said he'd noticed some tiles on my roof were broken. That's not surprising, I suppose, what with the amount of shrapnel we have dropping on us during the air raids, so when he offered to get up there and replace them I said yes. Gave him ten shillings for his trouble, too. All perfectly normal, but he said while he was on the roof he'd noticed I hadn't got an Anderson shelter in my garden, and asked whether I'd like one. I said yes, as a matter of fact I would.'

'You didn't get one when the council were installing them last year for free?'

Hunter gave him a bemused look.

'That was for the poor, my dear fellow. I may be retired, but do I look like a man with an income of less than two hundred and fifty pounds a year? No, the reason why I didn't get one was because I didn't want one. There was a lot of panicking going on at that time, and I'm not a man to panic. I saw no reason why the Germans should ever get close enough to bomb us if the powers that be had the gumption to organise our air defences efficiently, and it seemed to me that rushing about putting shelters in everyone's gardens showed a lamentable degree of defeatism.'

'But you've changed your mind now?'

As the words left his mouth, Cradock wondered whether Inspector Jago would have phrased the question more tactfully, but the deed was done. Hunter made a noise in his throat that suggested contempt.

'How was I to know the government would act like a bunch of blithering idiots? Of course I've changed my mind. Since these air raids started my wife has been obliged to share our neighbours' shelter, and I don't consider that appropriate for a woman of her standing, so I decided to get one of our own installed. People of your generation probably think I'm just an old fool, but I happen to believe it's a man's duty to protect his womenfolk. Give me a gun when the Nazis arrive and you'll see what men like me are made of.'

'Yes, sir – but tell me about the shelter, please.'

'Yes, of course. Well, it was simple. I applied to the council to buy one, but they said it was first come, first served and I was too late because they'd all gone. Typical of this council, isn't it?'

Cradock knew better than to answer a question like that, so he asked one of his own.

'But this man could get a shelter for you, presumably?'

'Yes. He said he was a builder and knew where he could get his hands on one, and could install it for me. He offered a special reduced price of fifteen pounds, including materials and labour.'

'And you said yes?'

'Naturally. If I'd bought one myself I'd still have had to dig the pit for it and assemble it. If my son were still alive he'd have done it for me, but I lost him in 1918. The only family my wife and I have now is her sister, who lives in Aberdeen, and my young niece. She lives locally, but I don't regard digging holes in the ground as women's work, so I wasn't going to ask her to help. I needed a tradesman who could provide the labour as well as the materials. I don't mind telling you I pride myself on my fitness, but I see no reason why I should go grubbing about in the soil when I can pay men who have nothing better to do with their time to do it for me.'

'Did he complete the job?'

'Of course not. That's the whole point, isn't it? He didn't even start it.'

'So what happened?'

'He asked me for a five-pound deposit, and I said I'd write him a cheque. He said he'd prefer cash – you know what these fellows are like – but I didn't have that much on me, so he said bring it to his office the next day. Always did his administrative work on Saturdays, he said. So I did exactly that.'

'Where were these premises, sir?'

'Somewhere off Manor Road. He said they were a bit difficult to find, so he met me on the corner of Gainsborough Road and took me down a back alley to the yard, unlocked the office, and I gave him the deposit.'

'Did you get a receipt?'

Hunter began to look a little exasperated.

'Well, no, I didn't – it was cash, wasn't it? But the point is, he said he'd come over in five days' time to install it. Ten days passed and no sign of the man, so I went down there on the next Saturday to find out why he hadn't come, but it was all locked up and there was no one there. That's the last I saw of the blighter – and of my money.'

'Thank you, sir. We'll see what we can find out.'

'I should jolly well think so. The man's obviously a criminal.'

Cradock looked up from his notebook.

'Did you get his name, sir?'

'Yes, he said it was Jones. Odd name for an Irishman, don't you think?'

'Yes, sir,' said Cradock. 'Very odd.'

CHAPTER TWENTY-THREE

Jago had told Cradock he'd be out this evening, but he hadn't mentioned he'd be returning to the centre of London. Not that it was a secret – there was simply no need to, because this was a private visit. He was meeting Dorothy. His original plan had been to take her out to dinner, but she'd said she already had a dinner engagement at the Savoy, something to do with her work. So it was a choice – either wait a few days for a whole evening to be free, or snatch the time for an early drink this evening. He'd opted for the latter, because it felt too long since he'd seen her.

They only had until seven o'clock – blackout time tonight was seven minutes past seven, so he'd chosen somewhere close enough for him to get her safely back to the hotel before it started. Part of him was therefore determined not to let their conversation venture into deep waters – all he wanted was a pleasant chat and some time with her, the Luftwaffe permitting. The trouble was, another part of him had something important that he felt compelled to ask her.

He met her in Savoy Court, at the hotel's front doors. She was wearing the blue coat he'd seen her in before, but in this setting its cut made her look more elegant than he could remember. He walked up to her and wanted to kiss her, but he knew he could not. Even a peck on the cheek would seem overfamiliar – it felt as though he would be crossing a line he had no permission to cross.

He took off his hat and stood before her, both hands gripping the fedora in front of him. He smiled awkwardly and greeted her, then realised he wasn't sure what to do next. Before he knew it, however, she had seized his arm and they were marching off towards the Strand.

'So where are we going, John?' she said. 'One of your favourite nightclubs?'

He knew she was teasing, and he found himself relaxing.

'The closest I've ever been to frequenting nightclubs was raiding illegal bottle parties, and that was a good few years back – they tend to happen more up in the West End. I don't think there's enough money down West Ham way to make it worth their while.'

'So not a nightclub, then. One of your good old English pubs?'

'Not quite. It's a place called the Blue Moon Bar, and it's just to the north of Covent Garden – you know, the big fruit-and-vegetable market.'

They crossed the Strand, and Jago took her through a succession of turnings, skirting the market. They came to Bow Street, where the Royal Opera House confronted the police station across the road, two grand edifices in white stone squaring up to each other like champions of the arts and the law in a clash for architectural supremacy. The Opera House had closed at the beginning of the war and reopened as a Mecca dance hall: now a queue of young people was stretching round the block, all waiting to spend their two shillings on a ticket for the seven o'clock evening session.

Along the side of the Opera House ran Floral Street, a cobbled side road which narrowed into a miniature canyon between steep walls of brick. When they were almost at the far end of the street they found a small frontage with the sign 'Blue Moon Bar' over the door.

'Your favourite bar?' said Dorothy.

'I don't know – I've never been to it. I chose it because it's only once in a blue moon that I go out for a drink anywhere west of the River Lea, and also because I've heard it has music.'

'So it could be a den of iniquity that you're taking me into?'

'Oh no, not at all,' he rushed, taking her remark as serious. 'There are places like that not far from here, but I took the precaution of asking a pal of mine at Bow Street police station, and he assured me this was a respectable establishment – and he said they don't jack up the prices like they do in the West End.'

'Isn't this the West End?'

'It depends who you ask – some people say the proper West End's only from Charing Cross Road to Hyde Park, but I'm not sure. But I do know West End prices when I see them, and they're not really designed for a policeman's pocket.'

Jago opened the door for her and they went in. It wasn't crowded inside, but still it had a warm and welcoming feel, and he found a secluded booth with a small table where they could sit in some privacy. From somewhere at the back of the bar came the sound of a piano, and a man singing 'The Very Thought of You', trying his best, it seemed, to mimic the voice and style of Al Bowlly. Jago liked the song, but he hoped Dorothy wouldn't think he'd chosen this bar in order to ply her ears with sentimental love ballads.

'What will you have?' he said.

'Do you think they'll have orange juice? That pub you took me to in West Ham didn't, but this place looks more classy. If they don't, make it a lemonade, same as before.'

He went to the bar and returned with a glass of lemonade, and a pint of mild and bitter for himself.

'Looks like oranges are a thing of the past,' he said. 'They must be pretty low on the priority list for shipping these days – in fact probably not on it at all.'

'This is just fine for me,' said Dorothy, taking the glass from him and placing it on a beer mat. 'So tell me, how's your new case going?'

'Just starting, really,' he said. 'You'll understand if I can't talk about it in detail, but we've found the body of a man who appears to have been murdered. He was a pacifist, and I think I've learnt more about pacifism in the last three days than in the previous three years. I've even been talking to a vicar today in the course of my enquiries – a nice man called Cardew.'

'Is that Henry Cardew?'

'Yes, actually it is. Why? Do you know him?'

'Only of him. If it's the man I'm thinking of, he's becoming quite famous, you know.'

'Why's that?'

'It's what he's doing. One of my political contacts in London told me he was virtually running the emergency relief effort down by the docks, right there in your borough of West Ham.'

'They say it's a small world.'

'Yes, but seriously – could you introduce me to him? I'd love to meet him. Maybe we could get together one evening, if the bombing allows. Could you ask him, please?'

'Yes, of course. I'll see what I can do. I hadn't realised clergymen in West Ham were of such interest to the world's press.'

'You'll see when we talk to him. From what I've heard, he's quite a guy.'

Dorothy took a sip of her lemonade and looked Jago in the eye. He had a nervous feeling that the conversation was about to become personal.

'I was wondering,' she said, 'have you thought any

further about what we were talking about – you know, about breaking free of the tramlines?'

Jago's sense of foreboding had been justified. He cleared his throat and tried to think of the best way to answer this question.

'I have,' he said. 'I know for you that's meant having adventures, reporting from wars, that kind of thing, but in a way I feel as though I had enough adventure, if you can call it that, in the war. Have you heard of J. B. Priestley?'

'Of course I have. The writer. He broadcasts talks to America on the radio.'

'Yes, well, he broadcasts here too, on the BBC, after the nine o'clock news on Sunday evenings. I heard him a few weeks ago – he said he'd lived dangerously through long spells in the last war, and once it was over he decided to be a pipe-and-slippers man from then on. I could really understand that, and I wondered whether that's what I am at heart – a pipe-and-slippers man.'

'Well, you don't smoke, and with the hours you work I don't suppose you get much time to put your slippers on. You know you'll never be a pipe-and-slippers man, not as long as people are committing crimes against other people and you can stop them.'

'But that's it – most of the time I don't stop them. I'm always coming along afterwards to clear up the mess and find out who did it.'

'But isn't that why you became a policeman? You told me once that it was because you wanted to keep everything in order.'

'Yes, that's right.'

'Well then, in that case you're doing something bold and brave and good – you're on the side of the angels, John.'

He didn't respond. Her words had brought storming back into his mind the thing he had wanted to ask her.

'On the side of the angels,' he said. 'That's reminded me of something I've been meaning to ask you.'

'Fire away.'

'You remember that time when you treated me to a meal at the Savoy, and I was worried because I didn't have a dinner suit to wear?'

'I do – that was a wonderful evening.'

'Well, it was something you said that night, when we were talking about your sister. You said you could vouch for the fact that Eleanor was no angel. What did you mean by that?'

'Did I say that? I guess it's true. Actually it was a rather painful story, and I've always kept it to myself, but I don't mind telling you. Would you like to hear the whole sorry tale?'

'Yes, I would, rather.'

'OK then, here it is. You remember me saying I'd met up with Eleanor in Spain, during the civil war, when I was there reporting and she came out to nurse?'

'Yes, you said she went there in 1937 but you'd only seen her once.'

'That's right – we managed to get together just before the paper sent me to Austria to cover the political situation there before the Germans finally marched in. I think I told you that just after I left she wrote me to say she'd met someone.'

'That's right – he was an American writer, you said.'

'Yes. Well, I have to confess that I didn't tell you the whole story. I was the one who inadvertently introduced them. He was a very talented man, and I'd seen him a few times. He'd take me out to dinner, you know, and we'd talk about books and things. There was nothing official between us, as you might say, but I'd gotten very fond of him and thought it might lead to something more. That time when Eleanor came to see me, I suggested he invite her to join us at dinner.'

'And things didn't go as you'd intended?'

'You guessed it. The shocking thing was the way Eleanor acted during the meal. She seemed smitten, and I soon realised she was flirting with him. I couldn't believe it – this wasn't the Eleanor I thought I knew at all. I'd always thought my sister wasn't like that. She was a nurse, someone who'd sacrificed her life for other people. She was like some sort of holy person in my mind. But now suddenly I could see that when the chips were down she was just like any other woman.'

'Feet of clay?'

'Yes. Anyway, to cut a long story short, pretty soon he was making eyes at her too. They fell in love, and she married him.'

'How did you feel when that happened?'

'It was a very difficult time for me. I felt kind of bereft, because I'd been beginning to feel something for the man, but then she swooped in and snatched him away for herself. But at the same time I wanted Eleanor to be happy, because I loved her. I didn't want it to come between us.'

'And did it?'

'No. I didn't see her for months after that, but then she got the chance to come see me, and we talked about it. I was honest with her about how I'd felt, and she clearly felt bad about what had happened – although why should she, if they'd fallen in love? She asked me to forgive her, and I did – what she'd done had hurt me, but I loved her and wanted our relationship to be restored, so how could I not forgive her?'

'And then?'

'Then the way I felt seemed to change – I accepted she was the right one for him, not me, and after that I was able to be with her as I always had been. I could accept him as a friend and nothing more than that.'

Jago sat in silence, staring down at the table as he digested what she'd said. This wasn't the Eleanor whose memory he'd cherished for so many years. But, he realised with a pain in his heart, this was Eleanor as a real woman.

'Are you OK?' said Dorothy.

'Yes, yes, I'm fine. I'm sorry, it just wasn't quite the kind of story I was expecting. But that's my fault, not yours. I can understand how you felt, and I'm beginning to understand something about myself. I think I've been keeping Eleanor on a kind of pedestal – since that time

I first saw her in the hospital, she's been like an ideal in my mind, a perfect woman who wouldn't do that kind of thing. But that's ridiculous, isn't it? She was just flesh and blood like any other person.'

'She certainly was, and still is, but that doesn't stop me loving her.'

'Of course, and why should anyone expect her to be more than flesh and blood? As I said, it's my fault. All these years I've thought I've been keeping a precious memory alive, but all I've done really is perpetuate an illusion. I think that's one of the things I need to change in myself.'

'I see. That sounds like a healthy decision to me.'

'You won't tell her, will you?'

'Not if you don't want me to, no.'

'It's just that it seems a bit stupid now.'

'It wasn't stupid, John. You were a wounded soldier and she helped save your life, cared for you every day. It's nothing new for a patient to fall in love with his nurse. And that's what you did, wasn't it?'

'Yes, I suppose I did. Or did I just fall in love with an illusion?'

'It sounds to me like it may have been a little of both.'

'Perhaps you're right. Anyway, it's all in the past now, and I want to leave it there.'

'Then that's where it'll stay.'

'Thank you.'

'You're welcome. Now it's my turn to ask you a question.'

Jago was a little apprehensive at the thought of what subject she might raise, but he couldn't let it show.

'Of course – what do you want to know?'

'How you see the future. What is it you all think you're fighting for? Your Mr Churchill talks about the British Empire lasting for a thousand years, so he's hoping everything will go back the way it was before. Is that what you want too?'

'To be honest, I don't know what I want. But I certainly don't want to go back to the way it was before. Whatever we do in the future, it's got to be something better than the past.'

'You're going to have your work cut out just getting your country back on its feet when the war's over, aren't you?'

'Yes, if there's much more of this bombing there won't be a lot of country left.'

'Mind you, I've heard some people are already saying the Germans may have done you a favour. They say bombing's done what the local councils never managed to do – like sweeping away so many of the old slum houses near the docks. They think now there'll be a chance to create decent homes for people to live in.'

'Yes, and a chance for some people I know to make a mint.'

'Who's that?'

'I can't tell you his name, but it's another man I've met in connection with this enquiry. He's one of the men who build things, and if the government put up as many new homes after this war as it did after the last, people like him could become very rich. He'd get two bites of the cherry.'

'What do you mean?'

'I mean there seems to be a suggestion that he's making money out of the war already. Except—'

'Except what?'

'I'm sorry, I was just thinking out loud. There's something that doesn't add up.'

'I won't ask you what it is.'

'Of course – thank you.'

Jago glanced at his watch.

'I'd like to get you back to the Savoy before blackout time, just so I know you're safe. If you decide to come back and dance the night away at the Opera House that's your choice, but I'll feel I've done my duty. The time's gone too fast. But look, I'm going to be back up this way in the morning – in London, I mean. Are you free tomorrow lunchtime?'

'I could be.'

'There's a place I need to take a look at – it's to do with my investigation, but nothing confidential – and I thought if you had an hour free you might like to come along with me. It's what you might call a British institution.'

'Which institution would that be?'

'You'll have to wait and see – but it's one of the things we reckon we're fighting for in this war, or some of us at any rate. It could be interesting for you.'

'Anything that can generate ten inches of copy is of interest to me. So yes, I'd like to.'

'Where will you be tomorrow morning?'

'I have to visit the Ministry of Information in Malet Street at ten o'clock, and then I'm seeing a man at Canada House to find out about pilot training for the RAF. I should be finished there by about eleven-thirty.'

'Good. In that case, meet me at twelve o'clock by Nelson's Column in Trafalgar Square.'

CHAPTER TWENTY-FOUR

Jago strode briskly into the CID office and hung his coat, hat, and gas mask on the coat stand. Cradock, who was standing on the other side of the room and staring out of the window, spun round to face him, instinctively straightening his tie as if interrupted by an unexpected inspection.

'Morning, guv'nor,' he said.

'Morning, Peter,' Jago replied in a cheery tone. 'Busy day ahead of us. I've got to pop up to Scotland Yard this morning, but I'll be back early afternoon. But before that, do tell me – how did it go?'

'With Mr Hunter, you mean?' said Cradock, reaching for the desk to pick up his notebook.

'No, not that. First I want to know how your big night out went, of course – the cinema.'

'Oh, that. Well, I didn't think much of the film. It was called *Turnabout*, some American thing, and it was supposed to be a comedy, but I didn't think it was funny at all. There was a husband and wife. He worked for an advertising agency and she hung around at home all day in their luxury apartment doing nothing, then some peculiar old oriental statue they just happened to have in the bedroom magically switched their bodies, so she became him and went to work, and he became her and stayed at home. Something about the two of them always arguing about wanting to be in each other's shoes, so the statue granted their wish. Ridiculous. I preferred the B film – that was *The Saint Takes Over*. More my cup of tea, that – at least it was a bit more like real life.'

'Real life? The Saint?'

'I mean it had crooks, cops, fast cars and guns.'

'I see. Sounds like a busman's holiday for you.'

'A what, sir?'

'Never mind. But listen – I wasn't asking about the films. I meant how was your company, the young lady you were escorting?'

'Oh, that.'

'She has a name, Peter.'

'I know. You mean Emily? Well, she was laughing all the way through – beats me what she found so entertaining about it. Do you think women have a completely different sense of humour to us?'

'I couldn't say. But apart from her taste in films, what about the girl herself? What did you think of her?'

'Well, er – she was very nice, actually.'

'Did you hold hands?'

Cradock looked shocked.

'Certainly not – I'd never met the girl before. But I enjoyed being out with her.'

'Rita was right, then. She seemed very confident that you two would hit it off.'

'Laid a trap for me, more like. How did she talk me into it?'

'Women can be very persuasive, Peter. And Rita is a woman among women. Would you like me to tell her off?'

'No, I don't think so.'

'In that case, the question is did you ask Emily whether she'd like to go again?'

'No. I wasn't sure whether I should.'

'Do you think she was disappointed?'

'I don't know. I mean I couldn't tell. How can you tell what a girl's thinking?'

'If I knew that, Peter, I'd be a rich man.'

Cradock's face registered disappointment at this answer, and a hint of despondency entered his voice.

'Well, all I can say is I've no idea whether she liked me or not, so I didn't like to ask her out again. Do you think I should have?'

'I'm not the best person to advise you on such things, Peter. You must use your own judgement – but if you like her, why not see her again?'

'I don't know. It's not as simple as that. I don't want to get—'

'Out of your depth?'

'Yes, I suppose that's it. I mean, it was Rita's idea, not mine, wasn't it?'

'But you liked her?'

'Yes, but all the same – I'm not sure. This sort of thing's too complicated for me. I'll have to think about it.'

'You do that,' said Jago.

He gave Cradock what he hoped was the sympathetic, reflective nod of an older and wiser man, but was not sure how convincing it looked.

'So,' he continued, 'tell me about the other thing – did you find Mr Hunter at home?'

'Yes, sir.'

'And how did it go? Less exciting than the Saint, I imagine.'

'Yes, sir, but I had an interesting time. I could see why he gets on well with Mr Soper, for example – he mentioned they were friends.'

'That doesn't surprise me. What did you make of him?'

'A bit stuffy, really. One of those "commanding officer" types, if you know what I mean. A retired something or other, but he didn't say what. Probably some kind of bigwig, I shouldn't wonder. He was quite steamed up about being done out of his five pounds.'

'What did he say?'

'He said something like he hadn't put a shelter in last year because he thought it was defeatist, and something about the government were all blithering idiots, but now the raids were on his wife had to share the neighbours' shelter, and that wasn't appropriate for a woman of her standing, and so he'd decided to get an Anderson shelter put in.'

'Sounds reasonable.'

'Yes, sir. Of course, he's too well-off to have one put in free by the council, but he said a man turned up one day and pointed out some tiles on his roof that were broken – something to do with the bombing – so Mr Hunter paid him to fix them. Then the man asked him if he wanted an Anderson shelter – said he was a builder and knew where he could get his hands on one and could install it for him. He offered a special reduced price of fifteen pounds, all in.'

'There's one born every minute.'

'Sir?'

'Never mind – carry on. I think I can see where this story's going.'

'Well, Mr Hunter said he'd like it done, and the builder—'

'Whose name was?'

'Jones, apparently. He asked for a five-pound deposit.'

'I see – Mr Jones. He shouldn't be hard to trace. And I suppose Mr Hunter handed over five crisp pound notes to this chap?'

'No, that was the clever bit. He asked Mr Hunter to bring it to his yard, so Mr Hunter went down there and gave him the five pounds. Jones said he'd come over in five days' time to install it.'

'But he didn't turn up?'

'That's right. When ten days had gone and he still hadn't shown up, Mr Hunter went down there to find out why not, but it was all locked up and there was no one there.'

'What a surprise. So Mr Jones had vanished from the face of the earth.'

'Looks like it, sir.'

'Right, we'll have to see what we can find out, then.' Jago glanced at his watch. 'But first, there's something that Gloria Harris said, and something that it seems Paul Ramsey didn't say, that's been bothering me. Let's go and see if she's in.'

They found Gloria at her digs in Kildare Road. She appeared to be working, and pushed away some books on the table when Mrs Grove showed them into the room.

'Good morning, Miss Harris,' said Jago. 'I'm sorry to disturb you again so soon, but something's cropped up that I'd like to ask you about.'

'That's fine, Inspector. My life here's rather quiet at the moment, as you can imagine, apart from the air raids.'

'Thank you. I'll come to my question in a moment, but first there's something else I'd like to know, and I'd like you to think carefully about it, please.'

'Yes, by all means. What is it?'

'It's quite simple, really. Can you tell me when was the last time you saw Paul?'

'Yes – it was weeks ago. I haven't seen him since the beginning of term.'

'But you wrote to each other?'

'Yes, we did.'

'So when was the last time you heard from him?'

'It was the Friday before last. That was the last letter I had from him. He said it was dull here without me, especially at the weekends, and he could see the weeks stretching ahead of him with nothing to do but work. That's what gave me the idea of coming down for a surprise visit.'

'To celebrate?'

'Yes, I've already told you – it was to celebrate his promotion.'

'And you've had no other contact with him since that letter?'

'No. Why? What's the problem?'

'Forgive me, Miss Harris, but the problem is that I find that difficult to believe.'

'What?'

'You're telling me you came to celebrate his promotion, so he must have mentioned it in his letter that you received the Friday before last – that's twelve days ago, if I'm not mistaken – but I happen to know that he didn't hear about that promotion himself until last Thursday, and that's only six days ago. So how could you have known about it if the last time you heard from him was a week before that? I'd like the truth now, if you don't mind.'

Gloria sat in silence, as if wrestling in her mind over what to say. Jago could see a tear brimming in each of her eyes. Eventually she sat up straight, wiped a finger across her eyes and looked directly at him.

'Very well. I did hear from Paul. He telephoned me – or rather, he managed to get through to the school and left a message asking me to call him. So I did, on Thursday evening. That's when he told me about the promotion, but the thing is, I had something more important than that to tell him.'

'And what was that?'

She hesitated.

'I told him I wanted to end our relationship.'

'Can you tell me why?'

'Oh, I don't know – I suppose you could say I no longer thought we were compatible, and I wasn't sure I wanted to spend the rest of my life with him. For one thing, he seemed to have changed since I moved to Bradwell – we spoke on the phone soon after term started down here, and it was as if he'd lost interest in me. His mind seemed to be elsewhere.'

'I see. That brings me to the other question I wanted to ask you. The headmaster told me Paul had seemed preoccupied, worried of late. Is that what you mean?'

'Maybe – I can't tell. All I know is he seemed distracted.'

'But you were his fiancée. Didn't he tell you about it?'

'No – I asked him if anything was the matter, but he wouldn't tell me. I felt he was hiding something from me.'

'Do you have any idea what that might have been?'

'No. I even wondered whether he'd found another woman – I was away in the country, and I thought perhaps it was a case of "out of sight, out of mind". His mind wasn't on me in the way it had been before I moved away, so I thought maybe it was on someone else.'

'Did you have any evidence to support that?'

'No, none at all. It was just what you might call a woman's intuition. There was probably nothing in it, but whether or not there was, the unfortunate effect was that once I sensed his feelings for me were cooling, I found mine for him cooled too.'

'How did he react when you told him you wanted to end the relationship?'

'He didn't take it well. He said he didn't want me to leave him – but not in a nice way. I felt he was trying to control me, even to threaten me. I couldn't see us resolving anything on the phone, so I ended the call as quickly as I could, then decided to come down here and have it out with him once and for all, face-to-face. So that's what I did.'

'You saw him?'

'Yes, I did.'

'But you told me you didn't. You said you were too ill to see him.'

She looked down into her lap and spoke quietly.

'I know – that wasn't entirely true.'

'And why would that be?'

'I'm not sure I can explain – it was a kind of panic,

I suppose. You'd just told me he'd been murdered, and I was shocked. My relationship with Paul had become rather – how can I put it? – complicated, and I didn't feel I could cope with going over it all with you. So I'm afraid on the spur of the moment I decided it would be easier all round if I hadn't seen him, and that's what I said.'

'So when did you see him?'

'I saw him briefly on Saturday afternoon. What I said about being ill wasn't completely untrue – I was feeling a bit under the weather when I arrived here, but I managed to see him. It was only later I felt really ill.'

'And what happened when you met?'

'We, er, discussed our future.'

'That sounds very calm and businesslike. It was only two days since you'd told him you wanted to end your relationship. Was it really nothing more than a discussion?'

'Well, if you must know, it was a row – he was furious. He still wanted me, but the trouble was, it was all or nothing for Paul – he wanted me on his terms, and on his terms only. And I was no longer willing to accept that. I'd been thinking a lot about my future, and I'd decided I wanted to have a career, not just be someone's little wife at home.'

'So it was a choice between marrying him or having your career – and he wasn't prepared to compromise?'

'He wasn't, but even if he had been, I'd still have run up against the marriage bar. I mean, can you believe it, Inspector? Women like me have had the vote for twelve years now, but the fact remains that any woman teacher who gets married loses her job. If I decided to get married, my employers would force me to resign, to abandon my profession. How can that be right? This is the twentieth century, for goodness' sake. Why should a woman have to choose between marriage and a job when men don't have to? They say it's because married women don't need to work – but what about married women who want to work? Whatever my feelings for Paul, I'd decided I couldn't sacrifice everything I'd hoped and worked for in order to get married. It's a barbaric system, but it's the way things are. So I told him I couldn't marry him.'

'How did he take it?'

'It's difficult to say – he became very emotional, but if you were to ask me what the real cause was, I couldn't tell you. Was he devastated by my rejecting him, or was he infuriated? Or was it both? I don't know. All I know is that he suddenly flew into a kind of rage – I'd never seen him like that before.'

'And the bruise?'

Gloria gave a sigh of resignation.

'All right, yes. That was him. He lashed out at me – but he was almost crying at the same time. He said if he couldn't have me, no one could. I was astonished and couldn't really make sense of it. He seemed so frustrated. It was like what people call a blind fury – there was no reasoning with him. To be honest, I don't think he could help himself. But whatever the reason for it, in that moment I saw a different Paul, and I didn't like what I saw.'

'And what did you do?'

'At first I just stood there – I was shocked. Have you ever known what it's like to love someone and then discover it's just an illusion?'

Her words struck a chord in Jago – it was as though she had heard his own words to Dorothy about Eleanor the previous evening. He waited for her to continue.

'But that only lasted a moment,' Gloria continued. 'I've told you about my cousin Harold, Inspector. I've had some bad experiences with him, and now if I see a hint of violence in a man I run away. I just told Paul our engagement was over and I was going straight back to Bradwell. It wasn't just bombs I wanted to be safe from.'

'And then?'

'I stormed out, and that was that.' She paused, and stared at Jago. 'If he couldn't have me, nobody could – that's what he said. You don't think—'

'Think what?'

'You said something on Monday – you said Paul had a gun. You don't think he would have tried to harm me?'

'I really couldn't say, Miss Harris. It doesn't necessarily follow.'

She shuddered. 'It doesn't bear thinking about,' she said.

'And that was the last time you saw him?'

'Yes. I went back to my room. By that point I was beginning to feel ill again, so I took to my bed and slept for as long as the bombers and the anti-aircraft guns would let me. The next thing I knew was you turning up on Monday to tell me he was dead.'

'One last question. Can anyone confirm your whereabouts on Saturday evening and through the night?'

'Of course not. I told you, Mrs Grove was away, and the house was empty apart from me. I'm a single woman, Inspector, and I spend my nights alone.'

'Yes, of course. There's just one more thing before I go . . . What can you tell me about Mr Ramsey's brother, Joe?'

'Nothing. I hardly know him.'

'Isn't that unusual? Not to know the brother of the man you're engaged to marry?'

'It may be unusual, but it's the truth. Why do you want to know about him?'

'It's just that I've noticed you've never mentioned Joe's name in our conversations.'

'There's nothing odd about that – I simply had no occasion to, and you never asked. I've only met the man once.'

'I mentioned earlier that people have said Mr Ramsey – Paul, that is – was preoccupied, concerned about something. The possibility has been raised elsewhere that this might have been to do with something his brother was involved in.'

'What do you mean by "involved in"?'

'I mean to do with his business.'

'Well—'

'Yes?'

'There is something that Paul said, but I didn't think it was relevant to your enquiries.'

'What did he say?'

'He just said something like he'd seen Joe, and Joe had had a bit too much to drink and was boasting about how much money he was going to make out of some deal. Apparently he always liked to remind Paul that he was making more money than him – I think Paul felt Joe was jealous.'

'When did he tell you this?'

'It was in that other letter, a week ago last Friday, the one I mentioned before.'

'Did he say what kind of deal it was?'

'According to Paul, Joe had said it was some nice little scheme he'd cooked up with the council – I think those were the words Paul used. Joe said the war had put a stop to house-building and had cost him a lot, so it was only right that he should make a bit of money out of the war if he could, or something like that.'

'And Paul was concerned about this?'

'Yes, he was – as I think I've told you before, he was a man of principle. He didn't like to think of anyone profiting from other people's suffering.'

'And was Paul going to do anything about it?'

'Yes, he said he was going to see his local councillor and find out whether he – the councillor, that is – could do anything to put a stop to it.'

'Do you happen to know which councillor it was?'

'Yes. It was . . . oh, what's his name? He's always in the local paper. Yes, that's it – Councillor Hampson. Do you know him?'

CHAPTER TWENTY-FIVE

Jago had finished his business at Scotland Yard and was now striding up Whitehall towards Trafalgar Square. The sun was bright and the air was quiet, with little more than the occasional growl of a double-decker bus to disturb the peace. The grand buildings that lined the street still lent a sense of calm permanence, and yet all around were the visible signs of how much had changed in the past year. Not just the white bands painted on the kerbs and traffic light columns to prevent accidents in the blackout – they could be seen everywhere – but most strikingly the odd structure that loomed directly in front of him. Thirty feet high and made from sheets of rust-stained corrugated iron, it was a conspicuously ugly contrast to the classical frontage of the National Gallery in the background. Inside this temporary eyesore, according to the newspapers, was the sandbagged equestrian statue of King Charles I, protected against enemy action in this way since the outbreak of war.

On reaching the square itself, Jago could see the disfiguring effect of other recent intrusions. First on the pedestal of Nelson's column, where the bronze relief panels depicting scenes from the admiral's battles were now obscured by jaunty placards urging the public to invest in national savings certificates, and then, in the distance, the complex of brick air-raid shelters which had been built along the northern wall the previous year.

Dorothy was waiting for him at the foot of the column. He increased his pace and waved to her.

'Sorry to keep you,' he said as he arrived. 'I've been in a meeting just round the corner at Scotland Yard – I had to see a man in the fingerprint department, and once those chaps start talking about fingerprints there's no stopping them.'

'Don't worry,' she replied. 'I only got here myself a couple of minutes ago. I've been trying to count the pigeons, but it's impossible. They don't seem to have been frightened away by the war – there must be thousands of them. I took a stroll round the square too, when I came out of Canada House, and I have a little question for you.'

'Yes? What is it?'

'I noticed you've got a statue in each corner of the square but nothing in that corner over there – just a base with nothing on it. Why's that?'

'Ah, yes, that's what people call the vacant plinth. It was supposed to be for a statue of King William IV, but there wasn't enough money to make one, so it's been empty for about a hundred years.'

'You're saying a country like this can't raise the cash to put up a statue to the king? Not in a hundred years? That's crazy.'

'Yes, and I've no idea why. But if you look towards the other end of the National Gallery, you'll see we do have a statue of your George Washington – who used to be our George Washington, of course.'

Dorothy peered across to the spot he was indicating.

'Not very big, is it?' she said. 'Did it have to be smaller than your guys?'

'No idea. It was a gift from your country – from the state of Virginia.'

'I see. So you put that one up because you didn't have to pay for it, right?'

'I suppose so. And apparently it even came with its own earth – there's a story that Washington vowed he'd never set foot in London again, so when your compatriots made a gift of the statue they sent some soil from Virginia for him to stand on.'

'Is that true?'

'I don't know, but I like the story. And now I have a little question for you. You said you'd like to meet Mr Cardew, so I called him this morning and he's invited us to visit him this evening. Would that be convenient for you?'

'That would be wonderful. I can take the train and meet you around five-thirty – is that OK?'

'Perfect. Now, we've got a bus to catch – we need a number 13.'

They crossed the square to a bus stop, where there was already a queue of people waiting – the new system of standing in line for a bus instead of the pre-war free-for-all seemed to have caught on quickly with London's population. The bus soon lumbered into view and stopped.

'Good,' said Jago. 'This one hasn't got the netting yet.'

'What?'

'London Transport's started sticking some kind of mesh fabric to the inside of the bus windows – it's to make them less dangerous in a bomb blast, but it means you can't see out. It looks like they haven't done this one yet, so we'll be able to see the sights.'

When their turn came to board, they stepped onto the platform at the rear of the bus.

'Let's go upstairs,' said Jago. 'We'll get a better view.'

He led Dorothy up the narrow, twisting staircase and along the gangway to the front of the bus, where there was a pair of empty seats.

'Here we are,' he said. 'Best seats in the house.'

The bus pulled away, and soon they heard the conductor's repeated 'Any more fares, please?' as he approached. Jago pulled a handful of change from his trouser pocket and sifted through it until he found a threepenny bit and a penny, then handed them to the conductor in exchange for two tickets. The bus trundled along the Strand, passing Dorothy's hotel, the Savoy, on the right and then the Law Courts on the left – 'Mostly built by Germans,' said Jago, 'after the British masons went on strike' – then continued the length of Fleet Street and Ludgate Hill to St Paul's Cathedral.

After twenty minutes of stopping and starting, the bus arrived in Cannon Street and they got off.

'We'll go this way,' said Jago, 'so you can see the Monument.'

'Which monument would that be?' said Dorothy. 'You seem to have quite a few here.'

'The Monument – that's what it's called. It's where the Great Fire of London started, in Pudding Lane. We used to be able to climb up to the top, but it's closed now because of the war.'

They passed the Monument without stopping, and a few minutes later turned into a street that ran alongside the Tower of London.

'Here we are,' said Jago.

Dorothy took in the view of the stone castle. It had a sombre appearance, darkened by a century of smoke and soot from London's chimneys.

'You're taking me to jail for spying?'

'No, we're not going in there. We're staying outside – you'll see in a moment.'

They arrived at a large cobblestoned area packed with people, many of them in the uniforms of the armed forces. Beyond them a man could be seen standing slightly higher, his head framed by the towers and upper walkway of Tower Bridge.

'So what's going on here?' said Dorothy.

'This is Tower Hill. You've heard of Speakers' Corner?'

'Sure. By Hyde Park?'

'Yes. Well, Tower Hill's like that – one of the places in London where people can stand up on a soapbox in public and say anything they like.'

'Surely not absolutely anything they like? I mean, the newspapers are censored, and so is the BBC, because of the war, so there must be some limits to what these fellows can say. And look over there – it looks like there are guys in uniform telling some soldiers to make themselves scarce.'

'They're military police, and they're probably moving those men along because soldiers aren't allowed to speak on a platform or take an active part in a meeting like this.'

'So they can't say anything they like if they've got a uniform on? But why are they being sent on their way? Does listening mean they're taking an active part?'

'I wouldn't have said so, but the military police are nothing to do with me. Maybe they're being overzealous. Or maybe they're worried the soldiers will be annoyed by some of the anti-war speakers and start trouble.'

'So people are allowed to speak against the war?'

'Up to a point, yes, but there are some restrictions. We're living under emergency regulations now, and they say expressing opinions is fine, but anything that's intended to impede the war effort isn't. No one's allowed to try and influence public opinion in a way that would prejudice the defence of the realm, and they definitely can't incite people not to do their military service – if they do that they could be looking at fourteen years' penal servitude.'

'Which means, I suppose, that the guy over there is managing to hold a crowd and speak his mind without breaking any of those rules. Who is he?'

'Let's get closer so you can see.'

They edged their way through the listening crowd until Dorothy could clearly see the tall, imposing figure of the speaker.

'Beautiful voice,' she said. 'Handsome, too, whoever he is.'

'He's the man they call Dr Soapbox,' said Jago. 'Donald Soper – he's a Methodist minister.'

'Your boss is called Soper, isn't he? Any relation?'

Jago laughed. 'I don't think so. They've got different kinds of vision. This man always talks as though he's got his eyes fixed on the distant future – the New Jerusalem builded here in England's green and pleasant land, and that kind of thing. Our DDI Soper at the station usually seems to see not much further than the end of his nose. So no relation as far as I know.'

'And what do you think of this Dr Donald Soper?'

'He's a good man. The only thing I've got against him is that he supports the Arsenal.'

He noticed that Dorothy was giving him a blank look, but decided it wasn't worth explaining London football club rivalries to her.

'Seriously, though,' he continued, 'I'm sure he could

sit in his church all day writing cosy sermons if he wanted to, but actually since the bombing started he's been feeding people in the basement of his mission up near Holborn underground station. And he's out here every Wednesday lunchtime, speaking his mind and taking whatever questions or insults the crowd choose to throw at him. He talks about his faith, but he makes it relevant to real things that are happening, like the war, and I like that.'

'From what I can hear, it sounds like he's against it.'

'Oh, yes – he's a well-known pacifist. But that's why I wanted to come here today. The man whose murder I'm investigating seems to have been a pacifist, and I wanted to find out a bit more about what makes them tick.'

'I see. I wondered how a detective inspector in the Metropolitan Police was allowed to take a girl out in London in the middle of a working day, but now I can see it was just a matter of duty.'

'No,' said Jago, alarmed. 'I didn't mean—'

Dorothy laughed.

'That's OK. I'm not offended. But tell me, was it perhaps duty mixed in with just a little pleasure?'

'Yes, in fact significantly more pleasure than duty, if I'm honest. But I thought it might be interesting for you too – I imagine what you're hearing right now is a bit different from what you get at the Ministry of Information.'

'Yes, and delivered with a lot more style.'

241

'I'm not sure whether the government's keen for him to have a wider audience, though – he's been on the BBC in the past, but J. B. Priestley on a Sunday evening probably puts the wind up them quite enough already. I doubt whether we'll be hearing regular broadcasts by Dr Soper.'

'Let's listen to him for a while, then.'

They stopped talking. The speaker was in the middle of a story about being at school during the Great War, then going to Cambridge after it and hearing terrible stories from men who'd served in the war and were scarred for life, not just physically but mentally. Jago liked the way he dealt with the inevitable heckler who shouted out something about the speaker's own mental state, and the crowd laughed at Soper's wit. The minister clearly didn't want his own speech to become a comedy turn, however, and carried on in a serious vein, saying that faced with what he called the obscenity of violence he could see no alternative to being a pacifist. When he started explaining his conviction that war must be resisted, he got a mixed reaction from the crowd, some accusing him of being unrealistic, others of being a communist, but others giving him applause and cheers.

'You can see why people come to listen,' said Jago. 'Whether they love what the speaker's saying or hate it, it's jolly good entertainment.'

'And it's important too,' said Dorothy. 'You can't have democracy without free speech.'

He was about to agree but was distracted. Across the open space he'd glimpsed a hatless young man in a blue overcoat hurrying towards a group of soldiers in uniform with a package wrapped in brown paper under his arm. Jago couldn't see his face, but recognised the colourful scarf that flowed over his shoulder. At that moment the young man looked round. He locked his eyes on Jago and pushed his way through the crowd towards him.

'So I was right, Inspector,' he said as he drew close, breathless but almost shouting, as if he wanted the bystanders to know this was a policeman. 'Here to keep an eye on me, are you? We know you're watching us – I've just seen one of your men over there writing down every word Dr Soper says.'

'Not one of my men,' said Jago.

'Everyone knows he's a policeman – he's here every week with his notebook. I suppose now that you've seen me here that'll be going into my file too, won't it?'

'I've told you before, Mr Morton, I'm not snooping on you.'

'I don't believe you – and let me tell you, I don't care what you do.'

Without waiting for a reply from Jago, Morton launched himself back into the crowd and was soon out of sight.

'You know that guy?' said Dorothy.

'I've met him in connection with my enquiries. He's a pacifist.'

'A pretty steamed-up kind of pacifist. Is that what people call righteous anger?'

'Anger, yes, but whether it's righteous I wouldn't like to say.'

'Well, he may be right or he may be wrong, but he should be allowed to say what he thinks – I'm a strong believer in free speech and a free press. But I expect you know that by now.'

'Yes, and you're right. That's why I think having a place like this where people can speak their minds is very important. It's a very long tradition here. Do you have anything like this in America?'

'We do where I come from.'

'In Boston, you mean?'

'Yes. Ever since your evangelist George Whitefield came over in the seventeen hundreds and preached there, Boston Common has been the place to do just this kind of thing. People can just pitch up and talk about anything.'

'No restrictions?'

'Well, sometime back in the last century the city passed a law saying you could only speak on the Common if you had a permit from the mayor, and surprisingly the US Supreme Court backed them, so technically even today you can't make a speech like this in a public place anywhere in the USA without a permit.'

'So what do people do?'

'Well, I don't know what they do in other parts of the States, but I can tell you on Boston Common they

244

just ignore it. We still have people saying whatever they like there.'

'I'm glad to hear that. Now, how about a quick bite of lunch?'

They wound their way back through the crowd, with the speaker still in full flow, and walked down towards the Thames. Jago found a stall that had some cheap Ticky Snacks pies warming on top of the tea urn and bought two. The stallholder put them upside down onto a saucer, cut them open and poured spicy HP sauce into them, and handed them to Jago and Dorothy, followed by two cups of tea.

They found a wooden bench to sit on, overlooking the river. There was a breeze blowing off the water, but it wasn't yet laced with the icy cold of winter.

'Nice pie,' said Dorothy, taking her first mouthful. 'But not the finest I've ever tasted. Another of your English treats for me?'

'Naturally – part of the continuing process of familiarisation with British culture.'

'Maybe I'll write a piece about it for the paper, if your censors will let it pass. They can be a bit sensitive about how we report the food situation in Britain. I don't know why they worry, though. Could be they just like to flatter us journalists with the idea that people will actually read what we write, which I doubt.'

'I know what you mean – today's news, tomorrow's chip paper.'

'I'm sorry?'

'I mean, you think you've got a sensational story one day, but the next day the public's forgotten it.'

'What's chip paper?'

'Ah, yes. You've heard of fish and chips?'

'Of course, the backbone of the British diet – served with "a nice cup of tea", I expect. Right?'

'Exactly – when we buy it from the fried fish shop to take it home or eat it in the street, they wrap it up to keep it warm, and the cheapest way they can do that is to wrap it in old newspaper.'

'I get it – so you eat your fish and chips and then throw my prize article in the gutter.'

'You've got the picture. Have you tried fish and chips yet?'

'Not outside a restaurant.'

'You have to experience eating it on the street – it never tastes as good if it's not wrapped in newspaper. I'll treat you sometime.'

'Sounds wonderful.'

They continued to eat in silence, watching the boats and barges making their way down the river. After a few minutes Dorothy was the first to speak.

'You know, I've been thinking about something that preacher said – Dr Soper. He said when he was fifteen he thought there was something noble about being a soldier, until he began to think about what using a bayonet in real life meant. It made me wonder whether anything's changed since 1914 – I mean, boys and young men always see war as something exciting and glamorous, so there are always young men ready to serve in armies. Will it ever change?'

'I wasn't old enough to go to war in 1914,' said Jago, 'but I remember there was a lot of celebration when it started, as if the men were going off to a party. By the time I was conscripted we'd had two years of war, and it wasn't like that at all. And I noticed when war was declared last year there was nothing like that excitement of 1914. I suppose most people didn't want another war, and when it finally came there was just a kind of grim acceptance, as if they thought there's no way of avoiding it any more, so we'll just have to get on with it.'

'He said he's a pacifist because it's impossible to cast out evil by evil. Do you think that's true?'

'He may be right in theory, but what do you do when you're confronted by evil in real life? When I was a young copper I was called to a house where a woman had been cudgelled to death – someone had broken into her home and beaten her brains in. That was evil if ever I'd seen it. Could any words have persuaded that man not to kill? I don't know. But I do know that if I'd been there, I'd have used my truncheon and anything else that came to hand to protect her. I think sometimes you have to use violence to protect people against violence, and whether it's evil or not depends on the motivation – is it violence to harm or violence to protect?'

'I understand what you're saying,' said Dorothy. 'Black-and-white principles are never so straightforward in real life, are they?'

They sat in silence again until a tugboat hauling barges towards the docks sounded a mournful note on its horn.

'It's getting a bit chilly,' said Jago. 'I suspect real life is calling both of us back to our duties now.'

They got up from the bench and took a last look at the river. Jago brushed the crumbs off his coat onto the path, where the sparrows swiftly devoured them.

CHAPTER TWENTY-SIX

When Jago got back to West Ham police station it was just after three in the afternoon. Cradock was seated at his desk, with a sheet of paper in front of him and a pencil in his hand. As far as Jago could tell, he appeared to be doodling. Cradock looked up.

'Hello, sir. How was your visit to the Yard?'

'Helpful, thank you. I saw Detective Superintendent Cherrill in the fingerprint department, and he said the only prints he'd found on the gun were the same as the ones you'd taken from Paul Ramsey's body.'

'So that means Ramsey was the only person who'd handled it.'

'Not necessarily, but it does mean we've no evidence that anyone else had. It still doesn't tell us anything, of course, about what he might've planned to do with it, and we don't know whether the person who killed him knew he had it.'

'The killer would've known, if Ramsey had the gun

out, but then that would mean either Ramsey put the gun back in his pocket before he was killed or the killer did after he'd stabbed him, but somehow kept his own prints off it.'

'Which is not impossible, of course, but unfortunately it doesn't get us any further forward. Any news on whether he had a firearm certificate, by the way?'

'Yes, sir. I checked, and there's no record of one being issued to him. Not that that tells us much, does it? There's no evidence he used it for criminal purposes, so if we'd found him carrying it without a certificate he'd probably just've found himself up before the magistrate – fined a fiver and the gun confiscated.'

'Yes, and that's not going to happen to him now, is it? And what else have you been doing – drawing pictures?'

Cradock glanced down at the paper, screwed it up and threw it in the bin.

'Oh no, sir – I've been thinking, sir. About Gloria Harris and Paul Ramsey, and that suitcase of his. She told him it was all over and she was going straight back to Bradwell.'

'Yes – and?'

'Do you think that could be why he'd packed his suitcase? I mean, he was in a rage – what if he decided to follow her up there with that gun and threaten her? Or maybe even kill her?'

'The thought did cross my mind, Peter, but why would he need to follow her up there to do it? If that's what he really meant to do, he could've done it right here. When a man's in enough of a rage to kill someone, isn't he more likely to strike out, not wait till they've gone and then start packing his shaving kit in a suitcase?'

Cradock reflected on this for a moment.

'I see, sir, yes. But he did strike out, didn't he?'

'Yes, but not to kill. I think the way he reacted to her tells us something about the man, but not necessarily that he was intent on murder.'

'Right. But it does show us there were definitely two sides to Ramsey. One minute all he wants is peace, next minute he's violent. Like Gloria said, all of a sudden she saw something in him that she'd never seen before, and she didn't like what she saw.'

'Yes, and it reminds me of what the vicar said the first time I spoke to him about Ramsey – he thought Paul had seen something in himself that shocked him. But does that make him a potential killer?'

'I don't know, sir – it certainly suggests he wasn't everything he liked people to think he was.'

'That could be said of most people – even some vicars. And let's not forget Ramsey's the victim in this case.'

'All right, yes. But at least one thing's clear. We've cleared up the little mystery of who gave Gloria that bruise – she's finally admitted it was Ramsey.'

'Do you believe her?'

'What? Oh, I mean yes, obviously.'

'Why obviously? Because she's a pretty young woman?'

'No, of course not, sir. Because she sounded convincing. She'd just told him it was all over between them.'

'She sounded fairly convincing when she told us it was a rounders injury, but then she changed her story. When someone lies to you once they can lie to you twice. But let's assume she's telling the truth this time. What does that tell us?'

'That Paul Ramsey was the kind of pacifist who didn't mind hitting women.'

'Yes. And it also tells us that a young woman who hasn't told us the truth was being harassed by a violent man who's been found murdered. Might that suggest anything?'

'You don't mean she could've killed him, sir?'

'It seems unlikely, but she had reason to be afraid of him.'

'She may've had just as much reason to be afraid of her cousin, but no one's killed him. And come to think of it, Paul Ramsey had more to fear from him than he did from Gloria, didn't he? I mean, Shaw seems to have been obsessed with the idea that he had to protect Gloria – and judging by what Morton said, I get the impression Shaw thought he owned her.'

'It's a possibility I wouldn't rule out. All in all, Mr Shaw's been a bit cagey with us.'

Jago looked at his watch.

'In fact I think if we go down to his school now, we might just catch him for a little chat before he goes home.'

It was a quarter to four when they parked the car on the street in front of the school. Lessons were over, and the site was as quiet as the playground of the closed-down Custom House School had been. They found Shaw alone in a classroom, sitting at the teacher's desk on a low platform at the front and working his way through a pile of exercise books, wielding a fountain pen. Jago guessed that it was probably filled with red ink.

'You two again,' said Shaw, keeping his pen poised in the air. 'What do you want now? I haven't much time, you know – I've got all these books to mark before I go home.'

'We won't be long, Mr Shaw,' said Jago. 'I just need to talk to you a little more about Paul Ramsey and his unfortunate death.'

'All right, then. What do you want to know?'

'First of all, I'd like to go back to something you said to me last time we met.'

'Yes – what's that?'

'You said that as far as you knew, Mr Ramsey didn't have a girlfriend – that he'd never mentioned it to you.'

'What of it?'

'Are you saying you knew nothing of his relationship with Miss Gloria Harris?'

'Who?'

'Come now, Mr Shaw. Have you forgotten your own cousin?'

'My cousin?'

'Yes, your cousin. Are you denying she's your cousin?'

He put his pen down on the desk, looking suddenly anxious.

'Well, no, of course I'm not. But how did you—'

'How did I know? Is it supposed to be a secret?'

'No, but . . .' His voice petered out into an awkward silence.

'But what?' said Jago.

'If you must know,' Shaw replied, 'I didn't mention it because she hasn't told me she's been seeing him. She thinks I meddle in her life, but it's not true – I'm concerned for her welfare. I knew that if I told you, you'd go and ask her about it, and then she'd think I'd been reporting her private life to the police. It would only confirm her bizarre idea that I'm spying on her, or whatever else it is that goes on in that strange little mind of hers.'

'You think there's something wrong with her mind?'

'Listen, Inspector, that woman is trouble, and I didn't want my relationship with her to get even more complicated than it already is. What I said was on the spur of the moment – I thought it was better to let you find out for yourself, so I'd be spared more grief from her. Probably if I'd thought it through for a bit longer when you sprang that question on me I'd have answered differently. But I didn't, and there you have it. Does that mean you're going to arrest me?'

'No, Mr Shaw. But tell me something else. You said you're concerned for your cousin's welfare.'

'Yes.'

'Would you say you're a jealous man?'

'What on earth do you mean by that?'

'I mean that it's been suggested to me that you assaulted a man you suspected of seeing your cousin. Is that correct?'

'Assaulted? That'll be that Morton fellow, I suppose.'

Jago made no response.

'What a damned cheek!' Shaw continued. 'It was just an argument – it was all over before it started. I give him a little tap on the chest to emphasise my point and he runs to the police accusing me of assaulting him – just typical of that limp-wristed upstart. You don't want to read too much into what he says. If he wants to know what assaulted means, tell him to say it to my face and I'll teach him a thing or two.'

'Have you ever done that to Gloria too – taught her a thing or two?'

'What? Certainly not!'

'So it wasn't you who gave her that bruise?'

'What bruise? I don't know what you're talking about. I haven't seen her for weeks.'

'Would you describe yourself as a man with a temper? A short fuse, as it were?'

'No, no more than any other normal man.'

'But you feel things deeply?'

'Sometimes, yes.'

'How deep were your feelings for your cousin?'

'What on earth are you suggesting?'

'She said you wanted to marry her.'

'Well, what if I did? It's not illegal, is it? I might have mentioned that at some time – as I said, I'm concerned for her welfare. I've always felt a responsibility to look after her, ever since she lost her parents.'

'And you found out that she was in a relationship with Paul Ramsey?'

Shaw did not respond immediately: he seemed to be considering how to answer this question.

'Yes, it's true,' he said hesitantly. 'That man Morton told me.'

'Why did he tell you?'

'I don't know. I think he was angry about it.'

'What was your reaction to that news?'

'I was surprised. I wouldn't have thought she'd be interested in a man like Ramsey – or rather, I wouldn't have thought any woman would be interested in a man like him who doesn't want to serve his country in days like these.'

'And you do?'

'Look, Inspector, I've already told you – when I'm called up I'll go, and willingly. That was probably the biggest difference between me and him.'

'You didn't like him?'

'I was indifferent to him. I happened to be his colleague at school, but that didn't mean I had to be his best pal.'

'And when you found out about him and Gloria, did you get angry with him?'

'No. I never spoke to him about it.'

'Did you have any reason to believe he might be violent towards her?'

'No. Are you saying he was? If he'd laid a hand on her I'd have—'

'You'd have what, Mr Shaw?'

'Nothing. I'd have told her to stop seeing him, that's all.'

'I'm wondering whether you ever did the opposite, Mr Shaw – did you ever try to persuade Paul to stop seeing her?'

'Why would you think that?'

'When we examined his flat after his death we found a suitcase packed – he was planning to go somewhere.'

'What's that got to do with me? I knew nothing about it.'

'But he'd got his hands on the job you thought should be yours, and on your cousin. If anyone wanted him out of the way it was you.'

'So he got the job that should've been mine. So what? I've told you already, I took him out for a drink – no hard feelings.'

'No hard feelings? I find that hard to believe.'

'Well, that's too bad, because it's the truth.'

'Was anyone else with you and Mr Ramsey when you had that conversation?'

'Of course not. I don't like what you're insinuating, Inspector. Innocent, law-abiding people don't spend their time making sure they have witnesses for every conversation they have in a pub. I had a drink with a colleague, and that's it.'

'And you didn't say or do anything to warn him off, to discourage him from seeing your cousin?'

'Of course not. What a preposterous idea. I just wished him well and drank to his future.'

'A future that he didn't have.'

'Have you finished? If you don't mind, I'd like to get on with my work – teachers don't get paid overtime, you know.'

'Very well, Mr Shaw,' said Jago. 'Thank you for your time.'

'Peter,' said Jago as they got back into the car. 'That drink Shaw had with Ramsey at the Prince of Wales on Friday – I'm wondering whether it was as innocuous as he makes out. I want you to go to the Prince of Wales this evening, and take that photo of Paul Ramsey with you. See if any of the staff or regulars recognise him, ask them if they can confirm Shaw was with him, and find out whether anyone saw or heard anything of interest.'

'Will do, sir.'

'Good. But before you do that, we should just have time for the appointment I've made to see Councillor Hampson.'

CHAPTER TWENTY-SEVEN

'We're seeing Councillor Hampson?' said Cradock, looking at his watch. 'It's getting a bit late, isn't it? I always imagined people like councillors would knock off early.'

'On the contrary,' said Jago. 'They're very busy people – everybody wants a bit of their time. When I spoke to Councillor Hampson on the phone yesterday and said we wanted to see him, he gave a sort of sigh that sounded like this was the last straw. I said if he was busy we could come to his home in the evening, but he declined, and said something like, "I get the world and his wife beating a path to my door with their problems and complaints – doesn't matter what time it is, they think I'm at their beck and call morning, noon and night." He said we should meet him at the town hall in Stratford at five o'clock this afternoon.'

Cradock thought for a moment, then spoke so suddenly it made Jago jump at the wheel.

'That's it, of course, isn't it, sir?'

'That's what?' said Jago.

'T. H. Hampson – it's not someone's name, it's just Paul Ramsey's shorthand in his diary for where they were meeting. T. H. stands for town hall.'

'I believe you're right, Peter – as simple as that. So, we shall have to ask the good councillor exactly what happened when Mr Ramsey came to see him.'

The town hall was typical of its age – built in the middle of the previous century when Victorian municipal confidence in trade and progress was at its height. Adorned with columns, balconies, statues and a tower, it was clearly conceived as the proud heart of the borough, designed to make the appropriate impression on residents and visitors alike. On the inside it was all sweeping staircases, chandeliers and ornate plasterwork, albeit not quite in the condition it had been when new.

Councillor Hampson met Jago and Cradock in a high-ceilinged office at the back of the building.

'Remind me, please, Inspector, what this meeting is in aid of. I haven't got much time, you know. I can give you ten minutes, and that's your lot.'

'Thank you, Councillor. I have an engagement myself this evening, so I'll get straight to the point. Did you have a meeting with a gentleman called Paul Ramsey last Friday?'

'Who?'

'Mr Paul Ramsey.'

'I don't know. I'll have to check my diary – I have meetings all day.'

Hampson crossed the office to a mahogany desk. He was a grey-haired, balding man well into his fifties, and his lack of height accentuated the paunch which seemed to be putting a considerable strain on his waistcoat buttons. The gold watch chain draped across it was perhaps intended to convey an impression of experience and reliability, but to Jago it only drew attention to that part of his body which suggested possibly too many years of municipal dinners.

The councillor opened a leather-bound desk diary and found the relevant page.

'Yes, it seems I did – eleven o'clock in the morning. What of it?'

'Are you aware that Mr Ramsey has been murdered?'

'Murdered? My goodness. No, this is the first I've heard. And what are the police doing about it?'

'We're looking for his killer, Councillor, and we shall find him – or her.'

'So you obviously haven't got far then, if you don't even know if you're looking for a male or a female.'

Jago judged it would be wise not to be provoked, and ignored the comment.

'What was the meeting about, sir?'

'I'm not sure I can remember. Let me think. Ah yes, that's it. As I recall, he'd come to complain about something – it was about his boss. The young man was a teacher, I believe, and he was insinuating that his headmaster was fiddling the petty cash at school or some such nonsense. Quite frankly I've got far weightier matters on my mind than some little man's office politics. This war has made life very busy for people in my position, you know. The public has no idea how much we have to do, and for scant reward, I can tell you.'

'I'm sure you're right, sir. But you were saying?'

'What?'

'The young teacher.'

'Ah, yes. Well, you'll appreciate that I'm working flat out to protect the people of this borough from annihilation at the hands of the German air force. I sent him away with a flea in his ear. Come back when we're not being bombed to hell every night, I said. Arrogant young time-waster, if you ask me. Conchie, too.'

'A conscientious objector? Did he mention that?'

'No, but I recognised his tone of voice, then I remembered his face. I sit on the conscientious objectors' tribunal, you know. He was up before us a few weeks ago pleading his excuses and wanting to be excused military service on grounds of his precious tender conscience. We rejected him.'

'Had you met this teacher before?'

'No, of course not.'

'But he told you which school he taught in?'

'Well, yes, I believe he did.'

'And which school was that?'

'Prince Regent Lane – the secondary school.'

'Am I right in understanding you're the chairman of that school's board of managers?'

'Yes, that's correct. But what's that got to do with it?'

'Yet you didn't recognise him as a master at that school?'

'No, why should I? I may serve on the board of managers, but that doesn't mean I'm on personal terms with all the teachers, for pity's sake.'

'And you didn't consider you should look into his accusations about the headmaster?'

'Look, I may not know that teacher, but I do know the headmaster, and he's a fine man. I know what it's like when young men like that start nursing petty resentments or grievances against their elders and betters, especially when they're spineless conchies who get on their moral high horse but aren't prepared to soil their pretty hands. They need to spend more time in the real world. You may disagree with me, but I've got better things to do with my time than listen to men like that carping about the management. He made some allegations, and I made a judgement that the whole thing was a cock-and-bull story he'd made up to get his own back for some imagined slight.'

Hampson glanced at his watch and let out an impatient sigh similar to the one Jago had heard on the phone.

'Anyway, I shall have to ask you to excuse me. I have a meeting with the mayor in five minutes and I don't have any more time to speak to you.'

He began to move towards the door.

'Very well,' said Jago. 'Thank you for your help. We may need to see you again, and it may have to be at your home. Could we have your address please?'

'Of course. It's 72 Balaam Street. Now, have you finished? There is a war on, you know.'

'Yes, but just before you go, am I right in thinking you're related to Mrs Maud Hampson?'

The councillor began to look irritated.

'Yes, she's my wife. Why do you ask?'

'It's just that we met her on Sunday, in connection with her ARP duties.'

'Ah, yes. Well, she's very busy with her ARP duties, you know.'

'The address she gave us is not the same as yours, though.'

He gave Hampson a bland look with just a hint of expectancy.

'So?' said Hampson. 'She's temporarily living elsewhere – moved out about six weeks ago. She's very devoted to her work, and since the air raids got so bad it's meant long hours, out every night. She was promoted to post warden recently, and she's taken a little flat so she can be closer to the post where she's based.'

'Vital work these days,' said Jago. 'Providing a real service to the community when its needs are greatest.'

He hoped Hampson hadn't detected a hint of sarcasm in his voice – he'd said what he thought without pausing to think how the words might be taken.

'Yes, sterling work,' said Hampson. 'Now, if that's all, Inspector, I really must go.'

'Yes, thank you, sir. We'll leave you to your next pressing engagement.'

Hampson grabbed some papers and bustled out of the office. Cradock waited until his footsteps had faded down the corridor before speaking.

'What he said about that meeting with Ramsey – it didn't tally with what Gloria said, did it? She said Paul was going to talk to him about Joe's little scheme.'

'Yes – Hampson may have got the conversation mixed up with someone else, of course – he does give the impression of being very busy and he clearly didn't think much of Paul Ramsey. But even so, I've an idea we'll be seeing him again before long. We'll just have to hope he can grant us a few of his precious minutes between all those meetings on which it would seem the successful prosecution of the war depends.'

'You didn't like him, did you, sir?'

'Did you?'

'Too used to throwing his weight around, I reckon. That's the trouble with politicians, even when they're only local councillors – give them a bit of power and it goes to their heads.'

'It's a temptation, yes – and one that policemen are not immune to, in my experience.'

'Mr Soper, you mean?'

'Never you mind who I mean. It was a general observation, that's all – but I hope you never find yourself in a position where you succumb to that temptation yourself.'

'I don't see me ever getting to be a DDI, sir.'

'It can happen to the most unlikely people, Peter – you mark my words.'

CHAPTER TWENTY-EIGHT

Jago's keenness to take Dorothy to meet Henry Cardew had been motivated not least by his desire to be with her again. He'd been surprised when the vicar suggested they visit that very evening, and wondered whether she might think seeing him twice in the same day was too much, but her ready acceptance of the invitation had been more than reassuring.

As soon as he'd escaped from Councillor Hampson he hurried to the railway station to meet Dorothy from the train, then drove her to Leyes Road. By just after six o'clock they were sitting in Cardew's house.

'I'm so pleased to meet you, Mr Cardew,' said Dorothy. 'And it's very good of you to spare us some of your time, especially at such short notice – I thought we'd have to make an appointment days or weeks ahead.'

'The pleasure is all mine. I tend not to live by a diary these days, just take things a day at a time. I only hope we shan't be interrupted by our friends in the sky. Incidentally,

I must warn you that I tend not to scuttle off into a shelter as soon as the siren goes off. I find I'm often more useful out on the street – sometimes if there's somebody trapped in the wreckage, just holding their hand until the heavy rescue team can get them out brings real comfort. So I normally wait until I hear the bombs falling and then go out to see how I can help. Is that all right with you?'

'That's fine with me,' said Jago.

'Me too, I guess,' said Dorothy.

'Good. Now, if you're going to be here for a while I must get you something to eat. Entertaining at home nowadays isn't as easy as it used to be, but that's no reason not to be hospitable. I can offer you some bread and cheese – at least they're not rationed yet – but alas no butter or margarine, as I've already used up this week's allowance. I have some canned soup, though, and a tin of salmon.'

'Bread and cheese would be delightful, thank you, if it's no trouble,' said Dorothy.

'No trouble at all,' he said, moving towards the door. 'Just wait here for a moment while I fetch it.'

Jago jumped to his feet.

'Sorry – I almost forgot. Here, I've brought something for you.'

He reached into his pocket and pulled out a small package, then handed it to Cardew.

'What's this?' said Cardew. 'A present?'

'Two ounces of tea,' said Jago. 'I haven't finished my ration for last week yet, so I thought you might like to have this week's.'

Cardew held it up and laughed.

'Two ounces of tea – the perfect gift for a vicar!'

He noticed that Dorothy looked puzzled.

'I must explain. Here in England people think all a vicar does is drink cups of tea – and write sermons, of course.'

'From what I've heard,' she replied, 'that's not true in your case, Vicar – I've heard so much about you.'

'I wasn't aware my fame had spread so far. Now, let me make you some tea.'

He left the room and closed the door behind him. Jago and Dorothy sat alone in the drawing room. She smiled at him.

'He seems a nice man,' she said.

'Yes, a very interesting fellow.'

Jago returned the smile, but did not attempt to start a conversation, expecting Cardew to return soon. Moments later the vicar reappeared, carrying a tray laden with three plates of bread and cheese, and put it down on the table.

'There,' he said. 'Not sophisticated, perhaps, but nutritious enough to keep us going. Now, I'll fetch the tea.'

He went out again and returned a few minutes later with another tray.

'Shall I be mother?' he said, and poured cups of tea for them. 'Talking of fame,' he said to Dorothy, 'if anyone's famous in this room, it's probably you – you're an international journalist. I'm just an ordinary vicar, you know.'

'I guess it depends what you mean by ordinary,' she

replied. 'According to one of my contacts in London, when the first air raids happened the people who'd lost their houses had no food, so you went and broke into a government food depot, started a bonfire and fed the hungry. That sounds pretty unusual to me. So when I found out that John here – Inspector Jago, that is – had met you I immediately asked him to introduce us.'

'I see – so how can I help you?'

'Well, having heard a little about your work with the people who live here, I'd very much like to ask you a few questions about it.'

'You mean you'd like to interview me?'

'That's right.'

'I assume anything you write will be censored by the authorities?'

'That's right too.'

'In that case I suppose it makes the whole thing easier – I can tell you the truth as I see it and leave it to those fellows at the Ministry of Information to decide what information is unsuitable for the American or any other public.'

'I assume that means some of your comments may not be quite in line with the official view that we read in the newspapers?' said Jago.

'You assume correctly, Inspector,' said Cardew.

For a moment Jago's heart sank at the thought of what Divisional Detective Inspector Soper would say if he knew about this conversation. The DDI had clearly indicated that he expected Jago to chaperone Dorothy round the borough and see to it that she got the 'right' impression of how the people of West Ham were coping with the air raids. It seemed that now a maverick vicar who didn't deny breaking into official food stores was going to give her something quite different. But in the next moment he realised that he didn't care. If Soper didn't like it he could make his own case for practising deception on a journalist. Jago was a detective, not a censor, and if a vicar wasn't allowed to speak his mind in the middle of a war, what kind of freedom was the country fighting for? He decided to keep out of the conversation and let Cardew choose what he wanted to say to Dorothy.

Dorothy took a notebook and pen from her handbag.

'First of all,' she said, 'is it true what I've heard about that food depot you broke open?'

'I'm afraid it is.'

'Why did you do that?'

'Because people had been bombed out of their homes, many of the shops had been put out of action, and they needed help. You know what they say – "A little help is worth a pound of pity."'

'But what about the local authorities?'

'To be frank, I think when these huge air raids started, our local leadership in West Ham faltered. The system they'd put in place to deal with potential air raids was simply unequal to the task, so they weren't in a position to help, and I didn't know how long it would be before they got into action. The ARP and voluntary services were doing everything they could, but I couldn't stand idly by while people suffered, so I decided to, er, take the law into my own hands.' He glanced at Jago. 'I'm sorry, Inspector. I wouldn't normally do something like that, but it was an emergency.'

Jago waved his hand in a way that dismissed the vicar's concern, indicating that he would not be pursuing the matter.

'What do you mean by "unequal to the task"?' said Dorothy.

'You have to understand that West Ham is a poor borough. Before the war the government said local authorities had to pay for things like building air-raid shelters and training wardens, but incomes here are low and housing is poor, so the council doesn't get much money from the rates. Unemployment had been high in the borough for many years, so a lot of that had to be spent on unemployment relief.'

'So when the raids started they weren't ready?'

'Not as ready as they should have been, with hindsight, and I think those air raids knocked the council for six. Suddenly there were all these people who'd been bombed out and nowhere to feed them – that's why I had to do what I did. The thing is, before the war the council had been mainly pacifist, and in those days people like that thought making obvious preparations for war would be sending a signal to Germany that we were intent on having one, so it made sense not to go too far. Now, of course, we have reason to regret that.'

'Have things changed now?'

'Well, the council's not pacifist now – in fact they've

changed their views so much that this year they even decided not to allow pacifists to work in any of their ARP services, which some people think is ridiculous. I've also heard it said that the council's too old to handle an emergency on this scale – the average age of the councillors is about sixty – and because they're nearly all from the same party there's no real opposition to challenge them. Of course, I don't take a position on political issues like that, but I hope it helps you to understand why there's so much for the church in general and me in particular to do.'

'It makes me wonder how on earth you find the time to write those sermons you mentioned,' said Dorothy.

'Ah, yes, of course. If a vicar can't write good sermons, what use is he to man or beast? The truth is, at times like this I believe my work is my sermon. When someone's lost the only home they've ever known and they're feeling terrified and alone, if I can help them get through it and find some hope then I think I'm preaching my sermon in terms they can understand. As the apostle John said, "let us not love in word, but in deed and in truth."'

'And someone else said "faith without works is dead" – isn't that right?'

'Yes – that's in the epistle of James. Don't get me wrong – we need words to explain what we mean, but as they say in Scotland, sometimes these things are better felt than telt. Would you agree, Inspector?'

'Me?' said Jago, jolted back into the conversation. 'If you mean do I hate hypocrisy, then yes, I suppose I agree, but I don't think I'm qualified to take a position on such matters. I'm happy to leave that to professionals like yourself.'

'So you wouldn't describe yourself as a man of faith, then?'

'No. I've got nothing against it, but I think I'm like many men of my generation – the idea of an all-powerful God of love was all right in Sunday school, but not when it was kill or be killed at the front.'

'And you, Miss Appleton?'

'I was brought up by parents who had faith, so yes, I do believe, but I've seen some pretty bad things around the world too, and I have lots of questions.'

'There's nothing wrong with asking questions – that's how we find truth. And as for what you were saying, Inspector, I must say that if you hate hypocrisy I believe God hates it even more. I think he prefers a man who even says he hates God, if that's true, because at least that man is honest. And I'm sure a man in your profession knows the value of honesty.'

'Yes, indeed. But look, we should be going. There's just one thing I'd like to ask you.'

'Of course – what is it?'

'You've been talking about the local borough council. Do you happen to know Councillor Hampson?'

'Yes, I do.'

'I met him yesterday and he was quite scathing about what he called "spineless conchies". So was he one of those councillors who've changed their tune?'

'It's not for me to judge, my friend. My observation

of politics is that people sometimes change their position and become very committed supporters and advocates of policies they once derided. Even Mr Churchill has changed party twice – he was a Conservative, then a Liberal, then a Conservative again. Councillor Hampson is a lifelong politician. I shall have to leave you to draw your own conclusions about his convictions.'

'I think I've already drawn a few, thank you.'

Jago looked at the clock on the vicar's mantelpiece.

'Time's getting on,' he said. 'I think we should be on our way before the trouble starts.'

'You're right,' said Cardew. 'And I should get ready to go out.'

'Can we give you a lift somewhere?'

'No, thank you. I'll just be making myself useful in the vicinity if I'm needed, as usual.'

'I'm sure you will be.'

'Experience suggests I shall, sadly.'

'Goodnight, then, Vicar,' said Dorothy.

'Goodnight, my dears,' said Cardew. 'Come back and see me again – I'll save some tea for you!'

CHAPTER TWENTY-NINE

Jago drove northwards from Cardew's house, cutting through side streets to dodge obstacles left by the previous night's attacks and hoping to keep clear of whatever dangers tonight might bring. But by the time he and Dorothy reached New Barn Street a rain of incendiary bombs had started fires in a number of places, dispelling the darkness. They heard the first explosive bombs falling behind them, and Jago tried to go faster, but progress was difficult. When they reached the junction with Barking Road he braked sharply as a fire engine hurtled past, bound for somewhere to the west.

He was about to edge forward when a woman came running across the road towards him. He glanced at her in the half-light. There was something familiar about her headgear – a turban with a large feather stuck in the front.

She stopped, breathless, and tapped on the side-screen window, motioning for him to open it.

'Inspector Jago?' she said when he'd pushed it open.

'That's right, Mrs Garside. Can we help you?'

'Yes, yes, I need to get home. I'm worried something may have happened to Wilfred – Mr Morton. I was up the road visiting a friend when we saw some bombs landing over this way. I must find him.'

Jago jumped out of the car and helped Olivia Garside into the back seat, introducing her and Dorothy to each other briskly as she got in, then took his place behind the wheel again and drove down Barking Road in the direction of her shop. Heavy smoke was drifting across the road, alive with sparks of burning paper and timber. He eased the car over a number of hosepipes that snaked from the fire hydrant on the pavement and across the street to a fire crew who were tackling a blaze above a newsagent's shop.

'Looks like an incendiary got that one,' he said, peering through the windscreen as they passed.

He made out Olivia's bookshop through the smoke, and to his relief it didn't seem to be on fire. He nosed the car closer, then parked it out of the way in a side street.

'Come on,' he said. 'Let's see what's happening.'

He led the two women quickly down the street. As they approached, he could see that the property opposite the bookshop had been hit. It was impossible to tell what it had been before the bomb fell – the explosion had reduced it to a confused pile of rubble, timbers and smashed contents, with just one wall remaining.

A pair of masked blue lamps on the ground marked the position of the ARP incident officer, and they headed towards him. Jago noticed that while Olivia's shop and the flats above were still standing, all the windows were shattered and there was obvious damage to the roof, with most of the tiles blown off.

'I must go in,' said Olivia, heading for the shop, but the incident officer barred her way.

'Sorry,' he said, 'you can't go in there. Too dangerous. The blast has knocked the chimney down and the brickwork's all crashed through the roof. It may have taken part of the upper floor out too.'

'But I have to – my lodger may still be in there.' She turned to Jago. 'Mr Shaw said he was going to be out all evening, but Wilfred told me he was staying in to do some of his PPU work. He may be injured. I can't just leave him there.'

She began to weep, her eyes straining through her tears in search of help. Jago thought she looked on the verge of hysteria.

'Watch out!' came a voice from behind them. Jago whirled round in time to see the remaining wall of the bombed property collapse, spilling debris into the roadway in clouds of dust. The incident officer ran to the scene, and as soon as his back was turned Olivia composed herself and dashed to the door beside her shop, key in hand. Jago and Dorothy hurried after her.

They pounded up the staircase, the brick dust and soot in the air acrid in their nostrils. When they reached the top floor the door to Morton and Shaw's flat was jammed. Jago put his shoulder to it and stumbled into the first room. He could see the sky through a hole in the roof. That must be where the chimney came through, he thought – and he hoped with all his heart for Mrs Garside's sake that it hadn't caught Morton. Finding no sign of him, he moved on to the second room, followed by Olivia and Dorothy.

'Over there,' shouted Dorothy. 'I think I can see legs, by the bed.'

She crossed the room, knelt down, and started throwing pieces of brick and wood to one side. Jago joined her and could now see the body of Morton lying motionless on the floor, still half covered in debris.

'Give me a hand,' said Dorothy, a note of urgency in her voice that he'd not heard before. 'This is too heavy.'

She had her hands on a large lump of brickwork that was lying partly across Morton. Jago bent down opposite her and took the other side. Together they lifted it off him and dumped it with a crash on the floorboards. Olivia was standing to one side, a handkerchief clamped over her mouth. She was in tears, and it sounded to Jago as though she were praying.

'Is he . . . ?' she asked. 'O Lord, please don't let him be dead – please.'

'Just a minute,' said Jago. 'I'll just—'

He took Morton's wrist and felt for a pulse.

'He's not moving,' he said, 'but I think . . . yes, I can feel a pulse. He's alive.'

'Thank you, God, thank you,' said Olivia. She knelt down beside Jago and gently brushed the dust off Morton's face with her hand.

'Those bricks must have knocked him out,' said Jago. 'But we can't wait for him to come round – there's no knowing what state this place is in. We must move him. Dorothy, can you help me? We must try to get him out of here.'

'No,' Dorothy replied. 'Don't move him. If his back's injured we could make it worse. He needs a stretcher.'

'Right,' said Jago. 'I'll go and find that incident officer and ask him to get a stretcher party up here. He got to his feet, surprised to find himself deferring to her better judgement, and yet feeling strangely proud of the way she'd handled the situation. He strode across the room and clattered down the stairs to the street.

He returned moments later. Dorothy was sitting on the bed, and Olivia was still kneeling on the floor beside Morton, gazing silently at him as she stroked his face.

'Stretcher party's on its way,' said Jago. 'Should be here in a minute or two.'

Olivia's attention seemed so fixed on Morton that he wasn't even sure she had heard him. She looked up at Dorothy.

'Do you ever imagine yourself being a mother?' she said.

'Well, I'm not even married yet,' said Dorothy, 'so I guess it would be a little premature to do so.'

'I used to, you know,' Olivia continued quietly. 'I was married, but my husband was in the navy – he was killed in action before we had the chance to have children. That was twenty-four years ago. If we'd had a son he'd have been a man now, like Wilfred.' She cast her eyes

280

back down to Wilfred's mask-like face. 'Wilfred hasn't married yet, but I want him to. He's been like a son to me, and I want him to have children of his own, so that he can have what I was denied and be happy. This might sound strange, you know, but I want him to have children so that they can be like grandchildren for me.'

'I'm sure he'll find someone to marry soon enough,' said Dorothy.

'I fear he won't,' said Olivia. 'He's only loved one girl, and another man stole her from him. But it's all right now, isn't it, Wilfred? Everything's going to be all right. You know I'd do anything to make you happy.'

She lapsed into silence and continued stroking him, now seemingly oblivious of her companions.

Dorothy caught Jago's eye and noticed that he looked deep in thought. She was about to ask him what was on his mind when the sound of two pairs of boots echoed from the staircase.

'Stretcher's here,' said Jago. 'They'll have him down to the hospital in no time at all, Mrs Garside.'

'I shall go with him,' she said. 'I want to be by his side when he wakes up. Do go, and thank you, both of you. You've saved his life – and mine.'

CHAPTER THIRTY

When Jago woke the next morning he felt surprisingly refreshed. He'd actually slept quite well – mainly because he hadn't been kept awake half the night. In fact it seemed to him to have been the quietest since the air raids began. When he arrived at the police station just before half past eight he was still buoyant enough to think he might even get on top of some paperwork today.

He gave a cheery greeting to Station Sergeant Tompkins at the front desk and was continuing on his way to the CID office when he heard Tompkins give a polite cough behind him.

'Excuse me, sir. There's someone come to see you.'

Jago's spirits dipped briefly at the thought of a visitor wrecking his hopes for the day.

'A young chap, sir – said he was calling on his way to work. He only got here a couple of minutes ago – your boy Cradock's taken him up to the CID office to wait for you.'

'Thanks, Frank,' said Jago, and turned to go.

'And there's something else,' said Frank.

'Yes?'

'In the occurrence book – I noticed something about that Irish character who calls himself Jones. Young Cradock told me about him on Tuesday when he'd been to see the man who didn't get his shelter built. Pleased as punch, he was – Cradock, that is, not the other bloke. I reckon he thought this was his big case. Anyway, there's a note in the book by one of the lads on night duty saying he found a man injured in the street and took him to casualty at Queen Mary's. The fellow was a bit groggy, but he soon got talking. He had a strong Irish accent, which is a bit unusual for a bloke calling himself Jones, and he was short.'

'Thanks, Frank – that sounds interesting.'

'Good. The hospital said they'd be keeping him in for the night, so if you nip up the road this morning you might find him still there.'

Jago found the visitor with Cradock in the CID office. He was indeed a youngish man, as Tompkins had said, dressed in a nondescript black suit and clasping a bowler hat before him with both hands.

'This is Mr Hedges, sir,' said Cradock. 'He'd like to have a word.'

'Good morning, Mr Hedges,' said Jago. 'Take a seat.'

Hedges sat meekly on the chair facing Jago's desk.

'What is it you'd like to talk about?' said Jago.

'It's something I'm a bit concerned about – something that's happening at work. I didn't know who to talk to, but my wife suggested I go and see Mr Cardew, our vicar, so I did – and he said I should come and tell you about it, so that's why I'm here. He said he'd spoken to you about me but he hadn't told you my name. He's very good like that. I'm still not sure, though – I'm worried about what might happen.'

'In what sense?'

'It's my job, see. I can't afford to lose it, but I'm afraid that's what might happen if it gets back to my superiors at the town hall that I've spoken to you. Can you promise to keep my name out of this?'

'Mr Hedges, you're here on a voluntary basis and you may be about to give me some information which we may choose to investigate further. You're not under arrest, and I'm not asking you to make a formal statement. I shall regard what you say to me as information, not as evidence, and if you wish to remain anonymous I shall respect that wish. The only circumstances in which I would be obliged to disclose your name would be if a judge ordered me to do so.'

'All right, then, but please don't forget – I need that job.'

'I won't forget. Now, tell me what it is that concerns you. Mr Cardew did tell me you'd said it was something to do with building contracts.'

'Yes, that's right. It was just something I stumbled across in my work. I happened to see some papers that I wouldn't normally see – they'd go to someone higher up, but he wasn't in that day. They were documents signing off invoices for payment. Nothing unusual in that, but it was just that I was a bit surprised by how big the payments were for the jobs done.'

'What kind of jobs were these?'

'Building air-raid shelters. I don't mean providing Anderson shelters for people's back gardens – they're all right if you've got a back yard, but people living in flats haven't, so in March the government told us to build communal shelters, the ones that stand in the middle of the street. That was difficult, because by then we were getting short of bricks and concrete, and it got even worse after Germany invaded Belgium and Holland in May, because so much cement was diverted to military use. On top of all that, the local authorities have been arguing with the government for years about who should pay for the shelters, and for all I know they probably still are. All in all, it's been a bit chaotic, and I think some people may have taken advantage of that.'

'In what way?'

'Well, you see the government issued standard designs and prices for these shelters. I saw the ministry's guidelines on what it should cost to build one of them, and the payment instructions for the invoices I saw were all authorising significantly higher amounts.'

'What do you mean by "significantly higher"?'

'Well, I saw one from a contractor for building three fifty-person public shelters. The normal estimated price the government expects us to pay is a hundred and eighty-five pounds, so I would think if a builder got a contract to build three it'd cost no more than about five hundred pounds, but in this case the builder had invoiced for seven hundred and twenty pounds, and it'd been signed off. I think someone somewhere's been making an excessive profit on those contracts, and the shelters aren't even safe.'

'What do you mean?'

'I mean they haven't been built properly. There's going to be a scandal about this one day soon, you mark my words. I was talking to one of the council's building inspectors – I didn't understand everything he said, but it was something to do with the kind of mortar they used when they were building those shelters. Apparently there was a loophole in the regulations the government issued back in April, and the upshot was that the wrong type was used – something to do with using only lime and sand in the mortar and not adding cement, I think.'

'They're not up to standard, then?'

'So he said. Some people are saying the local authorities are to blame for not doing it right, some say it was the government's fault for not issuing clear enough instructions, and others say it was the contractors who deliberately misinterpreted it to increase their profits. But whatever it was, the end result was the shelters aren't strong enough to stand up to a bomb blast, so if a bomb lands nearby there's a strong risk that they'll fall down. I saw one myself just the other day – you could see the walls had collapsed and the roof had fallen in on the people inside. They'd gone in there to keep safe, and they'd been killed – they probably would've been better off sheltering under the stairs at home.'

'Do you know if the contractor you've been telling us about used this faulty mixture?'

'No, I don't. I think it's possible, though – if he's cheated on the price he might've cheated on the materials too.'

'So what you're telling me is that someone at the town hall has been signing off inflated payments to a contractor who may or may not have also built sub-standard air-raid shelters – death traps, in fact.'

'I suppose that's it, yes.'

'And who was that contractor?'

'His name's Joe Ramsey. That's all I know about him.'

'That's all I need to know. And who had signed off these payments?'

'One of the councillors.'

'And his name?'

'It's Councillor Hampson. I think it would normally be the chairman of the ARP Committee who does it, but he's been off sick. Mr Hampson's chairman of one of the sub-committees, and I think he's managed to get hold of these invoices and sign them off without anyone objecting, or perhaps without anyone even knowing. Things are a bit chaotic at the moment.'

'But you found out he'd done it?'

'Yes, and like a fool I went to see him, to ask him if

there'd been a mistake. As soon as I spoke I realised I should've kept my mouth shut.'

'What did he say?'

'He said, "It's none of your business. It's my job to approve the payment, and if I've approved it, it's your job to make the payment, so write the cheque and let's hear no more about it. If you want to keep your job you'll do as you're told." That's why I don't want to be identified.'

'I see. And the paperwork you referred to – where is that?'

'It's all at the town hall. I wasn't going to try to remove it – that would be stealing. But I tell you, after what Councillor Hampson said I wouldn't be surprised if all the paperwork on those contracts disappeared pretty soon. You know – mislaid in the chaos of war, accidental fire damage, something like that. It wouldn't surprise me either if that Ramsey had been paid for jobs he didn't even do – and presumably the profits got divided up between him and the councillor.'

'Thank you, Mr Hedges. You've been most helpful, and I can assure you we'll look into this matter. There's nothing for you to worry about now.'

Hedges got to his feet and looked nervously at Jago.

'I hope you're right,' he said.

No sooner had Hedges left than the phone rang. Jago picked up the receiver and heard the voice of Tompkins again.

'Sorry to disturb you, sir, but it looks like you're as popular as Lobby Lud today – everyone's looking for you. I've got another visitor here for you, only this time it's a young lady. She says her name's Miss Gloria Harris.'

'Very well,' said Jago. 'DC Cradock will come and fetch her.'

Cradock left the office and returned shortly with Gloria Harris. She smiled at Jago and Cradock in turn, but declined a seat.

'I'm sorry to disturb you, Inspector,' she began, 'but I thought you'd want to know – I received a letter this morning, from Paul.'

She opened her shoulder bag and took out an envelope, from which she pulled a single sheet of notepaper.

'It was postmarked last Friday, so I should've had it much sooner, but he addressed it to me in Buckinghamshire, of course, so the school had to forward it to me here. Listen – he says, "You may remember I mentioned my brother letting slip in an unguarded moment that he'd cooked up some little money-making scheme with the council. When I thought about that later I got angry. I know he's always been jealous of me because I did better at school than he did, and he's missed no opportunity to rub it in that he makes more money than me with his confounded business. I think he wants me to envy him, and I suppose being stuck on whatever salary the council decides to pay me is good enough reason, but really, I don't care if he makes more than me, as long as he makes it honestly. And that's the point: what he said sounded like he was making it dishonestly. I don't know anything about the council and its workings, so I decided to take it up with my own local councillor – he's called Hampson. I think I may have said something about that the other day. Well, today I went to see this man Hampson and told him I thought my brother might be involved in dishonest dealings with the council."'

Cradock interrupted her, his voice sounding excited.

'But that means—'

'Just a moment,' said Jago. He caught Cradock's eye and gave a momentary shake of the head to silence him. 'Please continue, Miss Harris. What does Paul say next?'

'He says, "I felt bad making accusations against my own brother like that, but I knew it was my public duty – I can't bear the thought of anyone dishonestly profiting from other people's misery at a time like this. I worried that perhaps it was all some misunderstanding, but why would my brother have told me if it wasn't true? You know what they say – *in vino veritas* – and he was drunk enough that night to tell the truth, the whole truth and nothing but the truth. Anyway, the councillor was very good. He heard me out, asked me lots of questions, and then said he'd start making some discreet enquiries."'

'Does he say anything about what those questions were?'

'No, he just says, "Councillor Hampson seemed determined to get to the bottom of it, so I expect I'll hear some more later. I can tell you, when I left his office at the town hall it was like a weight had been taken off my mind."'

'Thank you, Miss Harris, that's most helpful. And the letter was postmarked last Friday, you say, so you didn't know anything about this when you saw Paul on Saturday?'

'That's right.'

'And have you discussed what he says with anyone else?'

'No.'

'Very good. Now, I'd like to borrow that letter for a while, if you have no objection. It might be needed as evidence.'

'Evidence? You mean this might have something to do with Paul's murder?'

'I couldn't say, Miss Harris, but in an enquiry like this anything that sheds light on his movements before his death might be of value or significance. It's just routine, you know.'

'Very well,' she said, handing him the letter. 'It's not as though it's a love letter, is it? And even if it were, knowing what I know about Paul Ramsey now, if you didn't want it I'd probably burn it.'

'Sorry for interrupting like that, guv'nor,' said Cradock after he'd seen Gloria off the premises. 'It's just that it suddenly struck me—'

'I'd be disappointed if it hadn't struck you, Peter, but at the moment we're the only people who can make a connection between Paul's letter to Gloria and what was going on with those contracts. That could be critical information, and I saw no need to let Gloria in on it, no matter how charming she may be. That's why I didn't want you to go blurting it out.'

'Yes, of course, sir. So if we believe what Paul says in that letter, his meeting with Hampson wasn't about the school petty cash at all. It definitely looks like one of those men was lying, doesn't it?'

'Yes. And since one of them's dead, there's only one man we can put the question to. We need to have a word with Councillor Hampson before the day's out. Paul seems to have thought he was doing his public duty, but he may have just been signing his own death warrant.'

CHAPTER THIRTY-ONE

'So,' said Jago as he and Cradock took the short walk from West Ham police station to Queen Mary's Hospital, 'did you get down to the Prince of Wales with that photo last night?'

'Yes, sir. The landlord showed it round the staff and found one of his potmen who recognised Paul Ramsey and remembered seeing him sitting at a table with another man. I asked the potman to describe this other person, and he said he was a big fellow, heavily built, fair hair, the sort you wouldn't want to have to throw out of the pub without a couple of coppers to help you. It certainly sounded like Shaw.'

'And did you find out anything else?'

'Well, yes, actually there was something very interesting. The potman said he went past their table on his way back to the bar with some empty glasses, and he heard one of them saying something that surprised him.'

'Namely?'

'He said one of them said, "Stay away from her – and if you don't, I'll kill you."'

'And was he able to tell you which one said that?'

'Yes – it was Shaw. And apparently it sounded like he meant it.'

'I see. Well, on the basis of what we know so far, there's only one "her" Shaw could've been talking about, isn't there?'

'Yes. But people often say things like that without intending to actually do it, don't they?'

'That's true enough – you hear mothers threatening their children like that every day. But it sometimes means more when one man says it to another, especially when they don't get on – and even more especially when one of them gets murdered two days later.'

Jago and Cradock arrived at the hospital and made their way to the men's ward. The sister on duty emerged from her office at the entrance to the ward and barred their way with her considerable presence.

'Visiting time was yesterday,' she said. 'You'll have to come back on Sunday.'

Jago produced his warrant card for her inspection. She scrutinised it carefully before handing it back.

'Very well,' she said. 'You may enter, but mind you don't disturb the other patients.'

Jago entered the ward, followed by Cradock, but was immediately called back.

'I didn't say you could both go in. The rules have

changed – only one visitor to every patient. Air-raid precautions.'

'We're police officers, sister,' said Jago, 'investigating a serious case, and we have to speak to Mr Jones.'

The sister crossed her arms and looked him in the eye.

'In that case, Inspector, you may speak to him, but make it quick. I don't want any of the other patients to think this sets a precedent. Follow me.'

She marched them down the ward and stopped at the fifth bed on the left.

'Mr Jones,' she said, 'these gentlemen wish to speak to you. They are police officers.'

Jones was sitting up in his bed, smoking a cigarette, with an ashtray balanced on the sheet where he could reach it. He had his right arm in a sling, a bandage round his head and some bruising to his face. He watched as the sister walked back to her office, until she was out of earshot.

'Good morning, Officers,' he said brightly, blowing smoke towards the ceiling.

He extended a packet of cigarettes towards them with his free arm.

'Here,' he said, 'help yourselves. Nothing to do in here except have a smoke.'

'No, thank you,' said Jago. 'We shan't be here long. I understand a constable helped you to the hospital last night because he found you injured. Can you tell me what happened?'

'Yes, Officer.'

'Detective Inspector.'

A fleeting look of surprise crossed Jones's face, followed by a hint of wariness.

'Well,' he said, 'it's very kind of you to ask. As a matter of fact I was just coming out of the Blue Boar on Stratford High Street when some fellow came up and started haranguing me. That's what it was – haranguing.' He rolled the word round his lips as though it were a choice morsel of food. 'Next thing I know, he's setting about me, calling me every name under the sun and pulling me about as if I was some underling and he was the lord of the manor. Well, I thought, I'm going to have to teach this man a lesson in the noble art – where I come from, if you're not handy with your fists you don't last very long. But before I could get the measure of him he cheated – would you believe it? He swung a golf club at me and cracked me on the arm. It hurt like . . . well, you can imagine what it hurt like. The doctor here said it was broken. Anyway, I dropped to the floor, and he ran off before I could land a single punch on him. He wouldn't have gone off so jolly if I had, I can tell you.'

'Who was this man?'

'Oh, I don't know. Some Englishman, I expect. Tall, military moustache – looked like the sort of fellow who was used to giving orders. Probably thought he was a gentleman. But look – I don't want to press charges. He was probably just an escaped lunatic or something.'

'Tell me, Mr Jones, what do you do for a living?'

'Well, er, a little of this and a little of that – you know how it is.'

'Yes, I do. Would that include a little of the building trade?'

Jones drew back his head and fixed his gaze on Jago, as if weighing him up.

'Since you mention it, it would, yes – mostly doing the jobs no one else wants to do. I've dug a fair few holes in my time, I can tell you, but I'm getting a bit old for that now.'

'Have you worked for any local firms?'

'Yes.'

'Which ones?'

'Just one, really.'

'What's the name?'

'It's a fellow called Ramsey.'

'Where are his premises?'

'Er, down Gainsborough Road way.'

'I see. And do you still work for him?'

'No. He laid me off about a month ago. No skin off my nose, though – bit of a shifty character if you ask me. But I'm wondering why you're interested in him.'

'I'm interested in all sorts of people, Mr Jones.'

'Well, I'm always one to help the police if I can, you know. Maybe I could tell you something about him that might help you, if you know what I mean. For a small consideration?'

'Don't push your luck, Mr Jones. I've got a few more

questions for you before I decide anything like that. Just tell me what you know, and we'll see.'

'You're a hard man, Mr Detective Inspector, but I'll tell you, just to be helpful. It was just before Mr Ramsey laid me off. I was round the back of the office, and the window was open, and I could hear him inside, going at it hammer and tongs. He was talking to some other fellow, and he said, "You're messing with the wrong man. You've made your little pile and I've made mine, but I'm not prepared to let you back out now." Maybe not those precise words, but near enough. Then he said something like, "You make sure I get some more contracts, or I'll see to it that your political career comes to a stinking and miserable end." Well, that sounded interesting, so I pricked my ears up. Then the other fellow said something like, "Now look here, my good man," like as if he was in some kind of a huff, but old Joe just cut him off, said, "Shut up and do as I tell you" – or words to that effect, as they say. Quite ungentlemanly, he was.'

'Did you see the other man?'

'No, I didn't.'

'Did you hear a name?'

'I did, actually. Why, would that be of interest to you too?'

'It might be. Just tell me what you heard.'

'Mr Ramsey called him Hartson, or Hodgson, or . . . no, Hampson. That's what it was. He said, "You're messing with the wrong man, Hampson." There, is that helpful enough for you?'

'That'll do. Are you prepared to make a formal statement?'

'Of course, Superintendent.'

'Inspector.'

'Of course, Inspector, it'll be my pleasure. Is there anything else I can do for you?'

'Yes, there is. If I said I wanted an Anderson shelter installed in my back garden, would you be able to do that for me?'

Jones stubbed the remains of his cigarette out in the ashtray.

'Now what would a gentleman like you be doing, asking a poor ignorant fellow like me to do a job like that?' he said. 'That's technical, that is. Lots of measuring, assembling. You'd need a proper builder for that, I reckon. Not a job for the likes of me, sir.'

'Do you know a man called Hunter?'

Jones gazed at the ceiling as if deep in thought, then shook his head.

'No, I don't believe I do.'

'He says a man answering your description took five pounds from him and promised to build him a shelter – a promise which he did not keep.'

'Five pounds, you say? Why, that's a terrible shame. There's a lot of dishonest people about these days.'

'He says this transaction took place at a builder's yard in Gainsborough Road on a Saturday afternoon about three weeks ago.'

'Really?'

'And he says the man who took the money was Irish.'

'Well, would you believe it? I don't know whether that's true, Inspector, but if it is, I feel ashamed to think a countryman of mine could stoop so low. But look here, perhaps I can make a small gesture to help redeem the reputation of the honest Irishman. If you look in that jacket of mine you'll find my wallet. It just happens that I had a bit of luck on the horses up in Leicester the other day, and you'll find some crisp new English pound notes in it. I hate to see a man out of pocket, especially when someone's made a fool of him, and since your constable was so kind as to help me and bring me into this lovely hospital, I'd like you to take out five of those pound notes and give them to the poor man who was let down. I'd hate to think of this gentleman getting a bad impression of the building trade, or of the Irish too for that matter, and I wouldn't want him to think we're all like that – you can't judge a whole profession just because of one bad apple, can you? Give him that money and tell him it's a gift from an honest Irishman. But make it anonymous, won't you – I think public benefactors should always be anonymous.'

Jago thought for a moment – about Hunter, about the DDI, and about his own in-tray – and without a word removed five notes from Jones's wallet, ignoring the look of surprise on Cradock's face.

'I'll do that, Mr Jones,' he said. 'I'm sure Mr Hunter will be pleased to get his money back. And by the way

– since you've had a bad experience here, perhaps I could encourage you strongly to move out of this area at the earliest opportunity. Just make sure you leave a forwarding address. Do you understand me?'

Jones gave him a mock salute.

'Yes, Inspector. Very good advice, and most kind of you to be so concerned about my welfare. I was thinking about taking a little trip anyway. Some place where there's more racing than you have down here these days.'

'Come along, Peter,' said Jago.

The two men left the ward, leaving Jones smiling broadly as he lit another cigarette.

'Sir,' said Cradock as they went down the stairs.

'Yes?'

'What he said just now – about the five pounds, and the horses. You didn't believe him, did you?'

'Of course not.'

'So when he said he wanted to give the money to Mr Hunter as a public benefactor, was it all right for you just to take it like that?'

'Yes – I shall give it to Mr Hunter.'

'But shouldn't we be arresting Jones?'

'For what? False pretences? Tramlines, Peter. You haven't forgotten your *Police Code*, have you?'

'Of course not, sir. I remember copying it out over and over again when I was training, until I'd learnt it.'

'There you are then. So what did it say right at the front, in Lord Brampton's address to police constables on their duties?'

'You don't have to arrest someone just because someone else accuses them?'

'That's right. Hunter's accused him, but Brampton said you should exercise your discretion, having regard to the nature of the crime, the surrounding circumstances, and the condition and character of the accuser and the accused. So that's what I've done.'

'I see,' said Cradock. 'I think.'

CHAPTER THIRTY-TWO

'It's looking pretty clear then, isn't it, guv'nor?' said Cradock as they walked back to the station. 'I mean, Joe Ramsey and Councillor Hampson had cooked up some shady deal to do with building air-raid shelters, but then Joe had a drink too many and let the cat out of the bag, and his brother ended up reporting it to his councillor, unaware that his councillor was the very man Joe was conspiring with.'

'Yes, that's about it.'

'So when Paul went to see Hampson, it must have put the wind up our councillor – and brother Joe. They had to do something fast, or they'd both be ruined. That would give them both very good reason to keep Paul quiet – even to silence him for good. They both had a motive for murdering him, didn't they? Could it be a conspiracy to murder that we're looking at?'

'I think we need to see them – separately.'

'Who first, sir?'

'I think we should start with Joe, and do so immediately.'

When Joe Ramsey opened the door of his house in Godbold Road he already had his coat on and was holding his hat in his hand.

'Good morning, Inspector,' he said. 'You're lucky – I was just going out.'

'To work?' said Jago.

'Yes, I am, actually. Mind you, it's hardly worth it these days. I still have a couple of men at the yard to keep an eye on things, but there's so little work around there's not much for me to do down there – you can't get the materials, you see, and who's going to build anything round here when it might get bombed to smithereens as soon as it's finished?'

'I'm sorry to hear that, Mr Ramsey. I just wondered if you could help me with a small matter.'

'Of course – come in.'

Jago and Cradock entered the house and were shown into the living room.

'So what's it about?' asked Ramsey.

'It's to do with a man who I believe may have been employed by you until recently,' Jago replied.

'What's his name?'

'That I'm not entirely sure about, but he told me he was laid off by you a month ago – and he's Irish.'

'Ah, yes. That'll be O'Leary – Patrick O'Leary.'

'I see. He gave me a different name.'

'Would that be Jones?'

'Yes, it would. How did you know?'

'It's a little party trick of his. You'd think that made him English or Welsh, but I've heard him telling people before that his name's Jones, in a broad Irish accent. Seemed to think it was funny. Charming fellow, but a bit slippery – what you might call an artful dodger.'

'What was his job?'

'Mostly labouring, and I can always find someone to do a bit of that if I need it. The problem's with getting the skilled men – the government's taking all of them. They've even made it illegal for someone like me to advertise for bricklayers or carpenters, because it'll mess up their own recruitment. It's ridiculous, isn't it? Even if a customer wanted me to build them something, how am I supposed to run a business if I can't hire the men I need?'

'I'm afraid I can't offer you any advice on that, Mr Ramsey. But can you tell me whether your business premises are open on Saturdays?'

'They used to be, but not for the last couple of months – there's not enough work.'

'Thank you. And just one more question about Mr O'Leary, if you don't mind.'

'Fire away.'

'Did he have a key to your office?'

'No – but I did notice a while ago the spare key was missing. I wasn't too bothered, because I don't keep anything of value in the office. Do you think he might've taken it?'

'I can't say, Mr Ramsey. I just wondered. But thank you. Oh, and by the way, does the name Robert Hampson mean anything to you?'

'No, can't say it does.'

'Come, Mr Ramsey, you're a contractor for the council, aren't you?'

'Yes.'

'And you've been building air-raid shelters for them?'

'Yes, but that was a while ago.'

'But surely you haven't forgotten who Councillor Hampson is?'

'Oh, that Hampson. Yes, now you mention it, I remember – I'd forgotten.'

'Forgotten? I'm surprised you should've forgotten the man who pays your bills.'

'Yes, well, I can't remember everything. I just didn't connect the name when you mentioned it out of the blue like that.'

'So you do know him?'

'Yes, but only through business.'

'But you've done rather a lot of business with the council through him, haven't you?'

'I may have done at one time, but only because of this war. That's not my fault. Anyway, what are you getting at?'

'What I'm getting at is this, Mr Ramsey – unlawful practices with regard to the administration of public contracts.'

'What are you talking about?'

'Do you enjoy an occasional drink?'

'What? Now you've got me really confused. What's a drink got to do with anything?'

'I just wondered, because I understand you had a little drink with your brother not long ago. In fact you must've had more than one little drink, because your tongue got a bit loose and you said perhaps more than you should've done.'

'Hang on a minute – you've asked me a question and I've done my best to help you, and now you're throwing accusations at me as though I'm some kind of crook. What if I did have a drink with my brother – what's it got to do with you?'

'I also understand that once your tongue was loosened, you mentioned that you were operating a profitable arrangement with the council that was making you a lot of money on the side.'

'What? Who told you that?'

'Let's just say a little bird told me. And I have reason to think that arrangement involved Councillor Hampson, and that between the two of you, you were defrauding the council on a regular basis.'

'That's rubbish – it's a pack of lies.'

'Not according to the evidence we've collected, it isn't. You're in serious trouble.'

'Look, mister, I don't think this is very funny.'

'Oh, neither do I, Mr Ramsey, neither do I. In fact, I think nothing could be less funny than murder.'

'Murder? Are you mad?'

'Not at all – I'm just looking at the evidence. You were conspiring with Councillor Hampson in illegal activity, and it was your little secret. No one else knew – until you had a drink too many and told your brother. Then Paul started to stick his nose into other people's business – your business – and found out what was going on. So you decided he needed to be silenced – for good. Is that why he needed a gun – to protect himself against you? You murdered your brother, didn't you, Mr Ramsey?'

Ramsey jumped to his feet, a frantic expression on his face.

'No!' he shouted. 'I wouldn't kill my own brother.'

'But you told me yourself he had a vicious streak and made your life a misery. Perhaps you decided you'd had enough of that.'

'No, you've got it all wrong. That was years ago. I wouldn't murder him – you've got to believe me. That's the truth!'

Jago responded with an impassive stare, then spoke.

'Has Councillor Hampson ever visited your business premises?'

'No.'

'And that's the truth too?'

'What do you mean?'

'I mean we have a witness who says he overheard you on those premises having a discussion with Councillor Hampson. What's more, he's given us a statement.'

Jago took his notebook from his pocket and opened it.

'The witness told us this was a heated discussion, in the course of which you said to the councillor, "You're messing with the wrong man, Hampson. You've made your little pile and I've made mine, but I'm not prepared to let you back out now. You make sure I get some more contracts, or I'll see to it that your political career comes to a stinking and miserable end." What's the truth now, Mr Ramsey?'

Ramsey looked around the room like a cornered animal in search of a way out.

'Look, all right,' he said, 'I admit it. So I was making a little bit of extra money, and Hampson was in it too. Why shouldn't I? This war's ruined my regular business – no one's building houses any more. The only thing I've got to keep us going is the jobs I do for the council, so why shouldn't I add a bit of a mark-up to keep the firm afloat? But murder? No – that's never entered my head. That really is the truth, Inspector – so help me, that's the truth. You've got to believe me.'

He sat down in his chair, his hands shaking.

'I'll ask you again, where were you last Saturday evening to Sunday morning?' said Jago.

'In my Anderson shelter, of course, like I told you, trying to avoid being killed in that blasted air raid.'

'Can anyone vouch for that?'

'No, I was on my own. I'm not married, see – I prefer my freedom. I didn't see anyone from when the air-raid siren went off on Saturday evening to the all-clear on Sunday morning.'

'The all-clear siren sounded at a quarter past six on Sunday morning, yes?'

'If you say so. I don't recall exactly, but it must've been about then. I came out of the shelter a bit after that and saw my next-door neighbour coming out of his. We had a chat together over the fence for about ten minutes or so. He'll remember.'

'Thank you. So, you admit that you were colluding with Councillor Hampson and obtaining fraudulent sums of money from the council?'

Ramsey looked down into his lap. 'If you say so,' he mumbled.

'I do say so, Mr Ramsey. I do.'

Ramsey's shoulders slumped as he slowly nodded his head.

CHAPTER THIRTY-THREE

'And now for the other party in Joe Ramsey's cosy little business arrangement,' said Jago as he and Cradock headed for Balaam Street in the Riley. A phone call had established that Councillor Hampson was at home, and that they would be able to see him briefly before he went out for a lunch engagement.

'I don't see how he can deny it after what Joe Ramsey told us,' said Cradock. 'But I still can't quite work out how it ties in with Paul Ramsey's murder. What do you make of Joe's alibi for that, sir?'

'Well, he's got no one to confirm he was in his shelter overnight,' said Jago, 'but it's only where he was around the time of the murder that matters. If he was really chatting with his neighbour in Godbold Road at about half past six as he says, there wouldn't have been time for him to get over to that public shelter in Nottingham Avenue and kill his brother before the lad found the body. And in any case, would he have known which shelter Paul might be in if he wasn't at home?'

'I'll still check that alibi with his neighbour though, shall I, sir?'

'Yes, of course. It may prove he couldn't have been responsible for the murder, but I think we've got what we need from him for the other job.'

'You mean the Hampson business?'

'Yes. I don't think he'd have owned up that easily if the threat of a murder charge hadn't been staring him in the face, but it seems to have done the trick.'

'If it's conspiracy we'll have to get a warrant before we can arrest him, though, won't we?'

'That's right. And that means we'll need some more evidence for the magistrate, so we'll have to get a search warrant for his house and his business premises. That shouldn't be a problem.'

Jago parked the car outside Councillor Hampson's house in Balaam Street, a plain but substantial three-storey brick building that looked as though it dated from about the 1860s. Hampson himself opened the door and showed them into a large room at the front of the house. Jago was surprised to see a familiar face already there – a woman dressed in ARP uniform.

'I believe you said you'd met my wife, Detective Inspector,' said Hampson.

'That's correct,' said Jago. 'Good morning, Mrs Hampson.'

She responded with a slight nod of the head and a

brief smile which looked more formal than friendly. She was standing alone on the other side of the room from her husband and his visitors, and did not move to join them.

'Would you gentlemen like a pre-lunch drink?' said Hampson. 'A drop of sherry, perhaps? We only have British, I'm afraid, things being what they are – what they call "Amontillado style", whatever that's supposed to mean.'

'No, thank you, Mr Hampson,' said Jago.

'I'll have a gin and tonic, dear, if you don't mind,' said Maud, smiling sweetly at her husband.

Hampson glared at her but said nothing. He poured her a small measure of gin and added a little tonic water, then handed her the glass. She held her glass up and peered at it.

'Generous to a fault my husband is, Inspector. Now, you look rather surprised to see me here. You may have inferred from the address I gave you that I'm not residing here any more.'

'Yes,' Hampson interrupted, 'I told the inspector that you'd taken a flat to be closer to your ARP post.'

Maud continued as if he had not spoken.

'It's not a pleasure for me to visit this house, Inspector. It used to be my home, you know, but that was when I shared it with a man who I was not ashamed to acknowledge as my husband. My, how times have changed. The truth is, I only called in to pick up some old clothes – I'm getting through a lot of them these days, scrambling over bomb sites. That's about all this place is good for now – a repository for old rubbish that I don't really need any more.' She raised her glass in Hampson's direction. 'Plenty more fish in the sea, though. Cheers, darling.'

Hampson glared at her again.

'And what the devil do you mean by that?' he said. As he did so, he seemed to remember there were visitors present and cut himself short.

'You'll have to excuse my wife, Inspector. I'm afraid alcohol doesn't always agree with her. Don't you think you'd better go now, darling? I expect you have things to attend to at your ARP post. All those men for you to boss around.'

'Thank you for your concern, darling,' said Maud, 'but I wouldn't dream of it. I don't often see Metropolitan Police detectives turning up here wanting to talk to you. Perhaps they're going to arrest you for something. I really do feel I should stay – after all, I am your wife, aren't I?'

'I wonder,' said Hampson. 'But why should I care? You can stay or go – please yourself. It's all the same to me. What is it you want to know, Inspector?'

'You'll recall that you told us yesterday that a young man came to see you last Friday morning – Mr Paul Ramsey.'

'Yes.'

Out of the corner of his eye Jago thought he saw Maud look up at the mention of Paul Ramsey, but he wasn't sure. He turned away from her in order to focus his attention on her husband's reactions.

'He came to see you to talk about Mr Gilroy, and to tell you something irregular was going on. Is that correct?'

'Yes. My memory may be at fault, but as far as I recall that's what he said.'

'Did he talk to you about fraud involving building contracts for the council?'

'No – I don't know what you're talking about. Fraud?'

'Fraud that involved you, Mr Hampson. Is that correct?'

Jago became aware of a noise across the room. He looked round and saw that Maud Hampson seemed to be choking on her drink, spilling some of it on the carpet.

'Maud, please,' said Hampson. 'What's the matter with you, woman?'

'Nothing,' she replied. 'It's seeing a policeman questioning you about fraud – I wouldn't have missed it for the world. Pay no attention to me, Inspector. Do carry on.'

'As I was saying, Mr Hampson,' Jago continued, 'did Paul Ramsey talk to you about fraud concerning building contracts – fraud that involved you?'

'Certainly not,' said Hampson. 'How dare you make such a preposterous allegation?'

'We have evidence that Mr Ramsey actually came to talk to you about his brother's fraudulent dealings with the council, involving payments for air-raid shelter construction.'

'It's not true – the whole idea is ridiculous.'

'That's as may be, Mr Hampson, but I'm sure a man in your position would have no objection to coming down to the station to help us with our enquiries. Would you be so kind?'

'Well, er, no, I mean yes, I'll come, I'll come.'

'We'll go now, then, if you don't mind,' said Jago. 'And Mrs Hampson, I'd like to speak to you later this afternoon. Will you be at the ARP post?'

'I shall, Inspector,' she replied.

Hampson fetched his coat from the stand in the hall, and Cradock opened the front door. As he was about to step out onto the street Hampson turned back to look at his wife. She raised her glass to him from the living-room doorway.

'Don't worry about me,' she said. 'I'll let myself out. But I think I might have another little drink first.'

CHAPTER THIRTY-FOUR

'This is the interview room, Mr Hampson,' said Jago. 'We'd like to ask you a few questions about this business of the building contracts. Have you been in a police station interview room before?'

'Certainly not,' said Hampson.

'Well, let me just make it clear that you're not under arrest – you're here on a voluntary basis and you're free to go at any time.'

'What do you want to know?'

'I want to know what you can tell me about allegations that have been made concerning overpayments for the construction of public air-raid shelters.'

'I don't know anything about that.'

'The contractor involved is a Mr Joe Ramsey. Do you know him?'

'No.'

'We have a witness who says he heard you and Joe Ramsey having a conversation at Mr Ramsey's business premises.'

'Heard? I assume that means he didn't see me. He must have been mistaken.'

'But Joe Ramsey has also told us that he had some business dealings with you.'

Hampson's face went blank, his confidence gone.

'Oh,' he said.

'Mr Hampson, I must caution you that you are not obliged to say anything, but anything you say may be given in evidence. Do you understand?'

'Yes.'

'Mr Ramsey has suggested that you were involved in a money-making scheme with him, whereby he added what he called a "mark-up" to keep his firm afloat. This is a very serious matter – it's what English law calls a conspiracy to defraud.'

'I see,' said Hampson. He sat slumped on the hard police chair, his appearance changed in an instant. To Jago he looked like a deflated and defeated old man who knew his world had suddenly unravelled.

'All right, I don't deny it,' the councillor continued. 'But I didn't want to do it – Joe Ramsey forced me.'

'How did he force you?' said Jago.

'We had a deal, OK? It was just once, one contract. Yes, the price was a little bit higher than his original quote, and we agreed to split the difference fifty-fifty. I thought that was the end of it, but then once I'd signed off the first payment he threatened me. He said he'd expose me and claim I'd coerced him into doing it so that I could make some money on the side – said we'd both go down together, but he knew I had a lot more to lose than he did, what with my public office and the prospect of being the mayor one day.'

'But Joe Ramsey wasn't going to expose you, was he? He had too much to lose himself – the survival of his business depended on these contracts and payments you were fixing for him.'

Hampson hung his head in silence.

'And this is where his brother Paul enters the story, isn't it? Paul Ramsey was quite a different matter. He came to see you because he'd found out about a racket involving the council and he felt he had a public duty to report it.'

'All right – yes, that is what he came to see me about.'

'Unaware that his local councillor was in fact the man in the council who was running the racket. When you'd heard what he had to say, I'm wondering whether it might have suited you for Mr Paul Ramsey to suddenly disappear from the scene – in a way that meant he'd never be able to report you to the proper authorities.'

'But he's – he's the man who was murdered. Are you suggesting that I – that I killed him?'

'Where were you on Saturday evening and Sunday morning, Mr Hampson?'

Hampson looked up, like a man waking from a bad dream.

'If you think I was somewhere round here murdering Paul Ramsey you're very much mistaken. I was away for the weekend, in Croydon – there was an ARP conference for councillors from the London region. The regional commissioner was there.'

'Was your wife with you?'

'No – there was no need for her to go. She has her life and I have mine.'

'Indeed – you seem quite separate. I noticed when we were at your house earlier today that Mrs Hampson said, "I am your wife, aren't I?" and you replied, "I wonder." What did you mean by that?'

'Nothing in particular. I suppose I just meant I wish she acted more like it. She spends her time ordering those ARP men about, and I think she enjoys it. The fact is, I'm not at all sure she's faithful to me, and I think she's mocking me. For all I know she could've been gadding about the West End with some fancy man the whole time I was away, while I was working hard to serve and protect the public at that conference.'

'Were you there for the whole weekend?'

'Yes, I went on Friday and came back Sunday morning.'

'And can anyone vouch for the fact that you were on the premises the entire time?'

'The entire time? Well, no, not when I was sleeping. Do you expect me to have a witness for that?'

'I shall need some names from you, Mr Hampson – people who can confirm your movements over that weekend. Let's start with what you did on Saturday evening.'

'That's easy. Saturday evening we had a dinner, so

there would be about sixty witnesses who could vouch for the fact that I was there.'

'And after dinner?'

'I was discussing some strategic issues with my colleagues.'

'Where was that?'

'Er, that was in the bar. We were there for some time, and then I went to bed.'

'At what time?'

'I went back to my room at ten-thirty.'

'When the bar closed?'

'Well, yes, actually.'

'And the next morning?'

'I had breakfast with my counterpart from the London Borough of Stepney.'

'I'd be obliged if you could give me the names of all these people.'

Hampson reeled off a number of names and details, and Cradock wrote them in his notebook.

'And then?'

'Well, then I came home. I caught the first train from Croydon – East Croydon, that is – back to London. Then I got the District Line back here. I'm afraid I didn't note the exact time I got home – I wasn't aware that I'd have to account for my movements to the Metropolitan Police.'

'On this occasion you do, Mr Hampson. And I shall be speaking to you further concerning the payment arrangements you made with Mr Joe Ramsey.'

'So what happens now?'

'I'm placing you under arrest.'

'You're going to lock me up?'

'No. We shall be releasing you on bail to appear here in five days' time unless you receive notice from us that your attendance is not required. In the meantime we shall be continuing our enquiries, and I think you may assume that your attendance will be required.'

CHAPTER THIRTY-FIVE

Having left Hampson at the station to be bailed by the duty inspector, Jago and Cradock drove straight to the ARP post at Custom House School. As before, they found Maud Hampson in the small building in the corner of the former playground. She had a stirrup pump on the desk and appeared to be trying to mend it. She looked up when they came in, and put it to one side.

'Hello again, Inspector Jago, Constable Cradock. Would you like a cup of tea? I've just made a pot.'

'That would be very nice, thank you,' said Jago.

'And something to eat? We have some rock cakes here that I bought this morning.'

'Yes, please,' said Cradock, glancing at Jago in case he'd spoken out of turn.

'That would be most kind too, Mrs Hampson,' said Jago. 'We haven't had any lunch yet, and Detective Constable Cradock is probably starving.'

'Here you are, then.'

She found a couple of plates, put a rock cake on each, and poured a cup of tea for both men, then herself.

'I'm sorry I can't offer you something stronger, gentlemen – we don't have anything suitable to hand right now.'

'Not while we're on duty, thank you.'

'Quite. It's the same for me. My husband may have given you the impression that I'm overly partial to alcoholic beverages, but it's not true – I never drink on duty, although I may have a little nip before I start my shift, just to keep me warm.'

'Don't worry, Mrs Hampson, we haven't come here to quiz you on your drinking habits. I would like a little chat with you, though.'

'By all means, Inspector. Be my guest – literally and metaphorically.'

'Thank you. It's quite cosy in here, isn't it? I understand from your husband that you were promoted to post warden only recently. That must mean a lot more responsibility.'

'Oh, yes. Never a dull moment, you know. We're certainly earning our wages at the moment.'

'I'm sure you're not doing this work just _for_ the money, though.'

She laughed.

'Very perceptive of you, Inspector. Do you know how much an air-raid warden gets paid for risking their life and sanity on a nightly basis?'

'Three pounds a week, isn't it?'

She laughed again, but this time it sounded more forced.

'You've been talking to the men, Inspector, but as you may have noticed, I'm a woman. When the war started, the government decided to pay full-time air-raid wardens who happened to be men three pounds a week, but if they had the misfortune to be women it was only two. This summer they were kind enough to give us a rise, but they stuck to their principles – five shillings for the men but only three and six for the women. On top of that, you may be surprised to learn that being promoted to post warden doesn't mean I get any more money, despite the additional responsibilities. Put all that together and you'll see that I'm still paid one pound one and six a week less than the men I'm in charge of.'

'I'm sorry to hear that.'

'Thank you for your sympathy, but it's a scandal, isn't it? Why should a woman who risks her life in her job get paid less than a man doing the same work? It's about time something changed, don't you think?'

'That's not for me to say, but isn't that sort of thing changing? I saw something in the paper about one of the unions telling the government to give equal pay to women – women workers in the munitions factories, I think.'

'Yes, it was the engineering union. There's plenty of unions that won't lift a finger, though. Did you hear about what happened with the teachers' unions?'

'No.'

'Only last year we had one of them demanding equal pay for women, and another that represented the same profession rejecting it. And you know why?'

'No, I'm afraid I don't.'

'They said it would mean a lower standard of living for men teachers, because they'd have to support their wives and children on the same salary, and the women teachers wouldn't. I ask you – and they're the people teaching the next generation. Some of those unions are as bad as the politicians if you ask me – and I don't trust politicians further than I could throw them.'

'Not even your husband?'

'Especially him. Do you know what West Ham Council was doing while the engineering union was lobbying the government?'

'I can't say I do.'

'They were protesting to the government for cutting the expenses they used to be able to claim for hiring cars and eating and drinking in the course of their so-called public duties in the borough. It was in the newspapers. And that's a Labour council! Shoot the lot of them, that's what I say.'

'So you're not entirely supportive of your husband in his public service?'

'Public service? You listen to me, Inspector – those words stick in my throat. My husband told you why I'm not sharing the same roof with him, didn't he?'

'Yes, he said you were renting a flat so you could be closer to your ARP post.'

'Well, there's a politician for you. Their idea of the truth is always flexible, isn't it? Look, I'll tell you why I moved out. It's because while I'm watching men sift body parts from wreckage and seeing people lose everything they've got in one blink of an eye, he's still more concerned about feathering his own nest. He's one of those men who know what they like and who get what they want, and that's all that matters in their life. That's the trouble with you men – once you get what you want, you don't value it. It's why women suffer – you get what you want from us, use us up, and move on. You're all the same, and politicians are the worst of all.'

'Some would argue we still need politicians, though, even in wartime.'

'Only if they're useful. Don't you understand? Every night I'm trying to help people who've been bombed out of their miserable little houses that the council did nothing to improve, people who've got no adequate shelter to protect them during the bombing because in the years when everyone knew war was coming my husband and his pals on the council did nothing to put air-raid precautions in place. That may sound a bit harsh to you, but when I see that, I feel ashamed. With all this hell going on I feel I've nothing in common with him any more.'

Cradock, having polished off the last crumb of rock cake from his plate, suddenly broke into the conversation.

'So did you leave him because you'd found another man you had more in common with?'

Maud Hampson cast a look of astonishment in Jago's direction and slammed her empty teacup down onto its saucer.

'What an outrageous question! A temporary separation from my husband does not make me an adulteress.'

'Of course, Mrs Hampson,' said Jago. 'But in an investigation like this we often have to ask personal questions. All you need to do is answer it.'

'In that case the answer is no, certainly not – I have not left my husband for another man. I left him and my home – my home, Inspector – because I don't like him any more, and I don't like the things he's done. As far as I'm concerned, I don't care how much money he has in his pocket, he's got blood on his hands. I think instead of asking me impertinent questions you should take a look at his bank account.'

'As a matter of fact we have been talking to your husband about some irregularities in the council's accounts.'

'You mean he's been on the fiddle?'

'He hasn't been charged with any offence, but he's been helping us with our enquiries into some suspected fraudulent activities.'

'There you are then – I knew it. You can put him behind bars for all I care. But he'll drag my name through the mud too, the selfish pig – you mark my words. He has no concern for anything or anyone but himself.'

She paused for breath. Jago caught her eyes and saw a

pain and stress that reminded him of the faces of soldiers he'd known under bombardment in the trenches. It was time to move her off this subject.

'You mentioned the teachers' unions just now,' he said. 'Do you have a special interest in teachers?'

'What an extraordinary question. No, I don't. It's just that my husband's been on the board of management for a couple of schools in the borough for years, so I know a little about how they're treated, especially the women, and when I see something about teachers in the papers I read it.'

'Were you aware that the young man who was killed in that street shelter was a teacher?'

Her face registered shock, and a moment passed before she spoke.

'No, I didn't. Oh my goodness – a teacher? But that's . . . it's dreadful. I had no idea.'

'So you didn't know Paul Ramsey?'

'Is that the person you were talking to my husband about?'

'Yes. I had the impression when we were with your husband that you perhaps recognised his name when I mentioned it.'

She shook her head slowly.

'No, I don't think I know him. Is he the—'

'Yes, he's the man who was found dead in that shelter.'

'The poor dear man – and so young. What a waste.'

'What made you think he was young, Mrs Hampson? You were too far away to see him clearly when you looked in from the shelter entrance on Sunday morning, and you said you hadn't visited it during the night.'

'Yes, yes, that's right – it was just that you referred to him as a young man when you were talking to my husband, if I'm not mistaken.'

'I see – perhaps I did. But tell me – you're an ARP warden. Aren't you supposed to know everyone who lives in your area? I believe he was one of those people.'

'I'm afraid you're mistaken, Inspector. An ordinary warden working on a sector has to know who lives in every house and where they usually sleep, but I'm a post warden now, and as I told you, that means I cover an area of about two thousand people, so I can't possibly know everyone who lives in it. And in any case, you've never told me where he lived. What was his address?'

'47 Tree Road. That's within the area covered by your new job, isn't it?'

'Yes.'

'So who's responsible for the sector including that address? I'd like to speak to whoever it is to see if they can tell me anything relevant about Mr Ramsey.'

She took a notebook from her pocket and turned a few pages.

'Here we are – Tree Road. Yes, the warden covering that street is Mr Draper – Mr George Draper.'

Jago saw that Cradock looked surprised and was about to open his mouth, but on seeing Jago's warning glance he closed it again.

'Thank you,' said Jago. 'Can you tell me Mr Draper's address?'

'Not off the top of my head, but I should have it in here somewhere.'

She flipped through some pages at the back of her notebook.

'Here it is. I'll write it down for you, and his work address – there doesn't seem to be a telephone number.'

She wrote the information on a scrap of paper and passed it to Jago.

'Do you happen to know whether this Mr Draper has a son?'

'A son? No, I'm afraid I don't, Inspector – Mr Draper hasn't been a warden for very long. I believe he's some sort of labourer and has a wife, but I don't know about any children. I'm sure you'll understand if I say he's not the sort of person I'd have met socially.'

'Are teachers the kind of people you meet socially?'

'Yes, of course – some teachers.'

'But not Paul Ramsey.'

'No, as I've said – and now it's too late. But a teacher – who would want to murder a teacher?'

'That's what I'm going to find out, Mrs Hampson.'

CHAPTER THIRTY-SIX

Cradock clutched the address Maud Hampson had given them as they neared George Draper's place of work.

'Gainsborough Road,' he said. 'That's where Joe Ramsey has his yard, isn't it? Where that Jones fellow took Mr Hunter. We're looking for number 73.'

Jago drove past Godbold Road and took the next turning on the right, Gainsborough Road.

'There it is,' said Cradock, pointing down the street, '73. And there's a sign – P. K. Ramsey and Son. So Draper works for Joe Ramsey?'

'Looks like it. And if he does, he might have something to tell us about both brothers.'

Jago turned the car into the entrance to the builder's yard and stopped next to a parked Austin truck. It was covered in dust and didn't look as if it had moved for a while. The yard was deserted. He and Cradock got out and knocked on the door of a small office. A man in a boiler suit opened it.

'I'm looking for Mr Draper,' said Jago. 'Can you tell me where I can find him?'

'Yes, mate – he'll be over there, in the stores.'

Jago and Cradock crossed the yard and found the entrance to the stores. Jago knocked on the door, and it was soon opened by a middle-aged man wearing a brown twill warehouse coat.

'Yes?' said the man.

'Mr Draper?'

'Yes. Who's asking?'

'I'm Detective Inspector Jago and this is Detective Constable Cradock. We'd like to ask you one or two questions in your capacity as an air-raid warden.'

'That's fine by me. Things are a bit slack here at the moment, but I get paid for the hours I put in, so I'm not going to be sloping off early.'

'Have you worked here for long?'

'Best part of fifteen years – been in the building trade all my life. Started out as a labourer when I was a lad, with hopes of something better, but then the war came along.' He gave a sidelong glance at Jago. 'You look of an age to have been in it too. Were you?'

'Yes, two years in France.'

'Ah, you know what it was like, then, pal. It put paid to any hopes I had of making a life for myself, and I was one of the lucky ones.'

'Because you got through it?'

'Yes. I was at Neuve Chapelle, 1915.'

Jago recognised the bond he always felt with men

who'd served at the front in the Great War, even when they were strangers. He turned to Cradock.

'Does that mean anything to you, Peter?'

Cradock looked blank.

'Er, well, er – it was during the war.'

Draper gave Jago a look that signified resignation and which Jago took to be lamenting the ignorance of the younger generation.

'At the going down of the sun and in the morning, we will remember them,' said Draper. 'That's what they say, isn't it? How soon we forget.'

Jago nodded silently.

'Neuve Chapelle, young man,' said Draper to Cradock, 'was a battle – where we had eleven thousand casualties for pretty much nothing. I hope you never have to go through anything like it.' He turned back to Jago. 'I managed to come out of that alive, then somehow I got through the next two years without getting my head blown off. I copped a Blighty wound in 1917, and that got me out of it, but when I came home my nerves were shot to pieces and I had a gammy leg.'

'It wasn't easy to get work if you were wounded, was it?'

'Too true. They said we were going home to a land fit for heroes, but all I got was the dole. I was unemployed for a while, then in and out of jobs. Seemed I couldn't hold anything down for long. Then Mr Ramsey – that's the present Mr Ramsey's dad, the one whose name's on the sign outside – gave me a job here, minding the stores, and he kept me on even during the Depression. I've never earned a lot, but it's been enough to get by on. Three years ago old Mr Ramsey died, but young Joe took over and kept me on – said he'd make sure there was always work for me. I owe everything to that man, and his father before him. These are hard times, though – I only hope him not being here today doesn't mean the whole firm's up the creek.'

'Hard times?'

'Yes, same as for most other businesses – the war's hit us bad. We used to do a lot of houses, but that's all stopped now. The government's still building all sorts of things, but from what I hear the contracts go to big firms, not small ones like this. I think Mr Ramsey did well out of building public air-raid shelters, but that work's mostly dried up. Now we seem to rely mostly on odd jobs we pick up from the council.'

'So the business is quite dependent on council orders?'

'Oh, yes, without a doubt. Fortunately, though, Mr Ramsey's been very good at getting work from the council – but who knows for how long, what with the way things are? That's anyone's guess, isn't it? But anyway, what's all that got to do with me being an air-raid warden? I thought you said that's what you wanted to ask me about.'

'I understand you're a volunteer warden – is that right?'

'Yes. What of it?'

'And your post warden is Mrs Maud Hampson?'

'Yes.'

'She told us you were the warden responsible for Tree Road.'

'That's right – along with a few other streets.'

'One of the residents of that street was Mr Paul Ramsey. That's why I've come today – to see if you can tell me anything about him.'

'He was my Mr Ramsey's brother, but I expect you already know that. I heard he copped it on Sunday morning.'

'Did you know him?'

Draper looked thoughtful for a few moments.

'Yes, I suppose I did. Not well, mark you, but I'm a warden on the sector where he lived, and it's my job to know everyone who lives there. Each house has to tell us how many people they've got living there and where they sleep, and they're supposed to let us know if they're going to be away, so that if it gets hit we can check our records and see if there's anyone likely to be a casualty or trapped inside – otherwise we'd end up digging all night trying to find someone who isn't there. Not that they always remember to tell us, of course. Anyway, I don't think he'd been there for long – if I'm not mistaken, he only moved into Tree Road about six weeks ago.'

'Did he use the street shelter regularly?'

'I think so – there was no Anderson shelter where he lived, you see, so he'd have had to.'

'Would it be easy for someone to find out where he sheltered?'

'I reckon it would, yes. Most local people who use these shelters tend to go to the same one every night, so they'd probably get to know the other people using it.'

'Did you ever see him here at the yard?'

'Once in a while over the years, but hardly ever, really. He's never had anything to do with the business, and from what I could tell he and my Mr Ramsey weren't particularly close. He may've been the boss's brother, but that doesn't mean I knew much about him.'

'Did Mrs Hampson know him?'

'I couldn't say, but she's the sort that would, if you know what I mean.'

'No, I don't – what do you mean?'

'Friendly with the men – always chatty with them, in that way some women have. Not quite what you'd expect of a married woman – especially if her husband's something high up in the council, which is what I've been told. Why are you asking?'

'I just wondered whether you'd ever seen them together.'

'Can't remember – I've seen her with lots of men.'

'Thank you, Mr Draper. By the way, do you have a son?'

'Yes, I do, since you're asking. Just the one – young Jimmy.'

'I understand it was he who found Mr Paul Ramsey's body in the shelter in Nottingham Avenue on Sunday morning.'

'That's right.'

'How is he? It must have been a shock for him.'

'Yes, I think it was. Of course, he didn't know it was Paul Ramsey at the time – he'd never met the man. It's still upsetting, though, isn't it – finding a dead body at his age? His mother was quite worried about him. But I think something else had happened too, something that'd got him on edge.'

'What was that?'

'I don't know. I think he saw someone he didn't want to see – someone from his old school, I think he said. The truth is, he hasn't been very regular about going to school of late, and he's worried about being found out. I keep telling him he ought to get as much schooling as he can while it's free, otherwise he'll end up in a dead-end job like me. You can't get anywhere in life without education, can you?'

'That's true enough.'

'Look, Inspector, you're a man who's got on. If it's not too much trouble, I'd be grateful if you'd have a word with him yourself – not too strong, of course, just encourage him, like. That might persuade him to go back to school.'

'Of course. But can you just tell me where he saw this person?'

'It was down near that shelter, not long before he came across the body, I believe. You'd have to ask him yourself. He'll be out now, but he should be at home tomorrow with his mother if you fancied dropping in.'

'Thank you, Mr Draper. I think I shall.'

CHAPTER THIRTY-SEVEN

By Friday Jago was feeling tired. With no day off the previous Sunday, he was losing count of how many days he'd worked without a break. Cradock looked as bright as a button, but then he lived in the section house, and although Jago wouldn't wish that on anyone, it did mean the young unmarried officers whose home it was could more or less roll out of bed and be at work. To his credit, Cradock had already made a fresh pot of tea, and as soon as Jago closed the door behind him and hung up his coat and hat he found a steaming mug waiting for him on his desk.

'Thank you, Peter,' he said. 'Have you got anywhere with those alibis Hampson and Joe Ramsey gave us?'

'Yes, sir,' said Cradock, scrambling for his pocketbook. 'I've spoken to Ramsey's neighbour, and he backs up what Ramsey said, although he wasn't too sure about the times.'

'And Hampson?'

'Yes, sir. I've made a few phone calls.'

'And?'

'I've got people who say they saw him at dinner on the Saturday evening, in the bar afterwards and at breakfast the next morning. I've also checked the train times. On Sundays the first train leaves East Croydon at half past seven in the morning and gets into Victoria at a quarter to eight. Then he'd have had to get from Victoria to here on the District Line, so he probably wasn't home till getting on for nine o'clock. Even if he'd come by car instead of train, he couldn't have got here in time – if he was at breakfast when the witness says he was, he was still eating his eggs when the body was found.'

'Right. It looks like that lets him off the hook for the murder, then.'

'Yes and no, sir. There were plenty of people ready to swear they saw him on Saturday evening, but he only gave us one name for breakfast.'

'The Stepney man.'

'Yes, another councillor doing the same kind of work as him in a neighbouring borough. It just occurs to me that they might've been old mates, and Hampson could've asked him for a favour or something – I mean, we know he's a crook, don't we?'

'He's not convicted yet, but he hasn't denied it. We still need to get search warrants for his home and whichever bits of the town hall offices might throw up some relevant evidence.'

'Yes, I'll get onto that. But you see my point, sir, don't you? Councillor Hampson might've fixed himself up with a convenient alibi for breakfast and then come back here during the night – using someone's car, for example.'

'It's possible, I suppose.'

'And the same goes for Joe Ramsey – I mean, it's very convenient that he just happened to bump into his neighbour at a quarter past six or whatever on a Sunday morning, isn't it?'

'You're suggesting Ramsey and Hampson could've been in it together?'

'Well, we know they were conspiring on the fraud, so why not conspire to murder too? They both stood to lose if Paul exposed their little racket.'

'Enough to murder, though? I'm not sure.'

'Yes, I see what you mean.'

Cradock was silent for a few moments, looking thoughtful, then he gave a short chuckle.

'And that stuff Mrs Hampson came out with was a bit rich too, wasn't it?'

'What "stuff" are you referring to?'

'What she said about her husband, and about her leaving him.'

'I see. Yes, it was quite striking, although I thought your question was rather precipitate.'

'Rather what, sir?'

'Precipitate – it means sudden, as if you hadn't given it careful consideration before you came out with it. Asking her out of the blue whether she'd left him because she'd found another man.'

'Sorry, sir.'

'Don't worry – it served its purpose.'

'Thank you, sir. And I was wondering, why did you ask her whether she knew Paul Ramsey?'

'It was because of something Gloria said – do you remember? When she told us she'd broken up with Paul. I mentioned that business about Paul being preoccupied, and she said she even wondered whether he'd found another woman. She didn't seem to take the idea too seriously, but if it did turn out to be true, I just wondered whether that woman could possibly have been Maud Hampson.'

'Yes. I wasn't entirely convinced when Maud said she didn't know him, and her husband did say he thought she might've been gadding about with some fancy man while he was away at his conference, didn't he? I reckon he was right, you know – and that fancy man she was gadding about with was Paul Ramsey.'

'It's an interesting possibility,' said Jago, 'and you may be right – but where's the evidence?'

Lunch with Cradock in the station canteen was the usual substantial affair, and Jago was beginning to wonder whether jam roly-poly pudding with custard was a wise choice after all if he hoped to stay awake in the afternoon. Cradock, however, seemed undaunted by the challenge.

'Just what the doctor ordered, eh, sir?' he said, tucking into his dessert.

'A doctor who didn't want his patients to run off without paying, perhaps,' said Jago. 'I'm not sure I'll be much good for running if I finish this.'

'I'll finish it for you if you like, sir – they say you burn it up faster when you're young.'

Cradock realised what he'd said too late – the words had spilled out of his mouth as quickly as the pudding was being shovelled in. He hastened to change the subject.

'That lad, sir, young Jimmy Draper – are we going to see him this afternoon?'

'Yes. As soon as you've finished, we'll go.'

Fifteen minutes later they were on their way to the Drapers' flat. When they arrived, it was Betty Draper who opened the door. She was wearing a pink cotton pinny and a dark green headscarf from which her lank hair was escaping. She was holding a cloth, which she stuffed into the pocket on her pinny when she saw she had visitors. Jago noticed that she was glancing over his shoulder, as if she were on the lookout for someone. She seemed uncertain what to say to him.

'Hello,' she said at last. She pushed a stray length of hair back under her headscarf and stared at him anxiously.

'Mrs Draper?' he said in his most reassuring voice.

'Yes.'

'I'm Detective Inspector Jago and this is Detective

Constable Cradock, from West Ham CID. May we come in?'

'Er, yes, of course. Please excuse the mess. There's never any end to dusting, is there?'

She took them into a small room with sombre-looking furniture and wiped a fine layer of dust from a couple of Rexine-covered armchairs.

'Do have a seat, Inspector.'

'Thank you.'

'How can I help you?'

'It's your son Jimmy I want to speak to. Is he about?'

'Jimmy? He's not in any trouble, is he? He's a good boy, you know, always looks after his poor mum.'

'No, he's not in any trouble. It's just to do with something your husband mentioned to us yesterday.'

'Oh, right, I'll go and fetch him then. Just wait here, will you?'

She scurried out of the room. They heard her calling to her son, and then the stomp of boots as he returned with her.

'These gentlemen are from the police, Jimmy. They want to ask you about something.'

'Hello,' said Jimmy, shifting from one foot to the other. 'What's that, then?'

'It's nothing to worry about,' said Jago. 'We just want to ask you about Sunday morning, when you found that unfortunate man dead in the air-raid shelter. We happened to be talking to your father yesterday, and he told us you'd seen something or someone that worried you.'

344

'Me? No,' the boy began, his face anxious.

'It's all right, Jimmy, we haven't come to get you into trouble. We're here because a man's been murdered, and if you know about anything that was happening at the time it might be important.'

'Right. Have you found out who did it?'

'No, not yet, but we will.'

'Who was he? The man who was killed, I mean.'

'He was a teacher – he was called Mr Ramsey.'

'Which school?'

'Prince Regent Lane. Why? Did you know him?'

'No, not my school – I told you before, I went to Custom House School in Russell Road. Mr Gilroy was the headmaster. He was nice.'

Jago realised Gilroy had never mentioned the name of his previous school, and he had never asked him.

'Mr Jeremy Gilroy?' he said.

'S'pose so,' said Jimmy. 'He was always just Mr Gilroy to me. Anyway, I told you before, the school got closed down when the war started, and I suppose I got out of the habit of going.'

'But some of the schools round here opened up again in January, didn't they? Couldn't you have gone back?'

'Well, maybe, but I couldn't be bothered. Like I said, I'll be starting work on the market soon, so there's not much point going back to school.'

'Did you know the law says you can't be employed in street trading until you're sixteen?'

'No. Are you sure?'

'I'm afraid it's true. And if you don't stay at school until you're fourteen the local education authority can take out a school attendance order to make you go. So I think it'd be a good idea if you thought about going back. There's a new emergency school in Prince Regent Lane, and Mr Gilroy's the headmaster there, so if you like him you might like the school too. Think about it.'

'Maybe,' said Jimmy. 'We'll see.'

He moved towards the door as if intending to leave, but paused and turned back.

'Actually, that was what I was worried about.'

'What was?'

'It was seeing him that morning – Sunday.'

'Seeing the body?'

'No, seeing Mr Gilroy. I wasn't expecting to, but suddenly there he was.'

'And why were you worried? Did you think he'd report you?'

'No – I mean I don't think he even saw me, and it was on Sunday morning, so he wasn't going to think I was missing school. Besides, he's a nice man, like I said. He was strict, but he was always fair – I liked him. I nearly went over to say hello, but then I thought he might still ask me something about school, so it probably wouldn't be a good idea. No, it was the way the lady with him looked at me. That's what got me worried.'

'The lady?'

'Yes. You know how you can tell from someone's eyes

that they're looking at you? She looked straight at me, and she looked cross, just like the other time, like she knew I'd done something wrong.'

'The other time?'

'Yes, when I found that bloke dead – she gave me the same look then. I don't think she liked me.'

'Who was this lady?'

'The warden – you know, the lady you spoke to that morning, the one with the white helmet. At least, I think it was her – they all look a bit the same, don't they? But most of them wear black helmets – there's not so many with white. I don't know her name, but she was looking daggers at me.'

'And she was with Mr Gilroy?'

'Yes, they were standing quite close – it looked like he was giving her a hug or something. Then she stepped back a bit and looked over in my direction. I didn't like the look on her face, so I ducked back round the corner.'

'And this was after you found the body in the shelter?'

'Yes, after . . . when I was going home.'

'And where did you see them?'

'In Ilkley Road, not far from that shelter. Why? Is it important?'

'No – I'm just interested. I've no more questions – you've been very helpful.'

'Can I go now?'

'Yes, but listen – you're a bright young lad. You help

your mum, and that's good, but you might be even more help to her if you finish your schooling. Just think it over before the chance isn't there any more.'

'All right,' said Jimmy, 'I'll think about it.'

CHAPTER THIRTY-EIGHT

'Still here, Frank?' said Jago on their return to the station.

'My home from home, this is, sir,' said Tompkins, aiming a conspiratorial wink in Cradock's direction. 'Looking forward to putting my feet up, though.'

'Me too. I'm planning to do just that this evening – relax in the company of Mr Johnnie Walker and a glass of his twilight nectar, and remember the good old days before this war started and you could still get a bottle for twelve and six.'

'A bit more work for you to do first, though – you've just missed Mrs Hampson.'

'She was here?'

'No, she phoned. She sounded a bit anxious, said she had to speak to you. It was only a couple of minutes ago. I said I'd tell you as soon as you got back. Here's her number.'

He passed a slip of paper to Jago, who took the phone and dialled her number, inwardly urging the dial to move faster, although he knew it could not. He heard only one ring before Mrs Hampson answered.

'Mrs Hampson? It's Jago here.'

'Oh, thank goodness you've called, Inspector. I'm terribly worried.'

'Tell me what's happened.'

'I shall. I must be quick, though – I'm on duty at the ARP post in twenty minutes' time. The thing is, this afternoon I went back to my house – I mean the one my husband still lives in but I don't – to look for an old pair of shoes. My husband was out, but a man turned up, banging loudly on the front door. He said he was looking for him – my husband, that is. He was shouting.'

'What time was this?'

'I'm not sure. It must have been after four, but I can't be precise.'

'Did he say why he wanted your husband?'

'No – at least not clearly enough for me to be able to tell you. He was angry and aggressive, positively rude. I think he must have been drinking, even though it was a bit early for that. All I could make out was something like he'd been swindled, and they weren't going to get away with it. I said my husband was out, and he demanded to know where, but of course I didn't know where he was and said so. Then he started shouting again, saying I was just covering up for my husband, and that they were all in it together. I said I didn't know what he was talking about, and he said, "It's a damned conspiracy – they've deliberately passed me over, him and that headmaster together." I said, "What headmaster? What are you talking about?" and he gave me a nasty look and said, "You know who I'm talking about – your husband's pal, Gilroy." Then I realised – that must be Mr Gilroy who's the head of the school my husband's chairman of. I was worried – he was getting very threatening. I told him to calm down.'

'And?'

'He didn't. He called me all sorts of names, then kicked the door and said something like, "Tell your husband I want to see him – he can't hide for ever." He said if my husband wanted to find him, he'd be at the school, then he shouted at me again. He said, "I'm going to give Gilroy a dose of what I'll give your husband when I get my hands on him." Inspector, I'm worried he's gone to hurt Mr Gilroy – please do something!'

'Did this man say who he was?'

'No, but of course I asked him. He said his name was Shaw – Harold Shaw.'

CHAPTER THIRTY-NINE

Cradock held on to the dashboard and twisted round to face Jago, shouting over the noise of the engine.

'Do you think Gilroy's really in danger? She might've been reading more into what Shaw said than he meant, mightn't she?'

'You could be right,' said Jago, swinging the car tightly round a hole in the road, 'but from what we know of Shaw, we can't afford to take the chance. Morton said Shaw went for him when he found out he was seeing Gloria, and don't forget what your potman at the Prince of Wales said he'd heard Shaw saying to Paul Ramsey.'

'You think that was more than just a threat, then?'

'What do you think?'

'I'm not sure – depends whether his bark's worse than his bite. He's got a violent streak, though – no doubt about that.'

'And then there's the business of the suitcase,' said Jago, his eyes fixed on the road ahead.

'Yes, maybe what Shaw said at the pub was enough to make Paul decide to run for it – he just didn't get away in time. Maybe Shaw wanted him out of the picture one way or another, because then he'd get the two things he reckoned Paul had stolen from him – the job and Gloria.'

'He wasn't guaranteed to get either of them.'

'No, but when a man gets carried away like that he doesn't necessarily think it all through before he acts, does he?'

Jago yanked the wheel down without answering and turned into Prince Regent Lane. Two minutes later he pulled up with a squeal of brakes outside the entrance to the school.

'Come on!' he shouted as he jumped from the car and ran towards the front door.

He pushed it open and went in, followed closely by Cradock. The building seemed deserted. He glanced at his watch – a quarter to five. All the children would be gone by now, and possibly most of the staff. He started down a corridor, his shoes cracking like shots on the flagstones as he ran. A man came out of a classroom, his arms full of books.

'Hey!' Jago shouted. 'Police. Where can I find Mr Gilroy?'

The man swivelled round, extricated one hand from under the books and pointed down the corridor.

'In his study. It's down there, stairs on the—'

'Thanks – we know the way,' Jago shouted back.

The man jumped back as the two detectives thundered

past. They took the stairs two at a time, found the study and crashed the door open.

On the far side of the room they glimpsed Gilroy near the wall, and a foot or so in front of him a man they could only see from behind. Gilroy was staring at them over the man's shoulder, his eyes wide with fear. As the door banged against the cupboard behind it, the man looked back – it was Shaw.

He stepped to one side, and Gilroy stumbled against a bookcase. Cradock strode forward and stood between them, forcing Shaw back against the wall and holding him.

'OK, OK,' said Shaw through clenched teeth. 'No need to be so rough – we were only having a chat.'

'All right, Peter,' said Jago, closing the door behind him. 'Mr Shaw's not going anywhere for the time being.'

Cradock eased his grip on Shaw and walked him over to a chair, then told him to sit. Shaw complied, rubbing his arm.

'You nearly broke that,' he said. His voice sounded surly and resentful.

'You'll survive,' said Jago. 'Now, Mr Gilroy, perhaps you'd care to take a seat too.'

Gilroy was back on his feet and straightening his clothes. He crossed the room with apparent difficulty, one hand pressed against his ribcage, and eased himself into a chair.

'Right,' said Jago. 'Tell us what happened, Mr Gilroy.'

Gilroy tried to smooth his dishevelled hair with his other hand.

'I, er . . . well, nothing, really,' he said. 'Mr Shaw came to see me in a very agitated manner and indicated he wished to raise a matter with me. We, er, had a vigorous discussion and, er—'

'When I came into this room it looked as though you were having more than a discussion.'

'Yes, but it's all right, Inspector.'

'Has this man hurt you?'

'No, I'm fine, thank you.'

'Did he use a weapon?'

'No.'

Shaw looked up defiantly.

'Are you going to arrest me?' he said.

'No,' said Jago. 'Not this time. But Mr Gilroy, if you wish to pursue the matter, you may decide to take out a summons against Mr Shaw for assault. It's up to you.'

'Thank you, Inspector, but I'm sure there's no need.'

'Very well. Mr Shaw, you can go now, and I advise you to restrain yourself in future. If I catch you assaulting anyone you'll be in trouble.'

Shaw moved towards the door, still rubbing his arm, and left them.

CHAPTER FORTY

'Now, if you don't mind, Mr Gilroy, there's someone I need to speak to as soon as possible, and I'd like you to come with me. Is that all right?'

'Well, yes, I suppose so.'

Jago didn't tell Gilroy where they were going, but the journey was brief.

'My old school,' said Gilroy when they stopped. 'Why here?'

'Just come with me,' said Jago.

They crossed to the opposite corner of the playground, where Jago knocked on the door of the ARP post and went in, followed by Cradock and Gilroy. Maud Hampson was standing on the far side of the room.

'Do you know who this lady is, Mr Gilroy?' Jago asked.

'Yes, it's Mrs Hampson – her husband is Councillor Hampson, the chairman of our board of managers. Good evening, Mrs Hampson.'

Maud opened her mouth to speak, but Jago interrupted her.

'One moment, please, Mrs Hampson, if you don't mind. I need to ask Mr Gilroy something else.'

'Mr Gilroy, what is the nature of your relationship with Mrs Hampson?'

Gilroy looked shocked.

'Relationship? Well, I believe we may have met once or twice at meetings or functions where Mrs Hampson has been with her husband, but I don't know her beyond that.'

'I have a witness who saw you with her early on Sunday morning, and the report I have from that witness clearly suggests you know each other rather better than that.'

'Oh, I see.'

Gilroy looked round for a chair and sat down, his air of confidence gone.

'Mr Gilroy,' said Jago, 'I think you've been having an affair with Mrs Hampson. Is that correct?'

Maud began to sob. She pulled a handkerchief from her sleeve and buried her face in it.

'All right, yes,' said Gilroy. 'If you must know, her husband is a crook and a hypocrite and she couldn't bear to be with him any more.'

'And where did Paul Ramsey fit into this story?'

'What? Paul Ramsey? What's he got to do with this?'

'You tell me, Mr Gilroy. He was a colleague of yours, and you were seen close to where he was murdered, with

357

a woman whose husband he had recently been to see about an important matter. You've already lied to me, so I'd advise you not to lie again.'

Gilroy looked up at Jago and swallowed.

'All right – yes, he knew.'

'Knew what?'

'He knew that Mrs Hampson and I had – had become close.'

Maud Hampson gave a louder sob and sat down heavily in her chair.

'Delicately put, Mr Gilroy. And he made use of that knowledge?'

'How else do you think he became head of the department? I had to promote him and convince the board of managers he was the best candidate.'

'How did he find out about your relationship with Mrs Hampson?'

'It was my own fault. Maud – Mrs Hampson, that is – had moved out of her home into a small flat in Freemasons Road, which wasn't far from where Ramsey lived. One Sunday evening I was seeing her there and the air-raid warning sounded. I should have gone straight home there and then, but I didn't, and then the bombs were getting close and I couldn't. I, er, decided to stay the night. I shouldn't have taken the risk of compromising her, but I made the wrong decision. The irony of it is that by then she'd dashed off to do her ARP duty, so we didn't, er . . . well, as it turned out I spent the night alone at her flat.'

'Not in a shelter?'

'No, I didn't want to risk the neighbours seeing me. Obviously I knew I'd have to leave at some point, because I had to be at school the next day, so I thought I'd slip away early in the morning, before the blackout ended. But unfortunately when the bombing finally stopped I fell asleep, and by the time I woke and left, it was getting quite light. As I said, Ramsey lived nearby, and I found out later that he'd been up and about early that day – taking his morning constitutional across the recreation ground, he said – and he'd spotted me. He told me he'd seen me leaving the flat and he knew that wasn't where I lived, so he'd followed me home after school a couple of times and seen me go back there. He worked out pretty quickly what was going on, and then one day he saw enough of the woman I was visiting to recognise her as the wife of one of the school managers, Mrs Hampson.'

'And he threatened to tell someone? Your wife?'

'No, I'm not married, Inspector. I never have been. He threatened to tell Maud's husband, and that would've meant not just the end of our relationship but the end of my job, my career.'

'Blackmail, then?'

'Yes, he was nothing but a dirty blackmailer. You have to understand, Inspector – it wasn't just about me. It was about the school, the children. Hampson's the chairman of my management board and a borough councillor – if he'd found out about me and Maud he'd have got me sacked, and that would've brought the whole school into disrepute. What chance would the children have then? This new emergency school that I'm running is their last chance to learn – if we fail, it'll wreck their future. I couldn't let that happen. Do you understand, Inspector? Ramsey was threatening to ruin everything. I couldn't let one greedy young upstart force me out of my job. I must continue my work, for the children's sake.'

'What did Ramsey want from you?'

'I think I told you before that the previous head of English at the school was killed in an air raid. The first thing Ramsey suggested was that if I wanted things to stay sweet between him and me I should get him that promotion. And like a fool I complied.'

'So he got the job. But it didn't end there?'

'No. Of course, I suspected that wouldn't be the end of it, and I was right. But I had no choice.'

'What happened next?'

'He started demanding money. He said not to worry, it was only to buy a train ticket, but it was for a long journey, so it would be rather expensive. He said if I paid up he'd go away and never trouble me again.'

'But you didn't believe him?'

'No. I knew it doesn't work like that – and no train ticket ever cost as much as he asked for. I was sure that whatever I gave him he'd want more, and there'd be no end to it. I'm not a wealthy man, Inspector – all I have is what I earn, and that's not much.'

'So you decided to remove him from the scene yourself?'

'Yes. He was threatening to expose me, and I couldn't let that happen. I decided to silence him.'

Maud let out a gasp and looked at him with an expression of disbelief.

'Jeremy? You killed him?'

'Stay out of this, my love,' said Gilroy. 'There's no need for you to get involved.'

'But—'

'Don't say anything, Maud.'

Jago swung his gaze back from Maud to Gilroy.

'So what did you do?' he said.

'It was simple, really,' said Gilroy. 'I decided to turn the tables. I asked him for a few days to get the money together, then I watched him, just as he'd watched me. I found out his routine – what time he left for school in the morning, whether he always went the same way to and from school or took any detours. I watched his flat in the evenings to see when he went out, and where he went when the siren sounded. I knew he didn't have an Anderson shelter, because after that first weekend of air raids everyone was talking about it at school and he mentioned that he had to use one of the public shelters in Nottingham Avenue and how terrified everyone had been. I followed him for three nights in a row, every time the alert sounded.'

'And he went to the same shelter every time?'

'That's right – the third one along. The next day was Saturday, so that evening I followed him to it just the same, but this time when he went in, I went into the first one and spent the night there. It was dreadful, but I'd made a plan and I knew I had to stay. I waited near the entrance until the all-clear went early the next morning, then slipped out quickly so I could see him come out of his. There was a risk he'd have gone already when I came out, but the bombing was heavy that night so I thought it was unlikely, and if he had gone, he'd have had no idea what I was doing, so there was no danger to me.'

'Had you taken a weapon with you?'

'Yes, I took the poker from my fireplace and I was going to hit him over the head with it, like I've seen them do in the films. I must have been mad – I've never killed anyone – but that was what I'd decided to do, and once I've made a decision I see it through.'

'Carry on.'

'The other shelter – the one Ramsey was in – was only a short way down the street, so when I got there the people were still coming out. He was one of the last out. I walked past, where I could be sure he'd spot me, but I pretended not to have seen him. I reckoned the temptation would be too great for him, and I was right. He came over and said, "What are you doing here, Mr Gilroy?" I put on a guilty look and said I was, er, just on my way home. He sneered at me and said, "You've been with Mrs Hampson again, haven't you? Have you got that money yet?" My plan was to say yes, I'd got it, but then ask him to go into the shelter because I was scared someone might see me handing money over to him on the street.'

'So you lured him into the shelter, yes?'

'No. That was my plan, but before I could do that a passer-by stopped in a shop doorway near us and lit up a cigarette, then just stood there smoking it. I couldn't say or do anything. Ramsey knew nothing of my intentions, of course, and he just laughed and strolled off.'

'Did you follow him?'

'I was going to, but the man with the cigarette set off after him, so I couldn't. Then I saw the man go up to him, and they went into the last shelter, the one furthest away. That upset my plan, and it was as if I woke up from some kind of dream. I suddenly realised what I was about to do and I suppose I came to my senses. I just turned round and walked away – and that was when I spoke to Maud.'

'Did she know what you'd been planning to do?'

'No, she knew nothing of it. It was all my own doing.'

'And who was this other man, the one who went into the shelter with him?'

'He was an ARP warden.'

'Do you know his name?'

'No, but funnily enough I saw him as we drove in here just now – I recognised his limp.'

CHAPTER FORTY-ONE

'Mrs Hampson,' said Jago, 'could you please go with DC Cradock and bring that warden in here?'

They left together and returned within a couple of minutes. The warden entered the room, looking round nervously.

'Mr Gilroy,' said Jago, 'is this the man you saw entering the air-raid shelter with Mr Ramsey?'

'Yes,' said Gilroy.

As soon as the word left Gilroy's lips the warden stopped in his tracks. He grabbed a chair and threw it at Jago, knocking him to the floor, then hobbled out of the door as fast as he could.

'After him, Cradock!' Jago shouted, struggling back to his feet.

Cradock ran out in pursuit and soon returned with the man, who was now cursing his lame leg.

'Sit down, Mr Draper,' said Jago. 'I have some questions I'd like you to answer. You are not obliged to say anything, but anything you say may be given in evidence.'

Cradock pushed Draper down onto a chair and stood behind him.

'Now, Mr Draper, you've been working for Ramsey and Son for fifteen years, haven't you?' said Jago.

'Yes.'

'And how old are you now?'

'Fifty-one.'

'Not an age when you want to lose your job, is it?'

Draper looked down at the floor and shook his head slowly.

'In fact that would be a disaster, wouldn't it?'

'Yes,' said Draper, his voice almost a whisper.

'You said you owed everything to Joe Ramsey and his father.'

'Yes.'

'But not to his brother, Paul. When did you last see him?'

Draper looked up. He glanced from Jago to Maud Hampson and back again.

'I don't know.' He looked down at the floor again. 'A couple of weeks ago, maybe. I can't remember.'

'Mr Draper, you were seen with Paul Ramsey on Sunday morning, going into an air-raid shelter with him – the shelter in which his body was found soon afterwards.'

Draper didn't look up, but his shoulders twitched, and Jago saw a tear fall onto his dark blue trouser leg. Draper slowly raised his head. A look of agony filled his face, and tears began to flow freely down his cheeks.

'I'm sorry, I'm sorry,' he said. 'I didn't mean to. I only meant to frighten him off. I knew the business was in trouble, and I was scared about what might happen. The boss had said someone was stirring things up, and if he didn't manage to fix it the whole firm might go bust. He trusted me, see. I asked him who was making the trouble, and at first he wouldn't tell me, but then he told me it was his brother – his own brother. He said it was his own fault – he'd got a bit drunk and told his brother about some scheme he'd cooked up with her husband.'

He nodded his head towards Mrs Hampson, who was looking shocked.

'And now Paul was going to shop him,' Draper continued. 'I knew Paul Ramsey lived in my sector, so I decided to put the wind up him. I waited till the shelter had cleared, then said I needed to talk to him and took him back inside.'

'And you had a weapon?'

'I took a kitchen knife with me, but I didn't intend to use it. That's the last thing I'd do, but I had to show him I was serious. I told him to keep his mouth shut about his brother's business, or I'd shut it for him. I pulled the knife out to show him I meant it. He backed away a bit and said he had a gun. I didn't believe him, but I jabbed the knife a bit towards him just in case. I thought that would do it, but suddenly he pulled a gun out of his pocket and aimed it at my stomach and tried to grab the knife from me with his other hand. I pulled my arm back so he couldn't get the knife, but then he got hold of me. He was younger than me, and stronger, pushing me back against the wall. It was all I could do to keep upright, and then—'

He broke off, then stared at Jago with a look of horror and began to sob.

'He was right up close, his face in mine, pushing me back. It was gloomy in there, but he got so close I could feel his breath on my face, and then I saw – his eyes. All I could see was his eyes, and something came over me. I don't know what it was – it was like I was suddenly someone else, in a different place. I was back in Neuve Chapelle, in a corner of an empty trench, and there was a German in front of me – a young officer, with a pistol. That's when you know what war is, don't you? It's not about armies, or strategies, or defending civilisation. It's just you against him. One of you's going to live, and one of you's going to die.'

He paused, and when he spoke again his voice was cold, hard, somehow distant.

'It doesn't matter who you are then or what you believe – it's just about who's the strongest, who's the most ruthless, which of you has the least mercy. That German had a uniform and a weapon, but I was a killer and he wasn't.'

He paused again, and his voice dropped to a whisper.

'That's what happened in that shelter. It was like I was there with my bayonet again, just the same as in the war, and I'd been trained to use it. You had to strike, that's what the sergeant said – you couldn't hesitate or you'd be dead. Suddenly he stumbled back a bit and loosened his grip, and in that moment I brought the knife down on him with all my strength, and it went straight into him. All I can remember is his eyes staring into mine, like he was looking into my soul. They were wide open, as if he was surprised, and next thing they were just empty. I saw the blood and pulled the knife out as his knees gave way, ready to stab him again, but he just dropped. He was already dead.'

'And the gun? What did you do with that?'

'I didn't know what to do. I didn't want it on me, so I just stuffed it back in his pocket and ran.'

'But then your fingerprints would be on it.'

'What? Oh, yes – but I'd been out on duty all night and still had my gloves on, so I don't suppose I left any. But anyway, I wasn't thinking about anything like that. I was panicking by then, and just wanted to get away.'

Maud stared at him.

'How could you?' she said. 'You're a warden – you've pledged to help people suffering violence, to protect them. How could you deliberately take another man's life?'

Draper didn't acknowledge her, but looked Jago in the eye.

'Did you ever have to bayonet a German, Mr Jago? I don't think any man can do that and ever be the same again. I've had nightmares about it for more than twenty years, and when he was trying to get that knife from me in the shelter it was like – I was just there again, and it was happening for real. I'm so sorry.'

He held his hands out towards Jago, palms upwards and fists clenched, as if asking to be handcuffed.

'You can take me, Inspector. I don't expect mercy. The last shred of mercy was drilled out of me twenty-five years ago. What's going to happen to me now?'

'You're under arrest and you're coming with me. After that it'll be for a jury to decide.'

CHAPTER FORTY-TWO

Divisional Detective Inspector Soper was rarely seen at the station early on Saturday mornings, but he had turned up today. Reflected glory, thought Jago – the successful end to this case must have tempted him in. He briefly considered asking whether Soper had a meeting with the area superintendent coming up in the following week, but decided to keep his own counsel. Instead he recounted the details of the case and answered the few questions that Soper had to ask.

'Very good – I look forward to seeing your report on Monday,' said the DDI when he'd finished.

'Of course, sir,' said Jago, making a mental note not to take on too many social engagements for Sunday.

'And what about the other case?' asked Soper.

'The other case, sir?'

'Yes – Mr Hunter.'

'Ah, yes, sir, since you mention it, we have had what you might call a bit of a breakthrough.'

'Jolly good. Tell me more.'

'We found the man responsible – he was in hospital, having been assaulted outside a pub.'

'Typical, I suppose.'

'He was clearly the man who'd swindled Mr Hunter out of his deposit. Jones wasn't his real name, of course – it was O'Leary. He didn't exactly deny doing it, but he didn't exactly admit anything either. Still, he claimed he'd won some money on the horses and wanted to compensate the man who'd suffered at the hands of whoever'd pulled this trick on him – out of the kindness of his heart, as it were. And he gave me five pounds to pass on to Mr Hunter.'

Soper's face clouded in a mix of astonishment and outrage.

'And you believed him? Didn't you arrest him?'

'No, sir. I'd got Mr Hunter's money back, as you wanted, so I let him go and advised him to leave the area.'

'But this was the villain who obtained money by deception from my . . . from an honest and upstanding member of the public. You can't just let him pay up and walk away scot-free.'

'Perhaps not, sir, but he'd given us some valuable information about another case, and I exercised my discretion. It seemed fair to me.'

'Fair? What's fair about letting a man like that go?'

'Well, sir, because he'd said he wouldn't press charges.'

'Against whom?'

'Against the man who assaulted him, sir – with a golf

club. He declined to press charges because he thought the man was probably an escaped lunatic.'

Soper's eyes narrowed suspiciously.

'What are you getting at, John?'

'Mr O'Leary said he was assaulted on Wednesday night by a tall man with a military moustache and an imperious manner – and, as I said, a golf club.'

'I see,' said Soper, clearing his throat. 'Right, well, er, perhaps it was the best thing to do, send him packing, and so on.'

'Of course, I was wondering whether I should try to find this man who assaulted him – O'Leary did end up in hospital, you know. Perhaps you're right – I shouldn't let him get away scot-free.'

A faint trace of alarm crossed Soper's face.

'Well, er – I don't know, John. I mean, it sounds as though it's all sorted out now, doesn't it? You've got Mr Hunter's money back, and this O'Leary or Jones or whatever is leaving the area and doesn't want to press charges. I think we can call it a day – don't you? After all, as you said yourself, there are bigger fish to fry. I think you should concentrate on those and regard this matter as closed.'

Jago smiled.

'Very well, sir – as you wish.'

There was only one more job Jago wanted to do that morning, which was to let some of those closest to the case know that he had made an arrest. He found

Cradock in the office, and the two of them set off in the Riley, heading first for the Barking Road.

Upon arrival they could see that the repairmen had done everything they could for Olivia Garside's bookshop, but it was still closed. What remained of the ground-floor windows had been boarded up and the glass swept away. The empty spaces that had once been windows on the upper storeys were now hung with canvas, and the roof was patched with sheets of tarred paper. Jago crossed the pavement to the front door and read the handwritten note that was pinned to it.

'Here you are,' he said to Cradock. '"Reopening for business as soon as possible. All enquiries to 62 Luton Road. Mrs O. Garside, proprietress." Let's nip round there and say hello.'

Five minutes later they were standing outside a small terraced house with a black front door. Jago knocked, and it was opened by Wilfred Morton.

'Gentlemen,' said Morton, 'what brings you here? Won't you come in?'

Jago entered the narrow hall, followed by Cradock.

'You look a little surprised, Inspector – why's that?'

'Only to see you looking so well, Mr Morton.'

'Yes – it seems I got off very lightly, and I understand I have you to thank for getting me out of that place. I'm told the bomb blast brought the chimney down on top of me. The hospital people were very good, though, and only kept me in for one night. Mind you, with all the casualties they're getting these days I don't suppose they keep anyone in longer than they have to. So here I am, none the worse for wear – fit as a fiddle, in fact. But forgive me, Inspector, I'm keeping you standing. Won't you come and sit down?'

Jago and Cradock followed him into the small front parlour and sat on a pair of upholstered armchairs that had seen better days.

'I'm pleased to hear you're feeling better,' said Jago. 'Are you staying here?'

'Yes,' Morton replied. 'The flats over the shop are in a pretty poor state, so Mrs Garside is renting this little place until they're put right. She was good enough to say Shaw and I could lodge with her here for the time being – a typically kind response on her part, I must say.'

'Shaw too? You brought him with you?'

'Yes. I've told you before what my attitude towards violence is.'

'Sooner you than me. Are you back at work yet?'

'Almost. I've been off for a couple of days, but I'm going back on Monday morning. So as you can see, apart from a few bruises, no harm done, it appears.'

'And no hard feelings about whoever dropped that bomb on you?'

'Look, Inspector, unlike some people, I don't assume every German up in those planes is a rabid Nazi. It's just as likely to have been some poor young conscript who didn't want to be there and was just doing his job.'

'So you still believe in loving your enemy?'

'No, I never said I did. I don't think I could do that – I just don't want to attack anyone just because someone else has decided we're enemies. All I'm saying is I don't bear grudges.'

Jago nodded. 'Well, I'm glad I found you here, because I wanted to let you know we've arrested a man on suspicion of murdering Paul Ramsey.'

'That's a relief – I thought you suspected me. Is it anyone I know?'

'No, I don't think it is. But I wanted to ask you one last question, since you knew Mr Ramsey.'

'Of course. What is it?'

'I don't think I mentioned to you that Paul Ramsey had a gun, did I?'

'A gun? How extraordinary. No, you didn't mention that.'

'Well, he did, and we believe he might have been planning to go away somewhere and take it with him. I wondered whether you might be able to shed any light on why he had it and what he might have been planning to do with it.'

'Well, I certainly didn't know he had one. It's not what you expect a pacifist to have, is it? Do you know where he was going?'

'No.'

'In that case the phrase that springs to mind is "to thine own self be true". If Ramsey were really a pacifist he'd have been taking that gun to throw it into the sea. But I always rather suspected he was putting on an act, and if I'm right, then I fear he'd have had some other idea in mind – to harm someone else, or at least threaten to harm them.'

'Or to harm himself?'

'I don't think so – he was too ambitious for that. But then who can tell what a man will do? It just confirms in my mind that while he could sound like the perfect pacifist when it suited him, he had other motives in mind when he joined the PPU. If he was out to use that gun on another person, perhaps that was him being true to himself.'

'What do you mean by that?'

'I mean if he'd found himself in a situation where violence of some kind – or the threat of it – seemed to offer the only way out, I could imagine him swallowing his principles and doing whatever he needed to do to solve the problem. How can I put it? He always struck me as more pragmatic than principled.'

Jago shifted his position in the armchair. It felt as though a spring under the cushion had broken free from its moorings and was intent on doing him an injury.

'How's your PPU work going?' he asked.

'Not as well as I'd like, to be honest,' said Morton, taking a seat. 'Our membership's been declining. Dick Sheppard himself said that if war ever came he reckoned about fifty per cent of the people who'd signed the pledge would change their minds, and it looks like he was right, especially since the fall of France. And people have made it hard for us – members of conscientious objectors' tribunals accusing us of treason, university students calling the PPU a fifth column business and getting up petitions to have our meetings banned, our members even fined for obstructing the highway when all they were doing was selling copies of *Peace News*. That's why I was so cross when I saw you at Tower Hill. I do apologise – I shouldn't have blamed you for other people's actions.'

'That's quite all right, Mr Morton.'

'The fact is, we don't have the support we used to have – even prominent people like A. A. Milne and Bertrand Russell have pulled out. There doesn't seem to be the same level of commitment any more.'

'Why do you think that is?'

'It seems to me some men believe in peace and some believe in God. If you believe in peace you'll do everything you can to persuade politicians and the public to find a way of preventing war and finding peaceful solutions, but if that doesn't work – well, perhaps we're seeing the results of that now.'

'And if you believe in God?'

'Well, as I think I told you before, I don't myself, but I can see that it's mainly the Quakers, the Anglicans and other religious people who are, er—'

'Sticking to their guns?'

'Not the term I would have used, but yes. I can only assume that if you believe in God there's something different going on inside you.'

'So are you reconsidering your own position?'

'That bomb hitting the shop on Wednesday night made me think. There's no way of settling our conflict with Hitler by negotiation. Chamberlain made a noble effort but failed, and I can't see how we'll ever get the kind of outcome we've been calling for. I still believe it's wrong to take another person's life, so I refuse to take up arms for any cause, but people are suffering and dying every day because of this war, and I just want to do whatever I can to help them. I may not be able to love my enemies, but I can try to love my neighbour.'

'What brought this change about?'

'It started with something you said. When I told you I loved Gloria, you said it sounded like a one-sided infatuation. I preferred to use the term "unrequited love", but basically it means the same – when one side wants something but the other isn't willing to reciprocate. I'd argued for years that if we would only negotiate with Hitler we'd find a way to maintain peace and prevent the destruction of Europe. Even when he made his final offer of peace back in July I still had a small vestige of hope that he might mean it.'

'His speech to the Reichstag, you mean?'

'Exactly – but it was obvious he was just offering to leave us alone with our empire in exchange for abandoning the whole of Europe to his tyranny. That would mean peace for us but generations of subjugation for our neighbours, and that couldn't be right. And since then, of course, he's started attacking us too, bombing people in their beds. Unrequited love may be a fruitless quest, but I've learnt now that an unrequited desire for peace can be fruitless too. I'm not going to stop objecting to war, but I've decided I'm going to do something practical to help the victims. When I was at Tower Hill on Wednesday I heard Donald Soper suggesting men who are against war but don't want to do nothing should join the Friends' Ambulance Unit – that thing the Quakers run – so that's what I'm going to do. If we can't have peace, at least I can do something to help people.'

Morton fell silent and scanned Jago's face as if seeking approval. Jago was still reflecting on what he had said when the door swung open and crashed against the wall.

CHAPTER FORTY-THREE

'Mr Shaw,' said Jago, as the teacher appeared in the doorway. 'Mr Morton was just telling us that you're still lodging with him.'

'What's it to you?' Shaw growled. 'And what are you doing here? Come to rough me up again, have you? You're no better than the Nazis, you lot.'

'If you have a complaint to make, Mr Shaw—'

Shaw cut him off in mid sentence.

'Complaint? What's the point? You all close ranks whenever there's a hint of trouble, don't you?'

He took a step towards Jago, his face a scowl. Morton jumped to his feet to placate him, but before he could speak the doorbell rang.

'Excuse me, gentlemen,' he said, leaving the room.

Jago heard him opening the front door and speaking. He caught the faint sound of a woman's voice, and then two sets of footsteps approached down the hallway. Morton reappeared at the door, then stepped aside to show in Gloria Harris.

Before Jago could greet her, Shaw sprang forward and glared in her face.

'What are you doing here?' he said, his voice menacing. 'I thought I told you to stay away from this man.'

She glared back at him defiantly.

'Listen to me, Harold – I'm here because I choose to be. I was wrong about Wilfred. I've come to see that he's a man of principle, and I admire that – and what's more, he doesn't tell me what to do or what to think. He respects me as I am.'

'Respects you? He doesn't know the meaning of the word. Look at him – he's no better than that other good-for-nothing coward Ramsey. I won't have you seeing him.'

'And I won't have you bullying me any more, Harold. I've made my decision, and it's Wilfred that I want.'

'What you want is a damn good hiding, my girl.'

He lunged forward to grab her by the arm, but she dodged to one side. Morton stepped forward and stood between them.

'You heard her, Shaw,' he said. 'She wants me, and I want her. It's time for the bullying to stop.'

'Shut up, you pathetic little man!' Shaw snarled. 'Get out of my way. I stopped Paul Ramsey, and I'll stop you.'

He swung his right fist and caught Morton full in the face before he could defend himself. Morton fell backwards onto the floor, blood streaming from his nose.

'Get up, you coward,' said Shaw.

Morton began to struggle to his feet, but before Shaw could throw another punch Cradock leapt forward and grasped his arm, forced it behind his back into a hammer lock and held him.

'All right,' said Shaw, ceasing to struggle. 'I'm not going to hurt him.'

'Right, Mr Shaw,' said Jago, 'I've warned you before, and now I've had enough of your antics. For one thing, you need to understand that this young lady is free to make her own choices. And for another, you are not entitled to go around punching people you don't agree with in the face – especially someone who's only just recovered from being on the receiving end of a German bomb. Mr Morton may be accustomed to turning the other cheek, but my practice is to arrest any man who assaults another in my presence. You're under arrest.'

Shaw hung his head in silence while Jago handed Cradock the key to his Riley.

'Take him out to the car and wait for me – I'll join you in a moment.'

Jago watched Cradock leave the house with Shaw, then turned back into the room, where Gloria was tending Morton's injured nose with a handkerchief.

'He'll be charged with assault, Mr Morton. I can only suggest you reconsider whether you want to live under the same roof as him, but it's your decision.'

Morton nodded, holding the handkerchief to his nose.

Gloria took his arm and clung close to him, her head resting on his shoulder. Jago gave them both a brief smile.

'It sounds as though you've both turned a new page.'

'Yes, Mr Jago,' said Gloria. 'I've already apologised to Wilfred, and despite my cousin's threats I've been seeing him the last couple of days. We'll have to see how it works out, but I think we may have a future together.'

'And your career? You said women teachers aren't allowed to marry.'

Morton removed the handkerchief from his face to speak.

'Not yet, Inspector, but that can't go on for ever. I know what Gloria wants for her future – she wants to teach, and that's something I *am* prepared to fight for.'

CHAPTER FORTY-FOUR

By early afternoon Shaw had been charged and released on bail, and Jago could look forward to meeting him in the Stratford magistrates' court just up the road from West Ham police station at ten-thirty on Monday morning. What happened next to Shaw was out of his hands, so he could safely discharge him from his mind. By half past three Jago was in Rita's cafe and had found a table for four, where he was inviting Dorothy, Cradock and Dr Anderson to take their seats.

'You're all my guests,' he said. 'Peter and I have concluded the case, so I thought we should have a little celebration. I'd originally considered organising something for this evening, but our learned medical friend here has a prior engagement. Still, at least an afternoon gathering may be less at risk of interruption by the Luftwaffe. It means we can't drink anything stronger than tea, but Rita's promised to make us a fresh batch of her famous scones. So I decided we'd have a traditional English treat for Dorothy – a cream tea.'

'What does that consist of?' said Dorothy.

'Do you know what scones are?'

'I've seen them. Those little round things?'

'That's right.'

'They look a bit like what we call biscuits in the States. I haven't tried the English ones, but I've heard they're very good.'

'Well, it's them, and the way we eat them is we cut them in half, then put jam and clotted cream on them – cream on first if you're from Devon, or jam on first with clotted cream on top if you're from Cornwall. My grandfather was from Cornwall, and all my family before him, so I eat them the proper way, with the cream on top, but either way they're delicious. And all washed down with a pot of Rita's tea.'

'Sounds great,' said Dorothy, relieved that this was not one of Jago's more outlandish treats, such as the pie and mash with green 'liquor' sauce that he'd once induced her to try.

Rita cleared her throat.

'Before you all get too excited,' she announced, 'there's just one little snag. I discovered this morning I was running a bit short of flour, so it's only one scone each – and they're a touch on the small side.'

'Never mind,' said Jago. 'Quality, not quantity.'

'Hear, hear,' said Anderson.

'And there's another thing,' Rita added. 'As of

yesterday it's an offence to sell cream – clotted or otherwise. The government says we haven't got enough milk to go round, so we're not allowed to have cream any more.'

'Oh dear,' said Jago. 'I remember reading about that in the summer, but it wasn't supposed to be happening until later in the year.'

'Yes, dear,' said Rita. 'Well, now it is later in the year, and you can't have it no more. You'll have to make do with jam and a bit of margarine. Will you be wanting the margarine on top of your jam?'

'Of course not,' said Jago. 'That would be ridiculous.'

'And putting clotted cream on top of your jam isn't? I see. Anyway, there it is. Nothing I can do about it, unfortunately – another little sacrifice we'll all have to make for the war effort.'

'Never mind,' said Jago. 'If your scones are as wonderful as ever, I'm sure we'll manage – Peter will just have to make up for it with extra sausage and mash in the canteen this evening. Four cream teas, please, Rita – but without the cream.'

Rita bustled away to the kitchen, and Jago heard what sounded like a sigh of relief from Cradock.

'What's up, Peter? Was it something I said about sausage and mash?'

'No, guv'nor,' said Cradock. 'It's not that. It's just—'

He hesitated, and looked in the direction of the kitchen.

'Just what?' said Jago.

'It's just that I feel a bit awkward, being here.'

'Why's that?'

'It's Emily, sir. I was worried Rita was going to ask me about Emily, about how we'd got on at the pictures and all that.'

'Ah, yes, I see – Rita can be a little probing, can't she?'

'What's the problem?' said Dorothy.

Cradock cast an uncertain look in Jago's direction, as if appealing for help.

'The problem,' said Jago, 'is that young Peter here's been out for an evening with Rita's daughter, Emily, and now he needs some advice. Perhaps you could help, Dorothy.'

Dorothy gave Cradock an encouraging smile.

'I'm happy to help if I can, Peter,' she said in a sympathetic tone. 'Do you like her?'

'That's what Mr Jago said, and I said yes, but the thing is, I don't know much about girls – in fact I probably don't know anything about them.'

'Well, I'm a woman, and I'm impartial, so tell me what you want to know.'

Cradock gulped, and dropped his voice almost to a whisper.

'It's a bit embarrassing.'

'I won't be embarrassed,' said Dorothy.

He was about to unburden himself when Rita returned with tea, scones, margarine and jam. There was an awkward silence at the table, and having deposited the items, she withdrew. Jago took charge, pouring the tea and distributing the scones, which he noticed were indeed disappointingly small.

'Here you are,' he said. 'Eat up. Doesn't look as though it'll take you long, unfortunately.'

Dorothy cast a glance towards the retreating Rita as they began their tea.

'I think it's safe for you to speak now, Peter,' she said.

'All right,' said Cradock, his voice still hesitant. 'It's like this, you see. Emily and I went to the pictures, and when I told Mr Jago about it he asked me whether I'd held hands with her, and I said no, but now I'm wondering whether I should have. I didn't want to do the wrong thing, you see.'

'Is that something other people do at the movies here?'

'Holding hands? Oh, yes. I've seen lots of blokes canoodling with their girls at the pictures. Some of them put their arm round the girl or even kiss her.'

'Well, I certainly wouldn't suggest you should have put your arm round her or tried to kiss her on your first date – that might have scared the life out of her.'

'Yes, of course – I wasn't going to do that. But I wasn't sure whether I ought to hold her hand. Even that seems like a big thing. I don't want her to think I don't like her, but I don't want to frighten her off either. What should I do?'

Dorothy ate her scone thoughtfully and sipped her tea, then spoke. Cradock was distressed to notice that far from whispering, she was speaking in what seemed like a normal conversational voice. What was worse, he was sure Jago was listening to every word.

'I understand why you find it difficult,' she said. 'It's perfectly natural. First of all, holding hands is quite a sensitive issue – once you hold a girl's hand it means a significant change in your relationship. If this visit to the movies was the first time you and Emily went out together I think you were right not to try. It's quite a delicate operation, and you have to be very tactful.'

'That's the problem – I don't think I'm very good at tact.'

'You just need to know how a woman thinks.'

'Right. In that case perhaps I should give up now.'

'Don't be silly, Peter. Girls are different, that's all. Do you like Emily?'

'Yes, I do – but please don't tell Rita that. I'll never hear the end of it.'

'Does Emily like you?'

'I don't know.'

'Well, let's assume she does. What you need to know when it comes to holding hands is that a nice girl will never take the initiative.'

'Why's that?'

'Because her intentions might be misunderstood.'

'Er, right.'

'It's not the holding hands itself that's the issue – these days no one objects to a boy and girl holding hands in public – but she'll be concerned about what it represents. She'll want to be sure about you – that's why you have to be the one who takes the initiative.

But you mustn't rush. If you grab a girl's hand within minutes of knowing her you might frighten her. She certainly won't get a good impression of you. You have to choose an appropriate moment.'

'Oh, why is it so complicated?' said Cradock. 'How can someone like me possibly know when it's the appropriate moment?'

'You have to learn to read the signals – it's very important. The key question is does she do little things that show affection?'

'Like what?'

'When you're talking to her, does she look you in the eye, does she smile at you, does she nod her head or lean a little towards you?'

'Yes, I think she does, a bit. Do all those things mean something?'

'They might. She could be pretending, of course, if she wants to hook you, but you'll just have to take it gently and work out for yourself whether she's sending you genuine signals. It's more than likely that if she does those things she likes you. Just don't rush things, OK?'

Cradock sighed. 'So what you're saying is I need to learn how a woman thinks – but that means I'm right back where I started. This is as bad as memorising the *Police Code*.'

'You'll learn, Peter. Just take it one step at a time.'

'But what's the next step?'

'Well, I guess if you want to find out more you'll have to invite her out again.'

Cradock looked round the table, a helpless expression on his face.

'Dr Anderson,' he said. 'Can you tell me what to do?'

Anderson gave a good-natured laugh.

'I'm sure what Dorothy has said is very sound – after all, she's a woman, so she knows. I may be a medical man, but on affairs of the heart I'm no expert at all. I think I'd better stay well out of this discussion.'

Cradock turned to Jago and opened his mouth as if to speak, but then closed it firmly and looked down at the table.

There was a short silence. Jago wondered whether he should change the subject, but Anderson did it for him.

'There is something I'd like to ask, though. About your case.'

Jago noticed that Cradock looked visibly relieved.

'By all means,' he said. 'What is it?'

'It's about that gun we found in Paul Ramsey's pocket. What was the story?'

'Ah, yes, the gun. Draper – that's the man we've arrested – told us Ramsey was waving it at him in the shelter, and that's why he panicked. He stabbed Ramsey, and Ramsey fell back onto the bench, and Draper said he put the revolver back in Ramsey's pocket, where we found it.'

'Did you ever find out why Ramsey had the gun? There must have been some reason.'

'No, we didn't, and that's what still puzzles me, because the man was a pacifist. Not a perfect one by any means, but that's what he claimed to be, and I reckon for all his faults he did believe in it. And yet he was carrying a loaded gun in his pocket in the night. He had more cartridges packed in his suitcase, too, which would suggest he might've been planning to use it somewhere else. How do you explain that? It's a contradiction, to say the least. I mean, he believes one thing but he's doing something quite the opposite. You're the medical man – what's the psychology of that?'

'Well, I'm not a psychologist, but they did make us study psychological medicine when I was training. Now all I do is read the occasional article, mainly because there's not a lot of application for it in my field. I mean, my patients don't come to me until they're dead, so I don't get the chance to ask them questions.'

He looked round the table for response to his wit, but found only a weak smile from Dorothy, so continued.

'As for your contradiction, though, I'm tempted to say believing one thing and doing another is pretty much a definition of human nature. But no doubt one day the psychologists will come up with a fancy name for it – I do know it's something they have ideas about.'

'So what do they say?'

'They say we all try to make sense of the world, but life's full of conflicting thoughts and experiences, so we look for some way to reconcile all that into something that seems consistent. Take this war, for instance – suddenly life as we know it is turned on its head. People in other countries who might've been our friends a couple of years ago are now trying to kill us, and we're trying to kill them. We have to adjust our thinking to make sense of that, find some over-arching idea that explains and justifies it, to keep ourselves sane.'

'So what about Ramsey?'

'I can't say for sure, but my guess is that perhaps something happened to challenge his beliefs. He had a strong belief in pacifism, but then maybe he felt his life was in real danger and he had to protect himself. Could that have been the case?'

'Yes, possibly. Someone had threatened to kill him.'

'If that's the case,' said Anderson, 'I could imagine him finding a way to reason that it was sensible and right to protect himself with a firearm. It's sad to think that that decision led to his death.'

'So he was an idealist – and that was the problem,' said Jago. 'He believed in peace and he'd put pacifism up on a pedestal, but then life came along and challenged his ideal, and he had to find a way of reconciling it with the reality of his situation. That must've been what he was facing.'

'And there's nothing wrong with that,' said Dorothy quietly. 'I think you're right, John – that was the challenge, and he wasn't the only one of us who's had to face it. Perhaps we all do some day.'

Anderson noticed that she was looking Jago steadily in the eye as she said this. He checked his watch and jumped to his feet.

'Look here, Jago, old chap, thanks for the tea and all

that, but I'm afraid I really must be getting along. I, er, promised someone else I'd meet up with them tonight, and they'll be waiting for me. Sorry to leave you three, but I'd better bid you good evening.'

'That's OK,' said Dorothy before Jago could speak. 'We'll be just fine. Nice meeting you, Dr Anderson – enjoy the rest of your evening.'

Jago found his voice at last.

'Yes, yes, of course, my dear fellow. It's been very helpful to talk to you, so, er, goodnight.'

Anderson shook their hands and left. Cradock glanced from Jago to Dorothy and back again, and stood up.

'I think I'd better be getting along now too, sir. You know what they say – two's company, three's a . . .'

He faltered, realising this might not be the most appropriate thing to say.

'Very well,' said Jago. 'Off you go. And if you want any more advice on the subject of young Emily, you'd better talk to Sergeant Tompkins. He's an expert on women – told me just the other day he'd been married to his old Dutch for forty years.'

'His what?' said Dorothy.

'His wife. It's from a song Albert Chevalier used to sing in the music halls. He called his wife "my old Dutch", but I've no idea why, except that it rhymes – he said being married for forty years didn't seem a day too much.'

'In that case I say well done Frank for loving the same woman for forty years.'

'Yes, I suppose so . . . Mind you, I've never heard Frank Tompkins actually singing the song – the way he talks sometimes, you'd think he's hoping to get time off for good behaviour.'

Dorothy gave Jago a querulous look.

'Well, I hope he's had a long and happy marriage, and I hope you don't tease him about it. Now, I enjoyed that scone, but to be honest, it was very small. I don't wish to appear unladylike, but I think maybe we should consider moving on someplace else for a little supper before the air raids start up.'

'Certainly. What do you fancy?'

'How about that fish and chips thing you were talking about? With the old newspaper, of course. You said you'd treat me, and I think this might be the perfect opportunity – don't you?'

'Yes, I do,' said Jago. 'And I know just the place.'

CHAPTER FORTY-FIVE

By the time Jago and Dorothy were left to themselves the afternoon was almost over. They walked slowly down West Ham Lane, the street quietening as people made their way home in anticipation of the air raids, which seemed now as regular as clockwork.

'Where are you taking me for this treat?' said Dorothy.

'To a very fine fried fish shop down the road here,' said Jago. 'It's in Abbey Road, the next one we come to.'

'Very fine fried fish shop – is that what you get people to say when you think they may have had too much to drink?'

'Some people recommend "The Leith police dismisseth us", but I think we're getting a bit more scientific than that nowadays.'

They arrived at a triangular open space where West Ham Lane met Church Street and Abbey Road. On the opposite side and to their right, where Abbey Road began, stood a Victorian school, now emptied of children and serving as an auxiliary fire station.

'We need to cross over here,' said Jago, looking right, then left, then right again, and recalling with a flash of childhood memory being taught that same kerb drill in a school that looked very similar to this one.

They stepped off the kerb and into the road. There was no traffic, and Dorothy could hear birdsong somewhere nearby. She wondered how long it would be before this tranquillity was broken, before the whistle of bombs, the crash of explosions and the urgent jangle of fire-engine bells heralded the onset of another night's terror for the people who lived in these little houses.

'There it is,' said Jago, interrupting her thoughts. He was pointing to the other side of the road. 'The best fish and chip shop I know.'

He pushed the door open, and they were greeted by a rush of warm air and a smell of cooking that made them both feel hungry. The shop was small, with white tiled walls and a marble-topped counter, and they were the only customers. Beyond the counter a modern-looking range in art deco style ran for about eight feet along the back wall. A heavily built man in a white coat and apron was standing in front of it with his back towards them, making the oil sizzle as he rattled a metal basket in one of its three deep fryers. He turned round when he heard the door.

'Ah, Mr Jago,' he said with a smile as broad as his face, 'how nice to see you. I'll fetch the missus – she's just cutting the potatoes for a few more chips.'

'Ada!' he shouted through a door at the back of the shop. 'Come and take an order for Mr Jago.'

His wife appeared and took her place behind the counter, wiping her hands on her pinafore.

'Cod as usual, Mr Jago?' she said. 'We've got some plaice too, if you prefer.'

'Cod will be fine, thank you.'

'And the same for the lady?'

Jago looked to Dorothy for her answer.

'I'll have the same as you,' she replied.

'OK,' said Jago to Ada. 'So it's two cod, and a penn'orth of chips each, please.'

'Thank you. That'll be sixpence, then, if you please.'

Jago took a handful of change from his trouser pocket, found a small silver sixpence and handed it over to her. She put it in the till and smiled at him.

'Where else would you get dinner for two for a tanner, eh?' she said. 'While there's fish and chips there's hope, that's what I say. And no sign of the government rationing fish or potatoes yet, so I just hope it stays like that. Can't be easy for the trawlermen, though, going out to sea with all them horrible submarines and things lurking about.'

'No, I don't envy them. But how are you? Busy day today?' said Jago.

'Oh, yes, we've been on the go all day. Just slowing down a bit now as the evening comes on – people want to get home, you know.'

'Yes, I wasn't sure whether you'd still be open.'

'Oh, we always stay open till the sirens go, then we clear up as fast as we can. If there's any fish and chips left in the fryers I get it out, and Fred shovels out any coal that's still burning in the range and puts it in a bucket. Once that's all done we get down in the cellar. You're welcome to join us if you're nearby.'

'Thank you, we'll bear that in mind.'

'Ready now,' said Fred.

Ada took two portions of battered cod and added a generous helping of chips to each.

'Salt and vinegar?' she asked Jago.

'Please,' he replied.

She doused the food with malt vinegar and sprinkled it liberally with salt, then wrapped the two meals in several sheets of newspaper – the *Daily Mirror*, Jago noted.

'There you go, Mr Jago,' said Ada. 'I hope you find that up to our usual standards – and you enjoy it too, miss.'

Jago raised his hat to the proprietors, and he and Dorothy went back out onto the street.

'So the idea is we eat this on the street?' said Dorothy.

'Yes – but if you can resist eating yours immediately, there's a little place just round the corner that I think you might like.'

'Why is anywhere you need to go here always "just round the corner"?'

'Because this is a small country, I suppose – but I promise you, it really is just round the next corner.'

They turned right into Church Street and Jago stopped.

'There it is,' he said. 'Do you remember I once said I'd take you to see a really old church, but we didn't go, because you thought it was going to rain?'

'Yes, the parish church of West Ham – All Saints', wasn't it? You said it was about eight hundred years old.'

Dorothy could see a long, low building made of brick, with a square stone tower rising at its western end. It sat in the middle of a small grassy churchyard full of gravestones and occasional more imposing monuments, surrounded by a low wall.

Jago led Dorothy through the gateway into the churchyard and stopped by an old wooden bench.

'I thought we could sit here and eat our supper, then we might be able to have a look inside,' he said. 'It's very quiet here. It's nice in the summer, with lots of shade from the trees – I sometimes come down here to think.'

'You think a lot?'

'I don't know. Only as much as I need to.'

Jago unwrapped his meal and broke off a piece of fish with his fingers. Dorothy followed suit, and they sat in silence for a few minutes, eating. Dorothy was first to speak.

'You talked a lot this afternoon about the man who was killed, but what about the man you've arrested? Do you think it was murder, or was it just some terrible accident?'

'I suppose his counsel might argue that it was self-defence, because Paul Ramsey pulled a gun on him. But it'll be difficult for them to get round the fact that he went into that shelter intent on confronting him and was armed with a knife for that purpose.'

'You said Draper only used the knife because he panicked.'

'Yes, but he'd decided to take it, so if the jury decides it was premeditated they're going to find him guilty of murder. It's a basic principle in our law that a person intends the natural consequences of his acts, so if Draper's act results in Ramsey's death, it's regarded as murder unless his defence can prove otherwise. If they can do that, he won't hang.'

'What might count as "otherwise"?'

'He could plead insanity, for example. A young man in South London was sentenced to death at the Old Bailey a couple of years ago for murdering a woman. He'd given her some money and wanted it back, so he went to her flat. He said he took a knife with him to put the wind up her, but they quarrelled, she screamed, and he lost his head. Very similar to this case, really. That was his defence, and his counsel argued that he was insane at the time.'

'Did he get off?'

'No. The prison medical officer said he could find no history of insanity and he thought the man knew what he was doing. It only took the jury about ten minutes to find him guilty, and he was sentenced to death.'

'Would pleading insanity work for your man?'

'I don't know. I think Draper's mind snapped because of his experiences in the Great War, but even if he's suffering from a disease of the mind it doesn't necessarily help. If it doesn't prevent him from knowing what he's doing, and knowing that it's wrong, in law he's still guilty.'

'I wouldn't like to do your job,' said Dorothy. 'It's all so sad, and so complicated.'

'Let's change the subject then. Would you like to have a look inside the church?'

'Won't it be locked?'

'Probably not – churches aren't usually locked. They're supposed to be a place people can go any time to pray, or just to sit quietly and think. And I don't know about this one, but since the air raids started, a lot of churches have opened up their crypts so people can use them as shelters. Let's see.'

CHAPTER FORTY-SIX

They crossed the churchyard to the heavy wooden door and tried the handle. The door swung open with a creak, and they went in. The nave was deserted. Two rows of pointed arches springing from circular piers led towards the chancel, where the east window's fine stone tracery contrasted with the robust timber frame of the tie-beam roof.

'It's beautiful,' Dorothy sighed. 'And so peaceful.'

They walked slowly between the rows of Victorian pews, their footsteps echoing on the flagstones. As they neared the chancel, Dorothy stopped at one of the arches on their left. It framed a large stone memorial with statues of a man and woman in old-fashioned clothes.

'It looks so ancient,' she said. 'I wonder who these people were?'

She dropped to one knee to read the inscription carved into the memorial's base.

'He was James Cooper, and it says he departed this

life the fourth day of December 1743, aged eighty years. I guess the woman must have been his wife, but it doesn't mention her. And it says he wanted this written under his statue. Yes, look – it's a kind of poem.'

She read the words aloud.

'"I believed in one God, Father, Son, and Holy Ghost, also the Resurrection, and whilst I lived, I firmly put my trust in His divine protection. But now interred I'm covered o'er with dust. Reader prepare, for there unto you must."'

'A bit glum, isn't it?' said Jago. 'Especially when hundreds of enemy planes might appear overhead at any moment, intent on blowing us to kingdom come.'

'But that's just the point. Don't you see how poignant it is? He wrote those words two hundred years ago, but it could've been yesterday. "Interred, covered o'er with dust" – it sounds just like people today when they're dragged out of the ruins, dead or alive. The kind of thing you must have seen a lot more of than I have. If ever there was a time for "reader prepare", it's surely today.'

'What price "divine protection", though? Isn't he telling us that whatever we might believe in life, we're all going to end up dead just the same?'

'I'm not sure I can say what he thought he was telling us. Obviously we all die some day, but it seems to me most of us live as if that's never going to happen – and yet you said yourself there are men up in the sky trying to kill us, and we could both be dead before the night's through. I think maybe he's right – look death in the face and believe in God, accept your mortality but ask him to protect you.'

'So do you pray when the air raids start?'

Unusually, Dorothy looked a little awkward at his direct question.

'Yes, I do,' she said. 'I ask him to protect me – and you. What about you? Do you pray for me in the bombing?'

'I don't pray for anyone.'

'Well, I wish you would.'

Jago regretted firing such a personal question at her. He felt as though he'd somehow hit her when her defences were down.

'I'm sorry,' he said. 'It's just that I don't believe a bomb can differentiate between someone who believes and someone who doesn't.'

'I know – of course it can't. But the Lord's Prayer still says "Deliver us from evil", and if that's something only God can do, I'm sure going to keep asking him to do it.'

Jago didn't want to spoil their time together by getting into an argument. It seemed that when she was gentle towards him he repaid her with harshness. He wanted to be gentle too.

'Let's go back outside,' he said.

They found their way to the door and he opened it for her. They walked in silence back to the bench in the churchyard and sat down.

'I'd like to stop here for a while,' said Dorothy. 'How long have we got?'

Jago looked at his wristwatch.

'I want to see you back to your hotel before the blackout starts, and that's just before seven tonight, so that leaves us half an hour or so.'

He looked up again and saw Dorothy gazing at the clear blue sky above the rooftops.

'Good,' she said. 'It's just that when I come out of a place like that, the world outside feels different. It makes me start thinking about the universe, the stars – about how huge it all is, and what it all means.'

'Does it have to mean anything?'

Dorothy pushed her head farther back so she could see more of the sky.

'Yes, I think so – it's so complex and intricate, so beautiful. It's like a work of art. Do you think it can really all be here by accident?'

'I don't know,' he replied slowly. 'When I look at the stars it just makes me think how short life is, how small this world is, and how stupid we are – how pointless all our petty ambitions and jealousies are.'

'But what about the beauty of it all?'

'Well, yes – I'm not immune to beauty. It's just that when you're a policeman you see a lot of ugliness. And when you've been a soldier . . .'

He fell silent.

'Of course,' said Dorothy. 'I understand. But aren't there times – even moments – when you see beyond all that?'

Jago thought for a while, drifting through different scenes in his memory.

'Yes,' he reflected. 'There was a moment, but that's all it was.'

'Tell me about it.'

'It was when the army took me out of the trenches and sent me off to be trained as an officer.'

'I remember you mentioned that once – it was in Cambridge, wasn't it?'

'That's right – the officer cadet battalion. There was a day I can picture clearly, when I went for a stroll along what they call the Backs – where the river runs at the back of some of the big colleges. It was a warm day, bright and clear, and I looked across the river. There was the green grass, the blue sky, and King's College Chapel, rising up and pointing at the heavens, all creamy-white stone glowing in the sun.'

'That's the famous one, isn't it? I've seen pictures of it.'

'Yes, and I don't think I'd ever seen anything so beautiful. I walked over to it and went in, and looked up at the ceiling. That was amazing too – such exquisite stonework. I wanted to lie on the floor and stare at it, but I thought they'd throw me out if I did, so I just sat quietly looking at it until my neck ached. I was about to leave when someone started playing the organ – it was like thunder, rolling down the length of the chapel. It made me jump – I'd just come from a few months of being shelled, so I wasn't too good with sudden loud noises, but this sound was majestic, other-worldly. And it must have been practice time, because then a choir of boys and men started singing. I have to admit it – right then I thought if there is a heaven, this is what it must sound like.'

'So did it give you that feeling – you know, that it's not all there just by accident?'

'I don't know. Maybe it did, but not for long. Before I knew it I'd finished my training and been made an officer, and I was back in the trenches trying to kill people. Back where I started, really, the only difference being that now I had a pip on my shoulder to show I was a second lieutenant. Even more chance of being killed, too, because the German snipers tended to go for the officers. And worst of all was that now it wasn't just living with the prospect of being machine-gunned to death at any moment. Night by night I had to decide which men to send out on patrol, knowing that they'd probably die. That's not something I like to remember.'

'Did you ever consider becoming a pacifist yourself?'

He shook his head. 'What good would it have done? Those men would still have been sent to die, just by some other fellow with less pity than me. No, I decided to take my share of it with the rest. But all I could think once I was back in France was how can God be a God of love if he lets us slaughter each other like this?'

'I was taught that he loves us as a father and we're his children. Supposing you had children – would you make them your slaves? Or would you let them grow up and make their own decisions, even if they were bad ones?'

'I'd let them choose, of course.'

'Well, I think that's why things like wars happen – it's because he lets us make our own decisions. I haven't been a soldier, but in Spain I found out a lot about war. I saw the young men killed by someone they might have gone to school with. I learnt what a high-explosive bomb does to a child, just like people here are learning now. But it was all because of choices men had made. I didn't blame God – I blamed them, and I asked myself whether in their shoes I'd have made better choices.'

Jago was silent. Dorothy wondered whether he was thinking about what she'd said or about men who'd died.

'I've read about that chapel in Cambridge, you know,' she said, 'and the choir. But I've never been there.'

Jago turned on the bench to face her.

'I'd like to take you some time,' he said.

'Would you? Please do.'

'Then I shall.'

There was an awkward silence between them. The light was starting to fade, and the trees in the churchyard looked cold and shadowy.

'There's something else I'd like to say,' said Jago. 'It's just . . .' He hesitated, then forced himself to speak. 'It's just that I want you to know how pleased I am that I've got to know you – you've made a difference to my life in more ways than you could imagine. Do you remember that time when you first showed me a photograph of Eleanor and it was such a shock to me?'

'Yes. I said, "You look like you've seen a ghost."'

'That's right – and in a way I had. It was partly because she was the last person I was expecting to see in a photograph of yours at that moment, but I think it was also because in a way she really was a ghost – she'd been haunting me for twenty years or more. She'd been there in my mind all that time as the perfect woman, the one no other could equal.'

'Like an ideal, you mean?'

'Exactly. When Anderson was talking this afternoon it all just fell into place for me.'

'I know. I could see it.'

'Feminine intuition, you mean?'

'No. I could see it in your face.'

'Is it that easy to read me?'

'Sometimes. But carry on.'

'Yes, well, as I say, it fell into place. No other woman could match up to what I believed Eleanor was, and even when someone I really liked came along, that ghost was still there in the background, holding me back.'

'Someone? Who might that be?'

Jago looked up and down the empty street, as if nervous of being overheard by a passing stranger.

'I think we ought to go now,' he said.

Dorothy placed her hand firmly on his arm.

'No, John. I want to know who that someone is. I've been let down by men before, you know, and it can hurt.'

She saw an anguished look in his eyes.

'I'm sorry,' he blurted out. 'I would never . . . I mean, I didn't mean to—'

'Just tell me, John,' she said calmly.

Jago gulped and nervously fingered the knot in his tie. He knew what was in his mind but was scared to put it on his lips.

'All right,' he said finally. 'The thing is, I know it was only our work that brought us together – but we've become friends, haven't we?'

'We have.'

'Well, you see, I've realised I've been feeling something recently that I think is more than friendship.'

'And?'

'And, well, I'd – I'd like to see more of you, spend time with you, even if there are no crime rates for us to discuss for your articles. I'll quite understand if you don't want that, and if you don't I'll just apologise and we can go back to where we were, but it's what I'd like. Would that be all right with you?'

Dorothy was silent for a moment, but then she smiled. She leant forward a little towards him, looked him in the eye, and slowly nodded.

'Yes, John, I'd like that very much.'

ACKNOWLEDGEMENTS

Like the other Blitz Detective novels, this story is a mixture of historical fact and creative imagination. The fraud against West Ham Borough Council which it describes is of course pure fiction but was inspired by a real case elsewhere. In a trial at the Old Bailey in May 1940 the managing director of a company engaged to build air-raid shelters for a local authority to the south of London was found guilty of conspiring to cheat and defraud the council and sent to prison for fifteen months. He had submitted inflated bills to the council, partly by claiming a number of men had been working on the project while in fact they were deployed on other jobs. The chaos of war and the pressures that it put on local authorities must have been tempting for individuals who wanted to make some extra cash.

Those pressures were particularly intense in West Ham, which had to endure some of the worst of the bombing, but its council – like others around the United Kingdom

– did not escape without criticism. Commentators at the time highlighted shortcomings in its ARP arrangements, and questions were asked at government level.

Other scams were aimed at individuals, and the story of Mr Hunter's less than reliable air-raid shelter supplier is based on a racket reported in the press in September 1940.

More reliable, I'm pleased to say, is the help I've received for this book from a number of people, and I'd like to thank them. Some are not known to me – I think particularly of whoever it was in years gone by who had the pre-war and wartime minutes of West Ham Borough Council's ARP and education committees lovingly bound and preserved so that I could read them at the Newham Archives and Local Studies Library in pristine condition more than three-quarters of a century later.

Others who happily are known include Frank Chester, DSC, for sharing his pre-war and wartime memories with me; Ben Williams, for his warm welcome to All Saints' Church; Roy Ingleton, for his advice on wartime policing; Rudy Mitchell, for his help with the American language; and Dr David Love, whose medical explanations of spurting blood must have alarmed customers seated close to our enlightening coffee-shop conversation.

And as always, I could not have finished this book without the support and encouragement of Margaret, Catherine and David, and so many friends and readers old and new.

MIKE HOLLOW was born in West Ham, on the eastern edge of London, and grew up in Romford, Essex. He studied Russian and French at the University of Cambridge and then worked for the BBC and later Tearfund. In 2002 he went freelance as a copywriter, journalist, editor and translator, but now gives all his time to writing the Blitz Detective books.

blitzdetective.com   *@MikeHollowBlitz*